BALANCE OF FORCES:

TOUJOURS ICI

Visit us at www.boldstrokesbooks.com

Praise for Ali Vali

Carly's Sound

"Vali paints vivid pictures with her words…*Carly's Sound* is a great romance, with some wonderfully hot sex."—*Midwest Book Review*

"It's no surprise that passion is indeed possible a second time around"— *Q Syndicate*

Calling the Dead

"So many writers set stories in New Orleans, but Ali Vali's mystery novels have the authenticity that only a real Big Easy resident could bring…makes for a classic lesbian murder yarn."—*Curve*

Blue Skies

"Vali is skilled at building sexual tension and the sex in this novel flies as high as Berkley's jets. Look for this fast-paced read."—*Just About Write*

Acclaim for the Cain Casey Saga

The Devil Inside

"Vali's fluid writing style quickly puts the reader at ease, which makes the story and its characters equally easy to get to know and care about. When you find yourself talking out loud to the characters in a book, you know the work is polished and professional, as well as entertaining."—*Family and Friends*

"Not only is The Devil Inside a ripping mystery, it's also an intimate character study."—*L-Word Literature*

"*The Devil Inside* is the first of what promises to be a very exciting series…While telling an exciting story that grips the reader, Vali has also fully fleshed out her heroes and villains. *The Devil Inside* is that rarity: a fascinating crime novel which includes a tender love story and leaves the reader with a cliffhanger ending."—*MegaScene*

The Devil Unleashed

"Fast-paced action scenes, intriguing character revelations, and a refreshing approach to the romance thriller genre all make for an enjoyable reading experience in the Big Easy…*The Devil Unleashed* is an engrossing reading experience." —*Midwest Book Review*

Deal With the Devil

"Ali Vali has given her fans another thick, rich thriller…*Deal With the Devil* has wonderful love stories, great sex, and an ample supply of humor. It is an exciting, page turning read that leaves her readers eagerly awaiting the next book in the series."—*Just About Write*

By the Author

Carly's Sound

Second Season

Calling the Dead

Blue Skies

Balance of Forces: Toujours Ici

<u>The Cain Casey Saga</u>

The Devil Inside

The Devil Unleashed

Deal with the Devil

The Devil Be Damned

BALANCE OF FORCES:

TOUJOURS ICI

by

Ali Vali

2011

BALANCE OF FORCES: TOUJOURS ICI
© 2011 By Ali Vali. All Rights Reserved.

ISBN 13: 978-1-60282-567-3

This Trade Paperback Original Is Published By
Bold Strokes Books, Inc.
P.O. Box 249
Valley Falls, NY 12185

First Edition: October 2011

CREDITS
EDITORS: SHELLEY THRASHER AND STACIA SEAMAN
PRODUCTION DESIGN: STACIA SEAMAN
COVER DESIGN BY SHERI (GRAPHICARTIST2020@HOTMAIL.COM)

Acknowledgments

Imagination is something we start to cultivate as children, but at times it dulls with the responsibilities that come with age. Writing gives us some of that back, and there is nothing more freeing than letting my mind wander and listen to the voices of the characters that are always chatting away. What a gift it has been to find a boss who encourages me and gives wings and voice to those characters and stories. Thank you, Radclyffe, for your support and for giving me a home at BSB.

From the very beginning, Shelley Thrasher has been there as well, guiding me with an active red pen as well as kind words. Thank you for all you've taught me, and for the ideas that sometimes send me off in directions I didn't consider. With your help the stories always end up stronger, and something I'm proud of. I'm so glad you're a part of my team.

The first people who get to read these stories are Kathi Isserman and Connie Ward. Thank you both for your suggestions and for honesty. You guys aren't just the best beta readers in the business, but you're great friends as well.

Thank you to each one of you who has supported and encouraged me from the very beginning. Every book, every word is always written with you, the reader, in mind, and it will always be so. It's nice having you all along for the journey.

No matter what else is happening in my life, or what the story is about, there is one person who is at the heart of my life who makes me feel as if everything is possible. Thank you, C, for not only your love, but for all you've brought into my life. These past twenty-six years have passed in a flash, and I'm looking forward to the next fifty at least. I love you.

For C
My partner, my life, my love

CHAPTER ONE

Egypt in the year 1482 BC

"Our enemy is anxious for battle," Asra, Captain of the Pharaoh Hatshepsut's elite forces, told her second in command as they headed toward her tent. "They should wait until sunrise, but post extra men along the ridge of the dunes in case they want to start their journey to the realm of Anubis early."

"As you command." The man bowed slightly with his fist to his chest.

"Report if you detect any movement. If not, leave me to a few candlemarks of peace."

"It shall be so."

Asra's tent fluttered as the wind picked up and drowned out the quiet conversations, and as soon as she was alone, she stripped off her gear and placed it on the trunk near her pallet. She had craved solitude all day, but had wanted to be sure everything was ready for the impending battle. The encampment was quiet now, only a few fires ensuring safe passage through the maze of men and equipment but not producing enough light for enemy scouts to detect them.

Asra had learned that lesson by age four from her father, Raad, the leader of the pharaoh's great troops. His name meant "thunder," and many of the men he had faced and crushed found it to be no boast.

In the morning they would face an enemy from the east that outnumbered them three to one, but Asra wasn't worried. Her confident demeanor spurred those who served under her to live up to their reputation as the pharaoh's elite warriors. At first the soldiers at her command had not welcomed their assignment, but none of them had hesitated to follow her into battle, because of her father. After that, her skill on the battlefield had made them want to follow her.

That night Asra had sat by one of the campfires to eat with some of her new recruits, listening to their stories of home and the families who waited for their return. She'd laughed at their jokes and added a few, but now she was grateful for the time alone to study her maps and mentally review the next day.

She planned to conquer the fools camped not far from their position as quickly as possible, returning a few survivors to their ruler to prove Pharaoh Hatshepsut's strength. Surrounding rulers who thought to gain new lands at Hatshepsut's expense had sent forces before. Most of them quickly learned, though, that Hatshepsut's gender didn't blunt her willingness to send people like Asra to kill anyone who opposed her, and tomorrow would be no different. Asra intended to carry out her orders swiftly, and those lucky few left alive would carry back the tale of their comrades who lay dead under the Egyptian sun with only vultures to tend to them.

A fast, decisive victory would also allow Asra to head home to care for her ill father. The desire to sit and share a few more conversations with him made her want to run into the night and slice the chest of every enemy who kept her bound to her duty.

But Asra would carry out orders before she indulged in any personal matter, as had her father, and his father before him. Her family had served the ruling dynasty in battle for generations, and Asra would continue the tradition.

She poured herself a cup of wine and recalled the day her father had put his own future at jeopardy by asking the pharaoh for something unheard of. Hatshepsut had gazed silently down at her from the throne for so long she felt a chill in her heart. Then the pharaoh called her closer.

"The gods have blessed you with Raad's height and eyes," Hatshepsut said, studying Asra's dark-brown irises with a slight smile. "Have the gods also blessed you with his skill with the sword?"

"With time, My King, I will be as proficient as he."

"Honest as well as confident, Raad. You have done well." Hatshepsut motioned for one of the servants to pour wine for the three of them. "What plans do you have for young Asra?" Her father laid out his goals for her training. She would begin by working closely with him and eventually become a captain. "And if we grant you this wish, Asra, how will you serve us?"

"With honor, obedience, and courage. As long as I have life in me, I will fight to keep you safe."

Hatshepsut had kept an eye on her progress, gifting her with the rank of captain seasons before she or her father thought possible. The pharaoh had come to trust her as much as she did Raad and often had her as a palace guest when she was in Thebes. Hatshepsut apparently saw much of herself in Asra and wanted her to succeed so those who opposed her rule would realize how capable females could be.

Asra's boast to become as skilled as her father with the sword came in time and was one reason she rose so quickly in rank. Raad always remained her greatest advisor and teacher, happy to see at least one of his children carry on their family's traditions. Asra was Raad's greatest pride, but her brother Abez was his greatest disappointment.

"Abez, I pray you eventually find your way home before it's too late to make amends with Father," she said as her eyes lost focus on the maps. "His time grows short; may the gods grant him that comfort before his spirit soars to join our mother." She thought of Abez only at times like this.

He was four seasons older than she, but always different from her in every way possible. He seemed to have inexplicably hated her from birth, and that hatred had deepened when their mother died in Asra's third season. No matter how much Raad encouraged Abez to begin his training, he refused and pulled away, blaming the perfect little soldier who'd followed him.

Now a man, Abez spent his time in the gambling dens of Thebes ridiculing Asra and her growing favor with the pharaoh and the city's elite. He had nothing to do with them until he exhausted his fund of coin for his women, wine, and games. Only then would he come home and play the perfect son, making Raad happy for a few days. Once their father's purse was lighter, Abez returned to the sewer that was his life.

Asra sighed and dropped to the small bench next to her map table, then rested her head in her hands. Regardless of how far back her thoughts had pulled her, Asra heard someone pull the flap back and approach with almost silent steps. "What is it? I left orders not to disturb me unless the enemy is approaching," she said, standing and reaching for her sword. "Has their position changed?"

The person before her bowed low enough that she couldn't see their face. "Forgive my intrusion, Captain, but I bring news of your father."

Any melancholy over Abez's behavior disappeared, and she wanted to shake the messenger. "Speak."

When the woman stood straight Asra became momentarily lost in the beautiful eyes and equally beautiful face. She shook her head to clear her mind and focus on the woman's words. "I'm sorry that you must find out this way, and for my bluntness, but your father is dead."

She dropped to her knees and buried her face in her hands again to hide her despair. "Did he suffer?"

"He suffered very little, Warrior, because his end was swift and before his time. Again, I do not know any way to make this easier to hear. Your brother killed him."

Before the mystery woman could continue, Asra quickly drew her blade. Her father had used this sword in combat and given it to her when she was promoted. "A filthy lie you will bleed for, woman."

"Please, Captain, let me speak. Then I will submit to whatever punishment you wish." The woman bowed again. "That is all I ask."

The messenger gave a history of the forces at work within the realm and in places not yet known to Egypt. As in every battle, good and evil were at odds, and she sought those worthy of fighting for those who could not fight for themselves. Evil, the woman told her, if left unchecked, would plunge the world into darkness forever.

"You're speaking in riddles and wasting my time. What does this have to do with my father?" Asra stood in the middle of the tent curling her fingers tight around her sword. This beauty was perhaps more crazy than dangerous.

"The evil I speak of has seduced your brother, and he took your father's life as revenge for what he feels was denied him."

"You're lying," Asra said. The words fell easily from her lips, but in the pit of her stomach she felt sick. What this woman was saying was possible. "Abez was seduced away from a noble life a long time ago, but he's never been violent. My father may not agree with his choices, but he's never denied him the coins or attention he craves." This news about her brother and losing her father, the only person she trusted completely, made the strength drain from her legs, and she dropped to the bench behind her.

"Blood is now the only craving he will have for eternity. He craves it like we need air to breathe. Abez could have chosen anyone to satisfy his thirst, but he chose your father. That was the best way to draw you out. Then his revenge will be complete."

"We disagree on almost everything, but I cannot believe he hates me so much."

The woman slowly moved closer and knelt next to her, then laid a comforting hand on her knee, waiting until she lifted her head. "He's no longer the brother you knew, Warrior. Accepting this gift destroyed all the good in him. Now he desires only blood and death. It will be so until the end of time, or until he is destroyed."

"Only the gods live forever, and Abez is no god." Asra studied the woman's light skin and hair. This beauty was like finding a rare jewel in the sand.

"What will it take to convince you?"

"I need no proof since I plan no revenge. My brother is not perfect, but he is no killer. That would take effort, which he has very little patience for." She stood and wiped away her tears. "Leave me to mourn my father, and thank you for bringing me the news of his passing. If I can, I will repay the debt."

The woman left as quietly as she had come, and Asra lay on her pallet to give in to her grief. She would have to set her emotions aside in the morning. If what her visitor had said was true, she was truly alone in the world.

❖

Asra headed into battle like a woman possessed. Not an enemy soldier was alive by the time the sun reached its peak. Leaving orders with her second to send word of the victory to the pharaoh, as well as the ruler whom the dead men served, she galloped toward the city. She arrived at her father's home candlemarks before sunrise and again fell to her knees. The atrocity she found made her throw up.

It appeared as if a beast had ripped out the throat of every servant, leaving the bodies for the flies. The lack of blood amazed Asra. The wounds should have painted the walls and tiled floors red, but the bodies, faces frozen in a grimace of terror, were like dry husks of grain.

The stench of death overwhelmed her, and she breathed through her mouth to keep from becoming ill again. As her chest expanded she heard Abez laugh before she saw him. As in her camp, only a few torches were lit throughout the house, and it was difficult to see past a few feet.

"How it pleases me to see the mighty warrior brought to her knees."

"Abez, what have you done?"

"What is my right to do, Captain. You've looked down on me for so long, but that will soon change. I fed on these pathetic fools but now I thirst for you, sister. I am invincible." When he moved out of the shadows, she shrank at the sight.

Seasons of drink and abuse had hardened Abez's features, but he had never been this hideous. His deathly pale skin and his face resembled a nightmare. He kept stroking his new elongated canines with his tongue as if he couldn't stop himself.

She pulled her sword free and held it out in front of her. "It's true, then, you killed Father?"

He laughed so hard he braced his hands against his knees. "He wasted his last breaths calling for you to protect him instead of being in awe of the god he sired." Abez pointed to her sword and shook his head. "You are no match for my strength, Asra, so put your toys away. Face your end showing the same pride with which you serve the mighty pharaoh." He kicked the sword out of her hand and pounced on it before she could move. "This is just one more thing that should have been mine. You stole it from me."

"Father would have given you anything. Don't twist history or blame him for your failures," she said, her anger fueling her courage. "Be a man for once. Admit that you gave away every privilege you were born to because you were too lazy to work for anything. You would have been a lazy, drunken parasite with ten siblings, or as an only child."

"Enough talk, Captain. It's time to pay me in blood for your lack of respect."

"Leave now and I won't turn you to dust, Abez." The threat came from the shadows, and she and Abez turned in the direction from which it came. The speaker was nearby. "Your master warned you of your limitations. Do you wish to see how invincible you are?"

Asra recognized the voice as that of her visitor from the night before. Her messenger stepped into view holding a sword with an intricate design along the length, but from her stance Asra could tell the pretty blade wasn't for show. Abez stepped back as if in fear, and his face morphed back to the monstrous features. The woman only stepped closer, and rather than fight, Abez fled with a speed Asra had witnessed only in horses.

"Are you all right?"

Asra dropped her hands from their defensive posture, but didn't totally relax. "Who are you?"

"I am Morgaine, a member of the Genesis Clan, and I have come to offer you a gift, Asra." Morgaine returned her sword to the sheath strapped to her back and held her hand out. "I am sorry this was the only way to prove that Abez is as lost to you forever as your father is. You may not fully understand what has happened here, but after last night I stayed near and watched you in battle. You possess great skill with the sword."

Asra searched the floor where Abez had stood, but her brother had taken her father's most precious gift. "Thank you, but did my skill help them?" She gestured to everyone who lay slaughtered.

"It won't erase the pain Abez has caused here, but if you accept my offer to join us, you could change the fate of many."

"Who is us?"

As Morgaine had done the night before, she explained how and why she existed. Those who understood and fought the unexplainable had formed the Genesis Clan. "Ages before your birth, a great sickness swept through a mountain village in a land leagues to the north. The weaker villagers died after weeks of suffering pains that contorted their bodies enough to break bones. Only a few survived, and a new breed of human was born who possessed incredible strength and longevity. But their new powers had limitations that rendered them to dust. Those weaknesses killed the majority of the survivors, leaving only one: Ora."

"Why does Abez fear you?" She knelt before her father's body, his wounds grotesque in the soft light.

"Of the little we know of her, Ora is highly intelligent, despite springing from an unevolved society, and was the powerful witch or medicine woman of her village. She was apparently more interested in the dark arts than in the healing part of her craft."

"What do you call her if she's a monster like Abez?" she asked, looking up at Morgaine. The woman's vigor and beauty momentarily blocked out the gore around her.

"The Elders at first called her a succubus, but your brother didn't inflict the wounds you see here to satisfy demon lust. Eventually, like Ora, your brother will learn finesse to get what he needs—the warm blood from a living being." Morgaine stopped in front of a servant girl who had died close to Raad. "See how gaunt her face appears," she said, pointing to the girl's eyes and mouth. "Was she like this in life?"

"No, my father used to tease her about her plump cheeks."

"Abez is now a child of Ora, and, like hers, his body will survive only on blood. Because of this the Elders call her and her kind vampires."

"Why have I never seen or heard of anything like this?" Her voice sounded calm to her ears, but something seemed to be ripping her chest apart.

"We know of Ora, but she is elusive." Morgaine knelt beside her. "I followed her trail here, but she had turned Abez before I could narrow my search. Ora is smart, but she will gladly kill and sacrifice others to learn more about her power. She has acquired the ability to turn others into what she is by taking their life, then giving it back to them."

"What did my brother have to do?"

"She drained him to the point of death, then he drank from her like a baby at his mother's teat. Mingling his blood with hers made him a vampire, and he will find release from the darkness only in death."

"Then when I find him again I'll free him from this curse. I'll kill him even if I must sacrifice myself."

"You've listened to why this happened, Asra, so will you give equal measure to the gift I mentioned? At least listen to the rest of my tale."

She searched Morgaine's face for any sign of what she'd just seen in Abez. If a monster lay dormant under the beautiful façade, it was well hidden behind the eyes that reminded her of sunshine. "Please, finish your story."

"The legend of what happened in Ora's village was fodder for storytellers' tales for many seasons, but as with most old stories few facts of what really happened remained. Talk didn't begin again until Ora discovered that she could share her gift. As she started to increase her family, as she refers to them, strange deaths occurred, mounting until fear swept the northern territories."

"Where were your Elders then?" Asra focused her anger now on Morgaine because if what she said was true, she and her Elders had done nothing to save her father and the rest of their household. Actually, she thought Morgaine mad, but Abez's monstrous features were hard to explain.

"Ora is even older than the Genesis Clan," Morgaine said, leaning closer. "The villagers that Ora and her cursed followers preyed on tried to fight back but failed until a great shaman had a vision. His foresight told of a force that would restore balance to nature. As a young man he started searching for the secret to life, but his grandson perfected the elixir of the sun, bringing to fruition the old man's prophecy. We cannot completely destroy evil, but we can maintain a balance."

Her father's body was cold under her fingers when she closed his eyes, but her gesture did little to erase the terror frozen on his face. "Are you a freak like Abez has become?"

"I'm young compared to some of the others, but I have dedicated my life to fight creatures like the one you saw tonight. Very little of who Abez was still exists. Our numbers need no blood to survive, and we find strength and healing in the sunlight instead of from the misery of others." Morgaine rested her hands on her thighs. "We are the balance to the darkness Abez has given himself over to, and we do not extend the invitation to join our ranks often, but we have found you worthy."

"If I agree, what do you expect of me?"

"I will train you to fight the darkness that has stolen Abez's spirit. With that knowledge also comes a gift."

"What, you want my spirit as well?"

"No, I want to give you life—one that will outlast the great pyramids and temples of Egypt. We ask in return only that you serve when called." Morgaine held out her hand, palm up.

Asra laughed and took the hand. "No one can live forever, woman."

Morgaine smiled as she pulled Asra to her feet. "Then time will be my proof. Will you commit?"

Asra nodded and placed her fist over her chest, willing to take any risk to avenge her father and the others who lay dead at her feet. Fear of death held no sway over her if she could take her brother with her to the land of the dead. The life she had worked so hard for meant nothing to her now. Thoughts of vengeance replaced everything she had ever believed in.

Together they rode into the desert to a camp. Morgaine had set up a large tent next to the watering hole and under the trees of the oasis. When sunset came, Morgaine stripped Asra's bloody uniform, stained from battle and from burying her father and the others. Asra sat placidly as Morgaine bathed her and washed her hair. The attention threatened to make her forget the almost overwhelming sadness.

"Your brother has chosen the darkness, and he will dwell in darkness for the rest of his days because his thirst will blind him to any remaining humanity. But you, warrior mine, will walk a different path. The sun will bring you life, strength, and wisdom. For Abez it will bring only death." Morgaine spoke in soft tones as she cleansed Asra's skin. When she was done she led Asra to a blanket under the stars.

With fascination Asra watched Morgaine mix numerous strange ingredients with clean, fresh water. Morgaine told her the purpose of each item that went into the cup, how much she used as well as the incantations that she had to say in order for it to work. When she finished, the cup appeared to contain only the fresh water she had begun with, but it emitted yellow smoke that glowed as bright as the sun and seemed to boil.

"Drink and live forever," Morgaine said, holding up the cup out to her with both hands.

Asra took the first sip tentatively, thinking it would be hot. It was, in truth, extremely cold, but she felt like she was consuming the strength of a hundred men with each sip, and the feeling of power intoxicated her.

As she drank, her muscles twitched and jumped as they were infused with the power of the sun. Finally, she roused and Morgaine led her to the watering hole. Asra's eyes were now the same pale blue as Morgaine's, and a slight rim of yellow flakes around her irises made them resemble the daytime sky almost as a tribute. The elixir had worked. The Genesis Clan's newest warrior was immortal.

"You are one of us now, Asra. You cannot turn back, but for as long as you walk the earth I will be here to help you. Are you ready to begin?"

"Soon," she said.

Morgaine showed no reluctance when Asra pulled her forward and kissed her. Despite their difference in age and strength, Asra held Morgaine still against her.

"Do you feel it?" Morgaine tried to break free but failed. "Your strength and purity will make you the greatest slayer we have ever produced. No one will ever be able to seduce you as they have Abez."

Asra lowered Morgaine and ran her hand down the length of her beautiful body. Soon she would learn how to destroy not only Abez, but the bitch who had turned him. And if Morgaine was right, she would have an infinite number of tomorrows to make them pay for the life of her father.

CHAPTER TWO

New York, present day

The pink tendrils of dawn painted the sky outside Kendal Richoux's penthouse like no master artist could. She stopped her workout to watch the sunrise, letting the sweat on her body cool.

"That never does get old," she said, placing her sword back on the wall lined with various weapons. Her phone started ringing as she headed to the kitchen, but she waited to answer it until she stripped off her damp clothes.

"Have you been well?"

Kendal stopped and stood naked in front of the open refrigerator, not because of the question, but because of the caller. "Considering I haven't heard from you in years, I thought you'd lost interest."

"I've had my reasons, warrior mine, but a lack of interest isn't one," Morgaine said, and Kendal could picture her smile. "I've missed you."

"No more than I've missed you." She shut the door on the cold air and walked over to sit in the chair that gave her the best view of Central Park. A quick glance at her phone screen showed Morgaine's number was blocked; she could be anywhere in the world, even downstairs. "Or am I not allowed to say so?"

"We can argue later, but I called to tell you that the Elders think it's time."

She'd heard that line so many times she'd lost count. At first messengers had arrived carrying scrolls with her assignments, but the Elders of the Genesis Clan had embraced the age of technology with gusto. However, even after thirty-five hundred years, they still softened the orders they believed would bother her by sending the one she loved above all others. For those occasions Morgaine delivered their message, as she had all those years ago.

"Time for what? I haven't heard of any problems lately." Her skin tingled as the sun rose higher. "The bad guys seem to have learned some self-control."

"It's time for you to return to New Orleans, Asra, and finish what you couldn't the last time you were there."

"You cut deep when you choose to, Watcher." She called Morgaine by the title that defined their relationship and roles within the Clan. "I've postponed what I've wanted for centuries for you, so you might approach me more diplomatically."

"I haven't forgotten your sacrifice, or your promise, but your word no longer binds you. The Elders want to remind you of what they promised you, and it's time to go back." While Morgaine paused, Kendal opened her hand and raised it to catch the first rays that streamed through the window. The feeling still intoxicated her. "They've waited for you, and in that time the problem has festered. The balance we've fought so hard for is in danger of tipping, but not in our favor."

"When?"

"I realize your current identity makes it more difficult to disappear, but as soon as you can."

"I'll try to be there tonight. I'm sure I can find some business deal to make." She stood and walked along the wall of glass, not caring if anyone was up early enough to see her. "Tell your little minions to stay out of my way."

"Why Kendal Richoux, and Richoux International? You've always picked more noble pursuits than being a corporate raider."

"I'm not exactly pillaging defenseless villages, darling." She brought the computer in her bedroom to life so she could scroll through the list of prospects she kept constantly updated. "I have to be a little heartless at times, but I haven't used this much strategy since my time with Pharaoh Hatshepsut."

"Be careful, then, and don't let the old pains blunt your skills."

The softening of Morgaine's voice made Kendal reconsider her anger, and she gave an honest answer. "I choose places with no life left in them, and while I make money, I give the employees of each company back something their employers gambled with to stay afloat. All of them receive the retirement that's owed them, and we help find them jobs when possible."

"What you're doing is legal. You don't owe me an explanation."

"I didn't want you to think the nickname and the business have made me someone you won't recognize."

Morgaine laughed, which made Kendal smile. "I know the core of you, Asra, and whatever window dressing you have to assume doesn't change that. Besides, I'm sure the men you faced in battle the day after I found you would have agreed with the nickname 'Great White,' had they known what it was."

"A mindless killer, you mean?" she asked, teasing.

"Mindless? I'd never say or believe that." Morgaine laughed again. "Please be careful, though. Time has been our enemy in this case."

"Actually, this is the opportunity I've waited an eternity for, and once I'm done I believe the reward will be so fulfilling, it'll change my life forever." She stopped scrolling at a company that showed the qualities her team usually went after.

"What do you mean?"

"It'll finally put my past to rest, bringing peace to a pain so old it's part of my soul. Perhaps in the future I can learn to better enjoy your gift of immortality, but I have to avenge my father."

"No, warrior mine, you'll find your true purpose in something wonderful, not in vengeance. You've left a legacy of goodness through time because you aren't afraid."

Kendal e-mailed her office the information about the floundering company so her staff could start the process. "The ghoulies aren't hard to figure out, so I don't have much fear once I learn their weaknesses."

"That's not what I meant," Morgaine said, and Kendal heard her inhale deeply. "You're never afraid to open and share your heart, and that's what the evil beings you face fear in you. Don't let this encounter blunt your skills or your ability to find the good in any situation."

"You sound so poetic."

"The truth sometimes deserves to be expressed in such a way." Kendal gripped the phone, wishing she could guess where Morgaine was so she could see and touch her. "My brother's waiting and he's ready. I've waited as long, and I've been ready from the day you handed me that cup. This will end a cruel chapter of my history, but don't worry. I'm still open and curious about whatever comes next."

"Until tomorrow, then," Morgaine said, and Kendal knew their time together had come to an end.

"And whatever it brings."

❖

A quick trip to the office brought Kendal's team up to speed on their target, Marmande Shipyard and Construction, but to drag out her time on the project, Kendal decided to take only her executive vice president, Bruce Babbage, and a few associates. Their prospect was a dinosaur in a modern world that had sprung up around its facility, making it totally noncompetitive.

She had the reports on the owners and how they'd reached this point in her briefcase, but she'd save them for later. Depending on their demeanor, she'd decide what to do with them and how much leeway she'd give Bruce, since she had to keep him on a short leash to curb his natural killer instincts.

The flight attendant left a glass of brandy next to her without speaking, so she reclined her seat and stared out the window. The fields south of the airport reminded her of the patchwork quilts common in the South. It had been close to three hundred years since she'd first stepped off a boat in the port of New Orleans, and her time there had begun as an escape after she completed a grueling assignment with Morgaine and a few Elders on the outskirts of Paris. Sadly, it had ended in her exile from a place she'd come to love.

Not that she ever stayed in one place very long, another lesson she'd learned before Morgaine released her into a world she didn't recognize anymore. Since then, she felt more like a bard or a court performer as she morphed from one life to another, learning new trades, meeting people now studied in history books, but always remembering the one purpose for which she existed.

Egypt, 1442 BC

The oasis had changed some in the forty years they had been there. At least that's how much time Morgaine had told her had passed since their arrival. They were alone except for the small caravans that occasionally brought supplies they didn't really need but enjoyed, as well as news from the Elders Morgaine often spoke of. All the other travelers passed them by, never coming close, as if they didn't even see the lush spot in the leagues of sand and wind.

As she did every morning, Asra ran to the highest dune to look out at the emptiness. The only part of her that the sun hadn't bronzed was the part that the loincloth she wore during the day covered, unless some of Morgaine's company was there. She'd expected the effects of the mixture she drank to wear off, but only the length of her hair and nails changed. The rest stayed trapped in the body she'd had when she was twenty-four years old.

"Do you see anything new today?" Morgaine asked, suddenly beside her.

"This place is like me," she said, her fists on her hips. "Always the same."

"Why come up here, then?" Morgaine had become tan also, making her blond hair more vivid. Asra let her gaze drop to the milky white skin around her breasts and hips, since Morgaine had run naked. "Are you getting bored with my company?"

"Not bored, no, but I don't understand so much of what's happened to me." The sun was rising higher, and her blood was circulating through her like a swarm of bees around a flower. "Why give me the ability to live so long, train me every day, only to keep me here? I thought you and your Elders wanted me to fight for you?"

"We'll have this much time together only once, and we'll share it in peace until you're ready." Morgaine moved closer, bringing with her the unique fragrance Asra could never pinpoint. "When the time comes, I'll respect your desire to go do what you wish when you aren't fulfilling the Elders' wishes."

"You've been waiting for me to ask to leave?" She followed Morgaine to the sand, sitting on the crest of the dune and allowing Morgaine to sit in front of her on a small blanket.

"I've been waiting for you to feel ready to leave, and only you'll know when that is." Morgaine leaned back into her, running her hands from her knees to the edge of her loincloth at the top of her thighs. "Do you think you are?"

"We've been over the drills so often I can do them without thinking." Morgaine's right hand slipped under the flap covering Asra's sex, and she instantly wanted her. In their time together she'd learned as much about pleasing Morgaine as she had about killing the monsters that supposedly prowled the night, but neither subject ever got old.

Her morning runs were a sort of prayer ritual to connect with her father. She whispered her secrets from the top of the desolate place, hoping the wind would carry them to wherever he was, even if he never answered. The passage of time since Raad's death had eased the pain, but she still ached, missing him. The memory receded only when Morgaine touched her like this, and when Morgaine's fingers landed on her hard clitoris, she closed her eyes and thought of nothing but the pleasure of having Morgaine so close.

The first intense pain came from her leg, where Morgaine opened a gash from her left knee to the top of her thigh. It was so deep she couldn't move to stand up and defend herself, and with her hand over the wound, she couldn't stop Morgaine's next strike to her chest. The last blow, to her neck, sent a spray of blood so far that it seemed to dye Morgaine's skin and hair red.

It had been difficult to adjust to this type of training, but when the sun reached its highest point she had completely healed. She would have been dead without the elixir, and Morgaine's message had damaged her ego so thoroughly she spent the day at the top of the dune alone.

By sunset the temperatures had dropped significantly, but the cold wind didn't bother her as she stared at Morgaine's fire in the distance. In the quiet stillness, she finally accepted the reality of her situation and headed back down to her watcher.

"I hope you know I took no pleasure in hurting you." Morgaine spoke without turning around, seemingly fixated on the fire.

"This gift, like the one Abez accepted, has its limitations, doesn't it?"

"Yes, and because nothing in life is foolproof, you always must be vigilant." Morgaine faced her, pulling her light cloak closed at the throat. "You will live forever, Asra, but that doesn't mean you're free from capture or suffering."

"You did that today to prove I can trust no one?"

"I'm sure the only person you've had complete faith in was your father."

She nodded, unable to talk around the stone that had formed in her chest, as if all her sadness and mourning over his loss had fused into a mass.

"He's irreplaceable, but I'll never betray you. As long as we have sunrises, I'll treasure our friendship and do nothing to bring you harm."

"Then why almost take my head off?"

"The night you saw Abez for the first time, the sight of him was hideous, but not all of Ora's children will present themselves like that. Many of them are beautiful, and if you allow that face to cloud your senses, they'll exploit your greatest weakness."

"Total darkness."

Morgaine smiled but still looked melancholy. "That's right. They will rob you of what feeds their power, which proves the balance in all things. Never let anyone close to you without having something to defend yourself with."

Asra had taken for granted that the difference in their sizes would always put Morgaine at a disadvantage. That's why she laughed when Morgaine dropped her cloak to reveal she was as naked as that morning. "You *are* beautiful, but I won't fall for the same trick twice."

"You have my word that I have no blade. If you can subdue me, I will give you my blessing to leave." Morgaine stood with her feet apart and her hands in front of her, as if she were about to pick up a large vase. "You may go when you please, but I will believe you're ready to do so only when you can defeat me."

❖

Kendal had forgotten some aspects of her life because the nonimportant things had faded with time, but the glee in Morgaine's eyes when she accepted her challenge was still as fresh as the night it happened. She had stood there trying to determine how to grip Morgaine without hurting her when Morgaine flipped her into the fire. Her loincloth burned until it fell from her body.

She smiled at the memory of the next twenty years in that isolated place as she learned what the world now knew as martial arts. She had quickly mastered her skills, but the extra time with Morgaine had transformed her into more than a warrior. Asra of the house of Raad was now the Genesis Clan's most skilled and successful slayer—the perfect killing machine who had kept the balance heavily tilted in the Elders' favor.

"Do you need anything else?" the attendant asked.

"No, thank you," she said softly, since everyone around her was sleeping.

The scenery below her hadn't changed much so she concentrated on paperwork, trying to spot every loophole in the delinquent loans. The Marmande family business was still operating because of an old friend at the bank. Unfortunately, the boards of directors of financial institutions disregarded friendship and loyalty. The old-fashioned qualities seldom had anything to do with business, especially when it came to money and its repayment.

Kendal would offer substantially less than Marmande owed, but she was willing to negotiate. She intended to buy the loans from the bank and secure the collateral the family had put up—Marmande Shipyard and Construction Company and all the assets that entailed. It sounded simple, but New Orleans had a way of piling unforeseen surprises in your path. This trip, she wanted to do without those, especially the nasty ones.

CHAPTER THREE

"Did you try him again?" Macarthur Marmande asked his granddaughter Piper, his heart racing.

"Yesterday we were ready to sign contracts by next week, but now his secretary says he wants to freeze the process and review some things. He's not available to talk to me."

Mac, as all his friends called him, ran a shaky hand through his still-thick but white hair. He was beyond ready to leave the everyday operations to Piper, but not until they were on steadier ground. She didn't deserve any more disasters.

She had lost first her mother, then her father, Mac's son, not long afterward, leaving him and his wife Molly the responsibility of raising her. She was spunky and full of ambition, but Mac suspected it was a defense for the empty place left in her heart after his son took his own life, a place no one had been able to fill. Mac understood why his boy had given up, but he'd been the only parent Piper remembered. The death of Mac's daughter-in-law had devastated two lives.

"I don't need to explain how important this contract is to us, sweetheart."

"It's not enough to square with the bank, but I agreed to the deal because it'll prove we're still competitive and putting out the best product. Ideally not what we're looking for long-term, but it'll be a moot point since I can't force this guy to take my call. We need to concentrate on who got to him and why."

Piper stood and smoothed down her wool slacks in what Mac knew was a nervous habit, then paced to the window. The executive suites that overlooked their operations were comfortable, without the usual plush surroundings of a corner office. "Without something coming in, we won't make payroll much longer, and another credit line won't be an option, Pops, no matter how much they love you."

"You haven't heard any rumors lately?"

Piper glanced over her shoulder at him and smiled. "I've been swamped putting this together, so I've missed a month's worth of chamber stuff, and lunch out has been impossible." She sat on the edge of his desk close enough to take his hand. "Don't worry. I always have more than one plan, and I won't quit until I uncover what's going on."

"Just remember, sometimes there's a bigger dog on the playground than you, my little pit bull. I'm here to help, and not only as window dressing."

"You're always my first call, Pops, so keep your phone handy." She kissed him, then grabbed her purse and keys from her office. Something had blown up their best-case scenario, so she had to shore up her last option to keep the bank from foreclosing.

As Piper hurried to her small sports coupe, she dialed her cell phone and asked the woman who answered, "Is he in?"

"You saved me a call, Ms. Marmande. If you're available, Mr. Delaney wants you to join him for lunch on his boat."

"Great," she said, not meaning it, but she had few options left. "I'll try his cell and tell him I'm on my way."

"It's a beautiful day for a sail."

To hell, maybe, Piper thought, but kept that thought to herself as she disconnected. I doubt I'll find the answers Pops wants in the middle of Lake Pontchartrain, but I can only deal with one crisis at a time.

❖

The limo driver from the Piquant waiting for Kendal at the airport was, thankfully, not a big talker, and he led her to the car after he collected her luggage. Thus far she could've been in any city in the world—nothing reminded her of the place she'd left in 1728. As she felt the trunk close, an unfamiliar excitement started to build.

The ride went smoothly and Kendal studied the scenery, but still nothing looked familiar. Since she'd been on a late flight, they'd hit the interstate into the city long after five o'clock traffic and arrived at the hotel in less than thirty minutes. The five-star facility hadn't existed either when she left New Orleans so long ago, but the staff's hospitality made her think of those who'd been special to her.

"Your group's already checked in, Ms. Richoux, and left this for you."

The thick packet contained the missing pieces of their puzzle and a schedule of all the meetings Bruce and his team had already set up. "Thank you, and if you could, I'd like a copy of the most recent map of the city."

"We'll send it up in a few minutes."

A tremendous amount of paper covered every table and flat surface in the outer rooms of her suite when the porter opened the door for her. "Even though it's Saturday, we got to meet with the bank leadership," Bruce said, as if he never could start a conversation at the beginning. "The good-old-boys' club didn't act interested until I told them we'd organized a reception for their board tonight."

"An open bar and crab puffs usually grease the wheels of business most effectively," she said, and laughed. The staff Bruce brought with him had left the best chair empty for her, but she stayed in the middle of the room with her coat draped over her shoulder. "The reception's a good idea, but don't set any meetings with these guys until we meet with Mr. Marmande. I'd prefer lunch with only the two of us so we don't seem so hostile from the beginning."

"If I can get a quick vote tonight, you don't want me to close?" Bruce stood across from her, apparently trying to look and sound menacing.

Kendal kept what she hoped was a neutral expression because Bruce's short stature made him appear more comical than scary. "From what I've read of Mr. Marmande, he deserves a healthy dose of respect."

"You picked him this morning and you've never met," he said through barely clenched teeth as he ran his hand through his thinning brown hair. "Why give him the opportunity to rebound?"

"Because I said so," she said, her humor gone. When Bruce got this intense, he reminded her of his father, which only accentuated how short they both were. Granted, Bruce had helped her become successful in this lifetime, but unlike his father, he never knew when to stop. His life revolved around business, but the kill shot, not the thrill of the chase, drove him.

"We could set a new record with this one," Bruce said after taking a few deep breaths. "In and out in a few days so we can concentrate on the L.A. deal."

"Take a few more cleansing breaths and listen to what I'm telling you." The room became very silent and still. "If you can't, admit it now and I'll meet with Mr. Marmande myself."

"I have your back, you know that." Bruce had lost his ferocity and stepped closer. "This can still be quick after you finish with the board members tonight. No way they can resist your charm."

"You set it up, you handle it. I might have to sit with these guys eventually, but not tonight."

"Kendal, come on. They'll want to talk to you. It's not like they can read up on you like you did with the old man," Bruce said, referring to her unbending rule about granting any media access to her business or personal life.

"It doesn't matter if they know what my favorite color is." She stepped around him and headed for the door. "They just care about the health of my bank account."

"What's more important than this?" he asked, the lid coming off his temper.

She stared at his hand on her arm until he let go so suddenly he stumbled back. Her humor didn't return until she got to the elevator and still didn't hear a sound from the suite.

When the doorman opened the front entrance for her it was close to eleven, but the traffic on Canal Street was still heavy. The drivers didn't appear to be in a hurry to get anywhere, but they acted like they were enjoying the scenery even though they were locals.

"Could you have this sent up to my room? Kendal Richoux," she said, handing her coat to the doorman.

"My pleasure, ma'am." He tipped his hat. "Can I get you a cab as well?"

"Thanks, but I'm in the mood to walk."

"Please be careful. This is New Orleans, after all, and as much as it pains me to say it, sometimes the streets are scary."

She laughed, glad to drop the façade of Kendal Richoux for a while because it wasn't the way she thought of herself in this city full of life and frivolity. "Don't tell me, the place is haunted."

"I'm sure more than one goblin's running around, but I'm more worried about the ones who're alive and armed." He pointed his finger at her like a gun.

"That's true, but they should be scared of *me*." She laughed along with him but decided that the cargo in her coat pockets might come in handy. "On second thought, give me my coat back."

"What, is it bulletproof or something?"

Kendal smiled as she threw it over her shoulder and handed him a tip. "Or something is right."

As she walked toward the river, she noticed the line of cars waiting for the all-too-brief spans of green at the traffic signals. Some drivers had their windows rolled down to enjoy the cool weather, and apparently so anyone walking could enjoy the blaring music pouring out of speakers worth more than the vehicles they were riding around in. This part of the city was unfamiliar too, but each step took her back to the familiar. She welcomed it with an anticipation she could almost reach out and touch. Had the heart of the city changed so much that she'd feel lost after having been away so long?

A new aquarium stood at the end of Canal Street, near a long walkway that meandered along the banks of the Mississippi River to the cusp of the French Quarter. Water lapped against the pilings that held up the sidewalk where she was standing, and as she began to stroll toward the old section, her eyes blurred with tears as memories washed over her like a gentle rain.

Under the permanent gazebo built where the river made a slight bend, she stopped and gripped the railing. Kendal didn't want to remember, but her heart wouldn't listen. She had kept the history of her time here at bay long enough, and like the churning brown water below, it wouldn't be held back any longer.

New Orleans, October 1726

"Master, the captain says the ship should be in port by tomorrow." Lionel St. Louis bowed slightly, even though the person he was addressing faced away from him, his eyes on the Gulf. His master's gloved hand clutched one of the thick ropes that held up the sails, and he seemed lost in thought.

"Not a day too soon, eh, Lionel?"

"I could've lived without all those waves. If I throw up one more time, I may not be able to carry the bags down the plank." His French was almost as flawless as his master's, causing one of the crew to stop and stare at them disgustedly. Usually, slaves barely spoke broken English, but he routinely drew attention since he wore a suit that rivaled his master's and his French would have passed muster in the French royal court.

"Don't worry, Lionel, we may flout tradition, but I'll help if it comes to that." The Marquis Jacques St. Louis turned around and smiled. As always, Lionel became lost in the pale eyes rimmed in yellow that seemed to look into his soul and decipher all his secrets.

Jacques, a tall, handsome man, owned a plantation outside New Orleans, but unlike most of his counterparts who worked their slaves into an early grave, he was known for his gentle nature. The French royal had ventured out of his comfortable life in the north of France to make a name for himself in the New World and had achieved his goal in only five years.

Oakgrove Plantation cultivated sugarcane, tobacco, and cotton on over ten thousand acres of cleared land along the Mississippi River north of New Orleans. Jacques owned more than five hundred slaves, whom he treated like his extended family instead of chattel. Many people had asked questions about him since his arrival, but he gave them only a smile and wink. The city dwellers knew only that no wife or children shared the large home he'd built, and he came to the city only to sell his harvest.

"No, sir, even if I have to crawl off this beast from hell, I won't let you do my work. I wonder if anyone missed us?" Lionel fastened his cloak as the wind picked up and put an extra snap in the sails.

"I'm sure they've noticed our absence. As much as I miss my homeland at times, I'm glad to be returning to Oakgrove. After selling my family's land in France, I consider this my home now."

Their recent trip to Europe had taken a little over fourteen months, but now Lionel joined Jacques at the rail to scan the horizon for land. He couldn't think of anything sweeter than stepping back on solid ground and seeing his wife and sons again. Unlike most of the other landowners in the area, Jacques never split up couples, much less any children that resulted from the unions they themselves negotiated.

Since coming to the plantation, Lionel had received his own quarters to share with a young woman named Celia he'd fallen in love with. Their four small children often ran after Jacques's horse when he visited the large cluster of cabins the servants occupied, and it was common to see them perched on his lap talking him out of the candies he carried in his pockets. A slew of children usually sat at his feet listening to stories created from his extraordinary imagination about people who lived long ago. As on the other plantations, Oakgrove required plenty of work, but Jacques worked right next to his slaves and never carried a whip. No one at Oakgrove feared a lashing.

"Sir, will you tell me more of your family?" A few of the curls that had escaped Jacques's ever-present ponytail flew freely around his forehead. Some of the men in New Orleans used the powdered wigs popular in their countries of origin, but not Jacques. Lionel had seen more than one woman's lingering stare on his master when they did come into town. The combination of his thick black hair and his interesting eyes was unusual among the French and Spanish settlers who had made New Orleans their home.

The silence grew between them, and when Lionel saw Jacques's grip tighten on the rope, he thought he'd made a mistake. "I'm sorry, sir. I didn't mean anything. It's not my place to question you."

"It's all right. I've told you most of my history so far, and you have a right to the rest. I have only one family member left, but he's lost to me and I don't like to talk about him. You have to understand that some choose their lot in life and others have it thrust upon them. Those who get to pick are lucky."

"I don't understand, master."

"Could you perhaps, while we're talking as friends, call me Jacques? It's been years since I've heard anyone besides myself say my name."

Lionel laughed from nerves and tightened his grip on the railing. "But we're not friends, sir."

Jacques's expression softened but he didn't move from his spot. "In this moment we are much more, Lionel. I've watched you grow from an angry young man who didn't want to let his heritage go, to a fine father and husband. I may own you in the eyes of the law, but in your heart you'll always be free, my friend. Did you think I wouldn't discover that you're the son of a king in your homeland who teaches your four little ones your language and your traditions at night?"

For a brief moment, the long voyage to a new, cruel world after his capture returned to Lionel. The trip was in some ways more humiliating than being put on the auction block. Every day more and more lifeless bodies collected from the belly of the ship were tossed overboard. He came to think of those who found their freedom in the waves as the lucky ones. They were either dead or too weak to be worth anything once they docked.

The young men from his tribe who had been captured with him looked to him for guidance, but demoralized and shackled, he had none to give. Now he'd come to terms with his capture and enslavement and had found people to love. However, this man who owned him could end his newfound peace with one strong shove and have no fear of recrimination. "In this moment we are much more, Lionel," Jacques had said. Would he throw him overboard for teaching his children the way of his tribe like his father had done for him?

"Please, master, I only told them stories to put them to sleep. I didn't mean any disrespect." He spoke in a rush laced with panic.

Jacques moved his hand from the rope to Lionel's shoulder. "I meant what I said. I've watched you because for so much of my life I was you. No one's ever enslaved me, but I've been angry with the choices that I couldn't make but that affected me nonetheless. I value your friendship, Lionel, that's what I meant. Sometimes I wish I had sons like you to pass on the vast experience and knowledge I've accumulated through the years." He squeezed Lionel's shoulder and smiled. "See, sometimes you're the lucky one, even if you think your life could be better. We're both slaves to circumstance, my friend. That makes us closer than family."

"Thank you, sir."

"Won't you consider my request?"

"Thank you, Jacques." The name rolled strangely off his tongue since he'd never uttered it, not even when he was alone with his thoughts. His own enslavement was grossly unfair, but it could have been much worse. He didn't intend to disrespect someone who had treated him like a man.

"And I thank you, Lionel." They left the rail, walked toward a row of barrels the crew had lashed to the front for storage, and sat down. "Now let me try to make you understand what I said about my only family. My brother, Henri, chose his path and walked into the darkness alone. And because he did, I had no choice but to make my own future or face the same darkness. I received a gift as a way to escape my brother's wrath, and when I accepted, my fate was set. Like everything in life, however, it comes with a price." Jacques looked out at the water again and sighed. "I'm sorry, Lionel, that's all I can share with you now."

"Does Henri still walk the dark path?" Lionel asked, not wanting their conversation to end. Children weren't the only ones who got lost in Jacques's voice and stories.

"He revels in it and has only grown worse with time."

They sat together in silence until sunset, when it became too cold to stay on deck. As they stood to make their way back to their cabins for a bite to eat, Lionel spotted the signal fires the port lit at night to guide ships into the mouth of the Mississippi. With any luck they'd be in New Orleans by dawn and back at Oakgrove within days.

New Orleans, present day

Kendal had assumed so many personas through the decades, but her time as Jacques St. Louis had left a mark on her soul. The boat had docked the next morning all those years ago at the spot where she now stood.

So many lifetimes had passed, yet the memories and the bittersweet pain they brought with them were still fresh because she had left so many things undone. It still angered her that she couldn't save so many of the people she loved.

"Ah, Kendal, weeping still, sister? Always the sentimental one, weren't you? Tears are for the foolish and the weak. Aren't you above that by now? Not that I'm not happy to see you, but I thought we agreed long ago you were never to return here. We each must have our realms, and this is mine."

Abez's voice was the same one that haunted her waking dreams when she closed her eyes, and it still held traces of the French he loved to speak after he fell in love with his creation, Henri St. Louis. But a cultured accent along with the outer appearance of a French nobleman couldn't hide the monster he was—not then, and certainly not now.

"How did you know I was back?" she asked, trying to gauge how powerful he'd grown.

"Your blood, my sweet. Its distinctive scent is like no other in the world. I smelled you in my sleep the moment your plane landed. But that doesn't answer my question, does it?"

"I'm here on business, Abez, and as for our agreement, it ended eighty-four years ago. Aren't you going to introduce me to your pets?" Kendal had yet to turn around, since she wasn't without skills. She was content to watch the tugboats on the river haul barges in both directions. The Mississippi had changed and grown massive over the years, but its years of roaming free were over. The levees the Army Corps of Engineers had built kept it well confined, most of the time.

"I'm sure you've better things to do. Why now?" Something must have caught Henri's attention because he snapped his fingers, making one of the women with him move away at inhuman speed.

"Because as the old saying goes, brother, to every thing there's a season. It was my time to come back even though I didn't want to, believe me. Like always, you do whatever pleases you without thinking of the consequences. Experience should have taught you everything has consequences, some more costly than others. Did you think they'd give you free rein forever? Surely the Elders have sent warnings about your behavior before my arrival?" She turned to face him.

Time had also stopped for Abez, so he was still handsome and tall, but his white skin appeared almost like marble. His suit looked like black velvet, and the ruffled shirt seemed a better fit than the first time they'd met in New Orleans, but Henri was too much of a monster to display sentimentality.

"Yes, they have, but with time comes power, if you're willing to take chances. You always followed the rules and orders, the consummate perfect little soldier. Doesn't it ever bore you to be so good? The time of such obedience has passed."

"This isn't about you and me or your list of perceived wrongs the world has committed against you. It's about balance, so grow up."

"It's about both, don't be ignorant. You robbed me of Father's love and managed to always get the glory." The woman who had run to do Henri's bidding was back, appearing flushed. Her skin, which moments before had resembled carved alabaster, now looked warm to the touch.

"You sound like a petulant child."

"Stay away from me, sister. This will be *my* only warning."

She turned around again when he left, not afraid that he would return. So many things about Abez never changed, besides his face. He still couldn't face any conflict without a few of his minions to act as his backbone. He had never fought his own battles, yet his life revolved around constant conflict. But if he wanted a fight, it wouldn't come an hour before dawn. Henri was at home in New Orleans, a place he'd stayed since 1728, giving him an advantage, but he wasn't reckless enough to face her at a time that might leave him vulnerable.

This ancient city was filling Kendal's head with painful memories, yet some of them brought a sense of calm. In a city that seldom slept, an hour before sunrise was as close as it got to total silence; she focused on the sound of the water and turned her face to the east. She loved to watch the sunrise, but here it had a deeper meaning, as if the new day brought a new beginning. As pink fingers crept across the sky, she raised her hands and started to murmur a prayer her father had taught her as a small child in a temple near their home.

"Father Ra, bringer of life, protect me. Give me strength to do your work and make me true to my spirit and to my cause."

Any scholar would give their firstborn to hear the old Egyptian dialect spoken correctly and with the proper accent. The language was as dead as the men who'd spoken it, but it gave Kendal a sense of belonging. She opened her eyes as the sun first appeared, and as always, a charge traveled through her as if the ancient god Ra had answered her prayer. If only he would give her the wisdom to make the right decisions in the coming days.

With one final sigh, she turned and made her way to Café du Monde for a strong cup of Louisiana coffee with steamed milk. It was one of the things Kendal missed most about the city in her long absence. The French and Spanish settlers who built New Orleans had brought with them the recipe for strong, full-bodied coffee that had changed only slightly over the years with the addition of chicory. The filler, an inexpensive way to stretch the grounds during times of war and ration, had become as much a part of Southern culture as pecan pie.

CHAPTER FOUR

As Piper Marmande ran on her treadmill, she watched the sunrise on television when the weatherman cut to a camera stationed by the lake. The shower she'd taken after docking at ten the night before hadn't left her feeling clean, so she'd increased her regular speed to try to sweat Kenny's presence out of her skin. She appreciated his help, but the price was more than she was comfortable with.

As the guy on the screen droned on about enjoying the cool, dry air and clear skies before the massive storm to the north hit them in a few hours, her cell phone started to ring. She would've ignored it, but her grandfather seldom called her this early unless it was important. He'd left numerous messages, but after she'd turned her phone back on, she hadn't wanted to wake him.

"Good morning, Pops," she said, pressing a towel to the front of her neck. "Sorry about yesterday, but I was working on plan B." What she said was true and necessary, but the dirty feeling came back.

"I hope it's a good one, sweetie, because I think I know who killed our deal and why."

She gazed out her kitchen window at the dark clouds rolling toward her. Fate seemed to be on its way to crush her, and she wouldn't be able to face her grandparents if she lost the one thing their family had built for generations.

"Did you hear me, Piper?"

"Yes, sir," she whispered, holding on to the countertop to stay on her feet. "What'd you find out?"

"You ever heard of Richoux International?"

Piper closed her eyes and pinched the bridge of her nose so she could concentrate, but the name didn't raise any alarms. "Should I have?"

"Kendal Richoux owns it. She visited the bank yesterday and offered to make good on our loans."

It was hard to listen to the weariness in Mac's voice, but she tried not to let it swamp her as she booted up her laptop. She didn't remember the company, but she'd heard of Kendal Richoux. "Is she the woman the *Wall Street Journal* calls the Great White?"

"That's what Brad called her." Mac sighed. "Ms. Richoux came out of nowhere, and he tried to put her off, but she knows what she's doing."

Brad Howell and Mac had met in grade school, so if he was willing to forget the friendship he and Pops had shared for decades, they were in serious trouble. "What does that mean?" she asked as she found a few articles about Richoux International that barely mentioned its owner.

"He told her the bank was working with us, and he wasn't in a position to sell us out...literally."

"That sounds like Brad." There was more, but she felt better knowing Brad hadn't turned his back on Pops immediately.

"She hosted a reception for the full bank board last night, and it'll be hard for them to ignore the amount of money she's talking about."

"What in the world would she want with us?"

"That's easy," Mac said, as if he'd resigned himself to the inevitable. "We're worth more with our doors closed than operational, and people like Kendal Richoux thrive on situations like this."

"You're not giving up on me, are you?"

"We'll find out today if we have a fight left to wage."

"The board would act that quickly? It's the weekend, for God's sake." Panic sucked the air from her lungs.

"Brad said it'll take about a week if they decide to accept her offer, that's not what I'm talking about. Ms. Richoux's invited us to lunch to discuss why she's here, so I need you to meet me at the Palace Café at noon."

"I'll meet you there, Pops, but I need to make a few calls."

Piper hung up and hurried into the shower to try to organize her thoughts. She put on a robe after she dried her hair and skipped breakfast to head to her home office. Then she called Kenny, who assured her that the bank officers would consider their merger plan before they entertained anything from an outsider.

She felt better now about delaying Richoux, but was still uneasy about Kenny. Deals that seemed to have no downside when the other guy was explaining them usually ended in disaster for the one being buttered up, so the red flags were still flapping when she considered tying their future to Kenny and his investors.

"This absolutely sucks," she said as she scrolled through her contacts, searching for a number.

Hillary Hickman answered after the second ring. "Hickman Investigations."

"Hill, thank God you're in," Piper said. "I need a favor, hopefully before noon."

"Not a lot of time, but I'll do my best."

Piper gave her Kendal's name and company information, wanting as many facts as Hill could find before their lunch date. If she could send this woman back to New York, she'd have a better shot of getting them out of trouble without anyone's help.

"I'll give you a call."

She placed the phone back in its cradle and stared at the framed photo her grandmother had given her as a housewarming gift after she bought her condo. Mac and Molly had tried to talk her into a house, but she liked the sameness of this place. It wasn't different in any way from the other twenty-nine units, which matched how she felt about herself—common and mediocre. She lived here, but it wasn't home or permanent.

The picture of her parents that sat on her desk showed her mom, Jen, seven months pregnant with her. She sat in front of her dad, Mackey, mid-laugh, her hands holding her midsection as if protecting the life within from being jostled too much. It was their only family photo, capturing perfectly Jen Marmande's joy that everyone remembered her for. The black-and-white moment teased Piper with the possibilities she'd never have. The happy memories stopped there, and she'd had no chance to build on them.

Her mother had died in childbirth, leaving her father to deal with the pain and loss along with their baby, but Mackey didn't have the strength to start a future without the one person he'd invested all his happiness in. They didn't talk about it, but her father took his life, or threw it away, as she considered it. He selfishly gave up, never thinking of the wreckage he'd left behind. Mourning his loss, Mac had been walking around in a fog for years, which inevitably led them to the scary cliff they were teetering on, but she never blamed him.

"We all process differently, and I refuse to lose another thing," she said to her father's smiling face. Her life had been cursed almost from the very beginning, and she had survived by finding a place that insulated her from as much pain as possible. She kept people from seeing who she truly was, even if that perpetuated the loneliness. She had earned her reputation as a bitch, but she dictated the terms of every relationship she had. That way no one ever mattered enough for her to consider death as a remedy for the lost happiness.

"That's where you and I differ, Daddy." With a deep breath, she buried the pain of losing him so she could try to salvage what was left of their family's legacy. "Giving up isn't in my nature."

❖

Tourists as well as the locals flocked to Café du Monde, a New Orleans tradition. The open-air shop served only coffee and beignets, small pieces of fried bread dough covered in powdered sugar that, like fingerprints, were individually unique even though machines now cut the dough. To Kendal the coffee shop with its brass kettles of steamed milk and constant motion was a microcosm of the city.

The waiters, an interesting reflection of the face of New Orleans, had originally been white men who later moved to finer establishments in the nearby French Quarter. Then African Americans moved into the vacated positions and were replaced in droves by Hispanics, who in turn lost their jobs to the new Asian immigrants. Strangely, the new minority in town was once again old white men.

History's most valuable lesson was that oppressors eventually became the oppressed. Or, as Kendal often thought, it was fate's way of displaying its sense of humor as it balanced the scales of justice.

"You want beignets with that?" the waiter asked.

She chose a seat at one of the tables along the rail, a prime spot for people-watching, but the streets were mostly empty that morning because of the chill blowing off the river. Most of the customers were jockeying for one of the seats under a heater inside. "Sure, why not."

"Make it four orders and another café au lait." Again Kendal didn't have to turn around to see who spoke. The voice was another familiar ghost in her head.

"What's the matter, Charlie, don't you trust me?"

"The Clan sent me to warn you. Henri knows you're here and he's preparing." He sat across from her and put his folded hands on the slightly sticky Formica-topped table. They knew each other well enough to be silent for a while.

"Tell me, Charlie, do you know how pistolettes got their name?"
she asked finally, cocking her head to the side and waiting for his
answer.

"Small French breads used for sandwiches? Those pistolettes?"

Her smile made him smile back. "Those pistolettes."

"No, but I have a feeling I'm about to."

"Once upon a time, before the technology that made all loaves of
bread taste exactly alike, bakers would rise early every day to make
dough. They mixed the same ingredients, in the same measurements,
and kneaded. The surprise always lay in the yeast. Would it rise? Would
it bake correctly? Finally one of the French bakers got smart. He mixed,
he kneaded, and he waited for the dough to rise. Only then, instead
of baking loaves that might or might not turn out, he baked small
individual loaves."

"So he could correct the dough accordingly, right?" Charlie asked.
Long gone were the days when he interrupted, wanting to know what
these talks were about. They were always educational and relevant, so
he sat back as if waiting for the rest of the story.

"Correct. When the small loaves turned out well, he would walk
outside and fire a pistol to signal the town. The shot meant he was
putting in the full loaves and they'd be ready within the hour. Those
who couldn't wait could buy the small loaves. In time they came to be
called pistolettes for the shot fired every day."

They were silent as the waiter filled the table with their order and
accepted a bill from Kendal, walking away with a bounce in his step
when she waved away the change. "As interesting as that story was,
I'm not sure why you told it."

"I already know my brother's aware of my arrival. He was kind
enough to visit last night or, rather, early this morning."

Charlie leaned forward in clear alarm. "Where?"

"By the river, close to dawn, and I wasn't surprised to see him
since I meant to draw him out. I'm always the eternal optimist when it
comes to Henri, but he's eternally predictable. He warned me to leave,
so obviously my arrival won't make him see the error of his ways or
motivate him to clean up his own messes in hopes of saving himself."

"That was stupid, Kendal. You know what he's capable of. You
shouldn't leave yourself so vulnerable."

She laughed before she bit into a beignet. "His visit was like a
pistolette, Charlie. The real loaf is in the oven baking. It isn't quite

ready yet, so I have time. Two of his little helpers weren't enough to do harm, just send a message."

His eyes, the exact shade of hers, narrowed and Charlie still didn't look happy. "The Clan wants—"

"I know what they want. They came to me, remember? And if they sent you out to pass along messages because they believe I have some misplaced family loyalty to Henri, tell them not to worry. He ceased to be my brother long ago." She seldom used this tone with Charlie, but she hated being spied on. "I don't need a babysitter. Make sure you tell them that too."

"I'm just looking out for you, old friend."

"I know, and I love you for it, but I understand the Old Ones just as well. They've already had Morgaine contact me about how out of control my brother has become. A few more converts and there may be a change in management within the Genesis Clan, and the Elders will spend eternity polishing Ora and Henri's boots."

"That's what they're afraid of."

"Yes, it is, but remember, Charlie, we live life in bits, one choice at a time. Some bits come out better than others, and some are worth remembering over and over because they were worth every minute."

She brushed off her fingers and stood. "Tell the Elders I know what needs to be done, so they don't have to worry. As for Henri, he's about to find out what price his choices have cost him." Charlie couldn't say anything that would affect her plan, so she left it at that. For once she didn't have a lot of time to finish this task. Ironic for someone who had nothing but time.

❖

Kendal walked through the French Quarter as it came to life for another day of tourists and fun seekers. Trucks were delivering various supplies in front of restaurants, blocking a lane of traffic, and the bars were busy restocking from the night before. None of them interested her as she strode in her usual brisk clip until she was at the other side of the neighborhood.

Here the buildings were more run-down, not by time, but by abuse and apathy. The rougher sections drove the crime statistics, but nestled in the middle of all the decay were the St. Louis Cemeteries I and II. These cities of the dead stood silent witness to all that had happened to make New Orleans the place it had become. Along the rows of raised tombs, politicians rested next to criminals and some of the city's founders. Firemen, policemen, and other heroes lay close to prostitutes and witches. Here it didn't matter who you were or what you did. You all ended up in the same place—dead and, for the most part, forgotten.

The Christians were fond of saying, "From dust you came and dust you shall become." True. The cycle of life had been the same for as long as anything had drawn breath on the earth. People lived, how well was up to them, and then they died. They had no escape. The monuments she passed testified to that.

It was a shame, really, that the living almost forgot the beauty people wasted on the dead. The two cemeteries were now full, and in such a bad neighborhood, people who tried to tend the graves gambled with their safety or lives. Kendal walked until she reached the center of St. Louis I. The brick tomb looked old. In fact, it was one of the first built, but unlike some of the others it had fresh flowers and a headstone mortared in place with a legible inscription.

Angelina du'Pon. My beloved.

Simple words for a beautiful woman, but they were still true. "You're never far from my thoughts," Kendal said softly as she ran her fingers along the marble etching of the name. She bowed and put a bunch of camellias in the empty vase to the right. The vessel held flowers only when she visited the grave. The one to the left was always full of fresh flowers, which the caretaker provided.

"Angelina, love, it's been a while but I'm back. I can't begin to express how sorry I am for all that happened to you. Everyone must face death, but for you it came much too early." She brushed away a few leaves that rested at the base of the tomb and gave her memories free rein once again.

CHAPTER FIVE

New Orleans, October 1725

Look, Master, we're in New Orleans." Lionel pointed at the little boys running along the riverbank as the big boat was guided to the docks. A majority of the other vessels in the port were being loaded for whatever journeys awaited them.

"Yes, we are, and it looks like the Fall Festival will have nothing but miserable weather this year. I'm glad to have some excuse to bypass it and head straight home." Jacques was also glad for his cloak and hat because the cold rain had been falling steadily since they left their rooms.

Lionel took his eyes off the docks and studied him. "If you went to some of these events, maybe you'd find a nice young lady who'd bear you sons to teach things to."

"I have you to teach things to, Lionel, so I don't need anyone else. Maybe in another lifetime I'll have time for women, but in this one I'm having too much fun building. It's been ages since I've concentrated on just that."

"Master, I mean no insult, but you're a strange puzzle at times," Lionel said, appearing confused. "Look, there's Joseph with the coach."

Their boots sounded heavy on the dock's wooden planks, but that was about to change as they headed toward the muddy street. From the look of the ruts it had been raining for days, and no end was in sight as a gentle mist still fell, making things messier.

"Did you have a good trip, sir?" Joseph removed his hat as he greeted Jacques, then embraced Lionel. The two had formed a close friendship after coming to live at Oakgrove, and Joseph acted as if he'd missed Lionel terribly.

"It was fine. Your mother didn't give you too hard a time before you left, did she?" Everyone on Oakgrove was familiar with Joseph's mother, Lola. The big woman ran his kitchens and, from time to time, told him exactly what he didn't want to hear, consequences be damned. Her only son Joseph was a bit sheltered, but no one was more loyal to Jacques.

"She made me promise not to leave the road for nothing, sir, and to tell you to get a move on when you stepped off that boat so she wouldn't worry. She said not to make her come down here and get us." They shared a laugh since each of them had been on the receiving end of Lola's wrath more than once.

"Then let's not keep the good woman waiting." Jacques was about to step up to his coach when he heard a very upset woman shriek, then a man laugh.

When he turned, he almost laughed too. In the middle of the street stood what he presumed to be a young lady and her maid covered in mud and glaring up at a driver, whose team had obviously done the damage. But the man wasn't getting down to help them, and their packages now lay scattered around their feet.

"Are you all right, mademoiselle?" The young woman stopped glaring and fully faced him, and just as quickly she zeroed in on his eyes. "Are you hurt?"

"I'm sorry, this is so embarrassing. I really thought he'd stop," the young woman said, wiping her face with a lacy handkerchief that only smeared the mud along her cheek.

"You should pay attention and watch where you're going. You're lucky all that hit you was mud," the driver said loudly.

"Excuse me." Jacques moved the woman behind him and pulled the idiot off his seat. After one punch the two teeth the driver had left were lying in the mud along with the parasol the woman had dropped. "I suggest you watch where you're going and how you talk to a lady, sir." When he was sure the man wouldn't fight back, he turned to the woman. "May I drop you someplace so you can clean up?"

"I live on Rue Bastille, if it's no bother." Her voice was soft and low, making Jacques bend to hear it. Despite the mud he could still smell her perfume, which made him wonder what was hidden under the filth.

"It would be my pleasure."

Without being asked, Lionel and Joseph retrieved the packages and moved to the back of the coach alongside the supplies Joseph had picked up while he was in town. They both put a hand up, trying to hide their smiles when Jacques helped the two women on board, holding the young woman's hand a little longer than was proper.

"I thought you were having fun building things," Lionel said, and Jacques ignored him as he latched the back gate of the wagon.

Once he was seated and ready to go, he said, "Please forgive my bad manners, mademoiselle, my name is Jacques St. Louis."

Acting with as much dignity as possible, the young woman wiped her mouth, smearing mud along her teeth before she answered. "Thank you for coming to our rescue, Monsieur St. Louis, I'm Angelina du'Pon, and this is my maid Dee."

"No need to thank me, Mademoiselle du'Pon. After a long sail I find nothing more refreshing than escorting two lovely ladies home," he said, and they both giggled.

They wound through the streets in silence, and at the end of the block Angelina named stood a good-sized home with a wide porch and matching veranda along the second floor. Jacques again helped the two women down and escorted Angelina to her door.

"I hope you fare better the rest of the afternoon, dear lady. I'll leave you to the comfort of your bath."

With a surprisingly strong grip, Angelina grabbed his wet sleeve to keep him from leaving. "Please, Monsieur St. Louis, my uncle would be furious if I sent you away without offering you at least a drink."

"Like I said, it wasn't a hardship to bring you home, so you don't need to repay me."

"But I want you to stay." As she spoke, Jacques noticed how green Angelina's eyes were and how fixated she was on his face, as if she'd spotted something different about him.

For a moment Angelina seem to strip away the façade of Jacques St. Louis and Asra felt naked, but she said, "Then I'll stay."

"Dee, get someone to see to Monsieur St. Louis and his men while we clean up. Sir, I'm sure you'll find my uncle's study a comfortable place to wait. Or would you like a room so you can change into something dry?"

"The study will be fine. We have to be getting along soon, but I promise to wait until you're done."

He pointed Lionel and Joseph to a small table with four wooden chairs in the room where the servant escorted them. It wouldn't be wise to sit on the upholstered couches with soaked clothes, so each of them sat on a straight-back chair with a cup of coffee before him and his hat in his lap. Angelina's uncle loved to read, if his bookshelves were any indication. Row after row of leather-bound editions lined the room, and the worn bindings showed that the books weren't just for decoration.

During the next couple of hours Joseph caught them up on the plantation's progress and the welfare of everyone who lived on the grounds. They had stripped down to their shirts and vests when the wool of their jackets had begun to itch in the warm room.

Angelina clearing her throat made them almost comically jump to their feet.

After Jacques's first look at a freshly bathed Angelina, he did a fair impression of a catfish out of water and tried to block out Lionel and Joseph's laughter.

"My apologies for taking so long, Monsieur St. Louis. I had mud in places that surprised even my maid." Angelina's blond hair was pulled back in a style that let the curls the maid had set cascade past her shoulders. That was eye-catching enough, but her smile made her face come alive in a way Jacques found stunning.

Only a few times in his life had he looked upon a face so beautiful. "A gentleman never minds waiting on a lady, Mademoiselle du'Pon."

"A rescuer of maidens and a charmer. It seems my mud bath has brought me nothing but good fortune, Monsieur St. Louis."

"Actually, my dear, it's Marquis St. Louis of Oakgrove, and by all accounts he's the epitome of a gentleman, if not a bit of a recluse. Leave it to you to pull the bear from his cave." The elderly gentleman at the front door leaned heavily on a cane as the doorman helped him take off his overcoat. "What mischief were you out creating today that you've come home with such a distinguished guest?"

"Uncle Tomas, I'll have you know this wasn't my fault. Marquis St. Louis, forgive me for not using your title."

With his hand out, Jacques walked toward the teasing old man with eyes the color of his niece's. "Monsieur and Mademoiselle du'Pon, forgive me for not calling on the two of you earlier. I've been enjoying the gazette you're putting out, Monsieur du'Pon. Reading about the goings-on around town makes me feel less hermit-like. I should have recognized the name when we met, Mademoiselle."

"What can I say? I'm an old hen who loves to gossip and found a way to make a living at it. Please sit and let's share something stronger than coffee. This weather makes my bad hip ache. I crave a good glass of whiskey." Tomas insisted on using the softer couches and, since Jacques was dry, he acquiesced. Tomas accepted a glass from his niece, who then handed one to Jacques.

"To good fortune, then," Jacques toasted as he tapped his glass against Tomas's.

"Good fortune indeed. Perhaps I can pry some juicy tidbits from the reclusive marquis for my next editorial. I won't be able to print enough copies for the ladies dying to know about you." Jacques laughed at the gentle teasing, taking an instant liking to the somewhat flamboyant man. "What do you say, Marquis St. Louis, are you up for an interview? The reading public is dying to know what bait to use to lure so charming and successful a fish."

"Please call me Jacques, and I'd be happy to give you one, but I don't want to be responsible for driving away readers from boredom, since my life isn't that interesting." Jacques smiled at Angelina, who blushed. "I was glad to be of assistance to your niece, but I'll have to ask your forgiveness for my hasty departure." He finished his drink and stood, motioning for Tomas to keep his seat. "Thank you both for a delightful afternoon. I enjoyed meeting you, but I have to be getting on the road home before this weather gets worse."

"Could I entice you with a dinner invitation once you're settled again? Finding such good company to share equally good conversation with is difficult these days. I promise to stick to safe topics," Tomas said.

"Thank you. I look forward to it."

Angelina followed him to the door and watched as Lionel and Joseph tipped their hats and headed to the coach. "Thank you for humoring him. My uncle can be a handful when he sets his mind to it."

"Believe me, this is the most fun I've had in ages."

"Then perhaps Uncle Tomas is right and you need to get out more, Marquis St. Louis."

"Would it be forward of me to ask you to call me Jacques?"

"Only if I could convince you I prefer Angelina to Mademoiselle du'Pon."

"Touché," he said with a deep bow, making Angelina laugh.

"Shall we expect you soon?"

Tucking his gloves into his belt, he moved slowly to take Angelina's hand. When she didn't shy away, he bowed again and placed a chaste kiss along her fingers. "I shall count the hours and send word of when I can come."

He might have preferred life in the country, but he knew enough about New Orleans's social circles to realize Angelina du'Pon was considered a prize catch, especially for any young man wanting to make a name in the growing city. Her uncle Tomas had raised her from an early age after her parents were lost to malaria in one of the epidemics that had ravaged the city. Being a man of considerable means, Tomas du'Pon had given in to her every whim, and Angelina thrived under the attention. However, she hadn't become insufferable, as had so many ladies of the same social status.

But Angelina hadn't found love, or even some nice young man to spend time with. At least that was the gossip of the day. Asra wasn't interested in becoming that *young man* because love wasn't in her plans. It was the quickest way to expose all her secrets. She wasn't ready for that since she had invested so much time and care into creating Jacques St. Louis, the plantation owner responsible for the lives of so many that *he* couldn't take the chance of getting close to someone like Angelina.

One dinner in their company then he'd return to Oakgrove, leaving the curious journalist and Angelina to the party circuit.

New Orleans, present day

"Sleep well, my darling, and know I'll never forget you." Kendal stood and brushed the dirt off her knees.

"How sweet, but you're talking to a woman who's been dead for a long time, idiot."

When she turned around she faced two punks, and the younger one was pointing a rusty 9mm at her head. They were trying to look like badasses, but she could see the slight tremor in the gunman's hand. The older one did all the talking.

"I can't really see that it's bothering anyone," she said, sweeping her arms around the deserted cemetery. Their expressions showed that it annoyed them that she didn't look intimidated.

"You're not from around here, are you?"

"I've spent time in New Orleans, but it's been a while." She widened her stance and calmly put her hands in her coat pockets.

"You have to pay a fee now when you come in here. My friend and

I own this place, and no one visits it for free. Get me?" The kid holding the gun laughed stupidly, at his friend's clever words, she guessed.

"A toll of some sort, is that what you mean?"

"It means, bitch, that I'll take whatever you got on you." The unarmed punk stepped closer and twisted his face into a snarl. "Give me your money and your jewelry now, or my pal blows your head off."

The only thing she was attached to was the signet ring on her right hand. It had been her father's, and he had given it to her shortly before he died. The rest was replaceable, but Kendal thought of all the other visitors who had run into her new friends while they were paying respects to their loved ones. "Money and jewelry, right?"

"You got a hearing problem? Hand them over and we make this easy. Play hard to get, and me and Zeke here get to have a little fun too. We might do that anyway since it looks like you could use a good man in your life. You a big dyke?" He grabbed his crotch and smiled back at his friend.

"Can I make a counteroffer?"

"What the hell's that supposed to mean?"

"You know, you told me what you want, now I get to tell you what I'm willing to do and what I want."

"You see yourself as having choices here?"

She rocked on her heels and smiled like she was negotiating the purchase of a pair of pants. "You always have choices. Today yours was to walk in here and point a gun at me. No one forced you to do that, and no one's forcing me to do anything I'm not willing to do. I was visiting someone who lost her life to someone just like you, but you're still young. You have time to turn your life around."

"You smokin' something, bitch? If you are, we'll take that too, along with the money and that nice watch and ring."

Relaxed and smiling, she kept her right hand in the pocket of her coat and slipped the other one into the front pocket of her pants. When she pulled out the money clip, she laughed at the talker's low whistle. She held probably more than the two had ever made in all their crime ventures. "This what you want?"

She knew his greed would make him move forward, into a web from which he couldn't escape. Not that distance would've made the difference. When he reached to take his booty she pulled her right hand out of her coat pocket and snapped open a wicked-looking switchblade. Just as quickly the money was back in her pocket and the blade was pressed so hard against his throat it drew a line of blood. She liked to practice her fighting skills when she could, but this guy didn't present much of a challenge.

"What's your name?" She grabbed the top of his head, exposing more of his neck. "Never mind. You aren't going to live long enough for me to care."

"Please," he said in a whisper as he stood on his toes, trying to get away from the blade.

"Please what? Please let me go, bitch. Is that the only inane thing you can think to say?" The gunman hadn't lowered his weapon and looked like he was trying to decide if he could get a clean shot off without killing his buddy. "Zeke," she said, glancing up at the armed thief. "You have one chance to put that down and run. Don't make me have to deal with you."

His hand shook but she could almost see him thinking that he had the gun, and all she had was a knife. "Let him go or I'll shoot."

"Another mental giant." Tired of the game, she kicked the guy she was holding in the legs and threw the knife in one fluid motion. The thump of the air rushing out of the talker's lungs came simultaneously with Zeke's scream. The gun was now on the ground at his feet and Kendal's knife was buried to the hilt in his palm.

"Who are you?" asked the one looking up at her.

"Someone you shouldn't have fucked with." Kendal stepped closer to Zeke and grabbed his injured hand. With one quick pull she retrieved her blade and wiped it along his cheek. The effect was chilling enough to make him stop screaming. "Only a lowlife would rob someone in a place reserved for grief. Today's going to be your chance to rethink your career path because, trust me, death doesn't pass you by very often."

"You're some kind of demon," Zeke said, looking like a macabre clown with his bloody cheeks.

"I've known a few of those in my time and I'm nowhere close, so get lost and think about what I said." Zeke jumped to his feet and took off, not glancing back. She watched him go and moved to pick up the gun he'd left behind. With one quick check of the clip she saw that it was full and hadn't been fired recently.

The talker was on his knees holding his throat over the spot with the slight cut. Despite the cool morning he'd started to sweat when she chambered a round and pressed the barrel to his forehead.

"You let Zeke go."

"I have a feeling you talked Zeke into being here today, so you don't get off so easily. Am I right?" When he didn't respond, she pushed the barrel harder against his forehead, making him nod.

"I didn't want to come by myself."

"A wise-ass who needs someone else to do his dirty work for him will never truly be a man. In some cultures they would've cut your dick off and fed it to the real warriors long before now." She moved the gun from his head and pointed at his crotch, and the growing wet spot made her smile. "Not so tough now, are you?"

Big tears loaded with fear ran down his face, but it was too late for remorse. "I didn't mean nothing."

She corrected him. "It's 'I didn't mean anything.' Tell me, did it move you to walk away from a victim when someone cried for you to stop? Tell the truth or I'll blow that little pecker of yours right off."

"No." He stuttered on the short word.

"How about a nice dirt nap to reconsider your options next time, then?"

She didn't give him the chance to ask what she meant. In an instant she used his gun to knock him out. When he woke up, anyone walking by the place would probably cross the street when they heard his screams since he would come to in a large mausoleum that the city used for paupers. He would be lying on a pile of bones he'd have to work hard to escape.

CHAPTER SIX

"Where have you been?" Bruce asked, sitting dressed and ready in Kendal's suite. "Not that you seem interested, but last night went well," he said through the bathroom door.

"You didn't set any time agenda, did you?"

"I was a good little soldier and followed orders, but it'll only drag this out, and that's not like you."

"I'm multifaceted, Bruce, so don't delude yourself into thinking you know everything about me." He turned around when she came out with her shirt unbuttoned. She guessed he knew he had no chance at a relationship with her outside of work. She'd made that clear from the beginning of their business venture.

"Those guys appreciated the meeting, but they really wanted to hear from you. I covered for you, but are you going to disappear on me for hours on end in the future? My father told me your family has some weird connection to this place, but this is business. You don't want to end up like your old man and mine, do you? Loading ships down on the docks isn't my idea of a wise career move."

"Wait for me in the other room."

His mouth clicked closed, but she knew why he was pissed. The money was all Bruce thought about, making him totally different from his father.

With a shower and a fresh suit, she looked like she'd spent the evening sleeping in the comfortable-looking bed instead of roaming the streets. He jumped to his feet when she opened the door.

"I take it Mr. Marmande accepted my invitation?" she asked as they stepped into the elevator.

"Macarthur Marmande wants to hang on to his family's business more than anything. He'll be there and I'm sure he's bringing his granddaughter, Piper. She's a Harvard Business School graduate he's grooming to take over for him, so don't try anything cute. I hear she's a real ballbuster."

Her low laugh made Bruce shiver. "Lucky for me, then," she whispered in his ear. "And Piper not only graduated from Harvard, she was first in both her undergraduate and graduate classes. She's not a ballbuster, Bruce. She's just smarter than most people who have a pair. So maybe you should worry."

"How do you know so much about her since you dropped this on us yesterday?"

"Every good strategist knows their opponent. You just heard about Marmande yesterday, but they've been on my radar." She didn't want to admit that she chose the company about twenty minutes before she informed him and the team. That was the beauty of her Kendal Richoux cover. Floundering companies all over the world helped her travel whenever necessary for the Elders.

The lunch crowd was starting to filter into the Palace Café on Canal Street when she and Bruce exited the limousine the hotel had provided for the ten-block drive. They stood back and let an older couple go through the revolving doors ahead of them, since they were a couple of minutes early. One of the attractive hostesses took their coats and asked for their names.

"We're here to meet the Marmande party." Kendal's smile made the girl trip over her feet, and Bruce sighed behind her. He loved to tell her that when they were handing out the goodies before birth, Kendal had obviously stood in each line at least twice. That was the only way to explain her looks, charm, brains, and physique.

"Mr. Mac's expecting you. Kendal Richoux, right?"

"The one and only," she said, making the woman blush.

"Right this way." They followed her to the staircase at the center of the restaurant; on the second floor at a table by the large windows overlooking Canal Street sat their adversaries.

"Mr. Mac, your party's here."

"More like the invading horde, darlin', but we'll let 'em join us anyway." He stood and studied Kendal before offering his hand.

Mac Marmande was in his sixties, but from what she'd read about him, he still ran around like he did in his thirties. Thick white hair framed an intelligent face and a warm smile, which, judging from the laugh lines around his mouth, seemed to be a permanent fixture. Others often described him as a likable good old boy who'd give you his last dollar if you needed the help. He was also as ruthless as she was if the right business venture came along, so she didn't let his friendly welcome fool her into thinking this would be easy.

Beside Mac sat a petite woman with a short shaggy haircut that Kendal thought stylish, though a slight frown marred her beautiful profile. For a second the woman's obvious displeasure amused Kendal. It was as if they'd taken her away from something far more important, like watching her grass grow.

"Mr. Marmande, it's a pleasure to finally meet you. Thank you for agreeing to this," she said as she and Mac shook hands, but his granddaughter had yet to turn her attention from the window. "This is my associate, Bruce Babbage."

"More like hired henchman," Piper hissed.

"Thank you for the opportunity, Kendal. May I call you Kendal?" Mac asked, all of them ignoring Piper's rude comment.

"Please do."

"Good, this is my granddaughter, Piper Marmande." When he made the introduction, Piper had to face forward. Kendal stumbled forward a step and her heart dropped.

Most people would have expressed concern at her reaction, but Piper's anger drowned out any sympathy. "I wish I could say it's a pleasure, but I'd hate to lie, Ms. Richoux."

Kendal wanted to run. Seeing Piper Marmande was like looking at a ghost. Though different in some ways, Piper's face was almost identical to Angelina's. Kendal's heart and lungs felt like they were in a vise. "I—"

"Are you all right?" Mac asked. He placed his hand on her shoulder as if to steady her.

His question allowed Kendal to take her eyes off Piper and focus on something else. "I hate to be rude, but would you excuse me for a moment?"

"Do you need to reschedule? You don't look well."

"No, sir, please give me a moment and I'll be fine."

In the restroom she stripped off her jacket and splashed water on her face. She'd experienced something like a panic attack, and, as shocking as that was, she was almost excited. It had been years since she'd felt anything nearly this intense.

When she made it back to the table, Mac asked again, "Are you sure you're all right?"

"I'm fine. Just hungry, I guess." Keeping her eyes on Mac's face, Kendal sat, unfurled her napkin, and placed it on her lap. "Shall we order something before starting our talk?"

"I'd suggest the turtle soup. It's the best in the city."

"Please, Pops, she's here to steal the company. I could give a rat's ass what she wants to eat." Piper didn't bother to keep her voice down this time.

"Kendal, would you excuse us? I'd like a word with my granddaughter."

"Call me crazy, but I'm guessing no amount of lecturing will change Miss Marmande's mind, so why bother? She's right, so save the trip to the woodshed. That's why I'm here, but what she should realize is if it weren't me, it'd be someone else. Since Miss Marmande is refreshingly blunt, let me be equally so. Marmande Shipyard is worth more in parts than as a whole, and no magic eraser on the horizon will eliminate the red tape that's about to choke out its remaining life."

"You are blunt," Mac said, and laughed. "We've been trying to break into new markets since, unlike you, I believe we still have something to offer."

"Please don't think I'm judging you personally. This is no one's fault. It's just the way of the business world. Luckily, I'm sitting here instead of someone who wants to outright plunder what's taken your family generations to build. I want to work with you so you'll get fair market value."

"What, pennies on the dollar? Should I kiss your ass now or wait until you hand us the big check?" Piper asked.

"Thank you for your suggestion on the soup, sir. I'll try it the next time I'm here." She stood and shook his hand again as Bruce jumped out of his chair like a trained monkey.

Waiting until she had Piper's full attention, she leaned across the table and rested her weight on her fingers so she could stare her down. "Miss Marmande, I came here to see if we could reach an agreement. I'm sorry you see it as a waste of time. Go ahead and cut what you think is your best deal with Kenny Delaney and his group, but before you do, take that expensive education your grandfather paid for out for a spin. Call Quill Contractors as if you work for Delaney and his group. Tell them to forward you the preliminary quotes so you can work on different sections of the contract having to do with the Marmande deal. You'll be surprised at what your supposed partner has been up to. Could be Kenny screwed you over in more ways than one."

With every word Piper turned a deeper shade of red. "You bitch." Piper's insult sounded venomous.

"True, but I'm an up-front one. I don't use my bed to cut deals unless everyone knows the score, and any screwing that takes place is only for mutual enjoyment." Piper might've looked like someone she'd cared about, but her heart set them apart. "I'm sorry to speak so crudely, Mr. Marmande. Perhaps we weren't meant to do business together after all. Have a pleasant lunch, and it was a real pleasure to meet you. I've admired your style for years."

"Wait, let's all calm down and start over."

She patted his arm and shook her head. The things she'd heard about him were true. Mac was extremely likable, but this wasn't the time to sit and get to know each other. "I'm always calm, Mr. Marmande, but sometimes people have to learn lessons the hard way, and this is one of those times." She then turned and looked at Piper again. "Miss Marmande, I wish I could say it's been a pleasure, but I'd hate to lie. Tell Kenny hello for me, and after you get that information I suggested, mention that I think he played this one beautifully. We go way back."

"You can't walk away and leave this hanging," Bruce said as soon as they were on the sidewalk outside.

"I can do anything I want, try to remember that. The day you hand out a card that says *Babbage Inc.*, you get to do whatever you like. Now we walk away and wait. Blondie's about to find out Kenny Delaney's as greasy as his hair, and after a long shower, she'll call. Have faith, Bruce."

"What choice do I have?"

"Endless. You can make a name defending drunks and hookers, because you did go to law school. That's my best suggestion, since you mentioned dock work isn't your thing."

He gave her an insincere smile and cocked his fist at her. "You're a riot, you know that?"

"It's just part of my charm."

"Want to head back to the hotel and grab a bite?"

"You go ahead. I think I'll resume my walk." She was down the block before he had a chance to ask to join her.

After answering her phone she asked, "Free for lunch?"

"Where would you like to go?"

"It's your city, you pick."

❖

Charlie was already seated when she walked up, and she laughed at the huge piece of bread he'd shoved in his mouth.

"You're still a pig, old friend," she said in French.

"You'd think you'd have learned to stop hanging around with me," Charlie joked. "It's nice that you're back. Except for tourists and pretty college students, I rarely get to practice my French anymore."

"Obviously age doesn't make all of us wiser." Kendal sat and poured her favorite brand of beer into the frosted mug that sat on the table waiting for her.

"How old are you now, anyway?" Charlie broke off another piece of bread and stopped to put butter on it this time.

"Over three thousand years, give or take a few. After a while the excitement of birthdays wears off."

"Mon Dieu, some of the pyramids are younger than you."

"Gods, why do I call you to spend time with?"

"Because after almost three hundred years you still see potential."

"Or maybe after I gave you the gift of immortality I can't kill you," she said, teasing him.

"I've missed you, Kendal." His eyes filled with tears and he reached across the table for her hand. Charlie was one of the few people in her life who'd been affectionate with her in a way that had nothing to do with seduction or romance. "Though that name doesn't quite suit you."

"And Charlie was your best effort?" She arched her eyebrow and smiled.

"To me you'll always be Jacques St. Louis, and in my heart I'll always be Lionel."

"Of all my lifetimes, that one holds the greatest mix of memories and is the only one still unfinished, even after all these years. It's the main reason I accepted the Clan's offer to return. I hope you know I left because I had to, not because I didn't care about what happened to you and your family. It still angers me when I think of the injustice the Clan let Henri get away with. I gave my word not to be the one to destroy him, but they should've had someone else drive a stake through his heart years ago."

Lionel squeezed her hand one last time before he leaned back in his chair. "I know, and that's why I accepted your offer. As much as I didn't want to go on after what happened, I'm glad I've lived to see this day. I know you always work alone, but I want to join you if only to watch. I don't have to tell you why."

"No, you don't, but let me sleep on it."

He laughed and pointed a finger at her. "I may be waiting awhile then. When was the last time you slept?"

She laughed as well and put her hand over her eyes. "After I left this city. I slept about fifty years in an effort to forget. After that I spent a hundred years in the East studying the way of the warrior."

"You were born with the heart of a warrior. What can anyone teach you?"

"You never grow too old to learn. You should spend some time away from here and expand your horizons. Stop thinking so much about the past. I've spent years at a time in places so I could learn the language, the culture, and their art of warfare. In the mountains with some of the masters of the Eastern clans, I learned to master the sword." Kendal pulled back so the waiter could put some dishes down.

"You're full of shit, my friend. I've seen you handle a sword. You're the one who's the master."

The spring rolls looked good, so Kendal picked one up and took a bite. She didn't need food to survive anymore, but she craved it nonetheless. In some ways it was like sex. If she saw a woman who interested her, she spent the evening with her. Then she was off to the next bit of fluff. She wasn't interested in long-term relationships. Who could outlast her?

"They helped with a number of things. No one's ever perfect, and no one will ever be perfect at anything, no matter how hard they try. We all have flaws and ways to be brought down."

"Is that why you stashed all the money and went to college as the poor and starving Kendal Richoux? To find more ways to perfect yourself and smooth over your flaws?"

She finished the spring roll and moved on to the dumplings. "You've become a better conversationalist with time. I'm glad to see the timid mouse afraid to ask questions is gone. And to answer you, no, I didn't seek answers to questions that have none. I went because I was losing touch with where the world is headed. Where better to find directions than from the young and overly opinionated?"

"And what has Kendal Richoux learned?"

"That a lot of really good-looking women hang out on college campuses."

He looked at her as he started in on his lunch but couldn't comment without talking with his mouth full.

"I'm kidding. It was just a diversion, and I wanted to hone my survival skills. I went, I conquered, and I made more money."

"Not that you need it."

"No, but it helps for those lives when I just want to bum around and drink wine all day."

"But hasn't this been the lifetime you've been waiting for?"

The question was interesting, but which of them was more qualified to answer? She was much older in years and in wisdom, but Lionel had matured much faster than she had. His growth came from a combination of intelligence and good tutelage. She'd been gone for close to three hundred years, but she'd never abandoned Lionel and his education.

"You'd think after so many days I wouldn't have anything to look forward to, but you'd be wrong. Every day I anticipate the moment the sun rises, and when it does, I sit in wonder of the world and my part in it. Do I look forward to some tasks more than others? I do, especially if they avenge the souls of the innocent."

The waitress put down two fresh mugs and bottles of beer after she cleared the appetizer dishes.

"Are you planning to stay in the city?"

"For a few days. I've other business aside from Henri and his collection of fools." Kendal shook her head, trying to clear it of any morose thoughts. "Promise me something, Lionel." She reached for his hand as she spoke.

"I'd do anything for you, Jacques. Just ask."

"Retreat into the cathedral until I call for you. Henri's left you in peace because he doesn't see you as a threat, but my being here will change that. I don't want to worry about you along with everything else."

He couldn't break away from her powerful grip, and she could tell his anger made him want to. "You promised you'd consider letting me stand with you. I deserve that."

"I haven't promised or denied anything yet, but I'll consider it if you swear to stay safe until I come for you. I won't do anything without talking to you first."

Lionel held his right hand out, knowing she'd never break an oath. "Swear it."

"On the spirit of my father." She took his hand and sealed their fate.

"Are you planning to go to the house after you finish your business? I had it cleaned when I heard you were coming."

"I look forward to it, merci."

❖

"I don't have time for lunch, Granddad. In case you weren't paying attention, the bitch who just waltzed out of here is trying to rip us off. If she was able to get the board off the golf course yesterday to make them an offer, tomorrow's going to be too late." Piper was dying to leave the restaurant and go back to her office since she'd assembled the management team to plug the holes from this surprise assault. She wanted to make a few phone calls and prove Kendal Richoux, the sanctimonious bitch, wrong, but she figured her granddad had heard enough cursing for one afternoon, so she kept the comment to herself.

"Sit your pretty little ass down, young lady, and tell this nice waitress what you want," Mac said.

"I really need to go."

"You need to listen to the old coot who's still your boss." Mac pointed to her chair. "You want to tell me what the hell that display was about?" he asked when she sat.

As she had learned to do when she was about six years old, she crossed her arms and tried to decide between throwing a fit or pouting. "I've read so many secondhand accounts about this woman and what she's capable of, I'm mad that she's got her eye on us. I don't think we're going to come out of this the same, whatever we do."

"And if given the choice, you prefer an alliance with Kenny Delaney?"

"Kenny promised we would keep control of the company so we'd have a chance to restructure. Once I'm able to do that, we can buy him and his partners out and tell the world to go to hell."

Mac nodded and took a sip of his whiskey. "Any truth to what she said before she left?"

Her anger dried up and she was mortified that she had to answer. "I…"

"I don't want to know who you're sweet on, Piper. I want to know if this guy is on the up-and-up."

She smiled at her grandfather's old-fashioned notions, or maybe that's what he let himself think so he wouldn't have to face the reality of his little girl actually sleeping with someone. "I promise you, we can trust Kenny."

The wait staff put down a fresh loaf of French bread and two bowls of turtle soup. Alongside each plate was a small shot glass of sherry to mix with the soup to accentuate the flavor. Mac picked up his spoon and looked at Piper before he began. "I hope you're right. The way I figure it, I've got one foot in the grave when it comes to what's left of my career, so if the worst-case scenario comes to pass, I won't have to live with it long. You, on the other hand, have years to look forward to. If this boy isn't all he's promising, you've got a lot to lose." He mixed in the liquor in slow circles, as if lost in thought.

"Don't you trust me?"

"With my life and everything that makes it up," Mac said, touching her cheek. "I'm not worried about me, sweet girl. I'm worried about you. The business belongs to you now, and I have every faith you'll do right by it."

"But you think I made a mistake with Richoux today, don't you?"

"You should give someone the opportunity to show their cards before you accuse them of cheating. Once they lay out what they have to say, then you scream and walk out if that's what you have a mind to do. If Kendal had something to offer, other than taking us over and selling us off in little pieces, we'll never know, will we?"

They ate in silence after that. Mac wasn't prone to outbursts unless provoked, and he didn't lecture her very often. She was the only daughter of his only son, and from the time she'd turned twenty Mac hadn't considered anyone else to replace him at the helm. As far as Marmande heirs, she was the last of the line.

Growing up with her grandparents had given her stability and more leniency than if her parents had lived, but she seldom gave in to what-ifs because they were a waste of time and energy. Her main goal was to make her grandparents proud, and it fueled her desire to succeed. The loss of her parents had made her vigilant about who she allowed close to her and who she shared bits of herself with. As much as she wanted to keep Marmande intact, she would control whoever she partnered with because she couldn't stand to be used.

"Anything else, Mr. Mac?" the waitress asked.

"Just the check, darlin'."

"It's been taken care of, sir. Ms. Richoux settled it before she left."

"Even the tip?"

"Yes, sir, and don't worry. She was very generous. Have a great day."

"She may be the enemy, but she's got style. You gotta give her that," Mac said as he pulled out Piper's chair for her.

As soon as they were outside Piper got on her phone and instructed her assistant, Amy, about what information she had to get from Quill. Amy knew some of the receptionists at the construction company, and Piper needed those connections now because they wouldn't raise any immediate red flags. She gave Amy the name of the Delaney Group's attorneys and had faith Amy would know what to do.

When Piper stepped into the suite where her and her grandfather's offices were located, Amy was having a conversation with the weakest link in the chain at Quill. She was doing a fabulous job of changing her voice to avoid being recognized, acting as if she was one of the secretaries at the law firm. A few moments later she hung up and the fax machine started humming.

The strangled scream Piper let out when she scanned the first few pages made everyone close their doors. Someone was about to die, and Piper wanted Kendal Richoux to be first.

❖

"So what do you want to do?" Bruce asked. Kendal sat beside him in the hotel bar watching the sun go down on the city. After her lunch with Charlie she'd returned in a somber mood. She had a lot to do on this trip, and if things turned out badly she'd have to abandon her life as Kendal Richoux and find another identity. Maybe she could create a new persona that'd keep her in New Orleans for a while.

"I'll give Mr. Marmande another couple of weeks or so, then I'll turn you loose on him and his granddaughter. That alone should scare them back to the negotiating table. Why don't you go get something to eat? You're in the most culinary delightful city in the country, Bruce. Live a little."

He turned his wineglass in his hands and looked a bit lost. "I hate eating alone."

"I promise I'll join you tomorrow, but tonight I want to spend some time alone."

"Anything I can do? I'll listen if you need a friend."

She laughed and slapped his shoulder before she drained her scotch. "Who are you now, Dr. Phil?"

"I just care about what happens to you."

"I know, and I appreciate your concern, but I'm okay. I've just got a lot on my mind, and sometimes it doesn't really help to talk about it. It's better for me to think it through, so go have dinner. I hear the turtle soup at the Palace is good." They both laughed over their disastrous lunch before shaking hands and parting.

She kept her eyes on Bruce as he walked to the bank of elevators after she ordered another drink. Then she remembered something important, so before the doors opened she caught up with him, sure that he'd take her advice to venture out for dinner. "Would you do something for me if I asked you to, without asking me a lot of questions in return?"

"Sure. You change your mind about talking?"

She pulled a chain with a small medallion out of her jacket pocket and held it up. "I want you to wear this and not take it off while we're in the city. Promise me you'll leave it on."

Bruce laid the likeness of St. Michael on his palm and looked at it closely. The archangel had his sword drawn and ready to strike the devil under his foot. "You're getting superstitious on me?"

"If that's what you want to call it, but promise me you won't take it off, especially if you leave the hotel after dark. It's important to me." She slipped the chain over his head and dropped the medallion down the front of his shirt so it rested against his chest.

"Why?"

"Because it marks you as belonging to me. Don't ask me to explain that because I can't, but it means something special to me, something others will understand."

"Are you sure you don't need to lie down or something? You're talking crazy." He reached up as if to feel her forehead.

"Bruce, has your father ever told you anything about my father?" She looked into his eyes as if daring him to lie. "Anything he found hard to explain?"

"He just said your father was his best friend, and then one day he left and never came back. Dad said he always felt protected when he was with Tony, like nothing could ever happen to him. He still misses him like crazy, but he gets regular letters from him." Then it seemed to hit him.

"The last time I was home for a visit, he was out working in the small garden he tends every year. You know, the one he keeps to stay out of Mom's way? It was hot so he opened his shirt and I noticed he was wearing one of these."

"The bond my father and yours share is special to him, and in his absence to tend to other family business, it's one Dad misses as well." Kendal rarely had a relationship with members of two consecutive generations, but Bruce Senior had asked Anthony Richoux to look out for his kid when he told him he was leaving. Bruce the elder might have been a dockworker all his life, but he seemed more aware of the world around him than his son, whom Kendal had paid to educate.

Bruce Senior hadn't been able to hide the shock when Bruce had brought her home for the first time after they'd gone into business together. He hadn't said much except that he was happy for his son. She knew Bruce Senior had figured it out, but the old man couldn't explain how her face was the same as the "man" he knew and loved as a friend. He'd just shaken her hand and whispered, "Welcome back."

"He has one of these, doesn't he?" Bruce asked again, with his hand over his heart where the medal had come to rest.

"Anthony gave him one a long time ago."

"Are you and your father religious?"

The question struck her as funny and she let out a laugh. If he only knew the gods she still prayed to on occasion had existed long before the thought of Christianity was even a blip on mankind's radar. "Not really, but St. Michael became a family tradition a while back, and it's tradition to give him to people who mean a lot to us." Moviemakers had cashed in on the monsters they thought they'd dredged up from the dark side of their imagination, and the rituals to kill the ghoulies were laughable to her, but St. Michael had become a symbol of her protection through the years. Some chose to ignore it, but the smart ones realized the sword raised and ready to strike wasn't a myth. "I can't force you, but it's a sign that I care for you."

"Thank you."

"You're very welcome. So do you promise not to take it off?"

"I promise, especially if it means so much to you."

"It does." She put her hand over his on his chest before she pressed the Down button for the elevator. "Go on, and have fun."

A fresh drink was waiting for her when she got back, and she nodded her thanks to the bartender as she unbuttoned her jacket and took her seat. The table she'd chosen was almost in a corner but stood in front of a window facing the street. It was still too early for the after-work crowd, and the cigar bar was a little subdued for the regular tourist, so aside from a few hushed conversations, Kendal sat in peace as she sipped.

"Would you care for a cigar, Ms. Richoux?" The bartender set another glass down, since the one in her hand was half-full. Everyone in the hotel seemed to know who she was, so the service had been perfect. "We have an excellent selection of Dominicans."

"Do you smoke?"

"Cigarettes, ma'am. I never got used to cigars."

Kendal pulled out her wallet and placed a hundred-dollar bill on the table. "I'll take a Cohiba, but it has to be Cuban. If I'm going to risk my health, I might as well make it worth my while."

"I'm sorry, Ms. Richoux, Cuban cigars are illegal. We carry the brand, only it has the Dominican Republic label."

She shrugged and started to pick up the money. "I may get a free night now, asking for something you can't deliver. Guest satisfaction and all that."

The man smiled and took a travel humidifier out of his apron pocket. "Yes, ma'am, we take guest satisfaction very seriously. Enjoy." It seemed she wasn't the only one who ran background checks on potential clients. The owner of the establishment took everything into account for a guest and their vices.

"What's the old expression?"

"Here, it's ask and you shall receive. It's a city-wide motto," the waiter joked as he clipped the end for her and provided a light.

The smoke filled her senses and the taste made her remember the next part of Angelina's story. She handed over the money, wanting her privacy back.

CHAPTER SEVEN

New Orleans, November 1725

"Don't forget to smile. Then maybe the girl will want to see you again," Lola said as Jacques mounted his horse.

He'd sent word to the du'Pon family that he'd join them for dinner, and he was trying hard to fight a case of nerves he couldn't explain. With his best suit packed, he saluted Lola and took off at a trot toward New Orleans. At dusk the next night, he knocked on the du'Pons' door, suddenly very glad he'd come when Angelina let him in.

"Marquis, how nice to see you again. I was hoping you hadn't run into any other maidens in need of rescue whom you might find more appealing."

"And miss an evening with you and your uncle, Mademoiselle du'Pon? I don't believe there's anyone more appealing to keep me away." He stood with one hand behind his back and his hat in the other.

Thanks to Angelina's clean face he was able to enjoy the blush his words caused. Angelina was truly a vision in a pale blue dress that brought out the green of her eyes. "I'm beginning to think you like making me feel a bit off-kilter, sir."

"And I believe you agreed to call me Jacques, Mademoiselle du'Pon. Or have you perhaps reconsidered?"

"I didn't forget. I just didn't want you to think me presumptuous." She rested against the door and simply gazed at him. "Would you like to come in, or would you have my uncle think I'm a bad hostess by keeping you confined to our porch?"

"I don't know. It might make good fodder for the next edition of his paper."

"I'm going to enjoy having you around. That is, if you grace us with your company in the future." She opened the door completely to let him pass and smiled when his other hand revealed a beautiful bouquet of camellias. He followed her into the parlor and blushed when Angelina gave him a full smile. "Are those for me, or did you wish to give them to my uncle?"

"I like Tomas, but these are for you. I hope they're to your liking."

"They're my favorites, thank you." The servant standing behind Angelina took the flowers, and his hat before, leaving them with only Dee doing needlepoint in the corner. "Please have a seat and I'll get you something to drink."

"Is Monsieur du'Pon not joining us this evening?"

"He sent word earlier that he's running late, so I'm afraid you'll have to make do with my company for the moment. I hope you don't mind." She poured two glasses of sherry from the bar and faced him.

"That's like asking a small boy if he'd like another treat. I hope you don't find the company lacking. Sometimes I feel I should get away from Oakgrove more often, so I can discuss more than planting and harvesting." As she handed him the glass, her fingers felt soft when they touched his.

"I'm sure both of our concerns are unwarranted. I've been looking forward to seeing you again. Would you tell me about Oakgrove?" Angelina took a seat across from him, smiling when he stood until she was seated.

From her expression and the way she nodded as he spoke, Angelina seemed to enjoy his animated description of the plantation he'd poured his life into for five years. Louisiana was still a wild place outside the city when he'd arrived in the territory, so it had been a Herculean effort to clear the trees off the property he'd fallen in love with. Now, with the help of the irrigation system he'd devised using the river, Oakgrove was producing substantial harvests. The farm was in its infancy, but his choice crops were making a good profit.

"You sound like you don't have enough time in the day to do all you have planned."

"I'm finding that the life of a farmer can be as fulfilling as that of a warrior or, should I say, soldier."

"Were you a soldier? In France, I mean."

"In a manner of speaking. Duty calls us to service at times, whether we want it to or not. Here I've tried to create something I can look on years from now and be proud of. The only thing that bothers my heart is the ever-growing slave trade."

"That sentiment won't make you a lot of friends here, Jacques. Whether you agree with the practice or not, those who wield power will never give up that right, not without a fight, anyway." Angelina spoke softly, as if someone were lurking in the hall ready to pounce and punish her for her words.

He nodded and leaned back in his chair. "And what of you? What are your feelings on the subject?"

"I'm just a woman who owns nothing, monsieur. No one cares what my opinion on the subject might be."

"I care."

"Then you're in the minority again."

He laughed, thoroughly enjoying the conversation. Women like Angelina were rare; most of the ladies he'd met in New Orleans cared more about the latest fashions than the welfare of others. "I usually am, but it makes life more interesting."

"Then we are birds of a feather, Jacques. Surely God won't bless any society that allows someone to own another human being. It makes me so sad to see families torn apart on the block day after day."

"I'm a hypocrite, I know, since I legally own so many, but I never split up families. I visit the auction blocks with my foreman Lionel, whom you met the other day, and my house overseer Lola whenever we're here to see if the relatives of any of our family are available for sale. Sometimes they're in such bad shape that the crowd thinks me mad, but reuniting families is cause for celebration at Oakgrove. It isn't much, but I try my best."

Angelina rose from her seat and walked toward the decanter to refill Jacques's glass. When she was beside him, she placed her hand on his shoulder and squeezed in soft affection. "Your best sounds like it's made a world of difference, so you're no hypocrite in my eyes. I feel the same way about Dee. We've been together since we were children, and her family lives here with us."

"Thank you, dear lady, that means a lot to me." Angelina moved back when she heard the front door open and Tomas's cane tap in the foyer.

"Ah, Jacques, you made it. Pardon me for being late, but it was an exciting day at the paper. Has Angelina been keeping you company?"

"She just now let me in. I was barred to the yard until she saw your carriage approaching," he joked.

"Oh, you." Angelina stepped closer to Jacques again and slapped his arm in mock indignation. "Don't listen to a word this heathen tells you, Uncle Tomas. I've been nothing but the perfect hostess." She moved toward Tomas and kissed his cheek in greeting. Jacques noticed her flirtatious behavior.

"Is she telling the truth?"

"About me being a heathen? Most definitely."

They shared the first of many laughs as the evening progressed. Jacques retold some of the stories from his earlier conversation with Angelina, but she listened with the same rapt attention. Before any of them wanted, the evening drew to a close and Tomas sent for Jacques's horse.

"I hope you join us again, young man. Perhaps you can find time for us?" Tomas asked.

"I'd enjoy seeing you both whenever it pleases you." He included both of them in the statement, but his eyes never strayed from Angelina's. "This week I'll actually be staying in town for a few days to arrange for the sale of our sugarcane harvest. Could I persuade you to join me for an evening out?"

"We'd love to," Angelina said before Tomas got a chance.

For the rest of the year, it was rare to not find Jacques sitting in the du'Pons' parlor enjoying a cigar with Tomas after dinner as Angelina needlepointed or knitted. Every so often she'd interject some witty comment to scale down whatever he and Tomas were arguing over. When the weather permitted, Jacques took Angelina for walks before their meal, always with a couple of trusted servants trailing behind as chaperones. After months, he and Angelina often strolled arm in arm, lost in conversation. Angelina had without effort become the envy of every woman in the Louisiana Territory.

New Orleans, present day

In the years since that special time, Kendal had rarely found as good a verbal sparring partner as Tomas or such a beguiling companion as his niece. The overwhelming sense of longing swamped her again as she stubbed out the Cohiba. Tears, which for so long had been a memory, welled in her eyes again. I'd give almost anything to see you again, she thought.

When she focused again she found Angelina's poor double sitting in the chair opposite hers with a strange expression. Giving Kendal time to compose herself, the bartender appeared and asked if Piper wanted anything. He seemed almost angry on her behalf that Piper had disturbed her.

"Come to finish your tirade, Miss Marmande?" she asked, clipping the new cigar the young man had left. A fresh drink had appeared along with it, and since Piper wasn't leaving, Kendal longed for the days when liquor could actually get her drunk.

"Actually, I came to apologize. If you don't have me thrown out before I finish, that is. I was rude earlier and don't have any excuse for my behavior."

Kendal smiled and tried not to gloat. She would have given Mac enough money to salvage his empire just to have seen Piper's face when she learned what Kenny Delaney had planned. She'd finished her research on Piper after lunch and found Piper had never mixed business with the inside of her bedroom, so in this instance she must've found her situation bleak. Those who'd been lucky enough to share Piper's bed had played strictly by her rules, if all her information was correct, and those liaisons had been few.

"Your being here can only mean one of two things, or perhaps a combination of the two."

Her triumphant tone apparently made Piper lose any trace of remorse. "What's your guess?"

Kendal guessed she was holding back a string of curses. "Macarthur reprimanded you after I left, and you found a snake crawling in your bed." She exhaled and blew a large smoke ring, followed by a smaller one that landed in the middle. "Am I on target?" A stream of smoke followed, cutting straight through the center of the rings like an arrow hitting its mark.

"I don't even have to be here for this conversation if you know every goddamn thing there is to know."

She didn't show any sign that the display of immaturity bothered her as she stared at Piper. "Can I ask you something?"

"Do I have a choice?" Piper asked hostilely, rolling her eyes and apparently waiting for her to rub her mistakes into her wounds.

"Yes, you do, and so do I." She stood, which sent the bartender running over. "Please put this on my tab. We're done."

"You're leaving?" Piper asked.

"Contrary to my reputation as a heartless shark, I don't enjoy playing with my prey. Nor do I enjoy the company of people who clearly detest everything about me. You hate me because I'm taking advantage of a business opportunity, and I can understand and appreciate that since I'm looking at your family's company. It doesn't, however, mean that I intend to sit here and take shit from you."

She leaned over the table like she had at their first meeting, making Piper press her back to her chair. "You want me gone from your life, fine. Consider it done. By tomorrow, though, you'll have ten other sharks circling the building and you'll long for the devil you know. Good luck, Miss Marmande. You and your grandfather will need it, because Kenny's going to carve you up without considering you or your workers."

Piper wanted to stop her, but no words would come out of her mouth. Only after Kendal disappeared out the door did she dig out her phone and call the car waiting downstairs.

"You strike out, boss?"

"In a big way. Keep an eye on the exits. Ms. Richoux says she's out of the deal, but she's put a lot of effort into us. She's not going anywhere." She fished out a bill for her drink that the bartender promptly gave back before leaving her alone. "It's time I know as much about Richoux as she knows about me."

"Will do, boss. I'll call you later."

CHAPTER EIGHT

From her position Hill Hickman could see Kendal standing at the valet station just inside the motor entrance of the hotel. "I've got you pegged as the limo type."

Expecting a boring sedan, Hill was shocked when the valet drove down a very large black motorcycle. Strapped to the back was a black leather jacket with gloves tucked into the pocket. Kendal handed her suit jacket to the valet and donned the heavier, warmer garment before roaring out of the garage headed out of town. At a red light she pulled out her phone and made a quick call. With a scanning device, Hill listened in from two car-lengths back.

"Bruce, pack it up and head home tonight, if you can. Take the team with you and scrub Marmande from our hot list."

"What? Why?" Bruce asked in such a high pitch Kendal had to move the phone away from her ear.

"Because I'm no longer interested. They could give me the whole damn thing and I still wouldn't want it. Mr. Marmande can keep that spawn he calls family, and they can both stew in the mess they've created."

"We can't just walk away. It's like throwing millions down the toilet."

"This isn't up for discussion, so get back to the office and find something else. This deal is dead." The light changed and Kendal walked the bike to the curb, making Hill have to pass her.

"And what do you plan to do?"

"I have some other things to attend to, so it may be a while before I get back."

"Like what?"

"Bruce, you don't own any part of me, and the attitude is getting old. I'm here and I have things to do, accept that and go."

"You have to attend to something more important than what we came for?"

"Marmande was something to do while I was here, that's it."

"Can I do anything for you? I'd be willing to stay behind and help," Bruce said, sounding like he was trying to heal any damage he'd caused their relationship.

"Thanks, but I've put this off long enough. Take care of yourself, and tell your father hello for me. You owe him a visit when you get home. He's different from you, but he's still a good man."

"Are you sure?"

"I'm positive."

"Take care, then. Don't take too long, okay?"

She disconnected the call as he inhaled to say something else, and Hill watched her through her rearview mirror as she put her phone away.

Kendal got on the interstate and opened the throttle. Miles down the road, she reached an exit just before one of the large bridges spanning the Mississippi River. Cold air blew through her hair as she started down River Road. With each mile the bike ate up, she moved farther away from the clutter of houses lining the road.

Here the homes were miles apart, and most weren't privately owned anymore. Every day, tourists from around the world followed docents dressed in period costumes to learn a little about life on Old South river plantations. A smaller plantation was the last she saw as the curvy road became dark with no streetlights or moonlight. To the right lay a long stretch of woods with a tall, simply designed wrought-iron fence surrounding it, and to the left was the high levee that kept the muddy waters at bay.

Finally, after a few miles, the woods gave way to cleared land with the same wrought-iron fence that gave passers-by only a small glimpse of what lay on the other side. All that was visible from the road were the massive oak trees that resembled spirits, with the Spanish moss blowing in the breeze, and ancient-looking azalea bushes lying dormant as they waited for spring to open the thousands of flowers they were known for. With the quick click of a button on the control in her jacket pocket, the gates opened to the bricked drive that led to the house. After almost three hundred years, the master of the house had returned to Oakgrove.

❖

Under Charlie's care Oakgrove looked very much like the last time Kendal had seen it, though now electric lights illuminated the porches and verandas where only lanterns had shone before. The house had been her joy for the time she had been in Louisiana, having overseen and helped in the original construction and additions they'd made. During the war the stories that it was haunted had saved it from serious looting and vandalism. In time Charlie erected the fence and allowed the trees to reclaim much of the land, leaving only the expansive formal gardens for the current staff to tend.

Besides modernizing the house for comfort, they had constructed a more modern barn and incorporated salvaged wood and relics from the original into the one now at the back of the house. The full stables housed some distant relatives of Jacques St. Louis's personal mounts, especially his beloved black stallion Dubois.

Per Charlie's directions the small staff had been given the night off so she could wander the grounds alone. She sat on the bike and just stared at her old home. The excitement of being there at last made her forget her run-in with Piper, and Kendal dismounted to start her tour. The front door was unlocked and on the center table in the foyer lay a note from Charlie.

Welcome home, Monsieur St. Louis. These walls have missed your presence, as have I. Enjoy, and call for me when you have need.

In the front parlor, wood was piled in the fireplace and the liquor bottles were all full, but none of that mattered. Kendal stood with her hands on her hips, much like she had the day it was hung, and studied the portrait of Angelina du'Pon over the mantel. The resemblance to Piper was uncanny, but the portrait showed the major difference: their eyes. Angelina's, a paler green, were filled with love for the person she was looking at when she sat for the likeness, whereas Piper's were more vibrant, but appeared hard and almost calculating.

Kendal walked through the house looking at and touching different objects. Finally, she visited the sword room. The priceless collection she'd amassed in her long lifetime hung along the walls. Some were older than any found in museums around the world. Each had a small brass plate that told the year it was purchased and where Kendal had acquired it. Under Charlie's care, each sword appeared almost new.

With a small bow, she took down the last one she'd sent Charlie for storage. The Japanese katana blade had been a gift from one warrior to another when she'd saved the son of a samurai during her travels. Light and sharp, it was perfect for the upcoming days. She took it with her upstairs and dropped it on the bed so she could change. A few minutes later she wore a pair of riding pants and a loose-fitting white shirt, the sword securely strapped to her back as she strode through the back door.

❖

"Where are you?" Piper asked in lieu of a greeting. After her meeting with Kendal, she'd decided to go home and relax with a glass of wine. Annoyingly, Kenny had left more than twenty messages apologizing for what he was sure was a misunderstanding.

"You'd never guess, no matter how much time I gave you," Hill said.

"A whorehouse?"

"As interestingly strange as that answer is, no."

"She talks about sex all the time, like she's a little obsessed."

"I don't know, Piper, you sound almost jealous."

"Please, I may need to hire someone else if you think I'm that desperate." She rested back against a pile of pillows in front of her fireplace and took a sip of her wine. "So if you're through playing games, tell me where you are."

"On the levee across from Oakgrove plantation."

"You're on a sightseeing tour?"

"Why I work for you is the real mystery," Hill said. "Your mark pulled up on a big Harley and the gates slid open like she owns the place. She's in the house right now."

"What's her connection to the St. Louis family? That place is one of the few that's still privately owned, though I've never seen any of the family in residence. And all the land the original owner acquired is still intact and the family trust controls it."

"If you do so well investigating on your own, why do you need me?"

Moving from irritated to distracted Piper sat up and stared into the flames. "To fill in the gaps."

"You don't sound like you have many. Or maybe you're just a plantation-history expert and I missed that."

"Pops's family owns the place next door, and since I was five, I've been trying to sneak over there and explore. I never get very far. This is getting more and more curious." Piper tapped her nail against her front tooth, remembering all her thwarted efforts to climb over the brick and wrought-iron fences. "Call me as soon as you know anything."

"Will do, boss. Oh, before I forget, I taped a conversation I thought you'd want to hear. I'll send you a transcript as soon as I get back to the office. She told someone named Bruce Babbage to pack up and get out. He wasn't happy about it, but believe me, she did all the talking."

"When did she make that call?"

"Right after she met with you. She phoned him from the curb before coming here. I had Mandy check it out. Whoever Bruce is, he walked back to the hotel and asked the front desk to settle the bill for the five rooms he'd booked, leaving only one suite occupied. Mandy's waiting to follow him to the airport. From what she said, he still looked as pissed as he sounded on the phone when Kendal treated him like the hired help."

"I know the type, though. Richoux's not going anywhere and she's not about to pass on this deal. We're worth too much to her dead and in pieces."

"Then she's going it alone if this guy leaves."

"We'll see. Keep your eyes open and call me if anything happens or if anyone else shows up. I don't care what time it is."

❖

"Look at you, big boy. Dubois would be happy to see that his line has carried on so beautifully." Kendal patted the large horse on the side of the neck, letting him get acquainted with her. With gentle words she bridled him and led him out of the stall.

"How about a little midnight ride, Ruda?" Not bothering with a saddle, she landed on his back with a fluid grace not often seen without the help of a stirrup. The black horse danced a little to the right when he felt her weight, but just as quickly waited for her command when she squeezed his middle with her legs. In a strong voice she said, "Ha," sending him toward the wooded area of the property, obviously glad for the freedom to run without the feel of the saddle since he moved as if he found joy in the long, fast stride.

She rode until they were well away from the house, then moved to the fence line. After a few sections she found what she was looking for and opened the hidden gate to allow them to move onto the road. Locking up before she crossed, she let a small laugh escape that Ruda's snorting echoed. He seemed to know what was coming next.

Ruda's powerful legs made quick work of the levee, and she let him loose once they were on level ground again, letting him set the pace. She slowed him only when she spotted the car. It was almost too easy to surprise the person sent to watch, especially if she was asleep.

Hill tried to decipher why her chin felt so cold so she could do something about it without waking. A move of her head to the right only increased the chill, and now a slight painful pressure made her open her eyes. When she did, she almost laughed at her hilarious dream. Got to lay off the nachos after nine, she thought. Sitting bareback was Kendal Richoux, holding a sword to the underside of her chin.

"Want to explain why you're parked on private property?"

She sounds so real, Hill thought, as she blinked rapidly. "Um…"

"Tell me, Ms. Hickman, are you a better detective than you are a talker?"

The steel was biting into her skin now, and she tried to pull back, only to have Kendal lean in farther after her. Any sudden moves might cause parts of her face to decorate her lap.

"This is public property and I was just taking a nap." It embarrassed her to be caught sleeping on the job, but a quick glance at her dashboard clock showed she'd been out there for hours, allowing the cool temperatures and silence to get to her.

"You got part of the story right, anyway. The drooling confirms the napping, but unfortunately for you, you're parked on Oakgrove property."

"I'm sorry to disagree with you, but the levee system belongs to the state." She stopped talking when she remembered her current predicament.

"Actually, most levees in this country belong to the feds, but the ten-mile stretch in front of this house is an exception. The estate stretches from the waterline of the river to the other side of a lake west of here so, in fact, you're trespassing. We don't know each other well, so let me explain how much trespassers offend me, and if that's not bad enough, being spied on makes me want to see how sharp this thing is."

"I'm sorry. If you'll move back I'll be on my way." Hill tried to sound in control, but the situation was so bizarre she couldn't keep the slight quiver out of her voice.

The sword pulled away from her face so Kendal could slide off the horse's back. "Not yet. Get out of the car," Kendal ordered. "And leave your weapon on the seat. If you think you're fast enough to draw on me you'll find your hand bloodying the grass before you can tense your finger on the trigger. If you don't believe me, try."

She removed the small pistol, not doubting the threat. "I meant no harm."

Kendal put up one hand as she sheathed the sword with the other. "You're doing your job, I can understand that. But why are you still here doing it?"

"What do you mean?" Hill relaxed a little when the chance of being sliced and diced diminished with the disappearance of the blade.

"Didn't you play the tape for her? I stopped so you'd get the whole thing." Kendal sounded reasonable, and it was a little spooky that she was so on the mark. No one she'd ever followed was this perceptive. "Tell Miss Marmande I'm not interested in her little company, so she can save the money this is costing her. She'll need it to fight off the next corporate raider."

"How'd you know?"

"By studying my opponent, Ms. Hickman. If you know your enemy, you know what to expect. It's not that difficult. Piper is predictable and you're on her payroll, so I doubt you're out here in the middle of the night soaking up the ambiance."

"Years of experience, huh?"

"It helps, but the concept isn't new. Master Tzu wrote it all in his book. In your line of work, you should be acquainted with it."

"Ah, you read *The Art of War*."

"So many times I feel like I know Master Tzu personally," Kendal said, whistling for her horse. "I'd say it was a pleasure, Ms. Hickman, but I don't lie that well. Please tell your client to stay the hell away from me. After tonight I don't have any plans for Marmande Enterprises. She has my word."

"Thank you, Ms. Richoux."

"You're very welcome. Just remember my warning. I won't be so nice next time, and you have such a handsome face. Pity something might happen to change that." Kendal arched an eyebrow before she mounted the horse again and kept riding along the levee toward New Orleans.

To Hill, she looked like a piece of the past brought back to life in vivid proportions. She could almost imagine the plantation owner riding along the river as the crops grew nearby, waiting for the fall harvest. It was a shame she wouldn't have a reason to follow Kendal any longer. Unlike most of the others she trailed, Kendal seemed like a fascinating subject.

Hill started her car even before she had the door closed, not anxious to still be around when Kendal returned. Her cell phone was on the seat, but she drove almost halfway back to the city before she called Piper. "She made me, and she knows who signs my paychecks."

Piper didn't answer for more than a minute. "What the hell doesn't she know? I'm beginning to think the only secret I have left is the color of my underwear."

"I wouldn't put even money on that. This woman's different, Piper. She said you have her word she has no interest in your company, so I'd stay clear." The memory of that blade biting into her skin made her shudder. She didn't doubt that if she were found on Oakgrove property again, Kendal would hand her her ass on a plate, literally. "You don't want her as an enemy, believe me."

"You show fear in business and you might as well hang the For Sale sign up. You have to realize that you don't put in that sort of time and effort to just walk away. Come on, Hill, you don't need an MBA to figure that one out."

"No, it's you who doesn't understand. She gave her word, and I get the impression that means a lot to Kendal Richoux. She rode up on a damn black horse and held me at swordpoint. I'm telling you, Boss, you don't want to mess with her."

"That's why I run a business and you lurk around after people. Call me tomorrow. I want to know a lot more about Richoux."

"As long as I can find it on a computer screen, lady. 'Cause no way in hell am I putting myself in striking distance again," she said to the empty car after Piper disconnected.

CHAPTER NINE

The ride was refreshing, and Kendal would've sworn Ruda enjoyed it as much as she did. With the minor annoyance gone from across the street, she returned through the main gates a little after four in the morning. It felt good to be on horseback riding through land that reminded her of the Shômû, or summer seasons, as a child when the world moved with the pharaoh to the southern palace and its rich fields of grain.

Those carefree times were the treasures of her past that helped her bridge the stretches of loneliness in her life. Her father had led the pharaoh's legions, and his best and most trusted men were among her first teachers, but in the trek up the Nile they were more of an extended family who, along with her father, had indulged her love of fun. All of them were long dead, but they still had an unforgettable place in her heart.

"I was beginning to think you'd run away." Morgaine seasoned the reprimand with a large dose of teasing, and seeing her standing on the porch made Kendal smile.

Through the centuries, in every lifetime Morgaine had known the names she'd gone by, the details of the identities she'd chosen, and why, sometimes, because of the society, it was easier to live as a man than a woman. Though Morgaine had so much information about her, in return Kendal knew her only as Morgaine.

In the life of immortality she had chosen, she had witnessed Morgaine become an Elder in the Genesis Clan, but she still remained Kendal's watcher. Morgaine now participated with the others in passing judgment when it was warranted so they could coexist in balance. For every powerful black force that was created, the Elders looked for a stronger white light to either control it or destroy it, if necessary. When things were quiet, Morgaine would be absent from Kendal's life for decades.

"Had I known such beauty was waiting on my steps, I would've beaten the horse back." She slid off Ruda and landed with a small thump on the pavement of the drive. One of Morgaine's men took the reins and led the horse away for a thorough brushing. "I mean, how often am I visited by the goddess of war?"

"I carry only the name, my warrior, but none of her powers."

"I'm positive the pagans named their beloved for you."

"Henri's growing stronger as we stand here talking. You cannot wait too much longer."

As with the first time Kendal laid eyes on her one constant for three thousand years, something inside her stirred. She was almost Kendal's opposite in every way. Petite in stature, pale skin extenuated by blond hair so light it seemed almost white. The eyes that had seen the passage of time were their only common feature.

"Is he ready to take over the world tonight?" she asked, stepping closer. Now that she had finished her ride and stopped moving, the sweat on her skin made the cold air more pronounced.

Morgaine laughed. "No, not tonight."

"Then let's talk about something else, since we both realize the price of failure."

Morgaine held her ground as Kendal moved closer. From the flare of Morgaine's nose, she had detected the citrusy cologne Kendal had started using during the French Revolution. Morgaine held her breath, as if anticipating the first touch of her callused hands made rough by years of wielding a sword.

She went slow, savoring the taste of the brandy Morgaine must have had while waiting for her return. Her lips parted, encouraging Kendal in to explore, so as she stroked Morgaine's tongue with hers, she slid her hands down her sides until she cupped her bottom.

"Better yet, I suggest we talk of nothing at all," she said, picking Morgaine up and moving to the front door. She didn't stop until they were in the master suite. There she put Morgaine gently on her feet and cupped her face in her hands. Just as gently she pressed her lips again to Morgaine's, enjoying the feel of her. "I've missed you."

Morgaine ran her hands up Kendal's chest and stopped at the cord holding the shirt closed. "And I you, warrior mine. I've never had your like in my life." With one tug the knot came loose and she laid her palm against the warm chest.

"The saddest day of my existence was when I had to give you the gift of immortality. As your watcher I'd never have a life with you, no matter how much I care for you." She pulled Kendal's shirt from the riding pants and up over her head. Kendal's body hadn't changed at all from the first night they had spent together.

By the time they had left the haven of the desert, everything and everyone Kendal had known was a memory, but Kendal told her that the only things she mourned losing were her father and her, once they had to part.

Over the years Ora had come to both hate and fear the best slayer Morgaine had ever trained. The exploits of the warrior Asra had become almost mythical, since none of Ora's followers had ever come close to defeating her.

Kendal was her greatest student not only because of the way she fought, but because of her ability to morph, always changing to fit her environment, serving whenever and wherever the Elders sent her to do their bidding. Now it was her time as Kendal Richoux, but it was also her time to finish the work she had begun as Asra.

"It's been so long," Kendal said as she placed her hand at the center of Morgaine's chest. The sound of Kendal's voice interrupted her memories.

"You're as beautiful as you were the night I gave you life, Asra."

"And you excite me just as much," Kendal said as Morgaine unfastened her belt and lowered her pants, dropping to her knees with them. With a little encouragement, Kendal pulled her head forward toward her sex. Morgaine loved sharing herself with Kendal since she understood so perfectly her needs and could match her strength.

Kendal moaned when Morgaine sucked her hard clitoris against her tongue. She smiled when Kendal flexed the muscles in her legs; only focused concentration kept her on her feet under the pleasurable onslaught. "Let go for me, Warrior, for the war begins tomorrow."

❖

The sound of birds in the branches of the oak outside the master suite made Morgaine turn her head toward the French doors that led out to the veranda. Standing naked in the dim dawn light, Kendal stared out at the front lawns. She had never visited Kendal at Oakgrove during her life as Jacques St. Louis, wanting to give her those years to pursue and romance someone who could have made her happy for a short while.

Since Kendal's life would never be normal, Morgaine would never deny her the few moments of happiness she could snatch along the way.

"What do you see?"

"The beginning of another day," Kendal said.

She rose and pressed her naked body to Kendal's back; the abdominal muscles she'd tensed the night before so she could rub against them twitched slightly under her hands. "Don't tell me you're getting bored with the prospect."

"In the beginning I thought I would," Kendal said, with her usual honesty. "Wandering aimlessly forever, with no chance at a family, watching everyone you love die, didn't seem too appealing once I gave it serious thought." Kendal turned in her embrace and led her back to the large bed. Morgaine snuggled up to Kendal's side as they continued their talk. "To know my life would revolve around killing brought an incredible sadness to my heart."

"Asra, your life was one of a soldier when I found you. Did you forget you were skilled enough to be the leader of the pharaoh's elite squad, even though you were a woman? Your duty was to kill on command. What was the difference?"

"Back then my life would've ended. The killing would've stopped with time, and someone else would've been waiting to take my place since some people are eager to face war in any lifetime, if history's any indication. Just look at the world today. How different are people now than those who lived when I served?" Kendal wrapped a strand of her hair around her fingers. "You always smell like roses, even when I'd never seen the flower."

She kissed Kendal as a reward for her continual sweetness. "The difference is the wise ruler you once served had more patience for talk. I would think that after all this time you would've grown bored with politics and the ups and downs it puts people through. My way's much more gratifying, don't you think?" She poked Kendal in the ribs, making her laugh. "Are you really tired?"

"Try some of that patience you're fond of lecturing me about," Kendal said, pinching her cheek. "Awe replaced the sadness quickly. It was the simple things at first—the forging of stronger steel, the printing press, the sound of an orchestra when I first heard it, and seeing man fly. These changes made facing each new day worthwhile. I've come to love life and those who cherish it like I do."

Morgaine lifted her head and looked into Kendal's eyes. "And the fighting?"

"I fight for those who can't do it for themselves. It's not only my obligation but also my honor. The killing doesn't bother me now because those I destroy really aren't human anymore. When I heard Henri speaking to me the other night, I couldn't bring myself to turn and look at him for the longest time," Kendal said, exhaling at length. "Three thousand years is a long time, but not enough for me to finally understand why he chose to become such a pathetic creature."

"Why didn't you want to look at him?"

"Because he may resemble my brother, he may sound like him, but he isn't him. From that very first night he came to kill me, I couldn't stand to see what he's turned into. I'm going to destroy him and hunt down the witch who made him," Kendal said, and the passion Morgaine wanted to hear was back after years of rest. Her warrior had awoken.

"He's grown powerful, you know."

"Yes, but so have I."

She laughed and bit the nipple closest to her mouth. "You sound incredibly sexy when you talk like that."

"Are you kidding? I sound incredibly sexy all the time," Kendal said as she rolled them over, pinning her to the bed with her hands above her head.

Morgaine had delivered the message from the Clan, so she would have to leave eventually to attend to other responsibilities. She planned to make the most of their remaining time. Kendal's life would become dark soon enough until the job was done, so now they should rejoice in the pleasures life could bring.

"Ah, I see the cocky captain I first encountered is back. And here I thought time would tame you."

Her clit got hard and she arched her back off the bed when Kendal sucked on her nipple hard enough to make her sex clench. "Do you really want to tame me?"

With almost equal strength she broke her hands free and squeezed Kendal's ass. "Never," she said, spreading her legs wide and feeling the morning air against her wetness. "But enough talk."

Kendal placed her thigh between her legs and kissed her in a way she seldom allowed because it was so possessive. They knew each other's strengths, so they had no reason to show restraint. With only the hard muscle against her clitoris, she broke the kiss by pulling on Kendal's hair. "Take me," she said as Kendal hovered over her. "I want you."

As if to torture her, Kendal went slowly after removing the little bit of relief by sitting up. Kendal held her knees apart, further exposing her, and the twitching in her clit made her want to beg, but she waited. The night before had been explosive since they'd tried to subdue each other, but now Kendal was looking down at her with familiarity.

They cared about and knew what it took to please each other, that had never been an issue, but they also knew not to become too attached. Their place within the Clan wouldn't allow them more than these stolen moments, so Morgaine savored these times when she could see Kendal's soul in her eyes.

"It amazes me still how beautiful you are," Kendal said, touching her as if she were suddenly made of porcelain. The calluses on Kendal's palms and fingers felt delicious as they skimmed her stomach and nipples.

"If I had the ability to dream," Kendal said as her right hand moved lower, scratching along the blond hair that topped her sex, "this is where I'd spend my nights when you aren't with me."

She couldn't help but close her eyes when Kendal wet her fingers and flicked them gently against her clit. "Please, Warrior, take me," she said, unashamed to plead.

The bed bounced when Kendal moved to put her face between her legs, blowing softly and making her arch off the bed again. "You taste as sweet as you smell," Kendal said after she dipped her tongue just deep enough for her to miss the contact when Kendal lifted her head.

"Do you taste as good?" Morgaine asked, suddenly craving the uniqueness of Kendal. Her question made it easy to roll Kendal to her back as she slid in the opposite direction. She bucked her hips as Kendal started sucking on her and had to concentrate on doing the same in return.

From this position she could enjoy almost the length of Kendal's skin under hers, moaning with Kendal's hardness against her tongue. Rocking her hips in time with Kendal's mouth started her orgasm, which washed through her so thoroughly that she shivered as her entire body tingled. She rode it out, feeling Kendal tense under her, and the moment ended too quickly, but left her boneless.

Kendal lifted her and lay back with her arms around her so they could enjoy the morning from under the covers. Their fire didn't burn often, but perhaps that was best. Anything this hot had to burn out if lit too long, and it was her responsibility that Kendal live forever.

❖

The sound of rain against Piper's bedroom window reminded her of all the times she'd spent daydreaming in her old room at her grandparents' place. Those hours pasting together fantasies of her future instead of sleeping whenever it rained had helped heal but not forget those parts of her heart she thought would always be broken.

She stared at the ceiling, not focusing on the moving patterns the streetlight painted as it filtered through the landscaping foliage her housing development prided itself on. The raging storm and the booming thunder that sounded close had woken her two hours before the alarm.

"The weather guy finally got it right," she said, turning toward the window. It was early, but she wasn't tired.

"Do you still see me, Daddy?" She spoke in a normal voice instead of the whispers she'd used as a child so she wouldn't upset her grandparents. Daydreaming when it rained always made her feel connected to her father. The report on Mackey's car accident had concluded it was just that—an accident. Only he'd lost control on the straightest part of River Road and hit the huge oak dead-center, almost as if he'd aimed right for it.

It had been raining that night too, and thinking about him dying out there alone still haunted her. She wished she'd fulfilled her most recurring daydream of having someone in her life who'd hold her when her head became too crowded with memories. A few moments of comfort, though, weren't worth saddling herself with anyone she'd ever met.

"Get a grip," she told herself, and laughed as she sat up.

The room was chilly when she pushed the covers off, but not enough to flip on the heater, so she pressed the control panel for the coffeepot. Today she'd enjoy the weather as she finished her proposal for the bank. It was a long-shot pitch, but she didn't have any tricks left to play since enemies had surrounded them.

Financially, with or without the business, she'd be fine because of the trust her parents had set up, but the hundreds of employees working at the shipyard didn't have that luxury. She didn't want them to remember her for stripping them of their livelihoods and futures.

When the coffee was done, she reread her proposal, then moved to the comfortable chair in her den with the couple of books written about Oakgrove and the man who built it. That mysterious place was often the subject of her rainy-day mental vacations because it was walled off from a modern world. Growing up next door had ignited her imagination about the house and Jacques St. Louis from an early age, but the fence was as far as she ever got to unlocking the plantation's secrets.

"What does Kendal Richoux have to do with Jacques St. Louis?" she asked the sketch of the house on the first page of the thickest book she owned on the subject. It was one of the only images of the plantation you couldn't see from the road, and since practically all the acreage was fenced, it wasn't visible from her grandparents' place either.

"You'd think someone would've cracked the story by now." She kept talking to herself as she flipped through the pages, trying unsuccessfully to find a picture of Jacques. She rested her head back, reading the almost clinical information, and before long it put her back to sleep.

❖

"Damn, just when it was getting interesting," Henri said to Troy, both of them standing outside Piper's place getting soaked. It was the first time he'd opened his eyes since Piper had woken up. "She's so accessible."

"Who is she, sire?" Troy asked, adjusting his coat as the rain made it heavier.

"Someone who could be useful to us." Henri opened his mind again, trying to reconnect to Piper's thoughts, but sleep had surprisingly raised her defenses. Her hatred of Asra was almost like an embrace. "Remember this place, but leave her alone."

When they reached the fence surrounding the complex, they both jumped effortlessly to the top. Sunrise was in an hour, but Henri wanted to feed before he returned to his sleeping chamber. He led Troy toward the older section of town, but kept searching for an easy target. He found it right outside the French Quarter when he spotted a middle-aged man slumped in the doorway of an abandoned house. From his appearance, the guy was probably homeless and drunk, but Henri only cared that he was alive.

He stopped close to him, smiling when the man opened his eyes and stared at him. "Can you loan me a few bucks?" the man asked, alcohol on his breath.

The silence seemed to unnerve the man since he straightened up some and looked startled. "I ain't got no money," he said, his voice slurred, but he talked faster.

"I'm interested in something else."

Henri grabbed him by the front of his coat and lifted him to his feet with one hand. The strength of Ora's blood never ceased to awe him, and he held the man almost completely off his feet, widening his smile so his canines were visible. When the guy saw them he tried to get away, making Henri laugh when only the tips of his toes hit the ground in a running motion.

The prickling in his skin signaled that dawn wasn't far off, but Henri could concentrate only on the hammering carotid artery that pulsed with blood and terror. The man's skin had a strong sour smell, but that wouldn't ruin the feast. As he broke through the artery and his mouth filled with the first gush of salty thick liquid, his euphoria made him hard. He was as excited as the first time Ora had pressed her wrist to his lips.

He remembered how his strength had left him one sip at a time, his fear and his life force abandoning him as he floated in Ora's embrace. That same bliss was making the man in his arms stop struggling. This brief moment was the only thing that reminded Henri of his life before Ora. As the heat of someone else's life force coursed through him, he almost felt his humanity again.

The man dropped like a rag at his feet, and Henri looked into his eyes until they completely dimmed in death.

"Please, sire," Troy said, standing behind him, "we have to go."

"Go on, and remember what I said about the girl. Don't take any of the others there."

He trusted Troy to follow his orders, so he turned and moved away so fast that Troy couldn't follow. Troy was his creation, but he trusted no one with the location of his resting place. No one could betray him with information they didn't have, one of the few lessons he'd retained from Raad.

He arrived at the house in the Garden District and closed the door to one of the only basements in New Orleans as the first rays of light cut through the sky, the storm now north of them. Henri stripped off his wet clothing and left it in a pile, having no problem moving around in total darkness.

When he shoved the heavy capstone over the crypt, he thought of Asra before he gave in to the oblivion of sleep. The Elders were getting ready to unleash their slayer, but he felt comfortable with his plan. "You'll be so busy with my young ones that you'll never see the trap I've set for you. Once I bury you, the old ones will bow to Ora's will or they'll face the same fate."

His laugh echoed in the confined warm space as he thought of the place he'd picked to put Asra where the sun would never touch her skin again. "We've come to the end of our story, Asra, and nothing will save you from me."

❖

Morgaine kissed Kendal before taking her seat at the breakfast table the house staff had set up on the porch. The unpredictable weather had again slipped into a more summer-like pattern, so Morgaine had chosen a sleeveless white shirt to go with her faded jeans. To the casual observer Morgaine was an All-American coed home for the weekend.

"My guys will stay with you until you're done. The regular staff Charlie hires on occasion might not understand some of the things that could happen if Henri decides to come visit," she said. The young server placed a crisp white linen napkin on her lap, and she smiled at him.

"You're leaving already?"

Morgaine broke a croissant in half and buttered it before she added the homemade strawberry preserves she recognized as Lola's recipe, which was now a common item at all of Kendal's properties. "Trying to get rid of me?"

"No, I just want you to say good-bye this time."

She put the bread down and reached for Kendal's hand. "That was a couple of hundred years ago, Warrior. Let it go and forgive me."

"What can I say? I know how to hold a grudge." Kendal shrugged, as if acknowledging her imperfections.

"And how," Morgaine said with a laugh.

"Speaking of grudges."

"He can't work with you, so don't even ask," she said, putting both her hands up for extra emphasis.

Kendal looked at the full plate of eggs and bacon the server had put down. "I'm not asking you, I'm telling you. Abez has kept the name Henri to taunt me about the past and my failures. One of the greatest of them was Lionel's family, so I won't deny him the satisfaction of ending this."

"He isn't ready. The Elders are still pissed that Charlie exists to be able to avenge anyone. Or have you forgotten that little infraction?" Morgaine tried not to sound like she was scolding a small child, but she crossed her arms over her chest, challenging Kendal to deny the truth.

"One," Kendal said, holding up a finger. "One in all the years you've given me. That's not a bad record. And I hate to disagree with you, but he *is* ready. If you try to stop him from helping me, then find someone else to go against Henri, because I won't do it." She leaned back and mirrored Morgaine's pose.

"You would defy the Clan?"

"Just because you and they are in a position of authority doesn't mean you're always right. In this case you're wrong, so my answer is, yes, I'd defy the Clan and you."

"He'll be your responsibility."

"He always has been. You'll see, Charlie will be an asset. If I didn't think so, he'd be a memory by now. That's why I gave him the gift. He's a rare man with a caring heart."

The corner of Morgaine's mouth quivered slightly, and she gave in to the smile. "That's the only reason the Elders upheld my wishes and didn't bury you under a rock somewhere. Take care of him because Henri will show him no mercy. And you're right about why Abez chose the name. I want you to take this business seriously, warrior mine. Age has made the enemy not only strong but extremely cunning."

"I should introduce him to Piper Marmande. After ten minutes Henri and everyone associated with him would volunteer to drive a stake through their own heart."

Morgaine laughed around her fork. "Don't tell me there's a woman alive who can resist you? What *is* the world coming to?" she asked after she swallowed.

"Hard to believe, isn't it?" Kendal laughed and looked through the window of the house to the painting over the fireplace. "The closest I've come to dying in generations is when I'm on the receiving end of her killer looks."

Morgaine clapped, then placed her hand over her mouth as if to not spit anything out. "You have to tell me more about her now. Start with a description."

"Darken the eyes and sharpen her features a little, and she looks like that." She pointed to the portrait.

"No way."

"I literally came close to passing out when I saw her. It was like fate was playing a cruel joke on me for my shortcomings."

The staff disappeared when Morgaine stood and sat in her lap. "The fault for what happened lies squarely on Henri. Stop blaming yourself for things you had no control over."

"Don't you get it? He did what he did because of me."

"Henri still did the deeds. Kendal, you can't control his actions and you can't be everywhere at once, no matter how hard you try. Henri is a vampire. He's a creature without conscience and soul." Morgaine caressed Kendal's face, wiping away the tears that had fallen.

"You sound so religious."

"And you sound like a smart-ass. Christians may think they invented the concept of the soul, but you and I know it's been there all along. Catholics find God in cathedrals, some think he's hanging around at tent revivals, and the lost tribes of the Amazon find him in every living thing. Who's right?"

Kendal stood, cradling her, and kissed her before putting her down. Morgaine enjoyed the speck of jam she'd missed with the napkin. "You will not drag me into this conversation again, so forget it. How about you gather your best swordsmen for later? I could use the practice before tonight."

"You're no fun," Morgaine said, pouting. They had argued about different topics over the years, the fights sometimes lasting for decades. "Where are you off to?"

With a quick slap to Morgaine's backside, Kendal moved toward her bike. "To a Catholic cathedral to find salvation. If I can't find that, I'll settle for Charlie."

CHAPTER TEN

"Well?"

"Well what?" Hill said, still shocked to find Piper standing in her office doorway. During their entire business relationship, Piper had always made her come to her office.

"Did you find anything?" Piper sounded exasperated. "Come on, get with the program. It's what I'm paying you for."

"I found the same thing I found the last time I looked. Didn't you read my report? She's like a machine, this woman. Have you seen her college transcripts? Even Einstein, in his science courses, at least, didn't get that many As." The computer behind her was finishing its search for any mention of Kendal Richoux, and even after the second time she'd run it she hadn't found much. She pulled her glasses off and rubbed her eyes because of the lack of leads.

"Did her pet snake slither back to New York?"

She handed a one-paged report to Piper detailing Bruce's itinerary from the time he'd received the call from Kendal and her associate watched his plane take off. "He checked everyone out and hopped a limo to the airport. But they flew to Los Angeles, not New York."

"What's in L.A.?"

"Aside from the obvious, you mean?" Piper put her fists on her hips in impatience, so she cut the jokes. "Webster International." She handed over another short report. "Old manufacturing firm on the ropes after the downturn in the economy a couple of years ago. Mr. Babbage is flying this one solo. Well, as solo as you can get considering the team he left here with."

"And?"

The last sheet at the center of her messy desk made Piper exhale loudly when she handed it over. "She hasn't left the property as far as we can tell from five miles away. Considering the estate owns all the land in every direction, surveillance is a little tough." The ringing phone stopped her recap since she was alone in the office, all her people out gathering more information for Piper.

"Hickman," she said, pausing to listen. "Stay way back and keep me posted if you head into town. I'll take over once you get here, and be careful. This woman has eyes in the back of her head."

"What's going on?" Piper asked.

"The big bike just rolled past our lookout, so it seems Ms. Richoux is headed back to town." Hill took her gun out of her top desk drawer. "I'll call you later and give you an update."

"You do that, and I want to know her every move. I'm not buying her I'm-not-interested act."

An hour later Hill paused at the back of the St. Louis Cathedral in the French Quarter, surprised that it was Kendal's first stop for the day. A security guard waiting on the sidewalk greeted Kendal after she dismounted. Obviously he was there to watch the bike she was leaving illegally parked on Royal Street. Kendal entered the courtyard through the wrought-iron gate Hill had never seen unlocked and walked past the large Jesus statue with his arms lifted and frozen in praise.

She dropped her head when Kendal took her sunglasses off and paused for a minute, and started breathing again when Kendal didn't turn around. "What are you up to?" She was interested in the answer whether Piper was paying her or not.

❖

Kendal stopped to admire the two massive oaks anchoring the garden in the back of the cathedral; the last time she'd seen them they were tall saplings taken from Oakgrove's grounds. As she removed her sunglasses, behind her she heard Hill's engine shut off.

"I must not be as scary as I thought if she's still on the trail," she said softly. The persistent Hill wasn't an irritation, though, and she decided to play along to see what Piper had in mind. "Could you do me a favor," she said, speaking the next part into her phone so softly that no electronic listening device could have overheard her conversation as she held up her hand to the priest waiting at the door. "Thanks," she said, ending her call and so giving the priest permission to move forward.

"Ms. Richoux, it's wonderful to finally meet you," the priest said, shaking her hand enthusiastically. "It's incredible how much you resemble your father Anthony." His eyes moved over her face as if he were trying to memorize it.

Before leaving the city and the identity of Jacques St. Louis behind, she'd made a substantial donation to the Catholic church to help finish the original cathedral and for the care of Angelina and Tomas's graves. She didn't usually bother with religion, but faith was the cornerstone of Angelina's life, so she'd played along. Through the years, she'd come to see what a wise decision it was, since the church seldom asked questions and the priests gladly traveled to wherever she was to collect the funds to replenish the trust.

"I believe this is the first time a St. Louis heir has actually visited the church," the priest said, making her smile since the same elderly priest had traveled to New York to meet with her as Anthony Richoux, her last persona. He'd changed significantly with age, but she remembered his thick hair, which had been so black it had reminded her of blackbird feathers, and how Times Square had fascinated him more than anything she'd had to say.

"Father, it's nice to put a face with the voice." She took his hands in hers before accepting his embrace.

"I'm so glad you've finally come. Your family has been absent from this house too long." He accepted her arm and led her inside to his office.

"After I finish my business in town, I hope to return more often, Father." They talked for an hour about the repairs Kendal was financing and the daycare center they were building a few blocks away.

"When you come back, please block out a day so we can take you around to see the fruits of your generosity. I would also enjoy showing you off to the parish."

"That's a deal, but now I'm just here to pick up Charlie, if he's ready to go."

"Oh, he's been sitting by the telephone waiting for you to call. Thank you for sending him, though. He did a bit of rewiring for us while he was waiting. He's really quite handy."

"Amazing what having time on your hands will do for a man." She helped him up and kept her pace slow to not aggravate the man's pronounced limp.

"You came," Charlie said when they entered the rectory.

"I gave you my word, and now's your chance to stay here where you'll be safe." She put her hand on his shoulder and spoke softly, her words changing his expression to one of disbelief and hurt.

"I can help you. There's no way I'll let you down."

"I'm not asking because I doubt your loyalty or believe you'll disappoint me, but you've never done this before. Could you kill one of those coeds you love to spend time practicing your French with if Henri's turned her into something that'll haunt your waking dreams? They look so vulnerable and sweet, but they're still deadly."

"But I can't die, you've seen to that."

"No, but they can bury you so deep you'll be as good as dead. Henri's as aware of our limitations as we are of his, and if he can't beat me directly he'll do it through you."

Charlie pulled away from her. Glancing at the priest still close by, he switched to French. "Then you don't want me to come with you?"

"Do *you* still want to come with me, my friend? Do you remember your boys and woman enough to avenge what happened to them no matter what we face?"

"Do I remember? Are you insane?" Anger poured off him, but she ignored his clenched fists and jaw. "Slavers took me from my home and my family in chains like an animal, and I could do nothing about it. I had to accept my fate, but then I was given Celia and four strong sons, only to be left alone again. Do I remember them? I've thought of little else for decades."

She held her hand out to him and smiled. "Then come on," she said before turning back to the priest. "Thank you for everything, Father." She embraced the priest, again noticing the painting hanging in the entryway where they were standing.

"I don't know if you've ever had the opportunity to see this, so I had it brought out of storage for your visit," he said, moving her closer to the wall. "It's uncanny how the St. Louis side of the family has retained their looks."

"Thank you," she said, studying the portrait she remembered posing for. The size of her contribution at Angelina's behest had moved the priests back then to have the tribute made. It was a gift she'd loaned the church before she departed to Europe.

"Even though I take my vows seriously, it's nice to see young love captured so beautifully."

"You're right. It gives us incentive to fight for what's just," she said before telling him good-bye.

On the street another bike was parked next to hers, and she threw Charlie a set of keys.

"What, no sunglasses?" he asked.

"They've invented places called malls, buddy. You should get out more."

The engines rumbled as soon as they were started, and she laughed when she saw Hill dive into the passenger side of her car when she looked directly at her. That Hill stayed put helped clear her mind as she and Charlie headed home. She didn't want another catastrophe on her hands, or to add any more targets for Henri to use against her. The upkeep of Tomas and Angelina's graves was enough for a lifetime, even one as long as hers.

"I wouldn't have pegged her as the religious type," Hill said to herself, waiting for her phone to ring. "Piper, you're wasting your time and money, because she doesn't act like someone interested in taking over your business." The call came, and one of her assistants confirmed that the two riders were headed in the direction of Oakgrove. Making a quick decision, she got out and headed to the rectory, since the guard was still there and the gate was still open. Piper's first question would be about the guy Kendal had picked up and what her connection to him.

"Can we help you, child?" asked the nun who answered the door. The full habit brought back an avalanche of memories from parochial school, making Hill shiver. Women with wimples armed with rulers were, in her opinion, brides of the devil.

"Could I speak to the priest who was sitting outside with the woman who came to visit just now?"

"He's in a meeting for the next few hours. Is there a problem, or perhaps something I could help you with?"

Hill was about to ask what Kendal's connection to the church was when the painting caught her attention. It depicted a group of men standing around what looked like a cornerstone. Standing next to a priest in brown robes was Kendal Richoux, dressed as a man, and on the other side of her was a woman who very much looked like Piper. "What an interesting painting," she said, moving past the nun for a closer look.

"It was from the construction of the first church in the territory. The original building was an important endeavor for Jacques St. Louis," the nun said. "Of course, that's not why we chose St. Louis as our patron saint."

"Wasn't Mr. St. Louis the owner of Oakgrove?"

"Of the original plantation, yes. The house that sits there now has been repaired enough through the years that I'd think it would be brand-new by now. Charlie does such a wonderful job keeping it up for the family."

"Charlie?" she asked, still staring at the image on the wall.

"The young man who was here that you were asking about. He's Oakgrove's caretaker."

"Do you know his last name, Sister?"

"Perhaps Father could answer that for you. I've always known him as Charlie. I've accompanied him to the estate a few times, but I was more interested in looking around than in Charlie's full name."

"You've been to Oakgrove?" The opportunity was too good to pass up, and Hill forgot all about the man who'd left with Kendal. Now that her sword-toting mark thought she was off the case, maybe this nun could point out any chinks in the security.

"Yes, it's lovely. You should see the lake toward the back. It's the only place where the fence separating the grounds from the property next door ends. The open space makes you imagine what it must have looked like way back when." The nun put her hand on her arm like she was telling her a secret. "It's so secluded it makes me consider skinny-dipping whenever I'm there."

Hill laughed as she noticed how soft the nun's hand was. "I'll bet it's lovely." Looking more closely at the nun's face, she wondered why such a beautiful woman had chosen a life of service. "Do you know the name of the young woman standing with Mr. St. Louis?"

"Angelina du'Pon was his fiancée. Tragic story, really, but I'm late for a meeting already, so perhaps next time."

"Thank you for your time, Sister. You've been very helpful."

Hill waved one more time, then hurried to her car. From the large window in the rectory, Morgaine unzipped the black garment and peeled off the wimple, finished with the favor Kendal had asked of her. The thought of masquerading as a nun any longer made her laugh, considering how she'd spent her evening. Asra could make her yell for the gods, but she doubted that was what the church had in mind.

"I consider this my good deed for the day, Asra, and you guessed right. Your stalker couldn't help but come in," she said, putting the outfit on a chair. She fluffed up her hair and decided to have it cut before she returned to the house. It would be only a matter of time before they had visitors via the lake, but she would leave it to Asra to find them. "Let's hope they decide to make their covert operation during daylight hours, because Henri will be sending his own welcoming party soon enough."

"Can I help you, miss?" asked a nun who entered the room.

"No, thank you, Sister. I was just doing a favor for a friend."

"Well then, God bless you. It's the Christian way to do for others, and it's a habit young people don't develop enough these days."

"That message never does get old, no matter how many times I hear it."

❖

"Yesterday you were deathly afraid of this woman, and now you want to sneak into her house. Am I understanding you correctly?" Piper asked.

As Hill weaved through traffic on the way back to the office, she focused on the painting in the rectory and the resemblance to Kendal and Piper. Now she was certain that even if Piper didn't pay her another dollar to work the case, she wanted to find out more about Kendal Richoux. She couldn't ignore the doppelganger coincidences in the painting. Genetics, no matter how perfect, didn't produce two people who looked so much alike after so much time. Having Piper in the scene was too bizarre to even contemplate.

"You don't have to go with me, Piper. I'm going no matter what. After last night she thinks I'm off her tail, so what's to lose?"

"Oh, no. Give me twenty minutes, then pick me up at my place. I have to change into something more comfortable for sneaking around."

A mental picture of sneaking anywhere with the impatient Piper made Hill want to kick herself for not calling *after* she returned from the plantation. It would've been much easier alone. "I could just take pictures and write a report by tonight. Besides, you don't know what's crawling in those woods."

"Twenty minutes, Hill. Don't be late."

The silence in her ear stopped her from making any other excuses. Hopefully the most dangerous weapon in Kendal's house was a sword.

It was illegal to shoot someone on their own property, but she'd make up some reason if it came to that.

"Next time just go first and talk later, moron, because if you're not careful, your old friend Piper's going to get you killed." She tapped her thumbs on the steering wheel as she talked to herself. No matter, though—she was going even if she had to carry Piper on her back to get there and gag her once they arrived.

When she reached Piper's condo she saw they were wearing similar outfits. Jeans, boots, and long sleeves would help if bugs infested the place they landed. Piper also had a pair of binoculars hanging around her neck and a bag with snacks. Had Piper misunderstood? She looked ready to attend a sporting event instead of trespass in someone's yard.

"Nothing in there crunches, right?"

"I didn't have lunch, so take it easy. We aren't sneaking into the house. Who'll hear us eating potato chips while we're hiding under a bush?"

The same woman who snuck up on me on a really big horse and threatened to slice me into little pieces, that's who, she thought, as she studied the tops of her boots when her chin dropped to her chest. "Let's go before it gets much later. We still have to find a way across the lake."

"No problem. Granddad keeps an old rowboat out there. I asked before I left the office. As long as he doesn't actually land on Oakgrove property, he has permission to fish the lake. Don't you find it odd that Kendal's so friendly with these religious types?" Piper asked as they walked to the car. "It would have made more sense for her to attend a cult meeting."

Hill opened the door for Piper, then headed around to the driver's side. "We don't know a lot about Kendal. If we're lucky, though, we'll be able to see and photograph more people there with her. Then we'll have some new outlets to find out more about her and what she's up to."

Hill stopped hitting her thumbs on the steering wheel when Piper stared at them. Piper would know she was stalling. "Maybe so. Let's hope so, anyway. Your little penguin friend didn't tell you anything else, right? Something that would help us out?"

"No." She shook her head for emphasis. They were sitting at a red light and she couldn't look Piper in the eye when she answered. She wasn't ready to tell Piper she'd seen Kendal in a really old painting done before her great-grandmother was even born. Piper would have her committed in a heartbeat, especially if she told Piper she had seen her likeness in the painting as well.

"There's nothing more you want to tell me?" Piper asked again, and from her peripheral vision Hill could see her staring at her now.

The light turned green and she floored it, crossing over two lanes of traffic to make it onto the interstate ramp. "That was it. She told me about the lake, that she visited the place a couple of times, and she explained a painting hanging in the hallway." Please don't ask me about the painting and I won't have to lie, she thought.

"What, are you becoming an art connoisseur?"

"They just seem eager for the public to take an interest in their history. It's not a big deal."

❖

Piper kept quiet the rest of the trip, content to watch the scenery and think about the summers she'd spent at her grandfather's place as a child. She was on the tire swing he'd strung up for her from one of the large oaks in the back when he told her of her father's death. At first the words "car accident" didn't sound so permanent, but her father was gone just like that. She figured he'd wanted to be happy by joining her mother, whom she knew only from pictures.

The memories of her father, though, were vivid, but she usually kept them buried since they brought her only pain. Her father had always worn his melancholy like a cloak. Despite his sadness he often read to her, walked the property with her skipping beside him, but nothing she did ever brought him true joy. From the time she could remember she'd tried to make him happy, but she couldn't reach the part of his heart that withered when her mother died.

That sense of failure had made her wary of trying so hard to please anyone again. She'd allowed only Granddad Mac and Grandmother Molly fully into her heart, especially Mac. When she'd moved in with them permanently, he'd laughed and danced with her and her grandmother every night when he got home from work, and never acted pressed for time when she asked to do something with him.

He and Grandmother Molly had done everything from attending her sporting events to volunteering for school functions so her life would be as full and normal as possible. From Mac she'd learned what exactly their family was built on, and a big part of that was Marmande Shipyard, as well as the extended family they employed and were responsible for.

Once she was old enough, she wouldn't stay away from the office. From her first day, she'd carried the company further than they should've gotten before someone like Kendal came along. However, the bleeding of red ink had been too severe for too long for Piper to make a lasting difference, though she wasn't giving up. To lose now would be to disappoint the two people she admired most in the world and put nearly four thousand people out of work. Mac and Grandmother Molly were everything to her, so she wouldn't let them die without Marmande Shipyard still being in business.

"Turn here to go back to the dock. Granddad said the boat should be tied up and ready, if someone didn't borrow it." She pointed out a dirt road where the Oakgrove fence line ended. The excitement she felt as a child when she made a break for the property line to explore Oakgrove's secrets returned. Back then, whenever she tried, Mac was always too quick and stopped her before she got into trouble.

"Go slow so we don't kick up too much dust."

"You want to row?" Hill asked when they reached the end of the pier.

"And deprive you of the pleasure? I wouldn't dream of it, Hill. Come on, chop chop. When we get to the other side I'll give you a potato chip."

They shoved off a little before noon, Hill plowing the water with powerful strokes. "Man, that nun said this was a small lake," Hill complained after thirty minutes.

"Call a nun a liar and lightning may strike you," Piper said. They were both whispering as the shore got closer. When they landed they couldn't tell how far back from the house they were since it wasn't visible from the road.

They tied off the boat in a stand of willow trees to keep it out of sight and waited to make sure they were alone. At least most of the foliage was still on the trees, giving them good coverage.

After a short walk to the east, they reached a clearing. They were in for a long walk around it if they wanted to keep from being spotted. They still couldn't see the house, and Piper hoped they could find their way out if sunset came before they were done.

With a quick pull, Hill yanked her farther into the trees, but she didn't complain about the rough treatment because she heard an approaching horse. They pressed themselves up to tree trunks big enough to hide them, chests heaving.

"I am one with the tree, I am one with the tree." Piper mentally repeated the mantra as the clip-clop of hooves stopped close to where they'd stood.

❖

Kendal reined her horse in at the beginning of the clearing, opting for no saddle again since she wanted Ruda to roam on his own while she worked out. Her skills never truly lost their edge, but because her brother had amassed quite a following, a little practice wouldn't hurt.

She didn't intend to let them capture her and lock her way from the sun. She always welcomed sleep, but to lose this fight would most probably result in a shift in power. Mankind could not afford any carelessness on her part. If Abez and Ora unleashed the kind of darkness they reveled in, she doubted that anyone would ever be able to fully rein it in.

The grass felt cool when she dropped to the ground. She slapped Ruda on the rump after taking the bit out of his mouth and watched him head for a small patch of clover the lawn crew had missed. She strolled to the center of the clearing, enjoying the midday sun on her shoulders and the soft grass under her bare feet. This was sacred ground, the one place on Oakgrove's lands where only the grass had grown; no crops had ever disturbed the soil here.

Those who had been under her care had put their dead to rest here using the ceremonies of their homeland, not in crude pine boxes like on other plantations. They had carried litters here and placed them on funeral pyres in solemn ceremonies. They had prayed in their native tongues as the flames welcomed the spirits of the dead.

From this spot, warriors who had died farmers and slaves were welcomed home to whatever afterlife they believed in, their ashes having long since become one with the soil. In Kendal's heart those ashes had blessed the area, and as long as she lived, she would make sure they would never be forgotten. She remembered every name they'd been given at birth and what place they held within their tribe. Even if she was somehow defeated and destroyed, the set of leather journals in the library contained a complete history of everyone who'd lived on the property back then.

When she reached the center, she dropped to her knees and lifted her hands to the sky. In the language those noble fighters had taught her, she gave thanks to their gods that these people had lived and that she had known them. After asking for strength to guide her hands and her heart in the upcoming fight, she asked forgiveness for disturbing their peace by drawing weapons here. Charlie had told her it did them honor for her to come here and practice, but she believed in covering her bets.

Finished, she opened her eyes and smiled at Charlie, who was kneeling next to her in the same position. The sweat on his bare chest probably meant he had run from the house. He waited as Kendal pulled a strip of cloth from the long pair of gi pants she was wearing. She'd picked a tight black sleeveless T-shirt instead of the traditional wraparound top. With her eyes covered, she stopped to center herself and let her other senses take over. The whispering among the trees meant her admirers had taken Morgaine's bait, but she figured Hill would've come alone.

"What's she doing?"

Kendal recognized Piper's voice.

"What's it look like? She's tying on a blindfold."

"What's with the big karate pants?"

"Piper, the secret of surveillance is to sit and observe. When you watch someone, you usually can answer the questions that might come up."

When she turned to face the river, they would get a good look at her weapons, which should scare the hell out of them enough to make them scurry back to their lives. In hindsight, she should've taken a vacation from being Kendal Richoux and just come back as whoever to take care of this problem. Had she done that, Piper and her friends would've never crossed Henri's radar like they might now. One look at Piper, though, made her almost glad they'd met. Once this was over perhaps she'd find out why fate had thrown Piper into her life, and why she looked so much like such a piece of her history.

The sword strapped to her back and a special belt holding two small axes prompted the next round of whispers, but she tried to tune it out. You wouldn't find the hatchet-looking weapons at the hardware store. These blades were longer and thinner, almost like quarter moons with handles.

Ready, she bowed toward Charlie and drew her sword. They would start with a drill she'd taught Charlie when they began their lessons together long before Henri had come back into her life. The two blades moved slowly in unison as if following some choreographed dance.

As they continued their movements, she heard Charlie stop, like he had many times, to watch. Her sword usually was invisible as she warmed up, moving the blade in a circle from hand to hand through the basic moves used in combat. The heat of the sun made her start sweating, and she widened her stance as she sheathed her sword so she could remove the axes at her back.

The leather on them felt new but soft, and she made a mental note to thank Charlie. One of the legion commanders who had fought against Genghis Khan had given them to her. The tanned warrior with the black hair and light eyes had been like a horde all by himself, the man had told the crowd as he held his gift up for everyone to see. It was a time of upheaval, but not a time of women warriors, so she had lived as a man in that lifetime to help rid the world of a more human evil. None of those she fought with had thought to ask why she had asked that pieces of wood be added to the metal when they were forged. That was the one common element in all her weapons except for the sword that had been her father's.

Wooden stakes through the heart and death by sunlight were the two things the movies had gotten right about vampires. While the thirst for blood was a given, she was always amused at some of the movies and television shows on the topic. The essence of wood was all that was necessary, so that's why her swords were able to destroy the little bastards she came across. Garlic and holy water, though, were Hollywood hype.

"What the hell?" Piper said, loud enough to make Kendal concentrate again.

She moved into a combative stance, twirling the katana slowly in her hand after she returned one of the small battle-axes to her belt. Morgaine's men had arrived and they fought to draw blood, if they could. Two of the men ran forward together and she met them stroke for stroke, not letting them get even close to gaining an upper hand.

The sound of metal hitting metal echoed through the clearing as she added a few new moves. She took out one guy who got too close with a kick to the jaw. Another two met a similar fate when she leapt up, then kicked both feet out. When the fight ended, less than twenty minutes had passed, and all five were unarmed and on their knees panting.

For a moment longer she stood with her head cocked, listening for any other threat. She tore the blindfold off when all she could hear was the men's heavy breathing. "Take as long as you want, then run through it again with Charlie, guys. And, Charlie, try not to add too many more bruises or they might not want to play with us again."

"Hill, we need to get the hell out of here before this nut figures out we're here."

Without the blindfold Kendal closed her eyes and tried to pinpoint where Piper's voice was coming from.

"Just stay calm. It'll be better if we wait until they're done," Hill said.

Piper nodded as she tried to even out her breathing. When they looked back to the field to watch Charlie go through the same dance, only without the blindfold, they just as quickly stared at each other in shock. They'd lost sight of Kendal.

"Where'd she go?" Piper asked.

Hill shrugged as she scanned the area through Piper's binoculars. Doing a good imitation of an oscillating fan, Hill's head turned from side to side as she looked where they'd last seen her.

As quietly as possible, Kendal climbed down behind them from the branch she'd picked to watch them from as real fear set in, as if they'd just realized they'd crawled into the cobra's lair, then suddenly remembered they were no mongooses. "Don't tell me, let me guess. You missed me so much you couldn't stay away?" she asked before pressing her lips to the side of Piper's head. She laughed when Piper gasped, then backed up so fast she knocked Hill over. The camera on the ground held her attention.

"I can explain," Hill said.

"Do you recall the last little talk we had, Ms. Hickman?" Hill nodded, still sprawled on the ground like she was frozen in place. "Did you think I was talking for the simple pleasure of hearing my voice?" Hill shook her head, the only part of her body moving.

Kendal straightened and sighed before offering her hand to Piper, only to have Piper shrink back in fear.

"You kill us and people will know. You won't get away with it."

With a smile, Kendal bent at the waist to get her face as close to Piper's as she could without pressing their lips together. "Want to make a bet?" She clicked her teeth shut a hair away from Piper's nose. Hill went down when Piper slammed into her again. "You two are quite a comedy act. Give me your hand, Miss Marmande. I only want to help you up, not skewer you." As soon as Piper was on her feet, Hill held her hand up, and just as quickly dropped it when Kendal reached for her sword.

"Well, it was nice seeing you, but we've got to be going," Piper said, motioning Hill to get on her feet.

"Not so fast. I'm sure you were just out here bird watching, but in case you weren't, could I have the camera? I promise to give it back," she said sweetly. With slumped shoulders Hill watched as she threw it into the air and cut it cleanly in two. "The next time, Miss Marmande, if you want to come to see me or the grounds, you'll find the front gate much more convenient. Do you want to talk about something now that you've slogged out here?"

Piper had turned to go, but Kendal's question and her tone stopped her. "Do you ever stop to think about what you're doing to people's lives when you come in and take everything they've worked for?"

Most of the warlords she'd faced off against didn't have as hair-trigger a temper as Piper. The fear Piper had displayed seconds before had given way to her angry question so fast, Kendal was afraid she might get whiplash if she had to deal with her for an extended period of time.

"Do you ask because people like me don't have feelings? That *is* what you think, right?" Her flip answer drove Piper's temper up enough that her eyes seemed to glisten, and Kendal almost made the mistake of smiling when Piper balled her fists and held them away from her body as she stomped closer. "Believe it or not, I do think about every step I make. Employees of failing companies I acquire get a fair deal. It's not their fault their bosses couldn't keep things afloat, even if they are running a shipyard."

"You sanctimonious bitch," Piper said, sounding like she savored each word. "It's easy to tear things down instead of working to build something meaningful. The way you rip things apart so easily means you're nothing but a liar. Don't make it worse by saying you care about the people who've been loyal to my grandfather for years. Once you sell us off like old scrap, you won't give us another thought. You might consider it a game, but you're ruining futures for your entertainment."

"You're a little sanctimonious yourself, lady, since you've done nothing but tear me down from the first moment you laid eyes on me." Kendal let a little anger seep into her voice. "I don't know what else you want from me. I told you I wasn't interested, so why in the hell are you here wasting time when I handed you the real thief on a platter?"

"Why are you still here, then, if you don't intend to take us over?"

"I could say none of your business and be done with it, but if I do, I assume I can only look forward to more of Ms. Hickman's company, since you aren't the trusting type. I'm here to attend to a family matter."

Piper crossed her arms over her chest and shifted her weight to one foot. The pose made her look like a bratty girl not getting her way. "I don't believe you."

"I tell you what. Have your attorney draft a statement saying that if I go after Marmande or get involved in your business in any way, I'll owe you whatever it'll take to get you out of debt."

"I'll do it," Piper said.

"And I'll sign it. It's the only way I can get rid of you." She looked at the hand Piper was holding out, noticing that if she wanted to shake it she'd have to close the gap between them. She moved forward halfway and held out her own hand. When Piper took it, she squeezed slightly and added one more thing. "Just remember, Miss Marmande, if you want my involvement, you'll have to come begging."

"I'll beg you for anything when hell freezes over."

"I've been to hell. There are no cold days."

"Then there's your answer."

Kendal let out a low whistle that made Ruda appear at her side. The stallion bent his head to accept the bit, pawing at the ground as if anxious to go. "I'd appreciate if you both would stay off the property. If you need to see me, call my office and make an appointment. Consider that your last warning, especially you, Ms. Hickman." With little effort she leapt onto Ruda's back and kicked his sides to get him moving.

"How rude, she didn't even say good-bye."

Hill picked up the two pieces of ruined equipment and snorted. "The nerve of her not to invite us up to the house for tea after you called her a bitch. What is the civilized world coming to?"

"She asked for it. Kendal Richoux walks around like she owns the world and everyone in it, but I bet she doesn't know what to do with herself when somebody stands up to her." She followed Hill back to the boat, making as much noise as possible now that Kendal knew they were there. "It's easy when you have everything handed to you. She probably doesn't know what putting in a day at the office is like."

Hill stopped so abruptly that she ran into her. "Not to defend her, but do you ever read my reports?"

"I'm busy, Hill. It's not like I've got time to read line by line."

"Her father was a dockworker. She made her fortune at the office one day at a time. The very little that's written about her business ethic says she's a straight shooter."

"Are you saying I'm not?"

"I'm saying that you might've been better off with Kendal Richoux in your corner than as your enemy. You're so angry with her because she one-upped you about Kenny Delaney you can't see straight."

"Straight is the last thing Kendal is, and watch yourself, Hillary."

Hill put her hands up and looked her in the eye. "I'm not telling you all this to point out your mistakes. I'm telling you because I'm your friend and it's the truth."

"Thank you, but it's all moot anyway. Now that I don't have to worry about this looter, I can concentrate on saving Marmande." Piper stepped into the boat and pulled out her chips, leaving Hill to grab the oars.

❖

"Good luck to you on that one, sweetheart, you're going to need it," Kendal said from the branch above their heads. They were so busy snapping twigs and talking they'd paid no attention to how far she'd gone or if she'd ridden off at all. "Today was one of those days you should have spent in the office instead of running after dead ends. The real looters are at the gate and about to storm the castle."

Hill pushed off before she sat in the center section to start rowing back. When they were far enough away that Kendal knew they were indeed leaving, she closed her eyes and tried to relax as she listened to the oars hit the water. Because it was fall, she had three more hours before the sun went down. Three hours closer to finding Henri and ending his miserable existence.

CHAPTER ELEVEN

New Orleans, October, 1726

The docks were lined with ships waiting for the deckhands to load them with the multitude of crops just brought in from harvest. Throngs of people walked around bundles of dried tobacco leaves, which sat next to bales of cotton ready for shipment to northern ports and their mills. Those who owned large farms, like Jacques, negotiated for fair prices before the lull of winter set in, and everyone who worked the land enjoyed a time of respite before the cycle began again.

"You finished unloading?" asked the merchant that Jacques dealt with.

"Twenty more bales of cotton and we're done." He took his hat off and wiped his brow on his sleeve. Despite the cool air, it was easy to work up a sweat unloading the wagons.

"You sure don't act like a landowner, Jacques. Don't take this wrong, but you're an odd man, or at least like no man from around here."

"That's because I'm *not* like any man from around here, or from anywhere, when you get down to it. I like to work. That's why I harvest more than any other place outside the city. Sitting on my porch drinking lemonade isn't my style." They shared a laugh before he helped unload the rest of the cotton bales.

"Lionel, take the men over to the general store and start on the lists we put together." All the people living at Oakgrove loved when he went into town twice a year to pick up supplies. A trip to the general store meant a new pair of shoes, work boots, dresses, shirts, and all the candy in stock. No one living on the plantation was left out, not even those who hadn't arrived yet. The loving hands of expecting mothers turned the bolts of cloth the men brought back into baby clothes. Jacques spent the majority of the profit Oakgrove's fields produced on his people. He used the rest to maintain buildings and buy seed for the coming spring.

"You got it, boss." In public Lionel always used a proper term of respect, but at home he now called him Jacques. The trip they had taken together, and all that came after, had made them friends.

"You weren't leaving without coming to see me, were you?"

After Angelina asked the question, sounding miffed, Lionel gently hit him in the stomach. "You're in trouble now, boss."

He turned around with a smile, now that he knew Angelina had a hard time resisting it. "And miss the pleasure of your company? I would rather be dragged behind my horse, dear lady."

"I'd rather you didn't. I'm rather fond of that handsome face." She moved closer but he moved faster. If anyone was watching, he wanted them to think he was the pursuer, not Angelina. It wouldn't become a lady of her standing, and when it came time for him to move on, he didn't want to leave a blemish on Angelina's honor.

"I'd give up my land for a bath at this moment." He whispered to her, "I'm so filthy I can't even kiss your hand."

"We may read about it in the *Gazette* tomorrow but I'm willing to chance the dirt." Without hesitation she put up her hand for him to take. "Please tell me you've finished cutting and gathering everything you had growing out there. I love Uncle Tomas, but I'd much rather spend my evenings looking at you."

He laughed and kissed her hand again. "I won't tell him you said so, and that sounds suspiciously like something I would tell you." He squeezed her fingers gently before he released her and stepped back. "I may be prejudiced, but my nights looking into your green eyes are a slice of paradise." Getting the blush he was after, he turned his attention to Dee. "And how is the second most beautiful girl in New Orleans?"

"Master Jacques, you'd best behave or Miss Angelina may lock me out of the house when we get home." Dee didn't protest, though, when he bowed over her hand and treated her to the same greeting as her mistress.

"It's this rogue who I may lock out," Angelina said, making them both laugh.

"Then should I cancel my visit for this afternoon?"

"Not if you know what's best for you. I haven't seen you in weeks." Angelina pulled her shawl tighter around her shoulders.

"I wouldn't do that to you. Just let me clean up and put on a fresh suit." He looked over Angelina's shoulder and whispered loudly to Dee, "Do you think you could persuade this lovely creature to don her prettiest dress and get the old coot to wear something appropriate for an evening out?"

"I'll do my best, sir."

"Good, I have a surprise for her, but you have to promise to keep it a secret."

"I'm sure she won't guess a thing."

He arrived two hours later in a hired carriage, thoroughly scrubbed. He had left the battered old hat he was fond of in the hotel room and replaced it with a tricorne hat more in line with current fashion.

The young man who answered the door relieved him of his cloak, hat, and the flowers he'd brought for Angelina. With the man's promise to put them in water and have them brought up to her room, he followed Tomas's voice into the study.

"Ah, good, I see my niece's moping has come to an end, and here stands the reason why. How goes it, Jacques?"

"I'm finished and we were able to surpass last year's totals, so I'm pleased. Actually I'm better now that I'll have time to spend with the two of you."

"Then perhaps you'll have time to show Uncle Tomas and me Oakgrove," Angelina said from the doorway.

Angelina's dress was the same shade of pale blue as his eyes, and the seamstress had even cut a matching bow for her hair.

"Do you like it?" she asked. She sounded a little uncertain when he stood there as if mute.

"No, my dear, I don't like it. I love it. You look better than any dream I've had of you over these past weeks."

Tomas cleared his throat and kidded Angelina. "Playing hard to get is doing wonders for you, sweetheart."

"Don't worry, Tomas, Angelina is perfectly safe in my company."

Tomas accepted Jacques's hand to help him to his feet. "If I were afraid of that, you wouldn't be here, young man. Angelina is precious to me."

"As she is to me, monsieur," Jacques said, just as seriously.

To break up the moment, Angelina looped her arm through her uncle's. "Where are you taking us this evening?" she asked Jacques.

"First to dinner, then I have a surprise for you two." He put his hand up before she could ask what. "It's not a surprise if I tell you."

The carriage took them to the city's finest restaurant where the du'Pons brought him up to date on what had been going on in town while he was stuck at Oakgrove. As they talked over coffee at the end of their meal, one of the young men who had tried unsuccessfully to court Angelina stopped at their table and interrupted Jacques mid-sentence.

"Angelina, Monsieur du'Pon, how are you both this evening?" the well-dressed young man asked as he bowed slightly.

"Rather well until just now, Winston. What brings you into our company?" Tomas asked.

"The production tonight at the new theater is supposed to be quite good. Since your niece looks so lovely this evening, I thought she might do me the honor of joining me as soon as you're done here." Winston pulled two tickets from his jacket pocket. "I have some of the last tickets available."

Angelina looked at Jacques in clear disbelief, as did Tomas, obviously because of his silence.

"I'm sure Mademoiselle du'Pon is free to attend with whomever she chooses, but I was rather hoping she'd join me in the box I bought for the opening performance." He pulled three tickets from his top pocket with a smile. "Surprise," he said to Angelina.

Winston crumpled the paper still in his hand and left without another word. The rest of the night they enjoyed the comedy, and Tomas smiled at Jacques when he took Angelina's hand and didn't let it go until the curtain went down.

At the end of the evening he escorted them both home and helped Tomas up the stairs to his room; sitting for such a long time through dinner and then the play had left his hip almost numb. Angelina was waiting for Jacques in the parlor when he came down.

"Thank you for tonight," Angelina said, holding her hand out to him.

"You're very welcome. I'm glad you enjoyed it as much as I did." Dee looked up from her needlepoint for only a moment. "It's late. I'll leave you to get some rest."

"Dee, would you please get me a glass of warm milk?" Angelina asked, her eyes never leaving his.

"Don't do anything I'll get in trouble for later," Dee told him before heading out of the room.

"Something like this, perhaps?" he asked when they were alone. Slowly he moved toward Angelina and gathered her in his arms. Her lips, which he had first seen splattered with mud, were too enticing to ignore any longer, so he lowered his mouth to hers but felt more awkward than passionate since Angelina didn't seem know what to do with her hands.

"No," Angelina said when he pulled away, until he placed her hands on his shoulders.

"Shall we try that again?"

"Yes, please," Angelina said in a soft, dreamy voice. Going against every argument he'd constructed as to why this was a bad idea, he took possession of Angelina's mouth until she felt limp in his arms.

"Go get some sleep because I have one more surprise for you," he said, pulling away reluctantly when he heard Dee's footsteps down the hall.

"You're leaving already?"

"I'll be back in the morning, so I meant what I said about sleep. Tomorrow, my surprise will make for a long day, and I want you to enjoy it." Jacques smiled at Dee, who stood in the doorway appearing uncertain as she held a cup of warm milk. "Good night to you both," he said, placing a chaste kiss on Angelina's cheek, then Dee's.

Standing outside staring at the moon, Jacques lowered his guard and let his persona fall away for a moment. As Asra, she dismissed the carriage and decided to walk. At the cusp of the residential area, the bars were still full of drunks enjoying the small bands and ladies that didn't cost too much for the evening. With a whiskey in front of her, she thought of what was happening and it slammed into her gut like a fist.

Angelina and Tomas had become important to her, and the way Angelina had paid more attention to her than to the stage made it easy to see Angelina's love for her strengthening. However, the man Angelina had fallen for was an illusion. What would happen when she peeled the veneer of Jacques St. Louis away? That only occurred in the dead of night when Oakgrove was totally still and she was free to roam the land while everyone slept.

"To fate and letting the girl down gently," she said before she downed the drink and fell back into her role as Jacques.

❖

The next day Angelina and Tomas boarded the coach he'd hired for their two-day trip to Oakgrove. They could have made it in one, but such a long stretch would've been murder on Tomas's hip, so on the second afternoon the du'Pons rode up to the entrance to Oakgrove for the first time.

Jacques stood outside waiting with all the families living on the plantation, who were enjoying the lull before they started planting again. They would spend the downtime using the mounds of supplies piled to the side of the house to improve the cabins out back. When Angelina and Tomas arrived, he stood back while everyone introduced themselves and their families. Then Lola announced that lunch was ready and on the tables under the oaks in front of the house.

"This is a little different than I expected," Angelina said as she walked the grounds with him after the huge meal.

"How so?"

"No one looks miserable," she said, glancing over her shoulder toward the picnic tables. "I believe you to be a fair-minded man, but even you have your limits."

"I can't do for the world, Angelina, but I can do for them. On this land we live by my rules, especially to show everyone tolerance and respect. The outside world has no say here about how I treat my family."

She pulled him to a stop. "What makes you so wise?"

"A long time ago I learned a valuable lesson from a ruler who was perhaps born before her time. She believed a person is born a slave by circumstance, not by choice or design. Sometimes, though, when given the opportunity, someone like that can conquer the known world without lifting a sword." As he told her his beliefs, he thought of the young Hebrew slave who had stolen the pharaoh's heart. Sadly, no history book had bothered to remember either of them and how, for one brief blip of time, things had been different enough that women had been able to serve as they pleased. Life had been fair, or as much as was possible without a total female society.

"How lucky for them to find their way here to you. Because, trust me, it could be so much worse."

"If they had luck on their side, they'd still be in their homeland. Given time, that's exactly where I'd like to see them. Can you imagine never seeing your child again and not knowing what happened to him or her?" He started them walking again until they reached the lake on the property. Under one of the trees shading the bank, he cupped her cheek in the palm of his hand. "As important as the state of the world and our place in it may be, I wanted to bring you here to tell you something even more so."

"I love you," Angelina said, appearing surprised by her own words.

"I…I love you as well," and in saying that, he knew he meant it. "I do have something to share with you, so perhaps you should refrain from any other declarations until you hear what that is."

"I'm glad you brought me here because I can see now it's where I belong. You are who I belong to, Jacques, and only you can give my heart away, so forgive me for not taking your advice." She pulled on his lapels and laughed. "Now I demand you reward my forwardness with a kiss."

Oakgrove, present day

Kendal thought about how different things might have turned out by this lake had she said what she had planned. She had loved Angelina as much as she had professed that day, but it wasn't fair to Angelina not to know the full truth about the *man* she had fallen in love with.

Had Angelina known sooner, might she have run back to someone like Winston? Would she have chosen someone who could give her a life and children to care for in her later years? Those questions were pure speculation now. After that one blissful moment on that idyllic spot, their lives had changed and the nightmare had begun.

"I owe it to you now to make things as right as I can," she said to the water. What had happened in that lifetime and what resulted from it still haunted her. The burden had made her lose a bit of her humanity

CHAPTER TWELVE

Henri's eyes opened as soon as the sun went down. Kendal was still there and she was coming, only this time nothing he did would stop her. He thought of all their meetings through the years and how her hatred for him had grown to rival his for her. He'd had an ideal life until their parents decided to expand their family. The perfect child was exactly what they'd gotten the second time around. Asra had grown taller, stronger, and smarter, and he'd tried to make her pay from the beginning. But nothing he did ever made his parents brag like they did about Asra.

The last time they'd faced each other, she'd left him wounded, and he'd had to run for his life. Only through good planning had he been able to run at all after that battle. He'd seen her look of satisfaction as she stood before him ready to plunge her sword into his chest. "That was then, Kendal, and as these sub-humans like to say, it's a new day."

He opened the lid of his resting place and climbed the stairs to the bedroom where he kept his clothes. Hopefully the weather had cleared, since he detested anything damp against his skin, which he noticed was still slightly pinkish from the late feeding that morning. Outside the street was still quiet, but he moved swiftly, anxious to set his plan in motion.

When he entered the house at the edge of the French Quarter, a large gathering of people bowed their heads as he passed. All of them were his children, his creations, made specifically to destroy the Clan's slayer. In the world, only one was left who was stronger than he, and he didn't want to disappoint her, so he'd stacked the numbers against Kendal heavily in his favor.

"The slayer is here and starts working tonight," he said, sitting in the chair set up at the head of the dining room. Some of those gathered looked at each other in concern.

He'd allowed them free rein in the city for years, not worried because Kendal and the others of the Genesis Clan hadn't sent a hunter. That misstep had given him the opportunity to build the army he'd need to battle the Clan's best. He was sure his diligence would work, especially after his brief meeting with his sister.

Kendal was still licking the emotional wounds he'd inflicted, so that preoccupation, coupled with battling his followers, would guarantee their success. If that failed, he was prepared to defeat her the same way again; Kendal's heart and caring nature were the chinks in her armor.

"We are here to serve you, master," Troy said. Troy had been a river rat who lived off whatever he could steal until Henri noticed him one night. In one moment Troy had been transformed from being one of the forgotten to one of the feared.

"Yes, you are, and remember one thing. Fail me, and I will haunt your place in hell for the rest of eternity. The slayer the Clan has sent is their best, so be extra vigilant."

"Everyone has a weak spot, sire," Troy said, running his tongue over his lips.

"True, but my sister is very good, so don't take her for granted. I made you and gave you dominion over man. Let me down and I'll put you out for the sun myself."

One of the young women close to him looked up at him in total disbelief. "Master, the slayer is your sister?"

"The one and only Asra, captain of the pharaoh's elite fighting legion. In life she inspired awe on the battlefield. At least those were the stories bards used to love to tell in taverns. As an immortal, though, I consider her godlike. The Clan chose well, but so have I in choosing all of you." He ran his fingers through the young woman's hair. She looked up again with an ecstatic expression, as if liking the feel of cold on her scalp. "I want you all to go out and seek until you find her, and when you do, bring her to me." When the girl began to get up, he moved from a caress to pulling her hair to keep her in place. "Not you."

"As you wish."

He smiled at her, showing the tips of his canines before he glanced back at the others. "Go." They moved rapidly out the door.

"How can I please you, master?" the girl asked when they were alone.

"What's your name?"

"Veronica, master."

"Veronica, this is what you can do to please me." He whispered to her, and she nodded at almost his every word. Then he licked along her ear, loving her shiver of pleasure. "Such loyalty deserves a reward, precious." He snapped his fingers, and Troy dragged a scared young girl who looked to be around thirteen out of the closet. "Enjoy."

Veronica pounced in a catlike fashion, holding the child close to the front of her body. The tender flesh tore open easily, and the gush of warm, salty blood almost caused Veronica to swoon. Slowly the body grew limp and Veronica cut the connection before the final life spirit was snuffed out, knowing better than to keep drinking until the girl was dead. Doing so wouldn't kill her, but drinking from a dead victim invited an illness that would leave a vampire weak and vulnerable for days because the blood turned poisonous instantly when the life force was extinguished.

With the same feline grace, Veronica walked toward him, leaned over him, and pressed her mouth to his. He accepted the kiss that filled his mouth with blood and made him hard, but Veronica was happy to take care of that need as well. When she straddled him, Troy left the room after bowing in his direction.

"I'll gift you her heart, master," Veronica said before the final shiver ran through her body.

❖

Kendal dismounted her bike and stood, eyes closed, for almost ten minutes just listening to the world around her. She left whatever guilt, anger, or other destructive emotion she was feeling at Oakgrove the minute she armed herself and headed into town. Next to her, Charlie was doing the same as he stood ramrod straight. She was able to filter out all the traffic and bar noises coming from the general vicinity, trying to find any abnormality.

"Kendal, can I ask you something?"

She opened her eyes in almost lazy fashion. "Sure."

"Aren't people going to freak when they see two people walking down the street with swords and enough sharp implements to start a small war?"

"Probably, if we decided to walk down the street, but we're not taking that route."

"We're not?"

She pointed up. "No. Two things about this city make it desirable to my brother and us." She bounced a little on the balls of her feet, ready to go. "It's heavily populated by people that society won't miss or cares little about when they show up drained, which makes it a good hunting ground if blood is part of your diet." She held up two fingers, smiling at Charlie's shiver, probably at the thought of an all-blood diet. "And because space is precious here, most of the buildings are connected."

"And that benefits us how?"

"If we want to take a stroll with enough sharp implements to start a small war, which we do, we can use the rooftops. Ready?"

He nodded and watched as she took off at a run. With ease she grabbed a flagpole hanging over someone's door, flipped around a couple of times, and propelled herself onto the roof. "Care to take a walk with me?" she asked from the edge.

Charlie followed quickly, as if not wanting to miss any of the action. "You're right," he said when he made it to the top. "Aside from a few short leaps and differences in the height of some buildings, most of them are connected." They walked until they reached the section of Bourbon Street most populated with tourists.

Bourbon was a popular strip because it was a smorgasbord of sin from one end to the other. In the whole country no place like it existed, and it was the one spot locals and tourists flocked to in equal numbers. It featured bars, strip joints, live sex shows, and a smattering of restaurants to round out the mix. When the sun went down, the barricades went up to close the strip to car traffic, and like a lazy river of humanity, people walked from place to place, doing a different kind of window-shopping.

One of the old joints, Big Daddy's, had a row of poles on the stage and lethargic-looking dancers, and the classier places like Rick's Cabaret had perfect, surgically enhanced beauties. If you were looking for tits, ass, alcohol, and fantastic seafood, this was the place to find it. For those who liked to study people, the real entertainment wasn't the naked souls trying to make a living, but the folks on the street.

Shocked visitors were taking pictures of the drag queens and leather crowd, who gladly posed with people with sensible shoes, who in turn felt slightly naughty for venturing out among the decadent. Sprinkled in to add more flavor were the religious zealots holding signs promising a fiery afterlife for participating in the moral decay the area was famous for. No one took the leaflets they were handing out, and the ones they did take littered the street several feet away.

Kendal stood at the edge of the building looking down at the street over one of the newer bars that focused on Gothic dress and hard rock. Only those appropriately decked out in black ventured inside. "Have a seat, this won't take long," she told Charlie. Since Henri knew why she was there, his people would be traveling in packs. If they couldn't defeat her by skill, they'd try by sheer numbers, proving that Henri had learned nothing from their father about strategy.

"Kendal, look." Charlie pointed his chin down the street.

"I see them. Now we just need to get them to see us." She stood and opened the long coat she was wearing enough so she could put her hands on her hips.

They were all laughing and walking shoulder to shoulder, harassing people as they went and putting out a vibe that warned everyone to stay away. From her vantage point she spotted others more used to seeing these groups of young punks and writing them off as sewer rats. The locals used the term to describe the young runaways who came to the Quarter to escape abuse and other misery at home, only to find prostitution and drugs on the streets. She knew better, though. These little punks might've started out that way, but from the pallor of their skin and their mannerisms, they'd evolved into something much more dangerous.

The one who appeared to be the youngest of the bunch glanced up first and stopped walking, making the guy next to her stop to see what she was staring at. Kendal waggled her fingers at them and smiled wide enough to show she wasn't afraid. The dare sent them moving like a pack of wolves after a wounded deer.

"Tell me where Henri is and I let you walk away," she said, facing all twenty of them once they'd made it up to the roof.

"We'll never betray our master. Are you the slayer he told us about?" asked the young woman who'd first spotted her.

"Please, let's not be so formal. Call me Kendal, and you, I'll call you Hoover bait."

"Hoover bait?" the girl asked.

"Dust, darlin'." Kendal's hand moved so fast the joke didn't register. The knife split the young woman's heart and instantly the wind blew away any proof of her existence when she turned to dust.

Kendal drew her katana next, along with one of the small battle-axes she'd worked with that afternoon. "Shall we dance?" she asked the others.

Charlie, she briefly noticed, was momentarily shocked into stillness when the rest of them charged forward. When their faces had transformed to their more hideous features—elongated foreheads with ridges, flattened noses, and snarling jawlines—the phenomenon paralyzed him. Had he been alone, he would've been an easy target even for this young, inexperienced group.

She'd known Charlie might react this way because of his good heart, but it wouldn't matter now. With her quick sword strokes and slashing axe, she made quick work of the group. Their lack of strength and fighting ability indicated how recently they'd joined Henri. She put her weapons away and placed her hand on Charlie's shoulder to bring him back from wherever his mind had flown off to.

"I'm so sorry," he said, looking everywhere but at her.

"Nothing to be sorry about. You okay?"

"It made me think back to when I first saw him."

She squeezed his shoulder. "You don't owe me an explanation, and you didn't do anything wrong. Come on, let's go hunt more trouble."

They found four more packs before they called it a night, and from the different accents it seemed that Henri had called his children from all over the world to gather for the fight. They'd found only a small percentage of Henri's numbers, from the information the Clan had gathered, but they had to start somewhere. Charlie had recovered and performed perfectly. Another couple of weeks and Henri would run out of pawns and have no choice but to send out his better and older fighters. Once she and Charlie destroyed them, they would soon flush him out.

Sunrise was an hour away when they got back to the house, and Charlie waved over his shoulder as he headed to his cabin. He refused to leave the only home he'd ever known since being brought to the States. Kendal was about to turn the knob of the front door when it hit her conscious brain. The birds in the oak by the master suite weren't cooing or chirping like they usually did.

She unclipped her whip from her belt and let the coil drop to the floor of the porch. She didn't use it often, but for what she had in mind it was perfect. Her adversary didn't have time to react when she moved. One second she was standing by the door, and the next she ran up the side of the large tree trunk and balanced on a limb. With a very accurate aim, she reached forward and wrapped the leather around the woman's throat like an extension of her hand. One strong pull and the trespasser fell off her perch.

The woman's legs kicked in midair as she pawed at her neck. After a minute the struggle stopped and Kendal dropped her bundle to the ground. To make sure she wouldn't have any unpleasant surprises, she hit the back of the woman's head with a closed fist before she lifted the limp body and flung it over her shoulder.

"You kill us and people will know." She laughed as she repeated Piper's threat. "Want to make a bet? See, people should take me more seriously about shit like this," she said to the night air as she moved deeper into the woods, heading for the lake.

At the end of a path cut through the trees was a long pier where Kendal dumped her load at the last piling by the water. "Wakey, wakey," she said, slapping the woman's face hard enough to get her attention after she used her whip to tie her up.

When the woman found she couldn't move, her blond hair whipped back and panic flooded her green eyes. "Please, let me go."

"We'll get to that, but first I want to know what you're doing here." She leaned back on the bench Charlie had obviously added to fish from, crossed her booted feet, and waited.

"You don't understand. You've got to let me go now."

With her eyes closed she took a deep breath. "Smell that? Don't you find the air changes just a tad before the beginning of a new day? It's sweeter somehow."

"Please, I'll do whatever you want. Just let me go."

"Oh, I'm thinking you're in no position to be making promises, and since time is of the essence…" She stopped talking and pointed at her.

"Veronica, master," she said, her head slightly bowed.

"I'm not your master, but I'm dying to see him, so how about you tell me where I can find him. If you do, I'll consider your request."

Veronica acted innocent and lowered her head in a submissive way to beg again. "Anything but that. I'll do anything but that."

"Okay," she said, not falling for the act. Veronica was beautiful, but she was just like the rest of them. No matter how attractive, they all had the same monster living inside, and the instinct to kill was all they knew. She stood and started back toward the house.

"Wait," Veronica screamed.

"Tell me or pray for a large vat of sunscreen to drop from the sky."

"I can't tell you what I don't know." Veronica sounded desperate.

She walked back and grabbed the bowed head. "Why do you think he sent you here, little idiot?"

"He loves me and trusts me," Veronica said with conviction.

"He sacrificed you like a piece of trash he cares nothing about." Kendal moved close to her, showing no fear. "Henri's a simplistic thinker when it comes to strategy, and nothing's wrong with that if you never care to learn any better. What's wrong or stupid, depending on how you want to look at it, is thinking everyone else has the same mind-set."

"What's that supposed to mean?"

"Look at you." She put her fingers under Veronica's chin. "Young, beautiful, blond hair, green eyes. He thinks your physical attributes will tempt me. What was supposed to happen tonight?" She ran her fingertips from Veronica's chin to her brow. "You seduce me into lowering my guard, and then what? What did you promise him?"

For an instant Veronica morphed and let the beast out to scare her back, she supposed, but it didn't work. "Your heart," Veronica said, sounding honest.

Satisfied with the response, Kendal moved back and sat on the bench. Her skin was starting to tingle, but for a completely different reason than Veronica's probably was. "How long ago did he change you?"

"Twelve years since I've been given the gift." Veronica fought with the knots she'd tied, her struggle and her expression becoming frantic. "Why do you thrive in the sun when we don't?" she asked, when the realization of her situation made her slump back against the piling.

"Because I was given life by someone who believes in the living. You were given time by someone who believes only in death." She sat in silence then, thinking hard about exactly how true her answer was. She took another deep breath before she stood and stepped closer to Veronica. "Today I'll give you something precious to make up for what's happened to you."

"What?" Veronica asked, as she started to sweat blood.

She wiped her finger along Veronica's brow, smearing the blood like war paint before running her finger along the woman's lips for one last taste of what had up to then given her life as well as pleasure. "Release."

As she moved back, the first pink fingers of dawn crept across the sky, and Veronica stopped squirming and stared as if in awe. Veronica looked up at her, but didn't make a sound as her skin began to blister.

"Such a waste," Kendal said as the sky grew brighter and Veronica started to moan. If the pain was severe it was short-lived, and with a small thump, the whip fell to the pier, no longer having a body to hold it in place.

❖

Morgaine was sitting on the porch with a cup of coffee as if waiting for her. "How'd it go?" Morgaine stopped her on the bottom step so they were at eye level.

The contents of the mug smelled so good, Kendal took a sip before answering. "What's that old Queen song you like so much?"

"'Another One Bites the Dust'? I always thought that should be your theme song."

"Multiply that by a lot and it sums up last night. I've been behind a desk so long I forgot how great it feels to protect and defend."

"You look like a caped crusader in this outfit." Morgaine kissed her, pulling on the lapels of the long coat.

"Yeah? You want to come upstairs and see my special powers?"

The joke made Morgaine turn away from her, but not to laugh, and she instantly realized why Morgaine was so quiet. They had been through this many times before, but it only got harder. "When do you have to leave?" she asked as she took Morgaine's cup and set it on the table.

"I've got time to have breakfast with you." Morgaine leaned back into her, laying her hands over hers. "They said I'm too emotionally involved to be of any use to you."

"That's bull."

"Maybe they're right. We need time apart so we can remember our place and our purpose. I care for you, Asra, but I'm not your destiny."

She laughed and kissed Morgaine's neck. "My destiny is to be alone. I've never had any other fanciful illusion."

"No, don't ever believe that. You've been so good for so long that life will reward you. Because of who you are in here," Morgaine placed her hand over her heart, "you won't continue this journey alone."

"I hope for my sake you're right," she said, turning Morgaine around and kissing her until she forgot why she was sad. "Are you hungry right this minute?"

"Let's go, superhero, show me your stuff."

The staff working nearby smiled when they heard Morgaine's laugh as Kendal carried her up the stairs. Morgaine was on a timeline to leave, and Kendal wanted to mess it up.

They left a trail of clothes from the door to the foot of the bed, neither wanting the encounter to end soon. They wouldn't see each other for some time. Once Henri was destroyed, Kendal could continue to find new ways to reinvent herself until the next challenge came along, and only then would Morgaine return to her life. The Elders would keep them apart to assure that no further feelings grew between them to upset the balance of their teacher/student relationship.

Morgaine slumped limply to Kendal's chest when the intense orgasm was over. "That was incredible."

"Thank you, and the feeling's mutual. I'm thinking those were your hands somewhere in there making me lose control. Unless you snuck someone else in here when I wasn't looking."

"Are you kidding? I know how you feel about group sex." Morgaine lifted her head and smiled. Morgaine had always kidded her about how old-fashioned she was.

"Sex is not a group activity. I don't care what other people may think."

Morgaine laughed and she joined her, thinking about the history of man and what was acceptable in different eras when it came to pleasures of the flesh. The Romans and their orgies certainly contrasted to the Inquisition. Whatever the era and whatever the practice, though, Kendal had been fairly predictable in her tastes—always women, and always one at a time.

"Lucky for me you're so focused," Morgaine said as she rolled off to the vacant side of the bed.

Kendal held her in place and kissed her. "Stay for just a minute," she said, running her finger softly along Morgaine's brows, then tracing her lips. "I'd like a long stretch of time with you like we had in the beginning. When we arrived at that oasis, I seriously thought I'd go insane in a matter of days, but when we had to leave I thought I'd lose a part of myself."

"Thank you. Of all those I've had to teach, you were the only one I wanted to share myself with. You have such a good heart, Asra."

"A large part of it belongs to you."

Morgaine nodded. "I treasure it, which is why I know you'll be rewarded for all you've done. Perhaps here where so much was taken from you, you'll find what you seek."

Kendal closed her eyes for a few breaths, losing her smile. "I haven't forgotten the bargain I made when you gave me that cup to drink from. Time never stops, and enjoying the gift of keeping pace with it doesn't come free."

That was true, but Morgaine knew not only how Asra's mind worked, but also her heart. She might not have constant contact with Kendal, but the reports she received often related not only where she was and what she was doing, but also who was sharing her bed. She could see only one potential problem that could derail Kendal's concentration in the coming conflict.

"Before I go, can I ask you something?" she asked.

"You have the right to ask me anything."

"Why are you taking time to mess with this girl? Can you really afford any distractions?"

Kendal ran her hands down Morgaine's back until she reached her bottom, making Morgaine's hips move toward her when she caressed the smooth skin. They wouldn't be getting up any time soon. "Are you talking about Piper Marmande and her trusty sidekick Hill Hickman? Thank you, by the way, for your excellent imitation of a nun."

"You know exactly who I'm talking about. But I don't understand why. Is it because she can't stand you?"

"If she just couldn't stand me, I'd be better off. She hates me, and I don't know why I'm fooling with her. Not because of a bruised ego, since I'm not narcissistic enough to believe every woman I've ever met has fallen madly in love with me. Maybe I tend to take my entertainment wherever I can find it instead of truly committing for short periods of time."

"So this is a quest for a short night of entertainment?"

"No," Kendal said, then sighed. "I feel bad for her and her family, but she doesn't want my help. The tragedy is, Piper has the potential to set the world on fire, but she's too angry to recognize it."

"It sounds like you like her." Morgaine's eyes dropped to her chest.

Kendal placed her fingers under Morgaine's chin and made her focus on her face. "Don't be jealous. It's only…well, do you know how much it takes to make me angry? I don't think I've felt a good case of outrage in decades, but it took her all of ten seconds to make my blood boil. And her grandfather reminds me so much…"

"Of Tomas du'Pon," Morgaine said, not needing any more guesses.

"Sounds crazy, huh?"

"No, but you do realize these people aren't Tomas and Angelina, right?"

She rolled them over so she was now covering Morgaine. "Trust me, the day I lose my grip on sanity, I'll throw myself down whatever pit you find suitable. I know who they are, and, more important, who they aren't. I probably won't get the chance to sit and talk with Mac like I did with Tomas, or develop the same relationship we had, but before I'm done here I might find some way to help them," she said as she put her hand between Morgaine's legs.

"Enough talk," Morgaine said when her touch became more intimate.

After they finally left the room, the staff served them a late lunch.

"Remember to be careful. And send word if you need me. This time I don't care what my colleagues say. If you're in trouble, I'm coming back."

"I'll be fine, but you can still tell them that the world won't fall apart if they let us see each other more often. They've got to know by now that we know the rules and are willing to somewhat abide by them."

"It's the *somewhat* that forces them to keep us apart, warrior mine," Morgaine said, laughing. Morgaine pressed her palm to her cheek one last time, her eyes glassy. "I'll miss you."

"Take care," Kendal said before she whispered the rest into a delicate ear. "I love you."

Morgaine nodded as some of her tears fell. "And I you." Her men moved to the car as their mistress kissed her one last time. "Remember to follow your heart in all things," Morgaine said before she closed the door.

The Genesis Clan had existed for decades, and their rules were literally set in stone. Because Kendal had broken so many, beginning with falling in love with her watcher, the Elders liked to flex their power to corral her back into the role they'd granted her eternal life to carry out. It was their way, and the Elders felt the rules had assured their success in keeping the sometimes-fragile balance between good and evil.

Morgaine was leaving her again, though, only partly because of that. This was a punishment for mixing the elixir for Charlie. She'd done it without the Elders' permission, and this was her payback for ignoring the first and most important rule about giving the gift of life to someone the Elders didn't deem deserving.

"When Henri's no more, my debt for Charlie will be paid," she said to the taillights of Morgaine's car as it disappeared through the gate.

CHAPTER THIRTEEN

After Kendal showered and dressed for another night of hunting, one of the servants gave her a note from Charlie saying he'd left for the city to search for clues as to where Henri and his followers were spending their days. It was admirable of him to try, but he'd find dragons in the bell tower of St. Louis Cathedral before he found Henri's crypt.

Her brother had survived so long because he never told anyone where he slept. His followers might not have the same self-preservation priorities, so Charlie might get lucky.

Kendal decided to go in early as well, to have a drink and think. She needed time alone to quiet the parts of her mind that still dwelled on the past.

She chose the same bar in the Piquant where she had enjoyed the cigars and scotch before, leaving her long coat and weapons in the back seat of the SUV she'd driven. The front desk had a few messages for her, none of them important, so she strolled through the lobby in the sweater and brown suede pants she'd chosen for comfort. The feel of the slightly rough material against her legs reminded her of her time as a trapper and hunter in what was once known as northern Britannia.

The same table she'd occupied on her last visit was available, and the bartender arrived promptly with a drink before she had relaxed in the leather seat. "Welcome back, Ms. Richoux."

"Thank you," she held up her glass, "and thank you."

He placed a small wooden humidor on the table and opened it to an excellent selection of cigars. "Ms. Morgaine called and said you might enjoy a smoke before you have to go to work."

"Never argue with an intelligent, beautiful woman." The bartender nodded and put down another glass so he wouldn't have to bother her again for a while.

She let her mind wander wherever it chose, remembering things from different lifetimes with no set pattern. In her time on earth, which she was still convinced wouldn't last forever, she'd tried to experience as many things as possible.

She still hadn't tried to learn and master a few trades, but she was willing to experience anything, so she'd never get bored unless she gave up on life. She'd put away the money she'd made in banks that only dealt in numbers, so she could live another three thousand years and never have to work again. To her, that wasn't as important as the knowledge she'd gathered. If she chose to sit and write a book, it would change the history books dramatically, if anyone believed it.

She laughed at people's notions about topics such as the importance of women and their place in the world of the past. Men had written most of the history books, so they'd had the edge on marketing their version of history. And like any writer, most men focused primarily on their accomplishments and conquests.

The same could be said of the Bible and other books men now used to keep their faithful flocks in check. The teachings of most philosophers and holy men lost so much in translation and the passage of time that very little of the lessons they'd hoped to teach their followers was left.

The heated voices across the bar stopped the mental collage of images of the people she'd met and what they'd taught her. When she saw who it was, she shook her head and concentrated so she could catch every word.

"The bank will be calling in your loans by the end of the week. Either you have the money to pay them off or we move in and take over. It's that simple, Piper."

"I trusted you, but you're nothing but a bottom-feeding scum sucker."

Kenny Delaney laughed and lifted his empty glass in the direction of the bar. "That's a mouthful, honey, but is that how you should be addressing your new boss?"

"I'd never work for you, and you're not taking the company from us." Piper held her glass in a way that made Kendal think she was about to crown him with the heavy crystal.

"You're so good in bed I might just give you a corner office. We'd never lose another contract if I put you in charge of entertaining the clients." He closed his eyes before the contents of Piper's glass hit him in the face, but he grabbed her arm and slammed her back in her seat. "You're going to pay for that one."

"Let me go, you're hurting me," Piper said, grimacing.

"I haven't begun to hurt you, bitch. You're going to find out what it's like to get fucked in every conceivable way. Your family's responsible for me almost losing everything, so I'm going to enjoy this almost as much as getting to fuck you. Allowing you into my bed was charity, but this is business, and we're not finished, so sit down and shut up."

"I believe the lady asked you to let her go," Kendal said softly, right next to his ear.

Kenny turned and looked up at her as he tightened his hold on Piper. "This is a private matter between me and her. Get lost."

"I'm sorry, did you think I was making a request?" She pulled the cigar lighter out of her pocket and turned the small torch on. "Care to see if that alcohol aftershave you're wearing is flammable?"

Kenny pulled back so fast he toppled over in his chair. "Crazy bitch," he said, pointing at Piper before he jumped up and left. "Friday at ten, don't be late, and don't forget to bring the old man with you. Tell him his payback is coming."

Kendal grabbed him by the back of the collar before he reached the door. She dragged him out and pushed him into the first empty bathroom she found. "Do you get a charge out of beating on women, Kenneth?"

"Get out of my way," Kenny said, his eyes darting around as if searching for a way out, but she was standing between him and the door. "That was a business meeting, Richoux."

"That was a pathetic man showing me he needs to be put in his place. Hitting someone who's already on the mat only makes you an asshole."

"You were lined up to do the same thing," he said, smiling. "What, she wouldn't fuck you so you're taking your frustrations out on me? Trust me, she wasn't that good."

She grabbed him by the neck this time and shoved his head in the toilet so fast he didn't have a chance to scream. Too bad the Piquant staff kept the facilities spotless.

"Are you crazy?" Kenny yelled when she let him up. "You'll pay for this."

"You need a new threat vocabulary, stupid," she said, shoving his head back in and flushing. The strong gush of water made him frantic, judging from the way he kicked his legs, trying to get his head out. "Stay away from Mac and Piper, or that cute hairstyle will be the nicest thing I'll do to you," she said, loud enough for him to hear her over his coughing fit.

When she let go, Kenny stood up and tried to hit her before he cleared the water out of his mouth. She easily sidestepped his sorry attempt and had enough time to decide where to land her fist. The size of the bruise that would cover most of his cheek and eye by morning was the best reminder of her warning.

"This isn't over, Kendal," Kenny said, both his hands covering the spot where she'd hit him.

"You're right. It isn't, so use your brain before you decide to treat Piper like that again."

Piper was still in the same spot, staring intently in her direction when she turned the corner. "Are you all right?" she asked Piper when she was close enough.

"Just peachy."

If she was expecting gratitude, she wouldn't get it from Piper. With a brief nod she turned and headed back to her table. Maybe Morgaine was right; she couldn't afford the distraction of Piper any longer, no matter how pretty and entertaining she was, especially if she couldn't be civil at all.

"I'm sorry," Piper said, standing behind the extra chair at her table.

"For what, exactly?" A fine mist had started to fall outside, painting the window she was staring at with water droplets that were getting thick enough to block the view. The thought of spending the night chasing bloodsuckers in the cold damp wasn't making her feel too sociable.

"I'm sorry for being rude to you just now," Piper said, sincerely enough that she looked up at her. "My fight's with Kenny, and considering how I've treated you, I'm surprised you'd come to my aid."

"Mental illness runs in my family," she joked, pointing to the chair Piper had a white-knuckled grip on.

"I could sue you for breach of verbal agreement for getting involved in any aspect of my business."

"Saving you from the wrath of Kenny and defending your honor is interfering in your business?"

"We were negotiating."

"Asking you to prostitute yourself with his potential clients is negotiating?" she asked incredulously.

"I was about to make my counteroffer."

"I can't wait to hear this one."

"It wasn't so much verbal as the glass to go with the drink I threw at him. I didn't get the chance or the satisfaction before you threatened to set his face on fire with that lethal weapon in your pocket." Piper smiled up at the bartender when he put two fresh drinks on the table, one of which was what she'd been drinking. "Want to tell me where you went just now?"

"I had something to flush down the toilet," she said, making Piper laugh. "And that's the first time you've strung that many words together in my presence that didn't have to do with wishing me bodily harm," she said, relighting her cigar.

"You have to understand the kind of pressure I've been under lately. I promise you I'm not usually such a bitch."

The tip of the cigar turned a bright orange as she sucked hard to get it going. "I don't think you're a bitch, Miss Marmande. You're feisty. If I thought you're a bitch, I'd have bought the company just to teach you a valuable lesson on manners."

"Why didn't you? Buy Marmande, I mean."

"My first sit-down doesn't usually go like ours did. People are usually so terrified of losing their business, they barely talk, so it was refreshing to find someone so passionate and ready to take me on. And, contrary to my reputation, I do listen before I make my offer. Even if you didn't say it, I realized how much Marmande means to you and your family, and I didn't want to be the one to take it away from you."

Piper nodded and held her drink with both hands. "Instead, you left us hanging so someone like Kenny could come along and take it."

"I offered to help you, if you remember, and you told me to go to hell. Life isn't always about people trying to screw you over, Miss Marmande. Your company is and has been in trouble for a while. You can't deny that."

"I'm not denying anything, but my grandfather isn't to blame. Life threw a lot at him, and he had a hard time climbing out of the hole he landed in."

"Please don't think I'm laying blame on anyone. I take over businesses like yours and turn a profit. History teaches us that there's a time and a place for everything, and business is no different. Marmande was once a giant in the shipbuilding industry, but now it's in the wrong location to compete for the really big contracts. You're landlocked, making expansion impossible, and you aren't competitive enough to go after the small contracts that could save you. That isn't anyone's fault. It's reality." The fire she was used to seeing in Piper's eyes was starting to burn. This time she gave in to a smile.

"What's so funny?" Piper asked, her anger clear in her voice.

"You don't like it when someone tells you the truth, do you?"

One of Piper's hands came off her glass, and Kendal put the cigar down just in case.

"The truth as you see it doesn't make it the truth."

"Okay, let's try this. Miss Marmande, do you want my help?"

"I can't afford your help. You want what's mine, and I'm not willing to pay that price."

She exhaled in a long sigh. Piper was the most annoying person she'd ever come in contact with, and considering she had thousands upon thousands of days under her belt, that was quite an accomplishment. "Why not ask what the price tag is before you turn me down? Haven't you ever heard that life is full of surprises? I might surprise you if you give me the chance," she said before downing the rest of her drink.

"Your first surprise was enough to make me wary, so forgive me for not jumping at your offer."

"My first surprise?" she asked, confused.

"You wanted us bad enough to kill the contract I worked hard to get. With no other work in our future, it was much easier for you to convince the bank to cut their losses."

"You have my word I never did that, but if you like, I'll find out who did. We both can make an educated guess. Kenny has a lot more to gain from watching you fold because he sold you out to assure his own survival. That isn't the case with me."

"Perhaps you're not as slimy as Kenny, but you both want the same thing so, I don't trust either of you."

Kendal stood, picked up her cigar from the ashtray, and leaned over the table. "Think about what I said before time runs out."

"Would you like to have dinner with me?" Piper asked, appearing surprised at her own invitation.

"I'd love nothing better, but I have work to do, so could I have a rain check?"

"You're going to work now?"

"Yes, ma'am, I'm not just telling you that to brush you off."

"Dressed like that?"

Looking down at herself, she spread her arms out. "What's wrong with the way I'm dressed?"

"Nothing, it's just not your usual business suit. Makes me wonder what type of business you have to attend to."

She laughed at Piper's usual lack of manners. "I could give you a lifetime of guesses and you'd never come up with the answer. Have a pleasant evening, Miss Marmande, and don't forget about my offer."

Piper let out a laugh of her own. "Why do I think accepting any offer from you would land me in the same position Kenny got me in, namely, in his bed?"

She moved closer, and for once Piper didn't back away. "I meant what I said about my bed the first time we met. If you end up there, it'll be because you want to be with me. I'll never force or obligate you. Right now the only shot you have is to beg me."

"Trust me, you're not my type."

Now only inches separated them. "Run along the straight and narrow, do you? And I'm putting emphasis on the 'straight' part of that statement."

"I'm not interested."

"And you think I am?"

Piper's eyes dropped first. "You sounded interested enough, but I'm sorry for assuming," Piper said, sounding uncertain for once.

"I do enjoy the company of other women, but my honor means everything to me. I'd never take advantage of you or anyone else when they're desperate." She stood straight and looked out the window again. The rain was now falling in a steady stream. "I've never had trouble finding someone who wants to share time with me, so you're in no danger."

She turned and left, hoping Henri would give her more of a challenge tonight. After a few minutes with Piper she couldn't wait to shove a sword into someone's chest.

❖

Henri entered the house and looked around to see who was missing. All the young ones he'd sent out were gone, including Veronica. Not that he had thought they'd have any chance against Kendal's skill, but he hoped the numbers of his followers had at least intimidated her.

However, it really wasn't important to him how Kendal felt or what she thought. For Henri and the woman he owed everything to, the time had come to fight and break the shackles the Clan and the damned Elders had imposed on every one of their kind. Taking Kendal out would give them the edge in the battle that would follow, because no matter what Kendal's position within the Clan was, she was their leading slayer. Not even the blonde who'd taught her in the beginning and remained her teacher came close to Kendal's skills.

As Henri moved to his chair, he studied the group of people in the room. It was small compared to those who would worship him once they announced their existence to the world and claimed their rightful place of power. He had always known he was meant to rule, and it wouldn't be long before he'd fulfill his destiny. Once he did, the world would either do his bidding or exist only to quench his thirst.

"Send out the more talented fighters tonight," he told Troy. "You don't have to defeat her, just capture her or her little pet. Asra's as predictable as the rising sun. Touch or threaten those close to her, and she'll drop her sword without hesitation."

"Yes, master. I'll send them out in force."

"Not all, just enough to do the job. I don't want to be left vulnerable if she's luckier than we give her credit for. Remember, all we need is just one of them," he said.

He stayed to see who Troy picked, then left the house headed into the city, hurrying to sate two hundred years of longing. When he slept he had no memories or dreams to cloud his rest, with only one exception. Her call had filled his head almost as if someone had screamed it so loud it had echoed off the stone of his crypt.

Most of the people he passed on the street never saw or felt Henri, and those who did simply shivered at the quick touch of cold of his skin. He didn't care about anyone who got in his way and only slowed down a block from where he was headed in the second oldest part of New Orleans. Uptown had been where the outsiders who weren't French or Spanish had built their big houses and estates.

The neighborhood that skirted the river had become more congested with time, but unlike the French Quarter that had held on to and protected its historic treasures, very few of the original homes from that era existed except the ones that lined St. Charles Avenue.

Henri stood before one of the survivors and tipped his head back to calm his excitement. The place appeared foreboding, with its dark shutters closed except for a few upstairs on the west side and the high, solid-brick fence that surrounded the property. Broken glass shards lined the top of the wall, an old security measure, but that's not what kept everyone out.

Anyone who stopped long enough to stare through the wrought-iron gates to the house didn't linger, and those who were brave enough to jump the wall soon went mad because of the strong protection spell in place. It didn't matter that commercial dock businesses, restaurants, and bars now surrounded the property—everyone had left it as untouched as a time capsule.

Henri stood on the cracked sidewalk, the cement no opponent for the roots of the large oak close to the fence, and the hair on his arms stood when he heard her call again.

"Abez, come to me. I've waited long enough for you."

This place was his, but he seldom ventured here. Through the years he'd modified and improved it so thoroughly he was confident it was safe for the treasure it would house for the fight to come.

He sniffed the air and closed his eyes in ecstasy at her scent before he unlocked the gate.

Their own Elders, who guarded the house, bowed to him as he moved to the door. Two other old ones sat at her feet with their swords across their laps when he entered the glass solarium with its good view of the full moon.

His eyes filled with tears. Ora was beautiful with her long red hair pulled back and held in place by a large comb that appeared to be made of bone. The black robe she wore opened to reveal her legs as she extended her hand to him with a smile.

"You've done well and have earned the right to sit beside me."

Without hesitation, he dropped to his knees. "My queen, welcome to New Orleans. I'm here to do your bidding."

CHAPTER FOURTEEN

"Piper, you have a visitor," the receptionist said.

"I requested no calls, and I don't have any appointments scheduled for today." The morning was as overcast as the previous day, but despite the dark luminous clouds, only a fine mist was falling. As Piper stared out the window, rocking slightly in her office chair, she felt like the weather reflected not only her mood but their future. "Who is it?"

"Are you sure you want me to say that?" The receptionist's voice was muffled but Piper still understood her question. "She said to tell you it's the sanctimonious bitch."

"Send her back," Piper said, laughing. Maybe her grandfather was right and she shouldn't have pissed Kendal off from the start.

"Good morning, Miss Marmande," Kendal said, stopping right outside her door and wearing another great suit.

"If you've come to survey the lay of the land to see what you can sell off, you can forget it." She smiled as she spoke, wanting Kendal to know she was kidding. "If that isn't threatening enough to keep you from running off with the furniture, Granddad has a gun in his desk."

"I've called off the invasion even if you don't believe me, so I left my invading-horde hat at the hotel."

"What can I do for you?"

"Even though you don't like me much, I thought I'd make up for having to turn you down last night by asking you out for breakfast." Kendal slipped her hands into her pockets. "If you'd like, you can ask Mr. Marmande to join us."

"He's actually out searching for buried treasure." It finally dawned on Piper why Kendal was still in the hallway, so she stood and walked around her desk. Kendal Richoux might have perfected the art of corporate raiding, but she had impeccable manners. "Please come in and sit." Her words pried Kendal's feet off the floor. "And breakfast sounds good."

"I thought if we talk without our original barriers, we could actually share a meal and not have it end in a food fight."

"The last few months haven't brought out the best in me, so I apologize again."

"I understand difficult positions, so you've nothing to be sorry for. Shall we?" Kendal asked, pointing to the door.

Piper guided her down the street to the café where she and Mac ate often. It wasn't fancy, but the woman who'd run it for years took pride in preparing simple homestyle foods. Once they'd ordered, Piper held her coffee cup with both hands to keep them still. Kendal had a way of looking at her that made her feel stripped bare.

"Can I ask you something?"

Kendal nodded. "What would you like to know?"

"Please believe I'm not asking to make you mad—I'm only curious." Kendal smiled, she guessed at her hesitation, and when she did it brought out the unique color of her eyes. They made her think of blue ice. "Why do you do this for a living?"

"You might get upset with me if I'm totally honest," Kendal said, stopping to take a sip of her coffee. "Would you like me to be?"

"If you say you do it for the hell of it, then no, not today." She shook her head for emphasis, and Kendal's smile helped lift her mood. As contentious a start as they'd had, Kendal hadn't taken too many shots at her.

"The strategy required to be successful at this challenges me. No two projects are ever the same, so they all teach me something. I'd never do anything just for the hell of it, unless you're interested in an afternoon of skinny-dipping. For that I might utter those words."

She laughed and couldn't look Kendal in the eye. "I'd admire you at any other time, but being on this end of things paints you in a different light, as they say."

"Actually da Vinci coined the phrase."

"He did? I've never read that," Piper said, lapsing into silence as the food arrived.

"You'll have to take my word for it, then," Kendal said as she covered her waffles in maple syrup, using almost the entire carafe.

Piper figured the stress was getting to her when she laughed at Kendal's answer hard enough to make her eyes water. Also, Kendal made her feel awkward and nervous. "Can I ask you something else?"

"Miss Marmande," Kendal said, locking eyes with her, "you may ask whatever you like. Believe me, I won't answer if I can't."

"Why did you come this morning?" Kendal's face was open enough for her to realize the question had confused her. "What I mean is, what is this?"

"A bacon omelet is my best guess," Kendal said, cutting a small corner off Piper's meal and eating it. "I was right."

"Now you're reminding me what I don't like about you."

Kendal laughed as if she enjoyed aggravating her. "It's my burden in life to be correct in most cases."

"I'm glad you qualified that with 'in most cases.'"

"So when I believed the report that you have a brilliant business mind, I was wrong?"

She had to laugh at that. "I can see why you're so successful."

"I'm successful because I'm motivated."

"You are that," Piper said, taking a bite of her omelet. "Eager beavers could learn something from you."

"It's something I believe we have in common." Kendal reciprocated by placing a piece of waffle on her plate without her asking. "It's also why I thought I'd like you."

"So much for first impressions, huh?"

"If more people fought as nobly and passionately for what they believe in, the world would have less turmoil. Marmande is yours, and I know in my gut you'll find a way to keep it."

Piper pushed her plate away after eating the piece of waffle Kendal had given her, her appetite gone. "Friday isn't enough time. I'm not that brilliant, and this is only breakfast."

"Don't lose faith now."

"I'm not a stranger to loss, so this won't kill me," she said, pausing to thank the waitress for clearing the table. "I've fought so hard for my grandparents and our employees. He'll never admit it, but Marmande means the world to Mac."

"Then you have to know that fate always rewards intentions like that."

"That's a pretty fantasy, but sadly reality has rewarded me more often than fate or destiny has, and that's going to happen again at the end of the week."

"When you do things for the right reasons, the universe has a way of paying you back tenfold."

"So I should buy a lottery ticket?" Piper asked, smiling.

Kendal put her fingers on the bill and slid it toward her before Piper had a chance to grab it. "Maybe you already have."

"You're an interesting person." After she said it, Kendal smiled at her, and Piper studied her face. Her eyes didn't seem to fit with the olive complexion, but Piper found the mix attractive. She wouldn't describe Kendal as beautiful, but her looks were hard to turn away from. That surprised her since she never got wrapped up in frivolous stuff.

"As are you, Miss Marmande," Kendal said, peeling two twenties from the clip she'd taken from her front pocket. "After all this, maybe you'll agree to have dinner with me." When the waitress came over, Kendal told her to keep the change, which was more than double the bill.

"Do you ask so you'll have another opportunity to impress me with your largess?" Piper asked, pointing to the server, who appeared smitten.

"I'm more known for my killer instincts, but you have nothing to worry about."

"That's right," she said, pointing her index finger in the air before aiming it at Kendal. "You aren't interested in us anymore."

"You're partially right." Kendal pinched her finger lightly, making her concentrate on Kendal's hand. "I peg you as a risk-taker, and having dinner with me is an opportunity to change your mind about me."

"What's the risk in that?"

"Tremendous, if you figure out what you're missing by holding back because you see your true self only one way." Kendal sounded incredibly honest. "It might be good to study the reflection of yourself I see."

"That could be a frightening proposition."

"You have nothing to fear from me," Kendal said in a way that made her believe it to be true. "If that's too deep, then saying yes means you get a free meal and nothing more before I head off to new challenges. After all, there's no rest from the wicked."

"Isn't it, there's no rest for the wicked?"

"That hasn't been my experience," Kendal said, and laughed, making Piper wonder what her game really was.

❖

The next two nights' hunting resembled the first. Henri sent his creations against them in packs, and Charlie and Kendal destroyed them, staying vigilant for the next group. It was the weekend, but the Clan's directive was still in force, even though the huge crowds in the French Quarter might see the immortals fighting on the rooftops. In a week, the city, already famous for its party potential, would shift into high gear for Halloween, and if they weren't any closer to finding Henri, he'd be in a better position to get everything he was after for Ora.

Kendal shook her head. Halloween would fall under a full moon this year. In a city like New Orleans that didn't believe in boundaries, if Henri planned an all-out attack for that night, he would be able to hide in plain sight. She and Charlie had already mowed through the younger of his followers, and the coming nights would become more difficult.

"Would you like breakfast, sir?" asked one of the men Morgaine had left behind to tend to her needs.

"Yes, thank you. Could you put these back in the sword room for me?" She handed over the weapons she'd used the night before. As she contemplated taking Ruda for a long ride, she heard a car stop at the front gate. With a wave of her hand, she motioned for the man to open it. She didn't need the intercom to guess who it might be. What did surprise her was the hour of the visit. It was only a little after six.

"Good morning," she said, not getting get up from the table and resting her elbows on the arms of her chair.

"I came—"

"I know why you're here. I'm more interested as to why you decided to come at all."

Piper stood next to her car fidgeting with her keys. "Can I talk to you?"

She stood and walked down the steps, not wanting to do what she'd accused Kenny of. "Please forgive my rudeness, Miss Marmande. Welcome to Oakgrove. Would you join me for breakfast?"

Piper looked up at the house before she took her arm, followed her to the table, and smiled at her when she pulled out her chair and poured Piper a cup of coffee. "If this is how you treat the enemy, I'd hate to see what happens to your friends when they come over. How do you ever get rid of them?"

"You aren't my enemy, Miss Marmande. You're more like a pesky annoyance buzzing around my ear." She rested her hands briefly on Piper's shoulders and laughed.

"Today's Friday," Piper said, appearing tired, probably from a few sleepless nights due to the stress of what she had to face.

"You're right. It's Friday, but you don't have anything to worry about. I meant it when I said noble battles are always rewarded."

"This isn't a joke."

"I'm not poking fun, but you have to accept that today isn't the end of the world as you know it. You have my word."

"I need your help, Kendal. At ten, Kenny will take everything my family has built." For the first time Kendal saw the frightened little girl Piper tried to hide from the world in her glassy, desperate eyes. They were so much like those from long ago when Kendal could do nothing to change what had to be done.

She knelt next to Piper and took her hand. "Pick up your grandfather, Miss Marmande, and go to your meeting. Have faith in what you and he have built together, and that you'll have what it takes to protect what's yours. You don't need anyone's help for that."

"If you want me to beg, I will," Piper said, squeezing her fingers.

"That's the last thing I want." She smiled at Piper. "I want you to call up that confident, take-no-prisoners, beautiful woman I first met and give Kenny hell."

You won't help us?"

"You don't trust me enough to believe me, but everything will be fine. You have everything you need to put Kenny Delaney and his partners back in the hole they slithered out of. When you realize I'm right, you'll have to make changes so no one will put you in this position again. You remind me so much of someone I knew, and you have her same spirit for life and ability to make the right choices no matter the consequences. Embrace that part of yourself and you'll be able to do anything you want."

Piper stood and moved away from her as if she wasn't interested in the comfort she was offering. "I'm sorry I bothered."

Piper walked away as if being led to the gallows, and Kendal came close to calling her back, but she'd done all she could. She needed to cut their ties so she could fully concentrate on Henri and his grandiose plans. She hadn't lied, though. Piper and Mac had made her deviate from "Kendal Richoux's" usual game plan, but it had been worth it. The fire in Piper had made Kendal notice her, and had it been another time she would've pursued her until Piper changed her mind on a slew of things.

But for once, she thought humorously, she was in short supply of time.

❖

Piper had controlled her tears by the time she reached Kenny's offices. When she entered, the rest of the thieves were already seated. The men gathered for the meeting stood until she had taken her place next to her grandfather, and from the head of the conference table Kenny smiled as if he would enjoy stripping them of everything. With a little more research, she might have discovered that Kenny thought Mac had stolen his family's business by exposing their less-than-honorable practices.

In an act of desperation, she'd dealt with Kenny because he was experiencing his own financial crisis. He had promised that if they joined forces, they could secure financing more easily because they jointly owned so much riverfront property. Now it was too late. This deal and the prime real estate it came with would infuse his construction company with capital to replace what he'd lost on bad projects. Kenny would profit by offering her and Mac up like sacrificial sheep.

She felt like a failure having trusted him so blindly, but when Kendal had appeared on her radar, she'd panicked. Her fear had caused her to be careless, and sitting and watching Kenny gloat was hard to swallow. In the end, Kendal was the only one who could have saved them, but Piper's pride and misbehavior had sealed that door shut. She'd made the mistake of believing Kendal was different from anyone she'd ever counted on to help her out of a bleak situation. Like her father Mackey, Kendal had left her to face the lynch mob alone.

Brad, the bank vice president of loans where Mac had borrowed from, sat across from them with a stack of papers before him. "We're here to discuss calling in your loans and the assets that come with their payment," he explained.

"Get on with it, Brad. We all know why we're here," Kenny said in annoyance.

"Mac, are you sure you want to go through with this? You have enough on your plate trying to stay competitive without taking on a new business as well." Brad spoke directly to Mac, and Piper's despair evaporated.

Kenny pounded on the table. "What? Are you delusional? My

partners and I are here to call in his loans and pay them in full. I know you all go way back, but the Marmandes are months in arrears, and we can make good on their debts this morning. Don't tempt me into getting the bank board involved. You do, and I'll make sure you lose big on this."

"I'm a banker, Mr. Delaney. Delusions of any kind are not part of the equation. As of the close of business yesterday, all of Marmande Enterprise's loans were paid in full, so the loans I'm referring to today have to do with your company. You're extremely delinquent on two of your three construction sites, and the board has already met on this matter." Brad glared at Kenny over his glasses. "If you don't believe me, the board president is on standby for your call."

"Yeah, right," Kenny said, sounding as childish as he looked when he laughed and rolled his eyes.

"The board has decided to give Mr. Marmande the same consideration they extended to you and your partners, especially after a large amount of cash as collateral accompanied Mr. Marmande's business plan for expansion. If you need it simplified for you, Mac put his money where his mouth is, whereas your plan involved risk to the bank in the form of additional loans."

Kenny looked at Brad like he was speaking a foreign language. "Stop fucking around. Unless he found a fairy godmother, he couldn't possibly pull this off," Kenny said, pointing at Mac.

"Mac, I can't tell you what to do," the banker said, "but I suggest that you take only the one site adjacent to your property, considering it will double your capacity and still leave room for future expansion. I know you don't need our money, but we have put some plans together to finance moving your dry docks to Mr. Delaney's property. We'll give you a competitive rate so you can invest the cash for upcoming projects, but we'll get to that over lunch. I only need your decision now so I can cut my counterpart here a check, if you're interested."

"That sounds reasonable. Piper and I aren't interested in taking over Mr. Delaney's other locations in east New Orleans, are we?" Mac asked her.

"No, sir. The property next door will be fine."

Brad handed Kenny's banker a check, since his investors had already left, and motioned for Mac and Piper to get going. Piper got to her feet, not wanting to subject her grandfather to Kenny's vile mouth any longer.

Once out of the office, Brad said, "Mac, Piper, I don't know how you managed it, but I really enjoyed putting that little moron in his place."

"You know how it is, got to keep your cards close to your vest," Mac said as if he knew what was going on.

"Well, next time don't wait so long to show them. I'm younger than you are, and I don't think my heart could take much more." They walked across the lobby to the front door of the building. "Are you two free? I really do want to talk to you about a line of credit, then I'll treat y'all to lunch and a glass of champagne to celebrate."

"I'll be happy to join you, but I can't speak for Piper," Mac said.

"Thank you, but I have to pass this time. After I eat my share of humble pie, I don't think I'll have room for anything else today." Mac smiled at her, appearing surprised. "Could I have a word with Pops before you two take off?"

"Tell me you didn't sell your soul to make that happen just now?" Mac asked when they were alone.

"I asked someone for help, and they came through. Now I just have to figure out what it's going to cost us."

"Who?"

"Kendal Richoux."

Mac leaned against the glass of the building and pinched the bridge of his nose. "The same Richoux who you called a thief a week ago?"

"More like the one you suggested I listen to before I jumped to conclusions. I'll tell you all about it tonight, but right now I've got to go." She led Mac back to Brad.

"All set?" Brad asked.

"You bet. You know something, I'm damned glad I'm retiring soon. You're right. I'm getting old and I don't think I can take much more of this either, but my Piper, she's something else. Your daddy would've been so proud of you," Mac said to her as she kissed his cheek. "You're my future and it's looking bright."

CHAPTER FIFTEEN

The grove of camellias planted close to the road still possessed some of the trees Kendal had planted when she'd decided to purchase the property that became Oakgrove. Over the years cold snaps or disease had destroyed some, but the new ones that filled in those spots were all hybrids of the originals Charlie had cultivated, knowing how much she loved them. These were the trees where she cut the bouquets she took Angelina when she went to call.

New Orleans, October 1726

On the morning of Angelina and Tomas's second day at Oakgrove, Tomas stayed inside to enjoy Jacques's library so Jacques could take Angelina riding. Angelina was excited about seeing the entire plantation, but appeared more excited that they were heading out alone. Dee, for all her loyalty, hated horses and everything to do with them, so Tomas trusted Jacques not to ravage his niece if given the opportunity to spend the day with her. At least that's the warning he'd issued before they left. With a packed lunch strapped to the back of her horse, they set off so Angelina could see what farm life was like.

"What do you want my role with you to be?" Angelina asked when they stopped for lunch and Jacques sat close to her on the blanket she'd spread out so they could enjoy their meal. Jacques had chosen the other side of the lake since Angelina had admired it the day before.

She stretched out and put her head in Angelina's lap. "What would you like it to be?"

"First, I'd like to be your wife and the mother of your children, but above all else, whatever will make you happy."

Jacques looked up at her and felt like someone had ripped her heart out for giving her something so precious she couldn't keep. Angelina needed to find someone new and wonderful to lavish all the things she deserved on her. Someone who'd love her and grow old with her, which was something Jacques St. Louis couldn't do because *he* wasn't real. She'd been trying to think of a way to tell Angelina that since the night they attended the theater.

"What would make you happy?"

"To always see the same expression in your eyes when you look my way," Angelina answered, pressing her lips to hers.

"No matter how much time passes, it'll always be so, but we have to talk before you make too many plans about our future together. You need to know some things about me."

"You don't want me?"

She stopped Angelina before she could move too far away. "No man in his right mind would refuse you, but you should know the truth about the man you're in love with. If we're to be together, we shouldn't have any secrets, don't you agree?"

"There's nothing you can tell me, Jacques, that'll make me change my mind about you."

Over Angelina's shoulder, she could see the dark clouds forming, and they were at least a couple of hours from the house. "I pray that's true, but let's get going before you ruin that beautiful riding outfit in a downpour." A few more hours of the illusion wouldn't hurt, she thought, as she helped Angelina back on her horse.

That evening they sat in the parlor and laughed at Tomas's stories of all the bribes people had offered him over the years because they didn't want to read about themselves in the paper. The afternoon storm was still raging with no sign of letting up. The noise of nature's fury and the distraction of Tomas's company kept Jacques from hearing the light knock at the front door.

"Yes, sir, may I help you?" asked the servant who opened the door.

"Is this the home of Jacques St. Louis?"

"Yes, sir, can I get him for you?"

"I'm his brother, Henri."

"I'm sorry, I didn't realize Master St. Louis had a brother." The servant stood there awkwardly. "Would you like for me to fetch him?" he asked, staring at Henri's face as if unsure what else to say.

"You have to invite me in, my good man. It would be rude of me to enter otherwise." Henri smiled and waited, knowing he couldn't step foot any place he wasn't welcomed first, especially any house under the Clan's protection.

"I'm sorry, of course. Please come in. I'm sure Master Jacques will be happy to see you."

"Wait," Jacques yelled, but it was too late. The young man who technically lived in the house had issued the invitation, giving Henri permission to enter. Once someone had granted that, Henri no longer had to abide by any rule of protection.

"Come now, Jacques, we are family, after all. Aren't you pleased to see me?" Henri stepped in and took off his cloak and hat, shaking his hair of any water. "It's been years, and I've gone through so much trouble to find you."

"Why are you here?"

Henri smiled before he spoke softly. "I've come to make peace. The years have made me strong enough that I don't need to feed as often to survive, so perhaps we can agree that the world's big enough for both of us and rebuild our relationship."

Angelina walked up and put her arm through Jacques's, looking at Henri. "Do I need to send for anything, love?" she asked, seeming unable to tear her eyes away from Henri.

"Just a towel if you have it, kind lady. Allow me to introduce myself. Henri St. Louis. I'm Jacques's brother." He walked forward and kissed her hand.

Angelina shivered, and Jacques knew it was from the cold white fingers. "Angelina du'Pon. Uncle Tomas and I are friends of Jacques."

"Don't be modest, my dear, I see how my *brother* looks at you. I'm willing to bet you're more than friends."

"Would you like a room to retire to, Henri, after your long voyage?" Jacques asked, wanting to cut him off and get him away from the du'Pons. Henri never reappeared in her life casually, but he knew he could take the chance with Angelina and Tomas in the house.

"And miss the opportunity to spend time with you and your lady? I think not." Henri's answer made Angelina smile. "Lead the way, Mademoiselle du'Pon. I'd love to meet your uncle."

"Go on, Angelina, we'll be right in." Angelina hesitated at her request, but left without a word.

Henri waited until they were alone, knowing that she wouldn't attack him in front of all these people, no matter how much she wanted to. "She's simply delicious, Asra."

"I want to know why you're here."

"I wanted a new start, just like you, brother," he said, laughing. "Does the little precious know your grand secret, or are you waiting to surprise her when it's too late for her to escape?"

"Get out of my house, or I'll—"

"You'll do nothing without risking everything you've built here. And have you forgotten, I was invited in." He moved closer until she could feel the cold skin that felt like death. "One night, Asra, then I'll disappear into the darkness. You have my word as a gentleman."

"Your word is worthless, Abez. It always has been, but watch your step here or I'll destroy you no matter what I have to sacrifice."

"Remember you said that."

❖

Angelina and Tomas watched as Henri simply pushed the food around on his plate, but none of it touched his lips. The same went for the sweet wine and fig preserves the cooks served after dinner in the parlor.

"Will you be staying long?" Angelina asked Henri.

"Long enough, but if there's to be a wedding I might be persuaded to stay for the festivities."

She laughed nervously and put her hand over Jacques's. "Like I said, monsieur, Jacques and I are only friends."

"Shame on you, Jacques. You'd best hurry and ask for her hand before someone else steals her from under your nose."

"Thank you for your encouragement, but I rather like Jacques's pace as much as his company," Angelina said without humor. "If you gentlemen will excuse me, I think I'll retire for the evening." They all stood when she rose to her feet. "Jacques, will you accompany me to my door?"

"Of course. Henri, I trust you'll be here when I return."

"Like I said, brother, we've much to talk about after all these years."

They climbed the stairs in silence and walked in equal silence to the door of the bedroom Angelina was using. Henri's arrival had disturbed her, and she could lose everything, but that wasn't as important as protecting all those she'd come to care about. If killing Henri would expose her charade, she'd gladly pay the price to save everyone from his evil.

Their last meeting had ended when she wounded Henri, but not enough to keep him from escaping. After that he'd vanished, and the only clue she'd found was the name of a ship he'd written in a journal when he'd stayed in Paris. The merchant ship had sailed to the new world a week after she'd last seen him.

Asra had followed with all the papers she needed to establish Jacques St. Louis in New Orleans. Oakgrove and the people she'd bought off the block hadn't been part of her plan, but the solitary plantation was a perfect location. No one was around to start gossip if she had to leave to hunt, and everyone who lived with her was tied to her identity, so they'd never turn her in even if they uncovered her secret. No matter how this place had come to be, she'd learned to love the life of a farmer.

"Are you all right, love?"

"Angelina, I want you to lock yourself and Dee in and don't leave the room until the sun rises."

Angelina put her hands on her chest, appearing frightened. "Why? What's wrong? Is that man really your brother?"

Kendal passionately kissed her to stop the litany of questions. She wanted Angelina to know how much she felt for her before, like Henri had said, it was too late. "I love you," she said before kissing her again.

"I love you as well."

"This isn't how I planned to do this," she said, holding Angelina's hand. "I have to speak frankly with you first, and if you'll have me, I'll speak to your uncle. Are you agreeable to that?" She didn't have time for romance, but proposing seemed so right. She'd deal with any fallout that her spontaneity caused after she got rid of Henri.

"Yes, of course. You have to know how I feel."

"Then get inside and remember, open the door to no one until morning."

"Jacques, please tell me what's going on. I'm frightened."

She held her close and kissed her one last time. "Get some sleep, and don't worry. I'm here to watch over you. In the morning I'll tell you everything I've put off until now, but please, no matter what you hear, keep the door locked."

"Master Jacques, is everything all right? I just heard screams coming from the back," Dee said, hurrying toward them.

"Lock the door and watch over Angelina and yourself. Remember what I said and stay safe," she said before she ran down the hall toward the stairs.

In the parlor Tomas stood by the window looking out at the rain. Henri wasn't there. "Where's Henri?"

"He said he was going out to check on his horse. Strange man, your brother. You two don't seem related at all." Tomas leaned on his cane, the pain in his hip evident in his grimace.

"Tomas, I don't have time to explain, but I need you to go up to your room and lock the door. My brother isn't the gentleman he pretends to be, and I have to find him before he harms anyone." She pulled one of the crossed swords from over the mantel. Doing so made her want to cry, because in the morning they were coming down anyway to make room for Angelina's surprise.

Not bothering with a horse, she ran toward the cabins to see if Dee was right. She wasn't prepared to find Lionel walking through the mud as if in a trance holding the lifeless body of his wife Celia. His white work shirt was covered with what was left of her blood.

"I don't know what it was, but it killed her," Lionel said through his tears. "It killed all of them, and I couldn't stop it."

She entered the cabin to find Lionel's children with their throats ripped open, dead as if a wild animal had come in and feasted on them. She ran back to the house, already aware of her mistake. The first body she found was the boy who'd invited Henri in, not far from Tomas.

"You old fool," she said from her knees. She closed the tired green eyes staring off into nothing before putting her hand on his forehead. Tomas's walking stick was backward in his hand as if he had tried to use it as a club to fight off his attacker.

Her boots felt like lead as she moved up the stairs. Angelina's door was almost ripped from its hinges, the lock no opponent for Henri's vengeance. Dee wore the same mask of death as Tomas. Her soft brown eyes were open, and in her hand the only weapon she had was the small gold cross Angelina always wore around her neck. The only thing missing from the room was Angelina.

She looked for the body until sunrise, but Henri had taken Angelina as a way to hurt her, and she swore she'd get even when the sun set again. Now, though, she had people to calm and bodies to bury after the night of death. Working together, they quickly assembled the pyres needed for Celia, her sons, Tomas, Dee, and the others who'd fallen to the demon they'd invited into their midst.

"Have them all pack and get them ready to travel soon," she told Lola, who was twisting a rag and appeared terrified.

"Where we going?"

"I'm giving you your freedom to go wherever you please, but I'd like you all to consider my estates in the northern part of England. You'll be welcome there and you'll be safe for as long you care to stay."

"I thought you were from France?"

She put down her glass of whiskey and turned her attention to Lola, who'd befriended her from the minute she came off the auction block and begged her for the life of her son. "I am Egyptian, but does that really matter now? This is all I can think to do, because after last night, I can't stay here, and I won't leave you all to suffer for my mistakes. Angelina and Tomas aren't worth more than the others Henri killed, but we both know the law won't see it that way."

"I'll get them ready, Jacques." Lola stood to go and spread the word. "And, Jacques, we don't blame you for what happened, especially Lionel. You're too good to be related to that monster."

"Thank you, but hurry and go. The sunset isn't far off. Lock your doors and invite no one in."

She waited in the study with her sword lying across her lap. Wondering why Abez had come back now was about to give her a headache. At midnight marking All Hallow's Eve, the front door creaked open and they entered together.

Henri followed the movement of the knife in her hand as she twirled it through her fingers. For the moment he didn't appear too concerned that she would throw it since he had Angelina pressed against his chest.

"Miss me, or should I say us?" He ran his hand through Angelina's hair, which hung freely down her back. The style made her look wild and sensual.

"For centuries I haven't struck the death blow when it came to you, Abez, because no matter how many despicable acts you've committed, I believed a small part of my brother remained in your heart. I was wrong. No matter what price I have to pay, you'll die tonight." She embedded the knife in the arm of the chair, put her glass down, and stood. The only noise in the room that followed was the sword leaving the sheath that housed it. "I'll take my revenge for our father and all the other lives you've ruined."

"Will you kill her too?" Henri pulled back on Angelina's head and, to her disgust, she kissed him. "Where has the love you have for her gone?"

"Angelina, come here," she said softly, and Angelina obeyed, acting as if she was drugged. Something had changed, and as she watched Angelina walk across the room, her heart broke because she knew what it was.

"Why didn't you tell me?" Angelina asked, running her hand up her chest. "Did you think that would frighten me away?" Her hand moved lower and squeezed between her legs to confirm what was missing from her anatomy.

"I intended to tell you, you have to believe me." Angelina's touch was overwhelming her senses, and she almost forgot Henri was still in the room.

Angelina pulled her head down, clearly wanting to share a kiss. Their lips were about to touch when the truth of Asra's suspicions registered in her mind and she felt like someone had dropped a bucket of ice on her soul. Angelina's strength was unnatural; she could feel it in the hand at her neck. Her lips went limp against Angelina's, but before she could move away, Angelina sank her teeth into her upper lip.

Henri's laugh rang through the house when she pulled back, her mouth cut and bleeding. "She belongs to me now, sister. I took what you so cherished last night, and I was right, she was delicious. What a wonderful wife she would've been, but you can delight in what an incredible bedmate she'll be to me."

"No." The word came out as a whisper, and she wanted nothing more than to run out of the room to find darkness and sleep. In darkness she would find emptiness and oblivion. That was the only way she'd find release from the pain of what she'd allowed to happen.

"Jacques, please." The voice sounded like her sweet Angelina, but this hideous creature only inhabited the shell of her body. Her Angelina was dead. Jacques opened her eyes to watch Henri run his tongue along her ear. "If you love me, release me from this hell. I killed Uncle Tomas last night. May God forgive me, but I couldn't stop myself." A tear of blood fell from the green eyes Jacques loved.

"I can't," she said in anguish. "Please don't ask that of me."

"Please, love, I'm begging you. If you care for me still even a little, then you'll do as I ask." When Jacques screamed, Angelina closed her eyes.

The sword flew from Jacques's hand like a javelin and pierced

Angelina's heart. She threw it so hard it tore into Henri's chest as well, missing his heart by inches. When Angelina exploded into dust, he staggered back, clutching the weapon that was weakening him by the second. When he looked up gasping, she was standing over him, intent on finishing the job.

"If you kill me, you'll never find the other blond bitch you sniff after all the time," he said as the sword slipped out, and she now held the point to the skin over his heart. "I buried your little teacher deep." He kept speaking as the sword drew its first blood on the way to its target. "Swear you'll let me go and I'll tell you where she is." Henri knew her sense of honor as well as her weaknesses, and her word would be his salvation. What he was saying was his ticket to escape.

"You believe I'd trust anything you say?"

"I'll take you myself. If I'm lying you can kill me, but if I'm not, you have to let me go after you get her out."

They arrived on horseback the next night, having to stop at daybreak; she'd watched over him when he crawled wrapped in a blanket under the bed in the room she'd rented. They had stopped at the church being built with Jacques's generosity after Angelina had convinced her to make a donation. This was where Angelina had wanted to marry the *man* she'd fallen in love with, but that fairy tale was over.

"Under the last pile of stones laid," Henri said as he held his hand over the festering wound. It would take extensive feeding and months to heal because of the essence of wood the blade was made with. Unlike when they were children and he showed no interest in learning battle strategy, he'd planned well for every possibility to escape, since his goal was to destroy her.

She braced her legs and pushed against the carved stones. She didn't believe Morgaine would be underneath, but she wasn't willing to gamble. She'd had no message that Morgaine was coming, but when the stones moved, she found Morgaine bound and gagged in an indentation in the dark soil.

"I kept my word, now it's time for you to keep yours," Henri said as he slowly staggered away.

"Kill him," Morgaine rasped from her arms.

"I gave my word not to kill him now, but I won't be bound to it forever. To the future I pledge my oath that Abez will die no matter the cost."

Two days later the sunrise came, bringing with it a sense of despair.

She gathered Angelina's ashes and arranged to have them buried in the church-run cemetery outside the city after Angelina's priest blessed them. Morgaine waited in the du'Pons' home until all of Jacques's slaves set sail to freedom in Europe. All of them accepted her offer and boarded ships except one.

Lionel stayed behind with her, wanting some explanation as to what had happened, why his family had been slaughtered. Her answers made no sense to him, and he cursed her for trying to finish driving him insane.

"No man or woman lives forever, and no one lives on blood alone," Lionel screamed.

The plantation was quiet and peaceful without the sounds of workers and playing children. They were standing in the field where they had lit the pyres of their dead. "I can only tell you the truth as I know it, but I can't make you believe me. I've lived almost three thousand years as a warrior of the Genesis Clan. Our Elders are the keepers of balance between good and evil in the world. You can say I'm their angel of death to the undead."

"You *are* mad."

She sighed and pulled a dagger from her belt and handed it to him. "If my words can't convince you, perhaps my blade can." She ripped her shirt open, and he appeared confused at the bindings wrapped around her chest. "I am Asra, born in Egypt under the rule of the only female pharaoh in history. The sun is my strength, and the Genesis Clan is my guide." She faced the afternoon sun and held her hands out. "Go on, try to kill me."

"So I can find myself at the end of a rope? I don't think so, Jacques."

She took the dagger back and drove it in herself, and Lionel lunged forward to try to stop her. "Pull it out," she said as they both lay on the ground. He watched in amazement as the wound closed and healed with the help of the sun. "Do you believe me now? These little demonstrations are rather taxing, and I'd hate to have to do it again."

"I want to be like you, if only to avenge my family."

She sat up, wiping her hands of her own blood on the grass. "I can't, Lionel. I promised the Elders, and to me that's very precious. A person is nothing without their word."

"Do you know how?"

"Yes, I remember how to make the elixir and recite the incantations necessary to draw the powers of the sun into the cup, but you don't know what you're asking."

"I'm asking for the time to find that bastard who calls himself your brother and drive him into hell, even if it means going with him myself."

CHAPTER SIXTEEN

Oakgrove, present day

Kendal had given in to his pleas, earning the wrath of the Elders for decades for breaking her oath. If she hadn't found and saved Morgaine, they would most likely have buried her and she'd still be a sleeping, dry husk.

She focused on her surroundings right before Piper's fingers reached her cheek to wipe away the tears that had fallen, and it surprised her that Piper would want to touch her. Kendal didn't move away, and when she met Piper's gaze, she saw a reflection of the same compassion Angelina's eyes had held for her once upon a time.

"Why do you always look so sad when you sit alone and think?" Piper asked with her hand still on her face.

"I cry for the things I cannot change."

Piper wiped away the last of her tears and smiled. "Then you must cry a lot."

"More than my share, but reviewing the list of my mistakes helps me try harder not to repeat them." She took a deep breath and tried to put aside the memories. Having to end Angelina's life had been one of her worst experiences, but that was easier to accept than leaving her to the existence that awaited her as a vampire. "To what do I owe the pleasure of your company twice in one day?"

Piper took a seat next to her and folded her hands over her knees. "You know why I'm here, and because you didn't bother to tell me what you did for us, I had a miserable drive into the city."

"I'm guessing you were wrong about the demise of Marmande," she said, tapping Piper's chin gently with her index finger. "At least the size of your smile indicates that you were able to handle Kenny."

"Don't get modest now," Piper said, shaking her head. "Since I didn't buy a lottery ticket, and no rich relative left us a hefty inheritance, you can admit you saved us. I'll always be grateful for what you did—"

Kendal almost laughed. "But," she said, knowing why Piper was having trouble finishing her thought.

"But...what do you want in return?" Piper got the question out in a rush, patting her knee once before sliding to the other side of the bench as if someone had placed a pile of nuclear waste between them. "You saved us, but my gratitude goes only so far. We can talk about how we're going to pay you back, and I promise a return on your loan. Anything else, though, isn't going to happen."

"You don't owe me anything, Miss Marmande, so you might look into your inheritance theory if you've found yourself in the black. If you remember, I'm a heartless bitch, so I certainly wouldn't be so generous. The only thing I'll add for future reference is this *homosexual* is perfectly capable of getting girls without a large financial transaction. No insult to hardworking girls notwithstanding." When she emphasized the word *homosexual*, Piper blushed.

"I'm not here to insult you," Piper said, her face relaxing a bit but her cheeks staying pink. "You can deny it, but thanks."

Kendal nodded and laughed at Piper's bull-in-a-china-shop personality. Someone would eventually have an interesting but fulfilled and happy life because Piper chose to love them. "I'm no one's rich uncle, Miss Marmande. But if it makes you feel better, you're welcome, even if your gratitude isn't necessary. You get to keep something that's important to you, and I'm glad because I know it's as much a part of you as your grandparents." She slapped her thighs before standing up and starting for the house. Piper and Mac might not have been part of her plan, but playtime was over. "If that's all, I really have to get going."

In reality, the gift that was to Piper the fortune she needed for a fresh start didn't add up to much, considering what Kendal was worth. Giving it had made her expect something more from Piper than a thank-you, with no strings attached. She wasn't confused or in denial about Piper's sexual interest, but something about Piper made her crave to be a part of her life.

"Can I ask why? I haven't exactly been on my best behavior every time we talk," Piper said, stopping her.

"It wasn't me. I can't put it any more simply," she said after turning around. Piper couldn't make her admit otherwise, since she had given her the money not only to keep the shipyard, but to keep her safe. Now that the crisis was over, Piper could go to work on her expansion plans, making her happy and, more important, keeping her off Henri's radar.

"If hypothetically you did help us," Piper persisted, "why'd you do it?"

She had to laugh and walk back to stand closer to Piper. "Perhaps you should consider a career in interrogation since you don't give up easily. Hypothetically, huh?" she asked, making Piper nod. "I'd consider playing your money fairy because you remind me of someone I used to know. Like you, she was beautiful, had a joy for life, and cared for others more than for herself. She was incredibly special, and I'm sure she would've been disappointed in me for not helping you." She paused and bent closer. "Hypothetically speaking, of course." She smiled since Piper's face got cherry red again when she'd said she was beautiful.

"Who is she to you?"

"The proper tense here is, who *was* she to me." It still stung to refer to Angelina as part of her past. "It's not important, so good luck to you and Mr. Marmande. Your business is simply that—yours, so enjoy your fresh start without any worry. You don't owe anyone anything for this, especially me. I give you my word," she said, ignoring Piper's question.

"But—" Piper stopped when Kendal raised her hand.

"There's nothing else to say but good-bye," she said, turning around and starting for the house. This time nothing Piper did would stop her. Henri was her priority now, so this would be the last time she'd see Piper. Before she got too far away, she turned around, finding Piper rooted in place, the slight breeze blowing her hair from her shoulders.

"Henri, if you'd picked her instead of Veronica, your strategy might've worked," she thought. Piper and Angelina were vastly different, even in their looks, now that she'd had the opportunity to spend time with Piper to compare. But those last days with Angelina would've been just that, even if Henri hadn't arrived. She would've come to her senses before revealing the secret of Jacques and let Angelina go. Piper, had she been willing, would've muddled her senses until she died in her arms years from now.

Piper Marmande wasn't a woman you walked away from, and she certainly wasn't one you forgot, but that's exactly what she planned to do.

❖

"Does anything in Richoux's past mention a girl who left her hanging somewhere along the line?" Piper asked. Hill looked at her like she'd lost her mind.

"Do you really not read anything I send when you have me investigate someone? Nothing, nothing tells me anything about her aside from her accomplishments in school, then as the head of the company she founded. She doesn't give interviews about business, much less about her personal life."

"Hill, this accomplished but extremely private businesswoman you know nothing about just gave me millions of dollars, and she doesn't want to admit it. She also doesn't want to look at me, much less tell me what she wants in return, so call me stupid, but I have a burning desire to know."

"You're stupid."

"What did you say?" She scanned Hill's desk for something heavy to throw at her.

"I called you stupid," Hill said again, obviously oblivious to any threat. "If she gave you the money, saved your ass, and doesn't want anything in return, what exactly is the downside?"

"You ever heard of a balloon payment? We're cruising along building boats, and whammo, Ms. I Want My Money Back comes waltzing along and we're screwed. You don't have anything to tell me, aside from thinking I'm an idiot?" In her gut she knew that would never happen, but Kendal wasn't getting off that easy.

She had a short window of opportunity to find out who Kendal really was before she disappeared. Once she was gone, no matter how much Hill dug, Piper would never find her. She'd have the shipyard, but nothing else. Remembering Kendal's face when she'd turned around and looked at her made that possibility unacceptable.

"You're not an idiot, you're stupid." Hill dropped her eyes to her lap. "Though I didn't tell you something about the day I followed her to the church."

"Now, Hill, I need to know now."

"The nun told me about this painting. The church that's there now is the second St. Louis Cathedral, but Jacques St. Louis mainly put the deal together and paid for the original."

Piper sat up in her chair. "The original owner of Oakgrove?"

"One and the same."

"What does that have to do with anything? I love history, Hill, but this isn't the time."

Hill rolled her eyes, so Piper closed her mouth. "The church must've commissioned a painting to mark the occasion or to chronicle the history of who was involved. That's what I was looking at the other day. It's a picture of Mr. St. Louis with the holy men who I guess were going to staff the place, other dignitaries involved, and a woman."

"Who was the woman?" Piper asked, again cruising the desk in case she needed to prod Hill into talking faster.

"I had to dig a little, but I finally found her portrait in the archives of the newspaper back then. At the time Tomas du'Pon, a guy who never married and had three brothers, owned and operated the *New Orleans Gazette*. One of his brothers, along with his wife, died in an epidemic, and Tomas was left to raise their only child, a girl named Angelina." Hill stopped and stared at her until she waved her on, impatient to hear the rest. "The girl in the portrait standing next to Jacques was Angelina du'Pon."

"What's so spectacular about that story that you just wasted ten minutes of my time telling me?"

"Okay, that's it." Hill jumped up, grabbed her by the arm, dragged her outside to her car, and shoved her into the passenger seat. They drove in silence to the church, where Hill grabbed her again and pulled her to the door of the rectory offices.

"Can I help you?" A young man in long priest's robes opened the door, then folded his hands in front of him.

"We're sorry to bother you, Father, but I was here the other day and one of the sisters showed me a painting hanging in the foyer. Would you allow me to show it to my friend?"

"Of course, come in." He waved them in and closed the heavy oak door behind them. A painting of the Last Supper hung there. "It's spectacular, isn't it? We just recently acquired it through a private donation."

"It's lovely, Father, but we were interested in seeing the painting that was here before," Hill said.

"I know the one you're referring to, and I'm sorry, but that's not possible."

"What, you want a donation or something?" Piper asked, about to flick Hill in the back of the head for dragging her down there, but now the priest was acting a little suspicious.

"No, ma'am, we sent the painting back to the original owner, or should I say the family who owns it. It only hung here on loan. It's a shame they didn't donate it or allow us to replicate it, but that's their wish." The priest smiled and folded his hands together again. "Can I help you with anything else?"

"Father, do you know much of the history of some of the church's more prominent parishioners?" Hill asked.

"Some, why do you ask?"

"Can you tell us anything about the du'Pon family or, more specifically, Angelina du'Pon?"

"That's easy. The Angelina du'Pon trust, set up shortly after the original church was built, funds a majority of the children's programs the church administers in this area. She's buried in St. Louis cemetery number one, though no reason for death was ever listed with the church." He closed his eyes as if trying to remember anything else of importance. "There's another perpetual fund set up to care for her tomb and place fresh flowers there every week."

"For hundreds of years?" Piper asked in disbelief.

"Yes, I'm a man of the cloth, but I've always thought it rather romantic to remember a loved one so long."

Hill squeezed her hand and made a motion for her to be quiet. "Who set up the trusts?"

"Her fiancé, the Marquis Jacques St. Louis. He left the city shortly after her death and was never heard of again. Some say he died of a broken heart, but he was most generous with us even in his absence." The young priest pointed to the door. "I have to return to my studies, if that's all."

"One last thing, Father. Who's the current St. Louis heir in charge of the trust?" Piper asked, the wild-goose chase Hill had involved her in making her forget her worry over the business. Suddenly it was crucial to know. If she wanted to keep Kendal close enough to build a friendship, the path to her was through the past.

"I'm sorry, I can't give out that information. They asked to remain anonymous. In these times the church must respect the wishes of whoever's willing to believe in our cause. I can only tell you that the money for everything Angelina's memory pays for goes strictly to the welfare of children, since they were supposedly Angelina's greatest joy, and the current heir carries on that commitment."

"So she and Jacques had children?" she asked.

"No, ma'am, they never married. Miss du'Pon died before they were able to exchange vows, so I assume Jacques St. Louis went on to have children. An heir has always carried on the family business since his death. Whoever that young woman was, she must've been very understanding to compete with the memory of Angelina's ghost. Jacques St. Louis's devotion affirms my belief in the afterlife. Maybe in their next life they had better fortune and were able to be together."

"Thank you, Father, you've been a big help." Hill motioned for Piper to follow her out. "What I'm about to tell you sounds crazy, but something was strange about that painting. I stared at it for ten minutes and still couldn't believe what I was looking at."

"Tell me already," Piper said, through clenched teeth.

"Jacques St. Louis was the spitting image of Kendal Richoux, and the woman standing next to him looked just like you."

Two things flew through Piper's mind, stopping her from telling Hill she was crazy. The day they met, Kendal had turned pale, as if she'd seen a ghost. Also, just that afternoon Kendal had said Piper reminded her of someone she knew. That was impossible, though. They weren't talking ten years ago. It had been almost three hundred years since Angelina and her boyfriend, Jacques, walked the city. "It can't be," she said, but her heart knew that's where the truth lay.

"I agree, but I'm telling you, Piper, the two were dead ringers for both of you. Emphasis on the dead part." Hill stared at Piper's forehead; she'd started sweating. "Are you okay? You want me to drive you home?"

"Hill, do you think Kendal is the current St. Louis heir?"

"Yes, but why would she want the painting back? Do you think one of the penguins told her someone was here looking at it?" Piper smiled at her description of the nun. "What difference would it make if anyone knew she was the current St. Louis heir?"

If Kendal was the current heir, her story of the miraculous Richoux success story would be a lie, Piper thought, not ready to share that possibility with Hill. "I admit I didn't read your report, so give me a break before I ask. Did it mention anything about family?"

Hill laughed at her honesty. "Nothing, why?"

"She told me the other night that she wasn't interested in Marmande anymore and was still in town on family business. I'm wondering who the family and business are."

"Why do you care?" Hill asked, getting up and offering her a hand. "You have control of the company again, and Kendal doesn't want anything else to do with you."

"I don't care," she said, even if it was a lie.

Why was Kendal walking the grounds and living at Oakgrove like she owned the place? Granted, Piper was more curious about why Kendal had helped her, but Oakgrove and its history had always fascinated her. Rumors of the original owner eventually became legends and ghost stories, but the history books weren't clear as to what had happened to Jacques St. Louis and all his slaves.

The official story was that the sheriff of the territory rode out to Oakgrove and found the place deserted. It was as if the slaves and the owner had never existed. They'd walked into the mist, leaving everything behind, but no matter how many years passed or events like the Civil War took place, nothing ever touched Oakgrove's property. It had all stayed intact, a vault that held the St. Louis family secrets, and very few possessed the key to unlocking it.

Perhaps the current heir knew the story, but Kendal was her own mystery, and the shark Piper had read about didn't compute with the image of Kendal crying on the bench that afternoon. Something haunted Kendal, and Piper wanted to know what it was.

CHAPTER SEVENTEEN

Do you think we're getting closer to the end?" Charlie asked. They were sitting on the rooftop of Pat O'Brien's, the famous bar, waiting for the next group of vampires to appear, since they had apparently declared the French Quarter their battleground. Their last fight had taken all of Kendal's skill and Charlie's help—the opponents were getting better.

"When we encounter the ones carrying the same weapons as ours, we're getting closer to the head slimeball. All these others who think their kung fu moves will make a difference are just bait." She peered down at the street and wondered if they could get away with what she had planned next. "Ready?" she asked, quickly descending the gutter pipe to the crowded street.

"Warrior, I am Troy," said the man she'd spotted as he pulled his blade from the sheath strapped to his back. The five Troy had with him followed his lead, laughing when the crowd dispersed, but remained nearby.

"Please, call me Redemption," she joked, twirling her sword slowly in one hand. In the other was a knife she had pulled from her boot.

"Why?" asked one of the fighters with Troy.

She moved forward a little, giving Charlie room to land to the applause of the crowd, which now thought it was a street performance. "What, Henri doesn't give you time to watch television? I'd contact my union rep about that. You need to have time to watch televangelists between all the killing and mayhem. They'll tell you to accept Jesus Christ because eternal life is only possible through redemption. That's me, and I want your soul."

"Kill her," Troy screamed.

Three of his men rushed forward, and sparks flew from their weapons when they clashed with her. "Watch my back, Charlie. These creeps have been practicing."

Everyone stared in awe as her katana met the other three swords stroke for stroke, driving them down one of the side streets. With one kick to the side of the shortest one's head, she sent his blade clattering.

When most of the audience clapped, she smiled before running up the brick wall of a building close by and flipping over two of the vampires' heads, landing in the middle of them. "Now you see them, and now you don't." The blade of the katana sliced through the one who was armed, and she threw the knife into the chest of the one who wasn't. When the oblivious crowd started clapping again, she took a bow after they turned to dust.

It was approaching midnight when the other two moved forward, Troy hanging back to observe. She took a short axe off her belt and stood waiting as the taller one twirled his sword in precision moves, as if trying to impress her. With no theatrics, she threw her axe and his exercise ended, his weapon dropping to the street. "Good form, but fancy sword tricks won't get it done, Troy," she said, keeping an eye on the guy standing between her and Troy, holding his sword still with both hands.

He suddenly dropped it and starting running, only to meet the same fate at the end of the other axe when she threw it with deadly aim. Because of the crowd, she followed the weapon's path to make sure it had hit its mark.

"Kendal, turn around," Charlie yelled, but before she could, Troy's sword sliced completely through her chest. The instant pain dropped her to her knees. His aim had punctured a lung and nicked her heart. She felt Troy yank a bit, like he was pulling it out to stab her again, when the crowd applauded again. The movement had stopped and she could still see the end sticking out of her chest, but she was getting weaker by the second. Had it not been for the elixir, her fight would've ended before the sword made it all the way through.

"I got him," Charlie said, kneeling next to her.

"Could you do me a favor?"

"Move faster next time?"

"There's that, yeah, but I was thinking more about you pulling this goddamn thing out of my chest so I can beat you with it." She laughed up at his concerned face. "If I've told you once, I've told you a thousand times, this hurts like a bitch."

A mounted policeman rode up and looked down at the bloodstain growing along her shirt. "Are you all right, lady?"

She stood on shaky legs and nodded, borrowing Piper's expression, "Just peachy." She sheathed the katana and accepted Charlie's help to get to her feet. "How'd you like the show? We thought we'd try a dry run out here before moving into the theater down the street."

"The disappearing acts could've been better, and the blood on your shirt is too dark looking to be real."

"Well, it's really old," she said with a smile. She took the axes back from Charlie before accepting his help back to the car. "Everyone's a critic, I swear."

"You're not still beating yourself up, are you, Charlie?" Kendal asked. She had been silent during the drive, reviewing that last fight. Something about the way some of the demons fought had nothing to do with Henri and his training. Their skill level was much more advanced, and the style wasn't the straightforward technique the younger ones had displayed, simply trying to overpower their opponent. These guys showed more finesse, which spoke of experience with the blade.

Charlie had been driving the speed limit since she didn't want to get pulled over and have to explain the bloody mess. She was in no danger of dying, but she wouldn't fight again until the sun came up and brought back her full strength.

"I'm turning out to be more of an anchor to you than anything else. You should start going out alone and leave me behind," Charlie said, finally breaking his silence.

"You took care of the big guy, or did the audience participate more than I realized?"

He put the vehicle in park and smiled at her. "No, that was me, and stop trying to make me feel better. I didn't get to you before he stabbed you."

"Time will make you better, but you're with me because I want you here. Would you like to wait until I'm done? I don't want to pressure you into something you'd rather not do."

The night was starting to fade with the coming of dawn, and he looked out toward the east. "If you don't mind, I want to be there for you, but mostly for Celia and my sons. They deserve for me to try to kill the bastard who did that to them. I'm sorry he's your brother, but I want nothing more than to kill him."

"I know how you feel. Have I ever told you who Henri or Abez's first kill was all those years ago when he became what he is?"

"Trust me, I remember all our talks having to do with him. You never told me much more than what he is."

She moved her hand from her chest and put it on his shoulder. "It was my father."

"Did you share the same parents?" Charlie looked at the steering column in shock.

"Yes, but that didn't stop him from killing the man who'd raised and taken care of him even as an adult when he came home drunk and broke, expecting to be bailed out again. I wasn't there, but I can imagine the betrayal my father must have felt as Abez drained him. Like you, it's what made me accept Morgaine's offer of eternal life."

He looked up at her in dismay. "You thought about not taking it?"

She studied her chest wound, which still bled freely. The blow would have killed her seconds after Troy inflicted it if she hadn't accepted the elixir more than three thousand years ago. "I didn't want to live forever. I wanted to serve my pharaoh, then find a woman to share my life with. Back then if you believed strongly enough, the gods would provide all that I could not, like children."

"But to never worry about death…"

She laughed. "Is replaced by the worry of living forever. Your family was different, Lionel. You watched them die and you wanted revenge, so I gave you the means to see it through. No one was left when I returned from battle; Abez's hunger and vengeance took them all. At first when I saw what he'd done, I wanted to join them in the valley of the dead, but instead I chose my honor and duty. My father would have expected me to destroy Henri and creatures like him, so I followed Morgaine into the desert willingly."

"Let's get you out of here to wait for the sunrise."

Her hand left a smear of blood along the door when she leaned on it to climb out of the car. She barely had the strength to stay on her feet. The purple of the night sky was turning pink behind the house, and she started walking slowly to one of the lawn chairs to sit and wait. It wouldn't take long for the healing to begin once the first rays of light appeared.

Behind them, an unexpected visitor announced herself by retching. When Kendal turned around, she sighed, watching Piper hold her stomach as if trying not to throw up again at the sight of all the blood she'd left in the car. She nodded when Charlie hiked his eyebrows in question.

"May I help you with something, Miss Marmande?" he asked while Kendal headed to the back of the house, leaving him to deal with Piper.

"I want to call an ambulance if you aren't going to."

"What do we need an ambulance for?"

"For the idiot bleeding profusely behind you," Piper said, making Kendal laugh at the insult. "Who's doing a good job of ignoring me, by the way." Piper raised her voice so Kendal would be able to hear her, even though she'd almost reached the chair.

"It's just a scratch, Miss Marmande, but I'm sure Kendal would feel better if you left her to rest and recover. I'll be happy to walk you out to the gate so you won't trip in the dark."

"I'm not leaving until I talk to her."

"Or I could carry you and deposit you on the road, your choice," Charlie said, making Kendal stop to hear Piper's answer. She turned around when she heard Piper scream, surprised she'd almost reached her before Charlie caught her. Piper continued yelling all the way to the entrance as Charlie carried her over his shoulder like one of the bales of cotton he'd lugged here long before. Every time she was able to land a fist on his back, she seemed to get angrier when he laughed. Even though the gate was some distance away, she heard the squeak when Charlie opened the small entryway.

"Have a good day, Miss Marmande," Charlie said, and Kendal relaxed and closed her eyes now that the area grew peaceful again.

"You'll be having a great day too when I come back with the police," Piper screamed at him.

A few hours later Kendal didn't get up when the sheriff's deputy climbed out of his cruiser. He'd arrived unannounced since she'd made Charlie open the main gates to show they had nothing to hide.

"Good morning, ma'am. Sorry to bother you, but could I have a word?" the deputy asked. She was sitting at the table on the porch eating a huge stack of waffles with syrup. Next to the plate sat another one with eggs and a rare steak. Not that she needed the food to repair the wounds, but eating the large breakfast that had followed Lola's old recipes made her feel better, and she gave in to the cook's wishes to feed her.

"Is there a problem?"

"Miss Marmande here—"

"If that's your problem, I can't help you. Annoyance isn't illegal. It just makes her a pain in the ass," Kendal said, pointing her fork at Piper, who stood with her fists on her hips after getting out of the passenger side.

He put his hand over his mouth to disguise his laugh. "I apologize for the bother, but Miss Marmande swears she was here this morning and you were knocking on death's door from an injury to your chest. Seems you were bleeding pretty badly, so again, I'm sorry, but we have to follow up on her report."

"I spilled a V8 in the car, but I can assure you I wasn't bleeding."

"V8, my ass," Piper said in a frustrated voice, taking the steps two at a time, then stopping next to her. "Stand up right now." Kendal's chair legs scraped the wood floor when she pushed away from the table to do as Piper asked. "Now we'll see who's lying."

Piper turned her around so as not to expose her to the deputy and opened her robe.

"If you wanted to come to my house and see me naked, you didn't have to bring the police with you. Asking nicely would've done the trick."

"Um, in your dreams. I was just worried about you, but you seem perfectly healthy." Piper's eyes never stopped slowly moving up and down her body.

"Miss Marmande, is everything in order?" the deputy asked, coming a little closer.

"Yes, I'm sorry. I must have misunderstood. She's all right. Nothing out of place and no holes that shouldn't be here."

"Are you done?" Kendal asked, amused.

"Hmm?" Piper sounded distracted as she stared at her abdomen.

"The visual tour, are you done?"

"Of course," Piper said, but her fingers still gripped the thick cotton of the robe.

"Of course," Kendal repeated, closing the robe herself. She turned to the deputy still standing by the steps with his hand covering his mouth again and gave him a smile. "Would you care for some coffee, Officer?"

"No, ma'am, we won't take up any more of your time. Miss Marmande, you ready to go?"

"You can go ahead. I'll see that Miss Marmande gets home. After all, she hasn't checked out the back for suspicious puncture marks," she said, making Piper blush.

"Yes, ma'am, I'll leave you to that." The leather of his utility belt creaked as he got into the car, and as he closed the door he couldn't hold back the laughter anymore, making Piper turn a darker shade of red.

"Thank you for not subjecting me to his company all the way back to the sheriff's office, but you and I both know what I saw this morning. You were hurt, and that guy threw me out instead of letting me call for help."

She pulled a chair out for Piper and put her hand on her shoulder to get her to sit in it. "I'm flattered that you were worried about me, but, as you saw, I'm fine. If I didn't know better I'd say you were stalking me."

"You must have gotten an A+ in your self-esteem class. Why in the world would I stalk you?" Piper watched as she poured her a cup of coffee and mixed it with the right amounts of sugar and cream. "I don't even like you all that much, remember?"

"At the risk of my sanity, why were you here at the crack of dawn?" She motioned for the young man at the front door to bring out the plate he was holding. "I ask because, for someone who doesn't like me all that much, you spend inordinate amounts of time trying to see me."

"You interest me. Is that a crime?"

"Interest you how?"

The red streaks of a blush ran up Piper's face again, and she tried to hide behind her coffee cup. "Not like that," she whispered, apparently so the server wouldn't overhear.

"Shall I call Charlie to carry her out again, sire?" the man said in Japanese.

"Let's wait on that. If worse comes to worst I'll carry her out myself." Kendal acknowledged his bowed head, then pointed to Piper's plate. "You should try them while they're hot. They're pecan hotcakes, an old family recipe."

"Whose family?"

"The St. Louis family, I would imagine." She buttered the stack and poured cane syrup over them so Piper would start eating. They weren't quite as good as Lola's, but the new chef had come close. "Shall I cut them up and feed them to you as well?"

"How are you related to the St. Louis family?" Piper asked, picking up her fork.

"I'm more like a family caretaker than a relative, and you haven't answered my question as to why you were here this morning."

"We'll get to that, but can you tell me about Jacques St. Louis and the woman he was going to marry, Angelina?"

Kendal ran the final piece of hotcake around her own plate to pick up the last of the syrup she had poured over them and chewed slowly, trying to avoid this conversation with Piper without making her crazy by putting her off. "What makes you think I'd have any of that history in my head, Miss Marmande?"

"Can I ask you something?" Kendal nodded. "Why do you call me Miss Marmande but call Hill Ms. Hickman?"

"You don't look like a Ms. to me, and it's impolite, according to old Southern tradition, to address you that way."

"Kendal, if I asked you to, would you call me Piper?" The question came out in a tired voice, and Piper's shoulders almost slumped.

"I would be happy to." Kendal pushed Piper's plate closer, cut one small piece, and held it up to her mouth.

One taste encouraged Piper to finish the plate, so Kendal enjoyed the silence that surrounded them. The only breaks came when she addressed or answered questions from her staff in whatever language they felt comfortable speaking.

"Would you excuse me for a moment? I'll run up and throw some clothes on and drive you home, if you like."

"What would you be doing if I hadn't barged in on you with a police escort? I could call someone to give me a ride if you had plans."

"I was going for a ride, but I'm sure Ruda won't mind waiting until this afternoon since I have all the time in the world." She stood up and cinched the belt on her robe tighter. "You're free to do whatever will make you more comfortable, like calling someone else to drive you, but I really don't mind." Piper nodded and smiled.

"All set?" she asked a few minutes later, now dressed.

"Will you take me riding?" Piper leaned forward in her chair in a way that made Kendal think she was ready to debate the issue until she gave in.

"You like to ride?"

"No, but I thought I could ride with you."

"That would require you to get really close to me."

"I want to get on a horse with you, Kendal, not do the nasty. Come on, I have a rare morning off since I thought I'd be driving you to the hospital, and you still haven't answered all my questions."

"I'd love to."

They walked to the stables with Piper looking around like she was trying to commit the grounds to memory in case this was her only opportunity on this side of the fence. Inside above the wide doors of the barn hung the St. Louis family crest Kendal had had made of copper years before. Charlie had relocated there from the house. Fixing and rearranging things around the property had kept him sane, she guessed, and some of his improvements such as the tile floors in the barn showed his growing craftsmanship.

Ruda had been brushed and stood in place clicking his heels and bobbing his head when he saw her. The stallion was a big boy, and Piper looked at Kendal with fear when she offered her a hand up after mounting. To make Piper feel more secure, Kendal placed her in front of her so she could hang on to her.

The gate opened for them as she led Ruda to the road, and Piper was clutching her forearms so tight, Kendal decided she would subject her only to a slow ride on the levee. She moved her arm to Piper's waist as the horse clopped up the incline.

"Do you have something against saddles?"

"This is better for the horse, less cumbersome. Just relax and go with him."

"Will you tell me about this place?" Piper squeezed her arm. "You didn't say you didn't know."

"Very perceptive of you, Piper. What do you want to hear?"

"How did Oakgrove come to be?"

New Orleans, Spring 1721

Jacques stepped off the boat and looked around the busy port. Most of the moored vessels flew French colors, a good number of Spanish, and a sprinkling of others. Here among the pirates and settlers would be a good place to hide for a while and forget her responsibilities. She also craved to work for something that wasn't born out of the privilege she'd known in France. Once her cover was secure, she could start searching for Abez, or Henri, as he called himself now.

"Carry your bags, monsieur?" asked one of the small boys hanging around looking for spare change.

It was a short carriage ride to the hotel, and one gold piece later she was walking with her new friend toward the stables. "Don't you want to sleep, monsieur? That was a long voyage you just finished."

"Sleep is for those who have time for it." She patted his head and sent him back to the docks with his earned loot, glad that her disguise fooled at least a boy.

After a quick negotiation Jacques St. Louis bought his first new horse and rode out of town. On the way she passed the main auction blocks, where most had lost their minds to greed and inhumanity. She would deal with that issue later, since she wasn't interested in anything now but being alone with her thoughts. Places like Paris and New Orleans were filled with the types of people she wanted to escape, so the countryside bordering the river was ideal.

She rode at a good clip until the sun went down, stopping at a general store with a stable where she spent the night to give the horse a break. The next morning she came to a clearing where the sun made the leaves on the new oak trees glimmer like they were wet. Immediately, she envisioned building a house there and making it her home.

Two weeks later she owned all the land that stretched from a large bayou to the north all the way to the river, plus the large lake at its center. During that trip to New Orleans to negotiate the land purchase, she'd also come back with Lola, her son Joseph, and Lionel to start building. The main house took a year, since that was all they worked on, and with Lola's help, she returned frequently with more haggard people from the auction block and any of their relatives being sold that day.

Alone she couldn't do away with the trade, but with Lola there talking to the ones who understood her as they came off the boats, they at least had the comfort of keeping together the family who'd survived the trip. Some, like Lionel, were highly suspicious of her at first, but after a few trips to town and seeing the whip scars across some of the men's backs, he grew to trust her and gladly helped her and Lola add to their numbers.

By the time she and Lionel had come back from France and she met Angelina, Oakgrove was one of the largest and most profitable plantations in the South. And it was the only one in Louisiana where the farm's cook, Lola, used the bedroom reserved for the lady of the house, with Jacques's blessing.

New Orleans, present day

Kendal stopped Ruda and looked back in the direction of the house. The trees had grown, but the levee made it possible to still see the roofline. It looked so different than the first morning she'd stopped here, but she still felt the same. Oakgrove had been the first house she'd built from nothing. All the other estates had been someone else's dream first, but not Oakgrove.

"The family history says that Jacques St. Louis stopped here one morning, seeing the potential others didn't. Back then, the trees were smaller and there was no levee or road."

Piper completely relaxed against her as she spoke. "It sounds like he was a man driven by what he wanted," Piper said, moving slightly so she could turn around and look at her. "It seems to still be a dominant trait in his gene pool."

Kendal smiled at Piper's compliment and pointed to the house. "It took him only two weeks to purchase, rather cheaply, I understand, all the land now surrounded by the fences erected much later."

"Was it all farmland?" Piper asked, turning around again so she could recline against her.

"Most of it, but some was left untouched for hunting." Kendal pointed out the area with the largest trees and densest vegetation. "From the stories I've read, he purchased close to a thousand slaves, who helped him farm the land and erect the buildings you see."

"What happened to them? I've read everything I could about this place, but because an extremely private family still owns it, no one knows for sure."

"Are you asking because you plan to write your own book?" she asked, teasing.

"No. I can keep a secret." Piper slapped her arm.

Kendal turned Ruda around so they could look out over the Mississippi. "After a tragic loss, the land and the house lost their appeal, so Jacques left for Europe but couldn't stand parting with a place he'd come to love."

"Do you mean after Angelina du'Pon died?" Piper asked, surprising her that she would've known the name.

"Yes, after Angelina and her uncle Tomas were killed, the dream of this place seemed to die with them."

"What about the slaves he owned? The official record states the sheriff found no one when he arrived with his men a short time after Angelina died."

"You really have read everything there is about the place," Kendal said and laughed. "Jacques bought them off the auction blocks, but once they came to live here, the shackles were taken off and melted for farming tools. In his mind they were forever free and a part of his family. When he left, he let them all choose where to go."

"How'd he move that many people that fast?"

"Jacques St. Louis was a resourceful man with plenty of friends who made their living at sea flying the Jolly Roger. With their help, he had boats brought here that sailed out in the afternoon, so they passed through New Orleans in the dead of night headed for Cuba, where his friends awaited his arrival."

Kendal stared at the water, remembering arriving in Cuba and offering to take them home, if that was what they desired, so they could reunite with the families the slavers had stolen them from. After a night to think about it, the entire small fleet she'd hired in Cuba followed her to England, where they adapted well to country life, learning to farm and herd in a vastly different climate. Their disappearance, accomplished so quickly, helped keep the plantation intact when the stories of evil deeds and curses spread like wildfire. Only Lionel stayed behind to maintain the land and buildings, having free run of everything. The cabin he'd shared with his family had been his home ever since.

"What an honorable man."

"He was someone who tried to do the right thing in evil times."

"True, and he would be proud to see that too still runs in his bloodline."

"I'm a thief, Miss Marmande, you said so yourself on more than one occasion. There's nothing honorable about that."

"There's another old Southern tradition you forget," Piper said, smiling. "A woman has the right to change her mind if she wants to."

"I must be losing my touch if you're starting to like me."

"Oh, the shame of it all," Piper said in her best Southern-belle accent and laughed.

It felt like sunshine to Kendal. Her laugh sounded so much like Angelina's, but in reality, when Piper relaxed and let down her defenses, she was much more beautiful than Angelina on her best day. Because of that, Kendal felt the need to raise her own walls to protect her heart. She couldn't bear to lose herself again; her vulnerability had come close to ruining her the last time. Piper wasn't Angelina, but Kendal could easily fall for those green eyes if she allowed herself.

CHAPTER EIGHTEEN

"Did you have a nice ride?" Charlie's question clicked through the intercom in Kendal's helmet and she glanced at him briefly.

"It's not over, as far as I can tell."

"Not this ride, and don't try and change the subject." He dropped his foot down as they reached the light at the bottom of the on-ramp to the interstate. "I saw how cozy that girl was up there with you."

"Clear that cozy girl from your mind before we get any closer to the city. I won't be responsible for the loss of any more innocents, and Piper Marmande's perfectly capable of taking care of herself from here on out. Don't count on seeing her again."

"Who are you trying to convince, you or me?"

"Drop it, Charles, she's history." She took off in a roar.

They headed to the French Quarter, stopping near the St. Louis cemeteries. When Charlie opened his mouth to speak, she put her finger to her lips. The sun was dropping below the horizon, and the church employees had padlocked the gates to keep vagrants out.

She took a running leap and landed on top of the brick wall surrounding the place. It amused some who visited the city from places where people were buried in the ground and marked by a small stone or cross to see the elaborate silent cities the people of southern Louisiana erected to their dead, but they had their reasons. When the first settlers from France disembarked their boats, they insisted on continuing the traditions they'd practiced in their homeland for generations, and burying their loved ones was no different.

After the first wave of sick and old died, the loved ones placed them in the dark soil of the delta in their pine boxes and prayed over them. But when the first rains of spring and summer came, they popped out the ground like macabre fish corks and floated down the city streets. No matter how much weight was put over or in the coffins, rain caused them to float to the top, breaking through the dirt. After a couple of years of chasing bones down the alleyways of New Orleans, the citizens built fences around cemeteries to hem them in and began to construct tombs.

Kendal jumped again and landed on one of the taller mausoleums in St. Louis number one, which allowed her to see any movement in both cemeteries. The grave belonged to one of the older families in New Orleans, and generations of remains were probably stacked inside. At the top of the marble structure, a large cement angel lifted her arms to the heavens as if in awe of God. Her flowing robes cast a deep shadow and made an excellent hiding place, but Charlie, who had joined her, looked as if he didn't know from what.

Kendal pressed her fingers to her lips, then pointed to her eyes and ears, motioning for him to watch and listen. Once the sky had turned dark and it was truly night, in less than twenty minutes they heard the first scraping of stone. She pressed her hand to Charlie's knee. Those who hid in cemeteries, especially those under the protection and blessing of the church, were the old ones who didn't respect what they called the superstition of organized religion and did everything to defy the Elders of the Genesis Clan. It took the best of their shamans to keep them under control.

These vampires were made before Jesus walked the earth spreading his message of salvation. But sometimes evil was just as capable of believing the diatribe of the church as its most faithful. Many young ones stayed away from the holy places, thinking the power of God would drive them into hell. The old ones knew better. Only warriors like Kendal had that power, and they were very real.

A tall bald man took the time to close the iron gate behind him as he stepped out to the walk circling the tombs in that section of the cemetery. He straightened his coat, which resembled Kendal's. The pommel of his sword was visible for only a second as he whirled and lifted his nose to the air.

"What is it, Wadham?" asked a thin man who had emerged from a grave topped by two small stone cherubs.

"A unique scent in the air. It almost makes me want to feed."

"We have no time for that. We must attend to the master's wishes."

"Don't worry, Jonas, I know my duties."

She watched them leave with incredible speed, joined by six others before the graveyard went silent.

"Who were those guys? They look different somehow," Charlie said.

"Just remember the names, because they *are* different, and I can think of only one place where we can find out why."

They left the bikes parked, and Charlie followed Kendal into the streets at the back of the Quarter. On Bourbon, an invisible line indicated the gay bars and establishments.

"Come on, Toto, you aren't in Kansas anymore, so watch your ass," she told Charlie, laughing as they entered a place called Oz. The music was blaring so loud the floor vibrated, and the dance floor barely had room for one more person.

"Why, are vampires in here?" Charlie yelled to be heard.

"Not the blood-sucking kind. I'm only warning you, since I think you look divine in those pants and so will every guy in here." Kendal had barely finished when a cute guy wearing leather palmed Charlie's butt and winked at him. She laughed and kept walking toward the bar.

❖

"Tell me why we're here again?" Hill asked Piper.

"I felt like having a beer," Piper answered, watching Kendal navigate the crowd. Kendal seemed to have a multitude of personalities, and this one was the most intriguing yet.

"You felt like having a beer? Okay, tell me why we're having a beer here?"

"Because I wanted to see what the fuss was about."

"Fuss?" Hill moved closer to her.

"Nature gave us certain parts, so why would you want to mess with that? Take you, for instance. Don't you ever wonder what it's like to have a guy who knows what he's doing show you what sex is all about?" Piper took a sip of her beer, watching two women dance together. She and Hill were sitting in the back corner away from the large speakers, so conversation wasn't impossible, but they still had a good view of the whole room.

"I'll answer that question if you answer one for me first." Hill snapped her fingers to get her attention.

"What?"

"How many men have you slept with who know what they're doing, and I mean in every category?"

"Category?"

"Oral and body-part utilization, as you put it."

"Some."

"I see. Well, I can tell you I've never met a woman who hasn't been able to satisfy every need I have, and I mean every need, without fail. You find the idea repugnant, but you have no point of reference as to why. You should try it first before you make any sweeping statements."

Piper looked away from Kendal and frowned at Hill. "I do not find it repugnant, I just don't get it. There's a difference. Nothing about women gets my motor running, so to speak. I mean, I can appreciate the female form, but I also admire pretty dogs. That doesn't mean I want to sleep with one." The label on the beer bottle finally lost the battle to her picking, and she crumpled it into a small ball. "Does that make me a bad person?"

"You're just honest, Piper. Nothing's wrong with that, but it still doesn't explain why we're here. We could find a more subdued place where folks of the same gender go to have a drink and hold hands, if you wanted to conduct a case study. This is the other end of the spectrum."

Piper waved her hand toward the dance floor before she opened her mouth. "It just seemed primal. These people left any inhibitions they even thought of having at home."

"What's that supposed to mean?"

"That they're having a good time and not ashamed to show it. Don't get your boxers in a twist. I'm looking, but it still doesn't make sense to me."

"Maybe you're looking in the wrong direction," Hill said, smiling and pointing.

"What?" Piper followed Hill's finger to the crowded bar where Kendal and her friend stood.

It should be a sin to always look that good, she thought as she slowly gazed at Kendal from head to boot. She sported a long leather coat, leather pants, and a pair of black biker boots. Her hair, as always, was pulled back and held in place with what looked from here to be a silk ribbon, which was the only soft thing about Kendal's outfit and attitude.

❖

"Why are we here?" Charlie asked, still having to shout.

"To see a woman about some history."

"You lost me." Charlie slid a twenty across the bar for the two drinks he'd ordered, handing her one.

"Everyone gets to do what they want as long as it's legal, Charlie. The woman who owns this place wanted to try her hand at being a club owner in this particular lifetime."

"She's one of us?" She nodded and took a sip of the cold vodka. "Why didn't you tell me?"

"You never asked and you rarely leave the grounds. See what you'd find if you were a little more adventurous and gave up your antisocial tendencies?"

A young Asian woman pouring drinks behind the bar looked over and made eye contact. She wiped her hands as a huge smile emerged and motioned for one of the servers to take over. With a quick leap she landed on the bar and strolled the length of it until she was standing over Kendal. The bartender accepted the hand Kendal held up and slid down her body until they were closely pressed together. The kiss she gave her felt like an invitation for later, if she was interested.

"You shit, you didn't tell me you were in town. I had to hear it from Morgaine while she was here."

"I wanted to surprise you, and I need to see your teacher."

"Promise me a dance and I'll take you up myself."

"Deal, now let me introduce you to Charlie. Charlie, this is Kim. Kim, my dear friend Charlie." She let Kim go so they could shake hands. "Kim's training to be an Elder archivist."

"Your teacher works out of this place?" Charlie asked.

"What's wrong with that?" Kim asked, putting her arm around Kendal's waist and resting her head on her shoulder.

"Don't you think it's kind of loud?"

"The libraries that pertain to our needs are a bit different than those you're used to. My teacher likes to be reminded of why she works so hard to keep the history of civilization chronicled correctly. Here she can feel the energy of who we're fighting for."

"Gay people?" Charlie asked, confused.

"Okay, Rush Limbaugh, that's not what she meant." Kendal laughed.

"Please don't compare me to that windbag."

"Then stop looking at the world in black and white. Kim's saying that people who aren't afraid to live gather here almost every night to celebrate life and who they are. Who better to fight for and, as you may notice, they're not all gay." A few couples in the crowd with someone of the opposite sex were obviously there for the music and a good time.

"Come, Lenore will be happy to see you." Kim walked them to the stairs against one wall, keeping close to Kendal.

❖

"See, she gets it," Hill said as Piper followed their progress across the room. She stretched her fingers out, not realizing how hard she'd gripped her beer bottle when the bartender practically sucked Kendal's tonsils out.

"I see that Kendal Richoux's as easy as I thought she was. Are you ready to go?"

"No," Hill said, sitting back and kicking her feet out.

"Please come with me. I don't want to walk back to my car alone."

"I'm not staying because I want to pick up someone, Piper. I want to see who Kendal's here to see aside from the cutie behind the bar. I don't know how you figured out she'd be here but," Hill pointed to the door the three had disappeared behind on the second floor, "that's the office, and as many times as I've been here, I've never seen anyone come out of there even though the light is always on."

They sat and waited with their eyes on the door. Every so often Piper would glance at the dance floor and the people packed on it. Would she be as free to express herself if it were Kendal she was grinding against? Could Kendal change her mind-set? She'd felt like shit when Kendal returned the woman's greeting so enthusiastically. That afternoon she'd been on the receiving end of Kendal's total attention, and she'd rather enjoyed it.

❖

The bar's office was actually the entrance to the building next door, and the cavernously large room Kim led them to contained volumes of old books, most of them handwritten in a variety of old languages. To add a bit of modern technology, a bank of computers sat in the middle of the first floor. Shelves lined the walls on the first and second floors, and a grand open space in the middle let anyone who entered enjoy the glass ceiling with its view of the night sky.

Lenore sat next to the railing in a comfortable chair, a cup of hot tea on the table next to her and on her lap a book entitled simply *Ora*. Lenore sat with her legs crossed, wearing a man's shirt and a pair of old jeans. "Asra, welcome. I was wondering when you'd come calling."

Lenore had become an Elder long before Kendal met Morgaine, and in her original life she'd been the priestess of her tribe, with an amazing memory for events. The Clan found her skills perfect for keeping an accurate, unbiased account of world events and the people responsible for making them happen. She'd been in the beginning of her thirtieth year when she drank the elixir, forever preserving the beautiful delicate features her people had been known for.

"I'm sorry I didn't come sooner, Master," Kendal said, bowing over her hand and kissing it. She moved aside so Charlie could follow her example.

"Please, Asra, let's not stand on ceremony. We haven't the time. Why are you here?"

"Charlie and I've been busy for the last few nights fighting Henri's forces in the city."

Lenore nodded and motioned them all to sit in the chairs surrounding hers. "Kim's kept an eye on you and hasn't reported any problems. Have you encountered something you can't handle?"

"No, the ones we've faced so far haven't been difficult to destroy, but tonight we went to the graveyard looking for bigger fish and found what appeared to be some old vampires arising for the night. Two of them talked as they waited for their counterparts to wake."

"Wadham and Jonas," Charlie said

"Are you sure?" Lenore leaned forward as if she hadn't heard him correctly.

"Those were the names they used," Kendal said.

"The tall one called Wadham, was he carrying a sword?"

"A large broadsword with a golden pommel. I saw it for only a second, but it looked like a—" She stared at the page Lenore had turned to in the book on her lap.

"An asp with its mouth open ready to strike, and from what I've read, the workmanship of the fangs is quite extraordinary."

"Who is he?" Charlie asked.

"Wadham and Jonas are the equivalent of the Clan's Elders. They serve and protect Ora, their queen and mother to them all. You see, Charlie, while demons like Abez have the ability to create more like him, there had to be a first. That was Ora, a witch who lived decades before Asra was born." Lenore told Charlie about the illness that had swept through Ora's village, leaving her the sole survivor. "She attributed her power and longevity to the black magic she practiced in life. The true gift for that had put her in the Clan's sights long before the illness that changed her."

"I wonder how she figured out she could make others like her, Charlie said.

"No one's ever learned all her secrets, but drink from her and you live forever as well, but with the same thirst for death."

Kendal barely heard the history lesson, since she'd learned the same things years before, and so had Charlie, but Lenore's voice was almost hypnotic. Something that Lenore had said, though, made the hair at the base of her neck stand on end.

"If they serve Ora, what are they doing here?" She looked at Kim and Lenore to see if they would withhold information.

"Ora has hidden herself well from us for hundreds of years, leaving only those like Henri to carry out her work. You've done well in the past at keeping their numbers reasonable, Asra, and hopefully Charlie will join the ranks of our elite warriors after this fight ends."

"But..." Kendal prodded Lenore.

"But no matter how we've tried, we haven't been able to figure out what she's been up to or what she has planned. Maybe our luck is changing, though. If you've seen some of her most trusted advisors and protectors in the city, their master isn't too far away." Lenore flipped the page and showed them the two men they had seen earlier sitting at the feet of a beautiful woman with long, flowing red hair. "The three are never without each other."

"Sounds kinky," Kendal joked, making Kim laugh.

"Laugh now, but if she's here and guiding Henri, we're all in great danger. Ora's extremely powerful and will stop at nothing to dismantle the Genesis Clan by burying us one by one. She's not only powerful because of the years the sickness that created her has thrived in her, but because she's also a gifted witch. She's not like anything you've faced before."

"I'm a slayer and I know what I'm doing."

"The Elders have never sent you to hunt Ora because she's more than simply a vampire."

"Then we have to keep fighting to even the odds. Most of the time, the easiest way to kill the snake is to sever the head so the body will wither. To draw this bitch out, I'll have to do it in reverse. I'll hack the body to bits and the head will have no choice but to show itself and face me."

"Don't try to face Ora alone. You are to destroy Henri and those he's turned. If you kill everyone who protects Ora, the Elders will find a way to rid the world of her for good."

Kendal nodded but stayed quiet.

"I need to hear you say it."

"I promise to stop at Henri and the others," she said, but didn't want to lie. "I'll face Ora only if she leaves me no other choice."

"Then may all that's good in the world be with you, Warrior, and protect you from Ora's strike. Call again if you have any other questions."

Kendal and Charlie kissed Lenore's hand again and followed Kim back down the stairs.

Kendal pecked Kim on the lips one last time before she headed out into the night to hunt. She wanted to kill the last of the fledglings before she took on the older and savvier fighters. The ones they'd seen in the cemetery had to be experienced; no one carried a sword like Wadham's only for show. An hour before dawn they waited in the St. Louis Cemetery, confident they'd eliminated the last of the young ones.

"The key to successful hunting, Charlie, is to trap your prey so it has no way to escape. The most successful hunters live by the credo, divide and conquer." She pointed from their place atop the tomb where they'd first seen Wadham and Jonas.

"Divide and conquer?"

"The two who arose first are the strongest in this bunch. The others are old, but they're only a few of the foot soldiers guarding the outside of wherever the queen bee has set up shop. Killing them will give us away tomorrow night, but they picked their resting place well. Plenty of spooks to keep them company in hell. When the sun sets again, Wadham and Jonas will wake up all alone."

The vampires moved back with the same speed as before, splitting up once they were over the wall. Wadham stopped before he entered his tomb and sniffed the air as he had done earlier. Jonas had already gone inside, but the other six were just opening the doors to their beds.

"All of you spread out and search the area. I think someone's here, and I don't want any surprises once the sun comes up," Wadham said, and while the others looked concerned, they didn't want to argue with him. "Go, you have time before the sun rises." He unstrapped his sword before closing the iron gate behind him.

"We can do this easy or we can take the hard route. What's your pick?" Kendal asked Charlie.

"I'm craving a hamburger and home fries, so I pick easy."

"You're no fun, Charlie, but that does sound better than going down there and playing with these guys." She stood up and pulled out the weapon she had retrieved from the bike before climbing back up to their perch. The quiver held arrows made totally of wood, with shafts sharpened on one end. They weren't good for the average bowman to hunt game with, but if shot with her strength they'd do nicely for what she had in mind.

She notched the arrow and drew the bowstring back. The man in her sights was short and stocky but held his sword competently. When it clattered to the ground the others drew back their lips and showed their fangs at the threat. A second later another sword hit the sidewalk, leaving the four survivors appearing frantic.

"Up there," one said, pointing up at her.

Kendal shot the two coming toward them as Charlie jumped down to fight the last one. Charlie met the man's downward stroke and the vampire's sword kept going—embedding in the grass next to the tomb Wadham had entered—since Kendal had shot him mid-stroke. Gazing up at her, he put his hands on his hips and glared, she assumed for taking the kill away from him.

"Hey, man, you said easy."

CHAPTER NINETEEN

Just tell me when she drives back home," Piper said when Hill dropped her off at home. If she goes home, that is, she thought. That kiss was still on her mind.

"And that'll serve what purpose?"

"Me knowing where to find her. I was planning to go over there and give her something as a thank-you for helping us, and I can't do that if I don't know she's there."

"What are you getting her?"

"Why do you need to know?"

"I'm curious as to what you think Kendal Richoux might want or need." Hill smiled at her, leaning toward the passenger-side window.

"I'll admit she's got expensive taste, considering what I had to pay."

That had been hours ago, and Hill hadn't called. Piper had waited until sleep claimed her on the sofa. At seven the phone on her chest rang, scaring her so much she fell to the floor. "What?" she yelled in annoyance when she found a line of drool running down her cheek and discovered her neck was killing her.

"They just rode by, I thought you'd want to know," one of Hill's employees informed her.

"What time is it?"

"A little after seven."

"In the morning?" Her brain wasn't functioning yet.

"Yes, ma'am. Will there be anything else?"

"No, thanks for keeping me informed."

After dragging herself into the shower, she picked a blue suit to wear, angry with herself for even caring enough to want to look good. It was worth swallowing her pride since she wanted to see Kendal again. She was looking forward to waking the party animal up as payback for the crick in her neck.

One of the men she remembered from the previous morning when she'd stopped by for breakfast opened the door and waved her inside after she drove through the open gate. "Good morning, Miss Marmande. Would you like me to take that?" he asked, referring to the box in her hand.

"Thank you, but I'd rather deliver it myself." She walked past him and headed for the stairs. "Want to tell me which room is hers?"

"Last one on the right."

"Aren't you going to try and stop me?" she asked, pausing on the third step.

"Would you like me to?"

She laughed at his answer and his friendliness. "No, but I don't want to get you in trouble."

"Kendal's expecting you, Miss Marmande. If she weren't, the gate would be locked and you'd still be buzzing out there."

"Is she now?"

He nodded before bowing his head slightly and heading to the back of the house.

She walked slowly up the stairs and down the long hall, taking the opportunity to look at the house. The colors were fairly neutral, which was good since they didn't compete with the beautiful paintings and furniture. Some of the portraits had small brass plates at the bottom with the subject's name. One in particular stopped her before she reached Kendal's door.

The woman wore a beautiful dark green gown and sat next to a grand fireplace that Piper hadn't seen in this house. She was older, but even her fragile condition couldn't hide the mischief the artist had captured in her soft brown eyes. Behind her stood a man who resembled her, with his hand on her shoulder, the family connection cemented in their smiles. She held the book in place on her lap as if it was precious to her. Unlike the others, though, this one didn't have an identifying brass plate.

She opened the door without knocking in time to see Kendal zip her pants up and start on her belt, seeming amazingly fresh and alert after a sleepless night. "You're late," Kendal said, sitting to put on her shoes.

"Why do you say that?"

"I'm dressed, so if you came over to see me naked, I'll have to take all this stuff off. Pain, really, but if you insist I'll go through the trouble."

Piper had a hard time fighting the urge to smash the box in her hand over Kendal's head. "Why do I bother trying to find things to like about you?"

"Because you find me irresistible. Face it, no matter how hard you try, you can't stay away." Kendal stood but didn't move closer.

Piper snorted and rested her gift against her chest. "You were right when you told me mental illness runs in your family."

"Does that make me crazy about you?"

"Here, before you embarrass yourself with any more corny lines."

Kendal accepted the box and ripped through the wrapping as soon as Piper let go. It was a box of the cigars she liked. "Thank you, Piper, I don't know what to say." She held her hand out awkwardly, as if not knowing what kind of thank-you gesture she'd accept.

"You're welcome. I hope they're the right kind."

"Best smokes on the planet." Kendal put the box down on the nightstand and reached for the jacket lying on the bed. "Are you ready?"

Thinking Kendal meant breakfast, Piper said, "I can't stay. It's Sunday, but I have a meeting this morning."

"How about giving me a ride into the city, then, since I do as well."

Kendal's request made her smile return.

When they stepped out into the hall together, she admired the painting of the two people again before looking back at Kendal. "Want to tell me another story?"

"Miss Marmande, it's my pleasure to introduce you to Lola St. Louis. It was Lola's family recipe you enjoyed yesterday. Her pecan cakes, as they were known back then, were the envy of the Territory." Kendal glanced at her and quickly added, "Or so I've read. Lola and her son were slaves here, and she ran the kitchens and household staff for Jacques."

"She sure dressed nice for a chef."

"Lola, like all the other slaves who worked this land while Jacques was in residence, was given her freedom and safe passage to England. This lovely woman spent the remainder of her life as the mistress of Farthington, Jacques's English estate. In her later years when she couldn't stand for long periods of time, she rather enjoyed having others cook for her. The man standing behind her was her only son, Joseph."

The thought of such a happy ending made Piper feel good. "What's the book in her hand?"

"That's the St. Louis family tree that chronicles Lola's branch of the family. Joseph, with a little guidance from his mother, went on to marry and have twelve children. All of them became successful, and the foundation Lola gave them all has remained firm, since one of her descendants is a current member of Parliament. One of her greatest accomplishments, though, and the thing she was most proud of aside from her family, was being able to record their history and pass it on to her grandchildren. Slaves in general were prohibited from learning to read and write, but like a great many other things, that wasn't the norm here." Kendal raised her hand and rested her fingers on the book in the painting. "Amazingly, Lola died at Farthington a week before her one hundred and sixth birthday, and her original book still exists, along with all the volumes that came after. Family lore says Jacques was quite touched when he saw his name written in Lola's hand along the roots of the first family tree in the book you see here."

"You know what I wish I could do?" Piper asked, staring up at Lola's face.

"What?"

"Go back in time and spend the afternoon with Jacques St. Louis."

"An afternoon well spent if he had any brains at all." Kendal offered her arm and escorted her down the stairs.

❖

The drive was slow. Kendal noticed they were going ten miles under the speed limit, as if Piper was trying to stretch out their time together.

"Where can I drop you?"

"I'm sure you'd like it to be off a cliff, but the Royal Sonesta is fine. I'm meeting someone for breakfast at Begue's. If that's out of your way, let me off on Canal and I'll walk the rest of the way."

"Really? That's where I'm headed, so it's no problem. Small world, huh?"

"You can fit it in a thimble at times." Kendal got out and waited for Piper to take her slip from the valet attendant. "I'll leave you to meet your party. Thank you for the ride."

"May I call you later?" Piper asked, reaching for her hand. "You can tell me more about Oakgrove's history."

"With all that's going on, I'd think you'd want to concentrate on the living and the here and now." She held Piper's hand for a moment before releasing it and turning away.

"Do you find something about me unforgivable? I'm trying to make amends for my mistakes, and I'd like to get to know you better."

"Why? You have plenty of friends, I'm sure. I can tell you all my stories if you want, but you'll never feel differently about me, so it's best if we part on the best terms we'll ever hope to achieve." For the first time since they'd met, she sounded immature and childish, but she had to pull back before Piper's allure sucked her in.

"Do you judge all women by whether they'll sleep with you?"

She lifted her hand and rubbed her chin. "No, I don't, but why do you want to get to know me? What do you think you'll gain?"

"A friend."

The image of thrusting her sword into Angelina's chest played out in Kendal's head, and she took a deep breath to still her emotions. Henri would use everything in his power to manipulate her, especially people she cared about. They were all her weaknesses, and no amount of training would ever teach her to develop a defense. Her love for Morgaine had helped Henri escape before, and if she were in the same situation she wouldn't change the outcome or question her choices that night. To protect and sacrifice for those people she held in her heart defined her humanity, so she refused to put Piper in harm's way, even if she had to hurt her now.

"Piper, I can't—"

Piper put up her hand to stop her. "Never mind, my mistake." The abandoned child seemed to come out in force, and Piper immediately put up all her defenses.

"Please, Piper, let me explain."

"You don't want anything to do with me. What's to explain?"

Kendal grasped Piper's arm to keep her from walking away. "It isn't you, little one, it isn't you at all."

Piper's laugh sounded harsh. "That tired line is beneath you. Go back to your life, Ms. Richoux, and don't worry about having to placate me." Piper broke her hold and walked away. "It's your loss."

"Hello, Pops." Piper plastered on a smile and kissed Mac's cheek as Kendal watched from the door.

"Are you done celebrating?"

"Yes, we have a lot to do now that we have access to the land next to ours. I've set a meeting with senior management for this afternoon to start reviewing our timeline."

"Someone's already done that, sweet pea. It's not set in stone, but a messenger delivered the preliminary surveys to reconfigure our setup to the office this morning. Our operations crew is reviewing them now, but they seem to be in order and have a good workable timeline." Mac lifted his orange juice glass and took a sip, finally noticing Kendal.

"Here's that someone now," Mac said.

"Stood up, were you?" Piper asked Kendal with a little heat.

"No, you're both right on time." She shook hands with Mac and took the seat next to Piper's. "Did you get the paperwork I had sent over this morning?" she asked Mac.

"Our staff's in complete agreement so far, but that's not why I invited you to join us. Even though Piper says you won't take credit, I wanted to properly thank you for your help. After our initial meeting, I sure never foresaw this turn in the road, but Piper and I are grateful to you for saving us. Aren't we, Piper?"

"You sent the outline?" Piper asked, and she nodded. "Thank you for the loan, but we're perfectly capable of handling our own affairs from here on out. Also, we plan to pay you back every cent with interest."

"Piper, apologize right now," Mac said, appearing mortified.

"Please, Mr. Marmande, Piper's entitled to her opinion. I did help you, but I truly don't expect anything in return. It was the right thing to do since you didn't deserve to have someone like Kenny take away something that means so much to both of you." Kendal reached into her breast pocket and pulled out a business card. "We've finished our business, but I thought I'd do one more thing before I go. It's up to you as to whether you take the offer."

"Who is this?" Mac asked, looking at the card.

"He's in charge of naval contracts and wants to talk to you about some Coast Guard cutters being bid out. The contract will prove you're capable of handling big construction projects, and with your reputation for fairness and honesty, it'll open avenues for potential future business." She took the napkin from her lap and placed it on the empty plate. She'd done everything possible to help them and could walk away with a clear conscience. "You have the inside track on this one, but if you need anything else or have any problems, please contact my New York offices. I left instructions to give you any assistance you require."

"Please stay for breakfast. The least I can do is buy you some eggs."

"That's not necessary, sir. Good luck to you, and hopefully some time in the future we'll have the opportunity to sit and talk again." She took his hand and returned the firm handshake. "Miss Marmande, it was nice seeing you again. Please take care of yourself." She held her hand out, but Piper ignored it.

It would've hurt less if Piper had slapped her. It seemed ludicrous to Kendal that she cared, but by ignoring her, Piper had wiped away any good will they'd built between them. Parting like this was for the best because it would be easier to wipe Piper from her mind before she entered any fight.

She let her hand drop back to her side and sighed. "I'm sorry, Piper. I wish things had been different," she said before leaving.

Kendal looked at her one last time, and Piper suddenly seemed to understand the finality of the farewell. It was fine if Piper wanted to believe that her last tantrum had ended any relationship they'd ever have, as long as she was safe.

Piper watched her go and was certain that Kendal's last glance meant she'd respect her wishes and disappear from her life permanently. Despite every insult she'd thrown at Kendal, and the anger she'd displayed, Kendal had helped and defended her. Piper forgot how to act in Kendal's presence because she couldn't control her emotions, but Kendal had, except for a few frustrated moments, remained steadfastly civil.

Kendal had displayed the patience of someone who cared, and she'd stupidly thrown it away. As soon as Kendal disappeared, an overwhelming sense of fear and loss grabbed her by the throat, making her stand up. If she didn't act, she'd never see Kendal again.

Running out to the lobby, Piper was sure she could catch Kendal before she left, but the only people standing around were a few tourists looking at street maps as if planning their sightseeing day. She ran out the front door and looked down the street in both directions, but Kendal was gone. It isn't fair, her mind screamed. They might've started off as combatants, but something was there now that she'd never be able to define without more time. She was sure Kendal felt the same way, yet she'd walked away like everyone else had. But Piper couldn't dredge up enough anger to blame her. This time she'd lost something precious and important to her happiness, and it was all her fault.

"You treated her like dirt, so you can't blame her for leaving," Piper said out loud, wiping away her tears. She wanted to sit on the sidewalk and give in to the despair suddenly building in her chest.

"Don't cry, little one," Kendal said gently from behind her, putting her arms around her, and the kindness made her cry harder. "Please don't cry. I'm sorry, and even if I can't explain my reasons, I was doing the right thing to keep you safe. It's nothing you've done, please believe that."

She turned around, pressed her face into Kendal's chest, and clung to her with her eyes closed. "Please don't leave me," she said in a shaky voice. She took a breath after she composed herself and gazed up at Kendal, looking at her as if this was the first time she'd truly seen her. Kendal locked eyes with her for the longest time but stayed quiet, as if making a decision about what would happen next.

Kendal hadn't imagined that Piper would run out of the restaurant frantically searching for her. She had fully intended to finish with Henri and disappear somewhere Piper would never find her, no matter how many people like Hill were on her payroll. But she couldn't walk away from the raw hurt that seemed to pour out of Piper.

Piper might not have been able to define her feelings, but what Kendal had feared most had come to pass. She looked into Piper's eyes and lost her heart again, but it was wrong to be so selfish. To care for someone she couldn't have a future with would cause years of frustration because Piper would never return her affections, but Kendal was willing to share this lifetime with her. After she killed Henri she'd give Piper whatever she needed to heal her heart, and it'd be enough. It would have to be.

"I'll never leave you, little one, don't worry." With a soft touch she wiped away the last of Piper's tears. "I'll always be here to look after you." She spoke the sentences, praying to any god that would listen that she could keep her word.

❖

"You promise you won't leave if I go in?" Piper asked, not letting go of Kendal's hand.

"I'll wait right here, I promise."

"I'll just be a second. I want to tell Granddad good-bye first so he won't worry."

Kendal stepped back and pointed to her feet. "Right here, word of honor," she said again, putting her hands in her pockets. Piper walked inside, glancing back every few steps as if to make sure she wouldn't wander. "If I had any sense I'd run as fast as I could to get the hell out of here. You'd think eventually you'd learn from your mistakes, Asra," she mumbled, glimpsing Mac and Piper's embrace before she looked skyward.

"I'm sorry, did you say something?" the doorman asked.

"Just talking to myself," she said, feeling Piper's hand come to rest in the crook of her arm.

"Now there's a sure sign of mental illness, Richoux. You should see someone about that." Piper smiled as she handed over her valet ticket. "Can we go back to your place?"

"I never said it was my place."

"And you never said it wasn't," Piper said, tugging her toward the car as soon as it arrived. The valet accepted a tip from Kendal, who pointed him toward Piper's door. "Drive on, Miss Marmande. The day is yours."

"Just the day?" Piper asked.

"I'd give you my nights, but I can't—not yet."

Piper looked at her before putting the car in gear. "You're not willing to persuade me to share, your nights, I mean?" Piper cocked her head into Kendal's hand when she pressed it to her cheek, as if suddenly wanting to explore something new.

"I'm sure you're more than capable of heading down that yellow brick road all by yourself, Dorothy." Kendal pinched Piper's cheek.

"You saw me in Oz?"

"And your little dog too."

Piper laughed. "I'm sure Hill will appreciate that. Why didn't you acknowledge me?"

"I could ask the same thing of you."

Piper concentrated on driving as if fishing for an answer, because the only thing that popped into her mind was that she'd been jealous when Kendal had kissed that woman. She couldn't admit that without admitting to a whole lot more when it came to Kendal and what she wanted. "I wasn't there because I thought you'd be." Piper slapped Kendal's arm when she put her hand over her heart, as if wounded.

"It's really the last place I thought I'd find you. I was just broadening my horizons, then you swoop in and lock lips with the bartender."

"Hey, you were there with a date."

"In Hill's twisted little brain maybe. I wanted to see women who prefer the company of other women. I was trying to understand the attraction."

"And do you, understand now?"

"I understand that I didn't find anyone in there remotely interesting," Piper said, pausing to run her tongue over her bottom lip, "and I understand I didn't much care for that woman kissing you." So much for her not admitting that, and making her sound like a wounded lover.

"Why, Piper Marmande, you sound jealous."

Piper shrugged. "Maybe I was."

"You don't need to feel that way. She's just an old friend, nothing more." She moved her hand to Piper's knee. "Get us back to Oakgrove and I'll make it up to you."

Now that Piper knew she would get her for the day, the drive to the plantation seemed shorter than ever. "This really is a beautiful place," Piper said as they turned into the drive.

"Do you have something more comfortable to change into? I'll give you a tour."

Piper followed her inside, carrying her gym bag, to one of the guest rooms with a beautiful four-poster bed. Kendal closed the door for her and waited twenty minutes before entering to total silence.

"You want to take a nap?" she asked when she found Piper on the bed with her eyes closed.

Piper raised her head at the question and grimaced. "No, I want my tour."

"Something wrong with your neck?"

"I slept in the wrong position, I guess." She got up and walked to the door, dressed in jeans and hiking boots.

"Turn around for me."

"Why? I said I'm all right."

She put her hands on the sides of Piper's neck. "No sense hurting when you don't have to." She twisted first to the right and then just to the left, feeling the bones go back into alignment, but it was hard to hear the slight crack over Piper's scream.

Piper turned around, appearing ready to yell at her when she moved her head around and dropped her poking finger. "Thank you."

"You're welcome, Miss Marmande." She held out her hand to Piper. "Shall we?"

Piper stared at it for a beat, then took it with such a strong grip Kendal thought she'd either made a life-altering decision or bet herself she'd accept whatever was within her boundaries in an effort not to be rude. Considering it was Piper, she could never be totally sure.

Kendal started their tour in the formal gardens Charlie mostly still kept up himself. They were so much grander than she remembered, and she enjoyed finally seeing them in person instead of through the pictures Charlie always sent. Through the years he'd not only mastered a variety of things like gardening, but he'd become a wonderful letter writer. In the thousands of pages they'd shared since Charlie had stayed behind, Kendal had glimpsed parts of his soul along with narratives about whatever project he was working on.

"The gardens were much smaller when the house was first built, but when Jacques left and the fields went dormant, the caretakers over time devoted their time here."

"It's gorgeous," Piper said, accepting a large pink rose bud she'd cut for her.

"Almost all the plants you see, like the horses in the stable, have something in common." She stopped at the bench in the gazebo Charlie had added in the early 1960s. "Except for a few of the seasonal flowers, the plants were cross-cultivated from the originals first placed here. Some are quite a few generations removed, but they carry plenty of history in their leaves."

"The horses have been bred that long too?"

"So much has changed since Jacques was here—some for the better and some not. Keeping alive some of the good things from that era pays homage to the families who made this their home. Horses were necessary back then, but also a passion."

"Do the family history books say that Jacques liked to ride bareback?"

"On occasion, but he used a proper saddle when he was out playing the role of the marquis."

Piper laughed before bringing the rose close to her nose and inhaling the scent. "Will you tell me what happened to him? When he left here, I mean."

"Jacques lived a quiet life in England, enjoying the company of those who left with him to build a future there. At least he did for a while."

Once she'd buried Lola, she traveled to the Himalayas. The cave she found at the base of a mountain had been her resting place until Morgaine had finally tracked her down. The world was again a different place, and she stayed there among the monks and mountain people, since they were so at peace away from the modern world.

CHAPTER TWENTY

Buddhist monastery, 1808

"To still your heart you must first heal your mind," advised the head master at the monastery where Morgaine had left Kendal as he circled her with a wooden sword. "To heal your heart, you must still your mind."

This was their ninth day of this exercise, and he'd done nothing but circle her, talking in circles. She kept waiting for him to engage so she could gauge how easy to go on him, but he only orbited in light steps that didn't compute with his age. As he said that damned line again, she recalled Henri limping away laughing. His taunts about honor and weakness still echoed through her head, and the anger she'd tried to bury with sleep finally broke its leash.

Still her heart? She wasn't listening to that nonsense again, so she raised the blade the monk had insisted she use and moved at him. She couldn't heal her mind because she couldn't forget or escape the rows of burning pyres the morning after Henri's arrival.

Before her sword met his wooden one, he smiled, and she pulled the force of her downward stroke at the last minute. He wasn't smiling because she'd finally showed a reaction, but because she still had lessons to learn. Using his inferior wooden stick, compared to her blade, he'd left more bruises on her than anyone had since Morgaine had first trained her.

"That's all you're going to say?" Piper asked, pulling her out of her memories. "Did he go on to marry?"

"Jacques never married."

"How did he have heirs?"

Training yard of the monastery, 1808

The last blow the monk landed was to her right wrist and broke it so badly it seemed that hairline fractures extended all the way down her fingers. "How do you define failure, Asra?" he asked, his sword held over his head as if ready to strike again.

"You know my name?" she asked through gritted teeth, the pain almost unbearable.

"Morgaine told me your name, but not who you are. Only you can tell me that, and only you can tell me how you define failure."

The story of Oakgrove came spilling out, taking long into the night to finish so she couldn't escape the pain in her hand, heart, and mind. While she spoke, the monk perched on a rock, the night sky lit with stars as his backdrop, listening intently as if what she was saying wasn't lunacy. No matter what she told him, he never appeared to judge her.

"What would you change?" he asked when she finished.

"I'd have let Angelina and Tomas go long before they were taken from me."

"And the others, they weren't important to you?"

"They were my family—of course they were important to me. I define failure as not protecting them all."

"What did that night teach you?" he asked, seeming oblivious to the cold.

"I'm destined to be a loner. I can't get too involved or care too much if I don't want the same thing to happen."

"If that's all you learned, your road is long before you learn the truth of yourself. You'll never still your mind or heal your heart until you find the one who challenges both."

Oakgrove, present day

"Kendal, are you all right?" Piper sounded concerned after she'd soared off to the past again. "We don't have to talk about any of this."

"It's okay." Kendal flexed her right hand, the memory of that injury still as fresh as the man's advice. "Jacques's bloodline lived on after an old lover came back into his life and led him on a journey to still his heart and heal his mind, as he later wrote."

She'd stayed with the monks until the grief became manageable, but they never convinced her that Henri was totally at fault. Originally she'd sailed to New Orleans to hunt him down, but she'd grabbed a brief opportunity for normalcy with Angelina and Tomas. The distraction had given Henri the chance to strike, and he'd almost broken her. She'd never forget, but knowing she was close to destroying him drove her.

"That sounds scandalous for the time."

"Jacques believed in duty to family and doing the right thing, like all the people on the family tree since."

"Thank God for that, especially for Granddad and me," Piper said, placing her hand on the side of Kendal's neck. "And it's good to know Jacques found love again."

"What about you?" she asked, taking Piper's hand again to continue their walk. "What's Piper Marmande's love history?"

"That's sadly a story yet to be written." Piper turned her head away. "My grandparents and the business have needed me more than I needed to be in love, and experiences like I've had don't make me want to change my mind on the subject."

"That's too bad," Kendal said, heading to the fields that trees hadn't reclaimed. Only knee-high grass grew here now. "Now that I know you, I'd like to think you'll make someone really happy, so don't rob yourself of the chance."

"Why do you say that?"

Kendal stopped and pressed Piper's back to her chest, so they both faced the house. "Neat rows of two rotating crops used to grow here where we're standing. Jacques and the others who worked this land from nothing wrote eloquently about how wondrous it was to see the plants at their peak."

"Do you not want to answer my question, or don't you know how?" Piper asked, placing her hands over hers.

"I'm answering your question," she said softly into Piper's ear. "You're like this place." Letting Piper go, she walked slowly toward the house, kneeling when she found what she was looking for. "You're full of history, made up of all the joy and sadness you've known, but it's good to remember your past because it gives you a good perspective going forward." She tore a leaf off the plant she'd found and handed it to Piper.

"They grew tobacco?" Piper took it and smelled it. "That's what this is, isn't it?"

"Yes. That's what mostly took up this acreage when it was the season."

"I still don't understand your point, unless you're telling me you think I'm fertile." Piper laughed.

"The seedlings from those crops keep popping up year after year." Kendal stood and pointed more out. "Some of this place's history is trapped in the soil, and when you compare that with the people in your family, it's the same. Your grandparents are only two of your history's great loves, and you were born with that seedling of love. When you find the person you're meant to be with, the seed won't have any choice but to grow."

"In addition to memorizing the family history, you must get lessons in romance. Thanks for saying all that." Piper held up the leaf. "Maybe some things are genetic as well, like enjoying tobacco."

"Maybe," she said, pointing to the house when she noticed Piper's blush. The day was about making Piper feel special, not pushing her into any future commitments. "And maybe we'll start planting again to keep me in cigars."

Piper took her hands but walked backward as if to maintain eye contact. "That isn't a very healthy choice. You ever think of quitting that nasty habit?"

"I've got a short list of vices, and cigars are in the top ten, so no. If it makes you feel better, I'll consider replanting the home garden instead." She turned Piper slightly to the area now covered sporadically with shade trees, flowering plants, and herbs. "That's what they used this land for, but I think it serves a better purpose now."

"What?"

"A place for lunch." She turned Piper the rest of the way. "Hungry?"

An elegantly set table stood between two massive oaks, with some of the house staff nearby. "You're too much," Piper said. Kendal smiled at her, and she felt as if she'd found shelter after standing in a storm for years. Plenty of people had tried to charm her with pretty words, but Kendal seemed to flatter simply because she was stating the truth as she saw it.

She moved to Kendal's side and put her arm around her waist, enjoying Kendal's partial embrace. "Thank you again for today. Well, for everything, really. You're like no one I've ever met, and even though I don't deserve what you've done for me, I'm so glad you gave me so many chances to accept your friendship."

"You deserve so much more." Kendal pressed her closer with the arm she had around her shoulders.

"Only my grandparents have ever thought so. Even my father didn't find me worthy enough to stick around for," she said, not believing she'd actually let the words escape her mouth.

"Perhaps he didn't have your strength. He let his seedling grow when he found your mother and didn't know how to keep it nourished once he lost her," Kendal said, stopping so she could hug her. "As for the rest, let me show you how wrong you are."

At the table Kendal pulled Piper's chair out for her and poured the wine while the staff served the first course. It was almost like being transported back in time, and any bad thoughts talking about her father had brought on vanished.

"To the future," she toasted when Kendal held up her glass, "and may it hold more days like today."

Kendal tapped her glass to Piper's and smiled. "That's something worth drinking to."

❖

The meal was simple but wonderfully prepared, which Piper enjoyed, but not as much as listening to Kendal answer every question she'd had about Oakgrove. After all her failed attempts to get on the property, the invitation and welcome she'd received from the owner were worth the wait.

"More coffee, miss?" one of the servers asked, holding a silver urn over her cup.

"It was wonderful, but any more liquids and we may have a problem," she said, holding her stomach. "Could you direct me to the ladies' room, please?"

"If you want authentic, you could use one of the oak trees while I hunt for some leaves for you," Kendal said.

"Don't make me laugh. It'll take more than one date to make me drop my pants, Richoux, even if it was wonderful."

"Let's go before you mess up the lawn furniture." Kendal helped her up. They entered through the kitchen, and Kendal led her to the nearest bathroom. "Take your time, then meet me on the front porch swing."

"Porch swing? You put me on that after all that food and wine, and you'll have to pinch me to keep me awake."

"I'd love to," Kendal said, winking at her, and Piper heard her laugh when she slammed the door on her.

Piper hurried, not wanting to waste time, and when she opened the door again the house was deadly silent. More paintings hung in the short hallway to the foyer, and as she walked past the front parlor and looked out the large bank of windows, she saw Kendal sitting outside. Above Kendal's head to the left, the sudden movement of a squirrel running across a branch drew her eyes up, and the image in her peripheral vision made her stop.

The portrait over the mantel made her quit breathing, and she put her hand on the door frame to keep from swaying. The woman was a reflection of Piper herself captured in oil paint. She didn't remember moving, but she walked only to the middle of the room. The sight of her smiling twin scared her because her expression was so lifelike her eyes seemed to follow and draw Piper in.

She didn't turn away from it when she sensed Kendal join her. She didn't need to break their silence yet to ask who this was because Hill had done such a great job describing the long-lost love who drove Jacques from his home—Angelina du'Pon.

"Why didn't you tell me?" she asked, not as an accusation.

"You would've thought me mad, and I really don't know why you look so much alike—you just do."

"Kendal, we don't look alike. Our faces are exactly the same."

"You're your own person, Piper, and you two have differences. Your eyes are darker, she was a tad taller, but it doesn't matter. You're both beautiful women in the hearts of those who care about you. To think otherwise would be to disrespect you as individuals. I didn't tell you because it's not important, merely coincidence."

"Are you sure? Is she why you didn't want to see me anymore? I'm not her, if that's what you're worried about. I understand she was set to marry Jacques and she died. This isn't history repeating itself." She glanced back at Kendal and felt like she was in a strange dream. "The same thing won't happen to us, even if you talk about her like you knew her."

"I'm not sure. Sometimes we can all learn from our past mistakes. Do you want to know how Angelina died?"

"The priest we talked to wasn't very forthcoming. Your family has done a great job of sharing only the history you want the world to know."

Kendal dropped into one of the chairs in the room and peered past

Piper's shoulder to the painting hanging there. "At the time, very few knew exactly what transpired the last night Angelina and Tomas spent in this house. And you're wrong—history can most certainly repeat itself. I didn't want to see you again simply because I wanted to keep you safe."

"Kendal, that was close to three hundred years ago. Don't let fear cloud what's in your heart."

"Our time together should prove how much I care about what happens to you, and that I'm not punishing you by sending you far away from me." Kendal looked at her with glassy eyes. "Piper, you've got to leave here today and never come back. I couldn't handle any harm coming to you or your family because of me."

"I don't want to walk away from you," she said, sitting next to Kendal. "I can't know how Jacques lost Angelina, but I'm sure the same thing won't happen again. Don't throw this away before those seedlings have the chance to sprout."

With a shaking hand, Kendal reached across for one of Piper's. "Listen carefully. I wasn't lying when I told you I was here on family business."

"I remember everything you said, but what does that have to do with people who lived a long time ago?"

"Angelina died at the hands of Jacques's brother because of an old rivalry that went too far. My brother has brought me to the city, and it would seem that history *is* repeating itself. I don't want to drag you into the middle of that, so please, as my friend, do what I'm asking."

"You think he's that dangerous?"

"More than Henri St. Louis ever thought to be, and he'll use whatever and whoever he can to get to me. I'll sacrifice anything before I let him touch you."

"What if I want to help you? You know, to return the favor for saving Granddad and me."

"I'd love you watching my back, but please just work hard to make Marmande a success and forget you ever met me. I gave you the opportunity to keep what's rightfully your family's, but it'll take your talent to make it work, so concentrate on that."

Piper moved closer and put her hand on Kendal's cheek. "If you can look me in the eye and tell me you want me to walk out of your life, I'll respect your wishes." She stroked the smooth skin where Kendal's shirt parted, and a new cascade of thoughts ran through her mind. "But don't ask me to like it if that's what you decide."

Kendal hesitated, but she lifted her head and looked torn. "I want you to go, Piper. I want you to go and erase this place and me from your mind."

"I don't know if I can do that," Piper said, meaning every word. She felt like she had to hang on to Kendal like she had outside the hotel so she wouldn't vanish like a mist.

"How do I face the rest of my life if something happens to you?" Kendal asked, framing her face with her hands. "I know what I'm up against, and it'll be hard enough making it through without having to worry about you."

Kendal didn't let her say anything else when she stood and helped her up and walked her to her car, as if not giving herself the opportunity to give in to what she really wanted. She went willingly when Kendal opened her arms and held her.

"This may sound strange, but it's the most important thing you have to remember. If anyone you don't know comes to your house asking to be let in, especially at night, refuse and lock the door. This is critical, Piper. I can't explain it right now, but you have to refuse even if they say they know me and I'm in trouble. If you do anything for me, do this. Promise me you won't forget what I'm saying."

"Why?"

Kendal's laugh was mixed with what sounded like exhaustion. "For the love of the gods, you're like a little pit bull at times. Don't ask why, just promise me."

"Okay, I promise."

"Thank you," Kendal said as she opened her door for her.

"This isn't the way I thought our day would end, so promise me something in return. You owe it to me for letting you get your way with so little information."

"If I can I will."

She felt completely out of her element, but she didn't want to leave without getting Kendal to reconsider what she was asking. "When you resolve this problem, call me. I just found you and I don't want to lose my *friend* so easily."

"I promise," Kendal said without hesitation, and she also didn't hesitate when Piper put her hands on her chest, then moved them behind her head.

"Hill told me your word is important to you, so I'm holding you to it." She stood on her toes and pressed her lips to Kendal's. What had started as a good-bye gesture took Piper by storm. Kendal's lips were soft but firm, and Kendal drew her in to the point that she never wanted to let go. Finally, she'd come home.

Kendal backed away first, severing the contact. "Go on, Piper, and stay safe."

"Are you sure?" she asked, making Kendal nod. "Then remember your promise." Kendal nodded again and closed the car door once Piper was settled in the driver's seat, then walked into the house without looking back.

"And I'm going to hold you to it whether you want to or not," Piper said, starting the engine. On the drive home she felt almost heartbroken, which didn't make sense to her. You didn't fall in love so easily in such a short time. "You'd think I'm twelve with a crush," she said, and laughed.

Only she'd finally found someone who woke her up emotionally, and Kendal Richoux had most certainly done that in extreme.

"Are you busy tonight?" she asked when Hill answered her phone on the first ring. "Good, grab your spy gear and pick me up in an hour."

She threw her phone into her purse and looked in her rearview mirror. The house wasn't visible, but damned if she was letting Kendal off that easy.

CHAPTER TWENTY-ONE

D o you want to talk about it?" Charlie asked.
       Kendal sat with a whiskey in her hand staring at the painting
of Angelina, and the longer she looked, the less Angelina resembled
Piper. If Piper had been in her life back then, she would've stabbed
Henri through the heart for dropping by unexpectedly and postponing
their conversation of their future together. Especially if she'd thought
she might hear a proposal soon.

"Do you know why Henri picked your family first out of the
hundreds he had to choose from that night?" she asked, keeping her
eyes on the painting and remembering the feel of those small pearl
beads sewn into the fabric. "It's not like your cabin was the first or the
last, yet he went right for it and killed them."

"I don't know," Charlie said, sitting across from her. "I just
remember him laughing as he dropped my youngest to the floor with
his throat torn out."

"Before the sickness took her, Ora was a powerful witch who
people feared as much as they sought her." Kendal stopped and took
a sip. "People always laugh, thinking that the dark arts are fake, but
they're wrong. They're not all parlor tricks and charlatans."

"The general public doesn't believe in vampires either, but they
exist."

"Imagine the ability to combine that craft with the abilities she
gained when her body turned," she said, accepting a refill from Charlie.
"Then think about how long she's practiced that craft."

"What does that have to do with my family?"

"That night, by picking your family and sparing you, Henri
showed me that his proclaimed queen gave him more than just the gift
of her blood."

"I'd think you'd remember Angelina and Tomas the most."

"We lit twenty-three pyres to Henri's savagery, and I remember them all," she said, sounding flat. "Ora can steal thought, a talent she's improved with time. Had Henri killed only Angelina and Tomas, I wouldn't have been suspicious, but the annihilation of your family wasn't to get at you, but at me."

He looked at her and opened and closed his mouth a few times. "I'm sorry, I don't understand."

"Henri stole my thoughts, and from them he plucked you and Lola. I loved both of you, but you had the most to lose. And if you blamed me, I'd lose you as quickly as if he'd drained you."

"Why didn't you ever tell me?"

"I've lived long, and in all that time I've trusted only two people completely," she said, looking him in the eye. "Morgaine and you, that's it, so forgive me, but I didn't want to take the chance of losing you."

"You worried a long time for nothing," Charlie said. "The men who brought me here stole everything from me, and I didn't feel a part of anything until you bought me. From that day my place has been with you, and like you said to me then, in the eyes of the law you owned me, but here I was a free man that Celia and you loved." They stood together and he embraced her. "I'm Lionel St. Louis and Charlie Richoux, but they're only names that change with time. What doesn't change is what we are together, Asra, and that's family."

"Thank you, so trust me when I say the last thing I want to talk about is Piper. I'm tired of losing to these monsters."

"Not this time, sister."

"Are you ready to go in? I want to get there early and talk to Lenore again. I have one more question before sunset." She strapped on all her weapons and touched her lips once before walking out the door. She could still feel Piper's lingering kiss, but now was the time to forget.

"It won't kill us to take a night off, if you need to."

"I'm an immortal, Charlie. I may get lonely, but I never get tired."

"I don't know about you, but sometimes I get emotionally tired. Nothing wrong with giving in to that."

"What I feel doesn't matter, since it won't change what I need to do or who I need to stay away from."

They took the SUV into the city so she could look out the window of the passenger side and brood until they arrived. When they were close to Oz, she pointed to the curb and asked Charlie to stop. Hill didn't have a chance to hide before Kendal stepped into the middle of the street in front of her car.

"I want you to drive to Piper's and spend the night with her." She leaned into the open driver's side window, and Hill moved back until she was against her door.

"We don't have that type of relationship. Trust me, I'm the last person she's interested in," Hill answered, gulping.

"I'm not asking you to sleep with her. I just want you to keep an eye on her. Whatever she's paying you, tell her you have a new boss who's paying you four times your fee and you couldn't refuse." She started back to the truck, then turned around. "Don't let me find you out here again tonight, Hill, I mean it. If things don't work out the way I have planned, I don't want her alone and unprotected. I'm counting on you to be there for her."

"I don't know what's going on, but I won't let you down. I'll make sure she understands that."

"I also know Piper, so don't think about taking her out if she asks. You do, and no matter what she threatens, I'll make you sorry."

Kendal was satisfied when she saw the car turn the corner and head back in the direction of Piper's condo. She wanted this to end so she could try to find some pleasure in this lifetime without the threat of Abez and his demon queen hanging over her head.

❖

"Which of them is stronger?"

"Which of who?" Lenore asked, looking up from her books. Kim was close by, reshelving some of the volumes they'd used that morning.

"Which is stronger, Wadham or Jonas?" Kendal put her hands on the table and bent a little so they were more at eye level. "I need to know before the sun sets tonight, and you can tell me."

Lenore was no warrior, but it wasn't easy to intimidate her, and she stared back without fear. "Wadham's the stronger and older. Why?"

"I'm back in New Orleans after all this time, so maybe it's time to revive some of those old traditions. I'm planning to kill his little buddy and call Wadham out, but only if he brings his friends Ora and Abez."

"Asra, be careful what you ask for, or you might just get it. I may not be as well versed in the arts of war as you are, but it'd be wiser to handle them one at a time. Together they'll be almost invincible."

"No one lives forever, Lenore, and no one's invincible." She moved even closer, making Lenore waver and sit back, unable to stand the intensity of her stare.

"You're proof that one can live forever."

"We cannot know what forever is, but I do know what fighting is, and that's what I intend to do. With Charlie at my side, I'll end this or die trying."

Lenore nodded. "Take care, Warrior, and go with just one more piece of advice."

"Watch out for the sharp teeth?"

"Your sense of humor has always set you apart, Asra, but I speak of more serious things." Lenore stood and put her hand on Kendal's head. "Wipe her from your mind or he *will* use her against you. Abez is your brother, so your mind is more open to him than most. Ora and Abez aren't the only gifted ones."

Kendal didn't need to ask who Lenore was referring to. If Lenore could sense Piper in her mind, what would happen when she faced Abez? "If something happens to me and they bury me where no one will ever find me, will you talk with her? Tell her how sorry I am I couldn't keep my promises."

"Go with a clear head and heart, Warrior. I'll be happy to talk with your woman."

"She's not—"

"Go, the sun is starting to set." Lenore pointed to the darkening skies visible through her skylights.

❖

Two flips got them over the graveyard wall, and without hesitation Kendal moved to the mausoleum Jonas had entered the night before. Together they moved the heavy stone lid that kept the light out during the day and looked down at the sleeping vampire. The little light left in the sky blistered his skin slightly, but Kendal didn't intend to let him suffer long. She sank her sword into his chest, truly turning this place into his grave.

They waited close to the iron gate of Wadham's lair, wanting him to see them this time. Minutes after it got dark, the stone slid open inside. "Draw your weapon, Charlie, because I can't guarantee he'll take me up on my offer."

When Wadham stepped out, he held his distinctive sword at the ready. "Ah, I should have realized last night who the scent belonged to, Warrior. Here to face me, are you?"

"In good time, Wadham, but I want you to bring all the troops when you do. I want Abez and your queen to come and try to bury me."

Wadham laughed hard enough for her to see his fangs. "I've no need of help to do that, Asra. I won't be like all those fledglings you've faced through the ages. In me you'll find your most worthy opponent, and you can praise my skill as I destroy you."

"Bragging and twenty bucks will get you a hooker down on Desire, but I just need an answer."

"Kendal, let's try not to agitate the big vampire," Charlie said through clenched teeth.

"I choose to face you now and gift my queen with the victory."

Kendal shrugged and pointed to a low gravesite. "Charlie, have a seat. This shouldn't take long." She drew her katana and faced Wadham, who was already circling her. "Windbag, are you here to fight or do the tango?"

Angry, he lunged with his sword out in front of him. Wadham then put his hand up and turned his head, frantically trying to find her. She kicked him from behind, knocking his face into the grass as she came down on his sword hand with the flat of her axe. With her foot on his head, he moved his hand around trying to locate his weapon.

"Swordsmanship 101, butthead, never enter a fight with your anger showing." Kendal kept her boot on his head and pressed the tip of the katana between his shoulder blades. "You end up either dead or really hurting." The blade slid in, but she stayed clear of his heart. For now she needed him alive.

"I'll never tell you where they are, so you may as well destroy me like you have my brothers." Wadham had lost all his bravado and sounded like he was in pain, the blood bubbling from his wound as if it were champagne spilling from the neck of a bottle.

She twisted the blade viciously, thinking of this man's victims through the years. Their spirits demanded some retribution. "I don't need you to tell me where they are. I already know, and they're now without protection. You've failed, Wadham, and Ora will haunt your afterlife for eternity for that mistake."

BALANCE OF FORCES: TOUJOURS ICI

With what felt to her like the last of his strength he turned, threw her off, and rolled to his knees. He saw his sword not far from him and made a desperate dive for it. Before Charlie could move from his seat, Wadham stuck it into Kendal's leg and ran to the wall. On the other side he ran as fast as he could, clutching his chest with both hands.

"Charlie, wait." She stopped him from following.

"But we can finish him off."

"I wanted him to get away. He's running off to the evil bitch who made him—to warn her."

"Should I follow him, since you so kindly took a hit in the leg for the cause?"

"Would you, please, and stay out of sight. Let me tie this up so I don't leave a trail, and I'll join you." She ripped off a piece of her shirt and bound the cut on her leg. The plan hadn't gone exactly like she wanted, but now maybe they'd discover where Henri and Ora were staying and if they had any other security.

Running was a bit uncomfortable, but she easily cleared the wall and followed the blood drops Wadham had left. He would have to feed for months to heal the wound she'd inflicted. Though the immortals enjoyed the power to heal quickly, their dark brethren didn't. Any cuts and punctures that wood caused would fester for months and drive their hunger to an almost painful state. Wadham wouldn't live long enough to worry about it.

❖

Piper gasped as she saw Kendal limp down the street. "See, I told you we were right in coming out here. Look at her, she's hurt," she said from the passenger seat of Hill's car.

"I'm telling you, she can take care of herself, and when she sees us, she's going to kick my ass."

"She won't see us unless she gets into something dangerous and we have to help her," she said, hitting Hill so she'd start the car.

"Oh, yes, she will. She's got a sixth sense that kicks in when we're around. Besides, she's jogging down the street at a fairly good clip. She doesn't look all that hurt to me," Hill said, looking through her binoculars. "Would this be a good time to mention again what a bad idea this is?"

"If you want to, you can go back to your office, but I'm not leaving her out here alone with some lunatic who wants to kill her. How horrible to know your brother wants to hurt you. I don't have any siblings, and now I'm glad."

"Did she tell you why he wants to kill her?" Hill started the car as soon as Kendal crossed the boulevard and entered the French Quarter. "She seems nice enough."

"She didn't come out and say it, but he sounds crazy. Of course, being related to Kendal Richoux could make anyone crazy. Just look at her. She's great-looking, has a body that makes you sweat just thinking about it, and she's outrageously successful. Those three things alone would fuel a sibling rivalry for eternity." She was bouncing in her seat, trying not to lose sight of Kendal.

"Have you seen her body recently in a different light than the rest of us mere mortals?" Hill asked, pulling behind another car for cover.

"By accident." She picked at the seam of her jeans. "We're going to lose her if you don't get going."

"We're fine, and don't try to change the subject. When did this happen?" They started down the street again when Kendal continued her jog.

"I went over there thinking she'd been hurt. Remember, I told you about it?"

"How does that translate to seeing her in something a little more revealing than a suit? And I sure as hell don't remember that being part of your story."

"It wasn't sexual, Ms. Dirty Mind. I was just checking to see she wasn't hurt. She found it quite amusing, actually."

"Spill it, Piper."

"I ripped open her robe and she was naked underneath it. Satisfied?"

"Extremely. I would've paid good money to see that." Hill pulled over again when Kendal went up the walk of an old house in the middle of the block. "Her athletic abilities are amazing," Hill said as they watched Kendal scale the wall to enter from a second-story open window. "Who do you think lives here?"

"Might be the crazy brother. I just hope she doesn't go out the back." As soon as she said it, Kendal walked out the front door.

They left the Quarter and crossed Canal Street, headed toward the Uptown area. Kendal never stopped or even slowed down the entire way to Louisiana Avenue, where she got down on her knees to look at something. When she stood, she held a small knife in her hand, and

Piper stared at it, momentarily wondering what it was for. The answer made her gasp when Kendal turned suddenly and threw it.

Their covert operation was over for the night when the front tire went flat. Another flick of Kendal's wrist and the back tire blew, and since they were both on Hill's side she figured maybe Hill was right about what would happen to her when Kendal caught up with her. For now, though, she could just watch as Kendal started to run again, disappearing into the Garden District.

❖

Wadham's blood trail ended at the wrought-iron gate in the Garden District, so Kendal climbed a tree across the street. From the higher vantage point she could study the large house walled off from its neighbors. The gas lamps on each side of the front door flickered in the wind, and that was all she saw moving.

Two men stood on the porch, and they seemed to be alone. They might've been trying to throw her off, but she was sure this was the place.

When the wind picked up, rustling the leaves in all the surrounding trees, the security guys became more alert, so she searched her side of the street for Charlie and anything out of the ordinary. It was three in the morning, and the neighborhood was quiet except for a few dogs and cats roaming the streets. It took her a few minutes to spot Charlie two trees over, fixated on the house.

"Did our wounded soldier go in there?" she asked, after she joined him.

"He stopped outside the Quarter before he ran inside here. I haven't seen him since. You okay?"

"Nothing a little sunshine won't cure," she said, noticing all the rooms illuminated with what appeared to be candlelight. "And I saw inside the place where Wadham stopped."

"He didn't linger. In fact, he was so fast I would've sworn some madwoman with a sword was chasing him," Charlie whispered, smiling. "If that place is Henri's, then who does this belong to?"

"This is Henri's humble abode. Wadham must've stopped at the other house to make sure we didn't snag my brother along with him. That was probably his gathering place for his young minions. I didn't stay long either, but I found some of Henri's things in the master bedroom and the decaying body of what looked like a teenager in the closet of another bedroom. Poor kid died with a scream on her face, but she was the only one there. The house was empty."

"This place isn't," Charlie said. "Look."

Henri stepped to the window in the middle upstairs room, wearing only a pair of pants. His naked chest gleamed almost brighter than the moon, and he held Wadham's sword. Charlie shivered and looked to see Kendal's reaction when Henri ran his finger along the dried blood and licked it off.

"They aren't going anywhere for the night, and if I had to guess, their resting place is on the grounds. We'll come back in the morning to look around and leave our calling card. If we have to fight these things, we'll do it on our terms and on our turf." Charlie nodded and looked back toward the house.

"Do you think they have any others in there?"

"A handful, maybe, but it won't matter. Tomorrow's the full moon, and at midnight it'll be All Hallows' Eve. We can't wait any longer."

Charlie's eyes teared, as if he hadn't realized another anniversary to mark the murders of his family was almost here. "We'll be ready."

"You bet your ass, Lionel. Tomorrow we'll fight for Celia and Angelina." They grabbed each other's arm in the greeting of warriors, sealing their solemn vow for vengeance.

❖

"Something's wrong," Ora said, whipping her head up from the book she'd been engrossed in since the sun set. "Are you sure you've taken everything I told you into account?" she asked Henri.

From the time she'd found him in a cheap gambling den in Egypt, Ora had seen the potential in Henri that his family had not. He had been a perfect choice because he was full of hate for almost everything and everyone in his life, which meant he'd never mourn what he'd have to leave behind.

By the time she'd discovered him, she was feeling the pressure of having to run from the Clan's henchmen. Having to feed regularly back then wasn't easy, since the bodies she left behind sent people like Morgaine a calling card as to where she was. The only person Henri ever valued had been his mother, but when she died shortly after his sister's birth, he had only a father who expected another god on the battlefield.

The fire in Henri's belly had kindled when Raad started pushing him, and it hadn't been hard to fan it to the blaze that had burned through their family home, leaving Raad and everyone there easy targets. With the power she'd given him, she'd put one more barrier between her and the Elders, and Henri had been successful so far, surprising even her.

"I realize how much you care for Wadham and Jonas," Henri said, sounding as if he didn't feel the same, "but you have to trust me." He was sitting across from her with his long overcoat on, but hadn't spoken until then.

"I wouldn't be here if I didn't trust you." She closed the book that was a replica of the one she'd started early in her life. "What you've put together here will allow us the freedom the Clan has denied us. Wadham and Jonas should be able to hold Asra off until midnight of All Hallows' Eve. I've worked for this night for a long a time as well, and with your sister out of the way, my spell will unshackle us forever."

"You have me," Henri said, standing and brushing his black hair back. "You don't need anyone else."

Ora moved closer to him, enjoying his looks even though his appearance had changed over the centuries. The dark hair was just as thick, but his skin was now alabaster instead of the darker complexion he once had. She'd seduced him the first night she'd found him, not realizing that he had a younger sister. Morgaine had beaten her to Asra, and she'd never forgive the Elder for that. Henri had been valuable, but with Asra she would've crushed the Clan long before now.

"Have any of your children come back?" she asked, sitting across from him.

"If any of them have, I wouldn't know it. Wadham has refused to let me return to my other house." The six men Wadham had scattered in the yard had made that clear. "We've lost the youngest of them, but I planned for that. They were here in numbers to keep my idiot sister busy while we waited for the time you need."

"Henri, you know your place with me," she said, with enough heat to make him lose his sarcasm, "but Wadham has served me well and has been as loyal. You'll have to learn to accept his place with me."

"Mistress," Wadham said, stumbling in and holding his chest.

"What happened?" She watched as Henri helped him into a chair. "Where are the others?"

"They're all gone." He appeared ashamed as he said it. "The slayer was waiting when I woke and was there when we returned before dawn.

She killed most of them before sunrise, and Jonas must have walked into her ambush since he wasn't there to help me."

"She wounded you and you came here?" Henri asked.

"I had to," Wadham said, looking not at Henri, but at her. "We must leave, Mistress. Asra has taken our best warriors, and I'm in no shape to defend you if she finds you."

"Of course Asra's going to find us," Henri said raising his voice. "You've led her right to our door."

"I'm not dust because I wounded her, and the man who fights with her isn't experienced. With the cut to her leg she couldn't follow me, and she ordered Charlie to stay with me."

"My sister's probably right outside, you fool," Henri said.

"Enough." Ora offered her wrist to Wadham. It wouldn't cure him, but it would shorten the time his wound would take to heal. "Are all your men still outside?"

"Yes, Mistress, and I've warned them to stay vigilant for any movement," Wadham said, licking his lips after he drank. "We have enough time to make arrangements to move tomorrow night."

"We get this close and you want to leave?" Henri asked.

"Nothing's worth it if we lose our queen."

Henri stripped off his coat off as if he'd suddenly grown hot. "Don't insult me by thinking I'd gamble with her life. If your men are gone, we'll replace them with some of mine, like Troy. Compared to us he's a child, but I trained him myself."

"Your simpletons are gone," Wadham said with a snarl. "Asra is a formidable opponent we shouldn't have goaded into this game of yours."

"What do you suggest?" Ora asked.

"We must move from here tonight while the sun is a few hours off to assure you're not in any danger. Tomorrow night we'll head back to the Ivory Coast." Wadham dropped to his knees and crawled over to her on them so he could place his forehead on her feet. "We've been there for years without problems from the Clan, and our day watchers adore you. From there we can plan how to trap the slayer. Next year I promise you'll have her heart for the spell you need."

"You plan to run away like a cockroach?" Henri grabbed Wadham by the hair and lifted him off Ora's feet. "Do you think so little of your queen?" he asked, bending down until their faces were close together. "Or do you have no faith in me?"

"This isn't a contest, Henri," Wadham said, pressing his hand harder into his chest. "Try to see past your hatred of me, Asra, and everyone else before we all lose everything."

Henri tore off his shirt and stood so he could tower over Wadham, slamming his chest with his fist. "You've bragged constantly how easy it would be to defeat my sister." Henri easily took Wadham's sword from him. "You've carried this around with you, preening for her," he pointed to Ora, "but after facing Raad's daughter you act like a frightened little girl. My father was skilled enough to rule over the pharaoh's troops, and he poured all that talent into Asra."

"Aren't you proving Wadham's point that we should leave and regroup?" Ora asked.

"Asra was good before the Clan came into her life, but after training with the Elders and the masters she's found in her life, she's almost perfect. I can admit that, but the blood that runs through her," Henri walked to the window and scraped off some of the blood on the blade, "is the same that runs through me. I know her intimately, so you must choose who you'll trust."

"Wadham, rest, and at tomorrow's sunset, if you are still unable to fight, we'll go home."

"You've never had to question me, Ora," Wadham said, making her smile since he seldom used her name. "I implore you to listen. We are all in extreme danger."

"Rest, my sweet." She placed her hand over the one he had pressed to his chest. "I might have lived long, but I'm in no hurry to welcome death."

"You've made up your mind, then," Henri said, still staring out of the window with Wadham's sword in his hand.

Ora let her eyes linger on his broad back and compared him to Kendal, based on the few times she'd witnessed Kendal in her role with the Clan. The siblings had inherited their looks from Raad, but only Kendal still retained the sun-burnished healthy color of the handsome man she'd seen moments before death. Raad hadn't begged for life.

That night as his household lay dead, Raad had watched his son stalk around him, displaying all the new powers she'd given him. Raad had risen from his sickbed to watch the others die, but if Henri had hoped to build his fear, he had failed. Raad's words had made her pause.

"Kill me, but I will live on in the spirit of Asra. Her sword will damn you, and as she plunges it into your chest, I'll be waiting to greet you in the land of the dead. On that day you will never know another moment of peace, and I will know paradise."

"I warned you about your tone," she said, heading for the stairs. "And I haven't decided anything." At the landing, she turned and glanced at Henri, finding him peering up at her. "Tomorrow night the bones will decide."

CHAPTER TWENTY-TWO

Y ou want to stay here today?" Charlie asked. They had walked back toward the car at a reasonable pace, but now Kendal was heading to the Piquant, where she still had a suite.

"I'd love to go home, but my fan club would only tail us, and I don't want them anywhere near Oakgrove tonight for any reason. I may have to tie both of them to chairs in Piper's condo if they don't start following directions. It's their choice."

"You're losing your touch, buddy."

Kendal punched his arm and laughed. "It's a new era, Charlie, and it makes me hanker for the days when I could club them over the head and drag them back to the cave. I have a feeling, though, if I tried that with Piper, I'd thank Morgaine every day for giving me the ability to not need sleep, because she'd kill me the minute I closed my eyes."

"You lived when people did that. I always thought it was a myth."

"It's a myth, at least when you consider all the women in my life. I've always thought it's not much fun if they aren't willing to go toe to toe with you. I bet that's why you still miss Celia."

"Celia was my friend and a lover, but she had a wicked temper. Thank the gods it only came out when I was doing something Celia disapproved of, so it wouldn't have mattered what era we lived in. I'd never have found a club big enough to intimidate her. I loved her with all my heart, but ooh she was scary when she got mad."

"We've been lucky, my friend. Those were women worth fighting for." They neared the hotel, and Charlie declined her offer of a room. He wanted to visit the field where the remains of his family rested. On the eve that this horror would finally end, he wanted to watch the sunrise from there and pray for guidance.

"I'll be back for you," Charlie said as they stopped at the front door of the Piquant.

She put her hand on his shoulder and whispered in his ear, "Put in a good word for me as well."

❖

"Good morning, Ms. Richoux. Are you enjoying your visit so far?" Edwin asked, recognizing her.

"It's been great, thank you for asking. They haven't given my room away in my absence, have they?"

"No, ma'am. You'll even find a chocolate waiting on your pillow. Would you care for anything else to be sent up? Perhaps a doctor to look at your leg," he said calmly. She had chosen a pair of light-colored buckskin pants, which were great for comfort but didn't hide bloodstains very well.

"It's not mine, but thanks again."

He opened the door and saw she'd left a bit of a bloody footprint on the tile. "Are you sure? We have a guy who makes house calls."

"Trust me, Edwin, you should see the other guy."

She unlocked the door and stepped into the closet to remove her weapons. The cut didn't hurt much, but it annoyed her, so she opened the curtains of the large window facing the city and propped herself on it. With the first sign of dawn, the process began again. She didn't need to remove the pants to watch what was happening, like she had so many times in the past. It was like watching a flower bloom in fast motion. The sun would knit the skin together, healing her body inside and out. When she was whole again, the door to the suite opened behind her.

"I knew it," Piper said, when she spotted her leaning against the window.

"I remember something about you and a promise. You can't blame forgetfulness since you made said promise less than twenty-four hours ago. I told you to stay away from me." She tried to sound angry but couldn't continue the charade as Piper stalked toward her. "It's the only way I know to keep you safe."

"And you swore you'd be careful and come back to me, and look at you."

"I don't remember promising that." Piper pulled Kendal's shirt out of the stained pants and she did nothing to stop her. "I'm fine, really. The blood isn't from a fresh cut."

"I'm not fragile. You don't have to lie to me." Piper poked her finger into the slash in the leather the sword had made. "Let me help you, don't shut me out. Please, Kendal."

"Little one, I'm all right. I wouldn't lie to you about something like this."

"So sue me, because I don't believe you." Piper held up the part of the shirt where she'd torn away her makeshift bandage. The tie of the pants came undone next.

"Is this some ploy to see me naked again?"

Piper's movements grew more frantic and her eyes filled with tears. "This isn't a joke. Hill had to hold me down when I saw you were injured. I couldn't stand to see you bleeding. Why can't you understand that? Why don't we just call the police? This isn't worth your life."

Kendal held Piper's hands and glanced down at her leg. Seeing her appearance through Piper's eyes made her realize how Piper perceived the situation. "This is something I have to do alone."

"But you don't have to. I'll help you so you can finish this. Then we can pick up where we left off yesterday." She released Piper's hands and let her pull the bloodied and torn pants down her legs. Piper removed the strip of shirt Kendal had tied to slow the stream as it soaked through and uncovered smooth, perfect skin. "I don't understand."

"I told you I was fine."

"Kendal, no one ties a bandage to their leg for nothing. What were you trying to do, make a fashion statement?"

"I was trying to fool someone into thinking I was hurt so they'd lead me to the people I really wanted. I'm sorry if you misunderstood and I worried you. I wouldn't intentionally try to hurt you."

Crying, Piper got back to her feet and appeared to be deciding whether to leave or stay. "You did hurt me by sending me away. I don't understand any of this, but I'm starting to understand how I feel about you. I don't know if I'm strong enough to stand by and watch you try to destroy yourself."

"What do you feel?" Kendal stepped out of her pants and moved closer to Piper so she could take her hands, needing a connection to her.

"I ache inside when I think someone's hurt you." Piper's shoulders slumped and her tears fell in earnest. "Stupid, huh?"

She held Piper against her chest as tight as she could without hurting her. "No, not stupid. That's very sweet, and I feel lucky to know you care about me." Piper's hair smelled like a citrus grove, and the aroma made Kendal relax. "Now you know how I feel when I think about someone hurting you."

"Why would anyone want to hurt me?"

"If you get too close, you become a weapon my enemies can use against me. This isn't a game, and you need to understand the danger before it's too late and you get caught in an impossible position." She relaxed her hold so she could see Piper's face. "Now that you see I'm all right, you need to go, and this time please keep your word. Stay away from me until I find my brother and deal with him."

"I don't want to go, not yet." Piper laid her head on Kendal's chest and tightened her arms around her waist. "Everyone I care about sends me away for my own good, and I think it's time to decide for myself what's best."

"Why do you say that?"

"My mother died after having me, and after that my dad checked out instead of trying to take care of me. From what I remember, if he was given a choice, I'm sure I'd never be it. He just gave me away." Piper's voice got softer as she spoke.

"Little one, from what I know of your family, your father didn't give you away. He was lost without the woman he loved. Apparently your mother, before you came, was his world, and her death killed a large part of his heart. It wasn't right that he couldn't show you how much you meant to him, but you can't keep thinking that he considered you lacking in any way."

"He blamed me for her death. He never said it out loud, but I could tell. If she hadn't given birth she'd still be here."

Kendal put two fingers under Piper's chin and raised the tear-stained face. "Your mother's death was nature's fault, not yours."

"You don't know that."

"I know lots of things, and I'm sure of this. Your parents were lucky. Their love and life together was short-lived, but they left behind the most precious evidence of what they meant to each other. They left the world you." She ran her hand along Piper's face, wiping away her tears and trying to comfort and heal the hurts of the little girl who had taken on her father's pain and guilt, which had become heavier the longer she carried them. "Open your eyes and see what the rest of us do. You're smart, driven, and beautiful."

Piper blushed and laughed at the compliment. "I thought you said I was annoying. If I remember correctly, you mentioned a pesky little thing buzzing around your ear."

"Lucky for you, I happen to like annoying. If we had dismissed each other right off, we wouldn't be here. I've found that, sometimes, anger's as strong an emotion as all the others combined. It hasn't been boring, has it?"

"No, and you're right. I can't explain why I'm here. Not that long ago I wanted your head mounted on my wall."

Kendal moved her hands down to Piper's waist. "And now?"

"Now I want to do everything I can to keep you whole so I can spend more days walking around Oakgrove with you, listening to your stories about interesting people who lived long ago. And in return, I want to build a friendship with you that we'll both treasure."

"I'd love that, but we had a deal, remember? You need to leave."

"I said I would, but we're not done." Piper moved a step back and took her hand, then looked around until she found the bathroom and started tugging her in that direction.

"Piper, can I ask what you have in mind?"

"I believe that the blood isn't yours, but it's disgusting, so I want to help you clean up. After that, I intend to order room service and then watch you sleep. If you're running around after people who want to kill you, you have to refuel."

Part of her brain loved the suggestion, but the more rational section applied the brakes. "As great as that sounds, we can't."

"Why not? It's not like I haven't seen you naked before." Piper's smile turned teasing as she pulled harder on her hand.

When Kendal set her feet, she was sure Piper would have more luck pulling up an ancient oak with her bare hand than getting her into the bathroom. "I appreciate it, but I don't need to sleep, and not to sound repetitive, but you've got to get going."

"Unless you're not human, you need to sleep. I was up all night trailing you and I'm exhausted, though I just rode around in the car. If you don't lie down and sleep, you'll force me to break my promise and follow you in case you need my help."

"Then let me be honest." She did the only thing she could think to motivate Piper to walk out the door. With a gentle pull she pressed Piper against her and kissed her with passion. This time she gave herself permission to let her hands wander as she took possession of Piper's mouth. She was sure Piper would want to get as far away from her as possible, and she didn't stop until Piper slumped against her.

"Um…" Piper looked up at her like she didn't really know what to say.

"I don't want to be, because I know how you feel about this sort of thing, but I'm attracted to you. It'd be torture to get in that shower and know I couldn't touch you like I want. With a little time, I'm sure I can get used to the idea of just being your friend, but I'm not there yet." Kendal laughed and patted the side of Piper's face. "That and remaining clothed at all times when we're together."

"Um…"

"Look, I'm sorry. I shouldn't have done that, and I'll understand if you want to leave now."

As she had before in their short history together, Piper did the unexpected by walking away from Kendal and putting her hands on her hips. She was clearly pissed and didn't appreciate being played, which only made Kendal's libido stand up and take notice. If Piper's eyes got any darker, Kendal would have to beg, she was sure, since she was ready to begin.

"Who said anything about me joining you in the shower, you big moose." Piper moved her hands from her hips to the top button of her shirt. It popped open quickly, and Piper moved to the next ones until the garment was close to undone.

"Um, Piper, sweetheart, you have to stop before we reach some place you don't want to be." Kendal's order sounded weak, and she kept her eyes glued to the black lace bra that was visible when the fourth button gave way.

Piper's shirt dropped to the floor behind her and she moved to the buttons of her jeans. "The way I see it, you big take-charge types look at women like me and have an uncontrollable urge to do our thinking for us."

"Big take-charge types?"

"You have some sort of conqueror complex. I'm sure you could find hundreds of books on the subject. You run around with your sword and swagger and think the rest of us are here to bow and scrape." Piper's shapely hips wiggled to help the jeans slide down her legs. When they hit Piper's ankles, the only moving Kendal wanted to do was put the Do Not Disturb sign on the door. The matching black bikini underwear was doing funny things to her blinking reflex.

"I do not expect people to bow and scrape."

Piper moved her hand to the clasp at the back of the bra, jutting her breasts out quite nicely. Drooling is not an option here, Asra, Kendal warned herself.

"Yes, you do. 'Piper, go home and don't worry your pretty little empty head about me.'" Piper lowered her voice to sound more like her. "'Only I get to decide when and where we'll spend time together.'" Piper had to stop and cough from trying to sound gravelly, making Kendal laugh. She took a step forward when the bra came loose and slid down Piper's arms. "Don't even think about it."

"You get naked over there and you expect me to just stand here?"

"I'm not naked." Piper put her fingers at the sides of her underwear and pulled down. "Now I'm naked." Her fists moved back to her hips. "Still want me to leave?"

"No."

"Want to get in the shower with me?"

"Yes." She couldn't stop sounding like an idiot. Piper's gorgeous body had reduced her to one-word answers. To remedy the situation, she closed her eyes and took a deep breath. "But you just said you didn't want to get in the shower with me."

"I don't, I want you to get in the shower with me. There's a difference." Piper closed the gap between them and pulled Kendal's shirt off, leaving her in a pair of plain white briefs. "How can you be so perfect?"

"Cigar smoking," she said, stepping over the pile of clothes, and scooped Piper off her feet. As they moved to the bathroom, Piper pulled the tie out of her hair and ran her fingers through it.

They stood under the spray simply enjoying the feel of each other's skin. With time to think, Kendal was able to control her urges. Instead of moving too fast, she touched Piper in a way that had nothing to do with sex, but more about giving reassurance and being someone for Piper to hold on to. Mac and Molly had provided everything within their power, but even their love had not been enough of a balm to heal the scars life had inflicted.

In her, she guessed, Piper had found someone with whom, perhaps for the first time, she could let her defenses down and fear no ridicule for who she truly was. And she believed Piper had been completely open with her, so as physically different as they were inside, they were two of a kind—people who projected an image that hid their true self, which almost no one was privileged to see.

She ran her fingers through Piper's hair to get it wet. She hated to use the hotel's shampoos since Piper smelled so good just as she was. When she was done, she stood still and watched as Piper gently washed away all the evidence of her injuries.

"You know what's funny?" Piper asked.

"Not me, I hope."

"Not you, but being here feels so right. Before you, personal closeness was never easy, and being with someone like Kenny made my skin crawl. I would've never done this with him." Piper ran her fingers along her collarbone. "But I can't curb the urge to touch you."

"In your defense, I think Kenny has that effect on most people," Kendal said, quickly pressing their lips together to erase Piper's pout. She had been with so many women before Piper, but very few had reached so deep inside her so quickly. Piper made her want to do what was necessary to remove people like Kenny from her life. The last thing Piper needed was a champion, but she'd gladly take the job if Piper offered it. "If I tell you something, will you try not to hold it against me?"

"I can't improve on my record of holding things against you, so I doubt it."

"It has to do with what you just mentioned, and it's the answer to what you've asked more than once." She looked at Piper and combed her hair behind her ear.

"You can tell me anything."

"I helped you and Mac for only one reason, and you owe me only one thing in return."

At the word "owe," Piper pulled violently away from her and opened the shower door to leave. "God, I'm such an idiot. Of course there's a price. Why would I think *you'd* be any different? At least you 'fessed up before we had sex."

She'd given the money freely, and Piper wasn't leaving until she heard why. She wrapped her hand around Piper's bicep to keep her close. "I respect your grandfather, especially for the kind of businessman he is, but I did all this for you." Piper still faced away from her, but she wasn't resisting, which made her hold unnecessary. "Unless you try to sink Marmande Shipyard, you'll never have a reason to feel you have to sacrifice yourself to someone like Kenny to keep what's yours. I never want an animal like that to put his hands on you, unless you ask of your own free will."

She finally let Piper go. "What do I owe you in return?" Piper asked as she faced her.

"I want you to be happy and strive to be whole, that's all. Take the freedom you have now and enjoy it. You do that and you'll never owe me a thing."

Piper stepped closer, but still seemed wary. "That's all?"

"This isn't a trick, Piper. I've finished my business with Marmande, and nothing in what I gave you binds you to me."

"So you're giving us millions? Forgive me for sounding skeptical, but who does that?"

"Stop searching for angles and loopholes—you won't find any. I just want what I asked for, but remember, the price is steeper than you think. Living a full life is more difficult than people imagine, because in most cases they plant the seed of doubt and misery themselves."

Piper moved under the spray with her, leaving an inch of separation. "How hard can it be to make myself happy when you've so freely given me everything I'll ever need?"

Kendal smiled before tapping a spot over Piper's heart. "Money makes life easier, but it'll never bring you happiness. So many have written about that subject that I don't need to explain it to you." She flattened her hand over Piper's chest. "Completeness comes from within yourself. No one and, more important, no thing can give that to you."

It was easy to acquire wisdom, given thousands of years to live, but in her time she'd been lucky enough to meet some who learned the answers to life's riddles in only one lifetime. A man living in the streets of Nepal had taught her the lesson she was repeating for Piper. He owned only what he was able to carry, but he believed he was wealthy because he understood what true fulfillment really was. He'd amassed knowledge, and sharing it with others only added to his bounty.

"Once you let go of all that baggage from your past, you'll discover true happiness. Then you can dismantle that fortress you've built around your heart and start to enjoy your life. With an open mind and heart, you'll be ready to welcome the person who'll share the rest of your days, and they'll bring with them the love and devotion you deserve."

"It's that easy, huh?"

"Your family's business is important to you, and you've become important to me, so, yes, it's that simple," she said, turning around for one last rinse.

"Then thank you." Piper pressed herself to her back and wrapped her arms around her waist. "I'll do whatever you want."

"Remember," she turned around and held Piper, enjoying the feel of her, "don't ever share yourself with someone who makes your skin crawl, as you put it. Save that gift for the one who holds your heart and sees you. If not, at least share yourself with someone who stirs your passion." She kissed the top of Piper's head and let her go.

"Who are you really?" Piper asked, holding on to her this time so she wouldn't leave.

"Why do you ask?"

"Because what you say doesn't compute with what you do. You sound like a warrior poet," Piper said, her smile back in place and her face relaxed and open.

"It's my pleasure to share my life's experiences with you." Kendal stepped out of the shower. Behind her, Piper shut the water off, so she handed her a towel before drying herself. Piper held her towel up as if she'd suddenly become shy, so Kendal put on a hotel robe and opened the door. "I'll leave you to finish up. Take your time, there's no rush."

Giving Piper her privacy allowed Kendal time to straighten the room, so when the bathroom door opened again she was sitting on the bed with Piper's neatly folded clothes next to her. She extended her hand in invitation to wipe the hesitation from Piper's expression. "Time for you to go, my friend, and time for me to get back to my battles."

"I'm not leaving yet. I want to make sure you get some rest before you start chasing crazy people around town."

"If I was tired, trust me, I would, but my internal clock works differently than most." When Piper didn't take her hand, she held up the delicate panties on the end of one finger, but Piper still wouldn't budge.

"If you lie down with me for an hour, you can ask me to leave and I will," Piper said, walking toward her. As if to encourage her to accept her offer, she lost her shyness and reached for the tie of Kendal's robe, opening it with sure hands. Kendal went willingly when Piper eased her down on the bed and climbed in with her. Once Piper pulled the covers over them, she opened her own robe and lay almost on top of her so they were skin to skin. "Close your eyes and hold me," Piper said, softly kissing her chin, then her lips.

She returned the kiss and gladly gave Piper her wish by putting her arms around her. "Sleep now, and I promise to keep you safe."

Piper's breathing hitched for a moment, but she stayed quiet, as if trying to find the right words for what was bothering her. "Don't you want me?" she asked finally in a small, fragile voice.

"Remember what I asked of you? This is about you and what you want, and need, so please don't think I'm deciding for you. Right now you're tired, which isn't the best time to make life-altering decisions."

When Piper didn't object, she began to speak again, but in Chinese so Piper would concentrate on the sound of her voice instead of her words. She recited a poem that a warrior who served one of the Chinese emperors wrote to the woman he left behind when he went to war. She carried his son in her womb, the testament to their love and his existence. His wife finished the verses for him when the boy grew to be a man and followed his father's path into battle. The warrior never knew the boy and entered the afterlife at the end of an enemy's sword, but his last thought was of his wife. In her face, in his mind's eye, he found his salvation and a way to push away the pain. His killer died years later, still wondering why the man faced death with such a blissful smile.

"Because he knew love," she whispered to Piper, who was sleeping deeply in her arms. "It is what gives our blades courage." She kissed Piper's temple and closed her eyes, trying to memorize every inch of her.

She gently rolled Piper over, not wanting to wake her, and got up to dress. If only she'd had more time. She smiled at the notion, but now she had to completely erase Piper Marmande from her mind, not only to keep her safe from Henri, but also to set her free before their feelings grew any deeper. Piper deserved someone to grow old with who would give her a life full of beauty, not the nightmares she had to face to keep the balance tipped toward the light.

She gazed at Piper one last time, feeling the years she'd lived like a weight on her heart. Piper, more than any woman she'd known, made her imagine how special it would be to share herself with someone so beautiful in every way. Be well, Piper, and thank you for making me feel alive, she thought, then walked out the door.

A few hours later Piper rolled over and opened her eyes, and she knew instantly that she was alone. The bed felt twice as empty with Kendal's missing heat, but on the pillow next to her lay a single yellow daffodil with a note under it.

> *These have always reminded me of sunshine. The woman I bought this one for, though, reminds me of the beauty in all things. Take the flower as a way of remembering all the sunrises you have left to enjoy and how beautiful you'll make each day by simply being you.*
> *Stay safe. Kendal*

Piper refused to accept the flower as a good-bye. Even if it took the rest of her life, she'd find Kendal again. "I have a gift to give you as well, warrior poet." She spoke the words to the card in her hand, and she knew now that the one who held her heart and had awakened her passions had written it. They would never have a moment of hesitation between them again.

CHAPTER TWENTY-THREE

The front door was unlocked, as if the owners were expecting them for a cordial visit. Kendal stood in the foyer and listened for any human guardians in the house left to watch over their masters during the day. Only the ticking of the grandfather clock in the long entry hallway broke the silence.

"If I were a bloodsucker, where would I hide from the sun?" she asked Charlie.

He put down the human skull with a candle melted into the top that he'd found on the desk in the middle of the study. "Must've been someone either Henri or Ora cared enough about to keep a memento of them, or someone who had insulted them in some way," she said.

"If we were anywhere but New Orleans, I'd guess the basement. Having one, though, is an invitation to an indoor swimming pool in a light rainstorm."

"Let's look around and see how creative they've gotten." They walked through the ground floor, and Kendal found the first unique piece of furniture. "Cute," she said, referring to the sunroom they were standing in.

The long piece was wooden on the bottom, topped with a slab of thick granite. In any other location it could've served as a buffet, but the skulls carved in the wood made her itch to remove the stone. "Want to see what's behind door number one?" Charlie asked.

"I thought you'd never ask, Monty." They worked together to make it easy. When sunlight streamed into the space, they didn't get a close look inside before the vampire burst into flames. "Makes me wish we'd thought to bring marshmallows."

Charlie laughed, leaning against the wood base. It didn't take long for the flames to die away and leave a pile of ashes. "We didn't get a chance to say good-bye, but I can tell you who the dirt pile was."

"Elvis?"

"Not unless he walked around with this under those shiny outfits." He lifted a sword from the ash. The snakehead marked the demise of Wadham. "And I don't think this guy could carry much of a tune."

"It would seem he's alone down here, so let's move up."

They opened five more boxes before reaching the house's master bedroom, which was empty except for two sarcophagi in the center of the room. On top of the longer of the two sat a coiled king cobra. The serpent raised his head when they entered, but then he only swayed from side to side without showing his hood.

"I never did like snakes," she said.

"It's not like it can kill you."

"Neither can polyester pants, but I don't have a fondness for them either." She stepped closer and the snake grew more alert. "My brother always did have a sense for the dramatic." She threw a dagger hard enough to pin the lethal reptile to the back wall.

She held her hand out for Wadham's sword. With a downward motion she buried it in the wooden floor between the two boxes. She pulled a small memento from her coat to show who'd visited and where to find her.

"Why not just lift the lids and be done with it?" Charlie asked.

"I would, but I gave him my word I'd face him like a warrior. I also want to see his eyes when he knows he's reached the end of his life." She ran her hand over the stone full of hieroglyphics telling the story of Abez's life. Her name was woven into the pictures. "Now it's just you and I, brother. Tonight you'll pay for the life you have chosen and for the death of our father. On my sword I swear you won't live out the night," she said in their native tongue.

In only four hours they would finish the saga that had begun in Egypt so many years before. The night of reckoning had arrived.

❖

Ora opened her eyes, and even in the dark confines of her resting place she easily found her family's crest carved in the stone in the area above her heart. The ritual she repeated before facing another night had worn the stone around the carving, but the circle strengthened the protection spell that enveloped her.

She took a deep breath and closed her eyes again when she found a new scent somewhere near. She pushed aside the heavy stone easily and found Henri already sitting up.

"Here's our proof that Kendal knows where we are." She stared at Wadham's sword and the camellia tied to the pommel.

"The flower is from Oakgrove," Henri said, looking at the same thing. "I came so close."

"Remember that coming close in anything focuses your enemies on defeating you."

Henri rose and took the flower so he could smell it. "Do you want me to wake Wadham for our retreat?"

"I sense she's left us to fend for ourselves. Our few defenders are gone."

Henri dropped Kendal's gift and walked to the wall to pull the dagger out, the snake dropping to the floor. "Do you want to run?" he asked, finding the rendition of the devil's face at the end of the dagger funny.

"We don't have time."

"If you want to leave, we can." Henri tucked the blade into his belt. "She won't be back tonight. The great slayer's too honorable for that. That's why she didn't kill us when the sun was at its peak. Kendal's waiting for us at Oakgrove."

"Did you think she'd come this close to us?"

"The only way we can survive is to join forces," he said, taking her hands. "You have to believe that Kendal has received too much credit for her fighting skills."

"What of the man who fights with her?"

"Him?" he laughed. "I took his family, and he's pretending to be something he's not. He'll be easy to contain."

From inside her sarcophagus, Ora removed a bag of polished carved bone and threw the pieces on the stone cover of his sarcophagus, then stared at them for five minutes before she spoke. "I'm not sure you have a true picture of your sister, my pet." Ora picked the bones up and threw them again. "She's strong and driven."

"Of course she is. How else did she come to lead her own troops in her mortal life?" He pushed aside her hair and kissed the back of her neck. "Kendal was too much like my father."

"Now would be a good time to remember Raad's last words." Ora looked at the position the bones had landed in. "Tonight is All Hallow's Eve, and if we accept her invitation, our lives will be forfeit this time."

He glanced at the markings but saw only lines in bone, since she'd never shared those talents with him. To distract her, he moved his hands up from her hips to her breasts. "Haven't you told me through the centuries that true power exists only in darkness?" When he circled her nipples with his index fingers, they grew rock-hard. "I revel in the darkness, and I won't let you down."

She threw the bones again and finally smiled and pressed her bottom to his groin. "We have something to use against her, something you've used before to assure success."

"Leave those for now," he said, leading her to the bed in the next room. "Kendal's driven but has never learned not to care so much for these weaklings she has surrounded herself with. Tonight I plan to drain her, then bury her in the grave with the ashes of her beloved Angelina."

"Don't underestimate her or overestimate how easy this will be. The bones never lie, and tonight will be the beginning of a new order." Ora dropped her gown, her body as perfect as the night she'd first revealed it to him.

"Tonight we will defeat the Clan's greatest warrior, and tomorrow you can take your rightful place as queen." He entered her as she bit the skin surrounding his nipple hard enough to draw blood. The pain made him move his hips faster, bringing their climax to its peak as she sucked only enough to enjoy the taste of him as she had so many times before.

"You have served me well, Abez, and your reward will be great," she said, running her finger along his eyebrows.

"Come, then. I've never tasted the blood of an immortal."

❖

Kendal and Charlie sat together on the porch of Oakgrove and watched the sun set over the far bank of the river. Kendal was smoking one of the cigars Piper had given her in silence, her mind blank. She'd put her memories away and made peace with what had happened to Angelina and Tomas. As painfully as Angelina's life had ended, she could only imagine Angelina's pain had she existed as a vampire. So gentle a soul could never have accepted living off the torment of others for survival. By sacrificing her own happiness at the time, Kendal had given Angelina eternal peace.

"The time is upon us, Charlie. They will arrive soon."

Charlie stood and held out his hand, and they exchanged a warrior's arm clasp before moving in for a friendly embrace. "For our women, then, and my sons."

She squeezed him one more time before letting go. "Celia and the boys are looking out for us, I'm sure. Fight well and stay away from pointy objects, especially teeth," she told him with a small laugh.

"You just remember the same thing."

Before she turned to go inside, she wanted to make one more thing clear before the heat of battle muffled their reason. "Promise me something."

"Anything, you know that."

"No matter what, these two die tonight. I'll make no more promises to let Abez go free. I want the same from you, because I'll sleep the sleep of the just or suffer an eternity of torture gladly if I know he's dead. He and the bitch who made him."

Charlie nodded slowly. "I promise to do what it takes, but you're going to fight like never before, right?"

"She'll need to, dear Lionel, for tonight the foe is like no other." How Henri got there mystified her, but suddenly he stood there holding a very familiar object. The sight of it momentarily stunned her. "Do you remember, sister, how many hours he held it in his hands trying to teach us the art of the sword?" Henri asked, holding their father's sword.

"It hurts me that what meant so much to him has ended up with you, but aside from my feelings, it can't hurt me."

"I never said anything about hurting you with this useless piece of metal." Henri raised his free hand, motioning someone forward. Ora emerged from the darkness with a struggling Piper. "Fight me, Asra, or I'll either take her like I did your precious Angelina, or I'll finally put this to good use," he said, pointing the sword at Piper's chest.

Kendal's limbs felt leaden with fear, and she could only watch as Henri grabbed Piper from Ora and pressed her to his chest. Piper's eyes were glassy with tears, as if she knew exactly what kind of evil had taken her. Kendal's smile did little to change Piper's expression. She had to change her attack plan, but no matter what happened to her, she'd get Piper back to her life.

"You're getting better at clearing your mind, sister, but when you love so deeply it's like leaving blood drops to her door. You made it easy for me."

"Be still, little one," she told Piper, still smiling to try to reassure her. "I won't let anything happen to you."

Henri ran his tongue up the side of Piper's neck and nipped the tender skin at the base. "My sister loves making promises she can't keep," Henri said softly into her ear. "I, though, swear you'll be mine before the sun rises."

Piper closed her eyes when Henri dropped his hand to her hip, but Kendal's anger rose with his hand as he started to caress Piper's body, ending at her right breast. She took deep breaths to keep calm, but something snapped when he placed his palm over Piper's breast and squeezed.

"I never have understood why you don't bed these women you find," Henri said, looking at her as he continued to touch Piper. "You've got talent for finding beauty, and yet you go through this courting ritual with such thoroughness that they become totally defenseless against that charm of yours. Is that the reason? You want them creaming their pants?" He laughed, then kissed Piper's temple. "You don't need to jump through so many hoops. Angelina struggled at first, but she was in ecstasy by the time we finished. She couldn't get enough."

Breaking every rule of combat, she ran forward and lunged at Henri with her sword, trying to stab him anywhere she could reach without hurting Piper. Sparks flew when Henri pushed Piper aside and stopped her attack with his blade. With a flick of his wrist, he dislodged her sword and kicked her in the stomach.

"This is the Clan's great slayer," Henri said, following with a kick to her face that made her mouth fill with blood. "You always thought me lacking, but I took what Raad gave me and improved it, just like I changed my life for the better by becoming something you'll never be able to defeat."

"What the hell are you talking about?" She spit the blood out and rose to her knees to deflect any more blows.

"Raad gave me life, then pushed me aside when you came, only to destroy our family." Henri stood in front of her, twirling the sword as if to impress her. "I paid him back by devoting myself to Ora and the power she gave me. I gave his sword to Wadham, and he made it over as many times as it took, waiting for this day."

"That's your problem, Abez," she said, grabbing his foot when he tried to kick her again. "No one pushed you aside." He fell on his face when she twisted his foot hard, flipping him. "You were nothing but a drunk who thought if he whined enough about the unfairness of his life, you could get by without having to earn anything." She didn't let go of him as she stood up. "That act got old by the time you were ten, so don't blame Father for your immaturity."

Henri tried to reach blindly for his sword, but she held him in place. "You became a monster so willingly because you didn't get enough attention? You're even more pathetic than I thought. I might have forgiven you if you'd told me that bitch forced you into this hideous thing you've become."

The moment she released him, Henri scrambled to his feet and looked frantically for his sword when he saw she had her katana back. "Pathetic better describes you," he said, doing well to meet her stroke for stroke. "You've lived all this time for what? To do the Elders' bidding but never join their ranks. That makes you no better than your slave Charlie. Ora gave me true life and, with it, the opportunity to rule with her." He struck so hard she had to use both hands to defend herself, leaving her open to his fist that landed on the side of her head. "The beginning of the Clan's end comes with you." Henri stopped talking abruptly when she got past his defenses and landed two kicks to his chest. As he lost his balance, he screamed when she jabbed him completely through the leg.

"It's not that easy," she said, slicing through his dominant sword hand. "You can say whatever convinces you of your importance, but don't pretend you know anything about me or my life. Tonight is about you and everything you have to answer for." She raised her sword, ready to bury it in his chest. "That list is long, and I'm here to collect."

"Then consider this my down payment, idiot," Henri said, smiling.

Kendal turned her head, but not in time to move before Ora drove her blade through her, and she saw the point when she glanced down. In dealing with Henri she'd taken her eyes off Charlie and Ora, and it had cost both her and Charlie dearly. He was behind Ora but holding his arm against his chest, and it appeared Ora had come close to severing Charlie's hand.

The pain was excruciating, and she tried to stay conscious so she could save both Charlie and Piper, but as the blood flowed freely from her wound she saw no way to destroy either Henri or Ora. She bit back a moan when Ora twisted her blade and drove it in until the hilt rested against her back. She hadn't blacked out because Ora's hit had missed her heart. From somewhere she couldn't pinpoint, Piper screamed in a way that haunted her.

"Let me go, goddammit," Piper yelled, apparently at Charlie. "I can't lose her."

"Charlie, keep her from seeing the rest," she said in French as loud as she could. "She doesn't deserve those nightmares added to the ones she already has." Her voice wasn't loud but Charlie must've understood, because suddenly the night went quiet again.

"All that loyalty wasted on Charlie, only to have him run at the first chance," Henri said, laughing.

"I owe you an apology, precious," Ora said, yanking the blade free with another twist. "I've thought for so long I'd chosen the weaker of Raad's children, but your sister shows the fight of a tame puppy. You've proven yourself smarter and stronger. Now finish it."

Henri picked up his sword with his uninjured hand and drove it close to where Ora had stabbed her. "I wanted Father's blade to taste your blood before I take your greatest weakness from you."

"What's that, my unfortunate luck in siblings?" she asked, gasping from the pain.

"Your heart, Asra, and its infinite capacity for caring, sets us apart. I'm going to rip it from your chest, and while you watch it beating in my hand, I'm going to drain whatever blood hasn't spilled down your shirt." He bent at the waist and pressed his index finger to her forehead to force her to look at him. "Will it taste as sweet as Father's?"

"If you sit long enough by the river of life, you'll see the bodies of your enemies float by," she said to Ora with effort.

"Henri, this is no time for games. Give me what I want," Ora said. "And does the pain make you talk in riddles, Asra? If so, you won't have to suffer much longer."

"Actually, the pain clears my mind." She looked into Ora's eyes and smiled. "My teacher said I'd never know death, but she couldn't erase pain. The answer to what needs to be done, though, lies in the pain."

"More riddles?" Ora asked, slapping her.

"The meaning of the proverb is that you should never claim victory until your enemy's dead and the lifeless body passes you by. Don't trust anything but your own eyes."

"What does that mean?" Ora demanded, holding her hand up to stop Henri.

"It means I know Abez better than you ever will, no matter how many years he's been your lapdog. It also means my body is neither lifeless nor dead, witch." She struggled to her feet and raised her hand, stunning both of them into watching her. Ora noticed the katana flying toward her, but couldn't reach it before Kendal grabbed it. Charlie had followed her directions and not tried to help as Ora and Henri used her as target practice. He'd waited to throw her weapon back when she was ready.

Once she was able to stand upright, she took a deep breath and tried to bury the pain like Morgaine had taught her. Henri had snapped out of his stupor and screamed as he ran toward her, holding his sword above his head. She used the dagger she'd taken from her boot to parry. Ora had also armed herself again, but Kendal stood between them with her back against one of the porch's pillars, fending them off.

Moving made her feel like the wounds weren't bleeding as much, so she came down with both hands, driving Henri and Ora's sword points into the dirt. Pushing off from her support, she gained enough momentum to get her foot high enough to reach Henri's throat, making him pitch forward. With his head so close, she grabbed it and twisted, snapping his neck. Not a death blow, but she only needed to disable him long enough to deal with Ora.

"What of your choices now?" she asked Ora. "If Henri had ripped my heart out, all that stood between you and victory was Charlie. I love him, but he wasn't ready for that."

"You're telling me you planned this?" Ora asked, laughing.

"I planned on Henri being Henri, and he didn't disappoint me. He doesn't only live to kill, but also to inflict as much torment as he can." She moved forward and disarmed the inexperienced Ora.

"I can give you power, or I can give you pain—your choice," Ora said, backing up with her hands in front of her.

"I choose peace of mind."

Ora laughed as she reached for the pouch tied to her waist. She released the inner monster and morphed into the grotesque being Kendal had seen so many times. Here was the source of so much misery. "I'll never allow you peace as long as I live."

"There's your answer, then," she said, moving closer toward Ora.

"What answer?"

"That I need to kill you to know peace."

Ora held her fist up as if she was going to throw something at her, but Kendal held her ground. Ora backed up, murmuring softly as if reciting a spell. Kendal held her sword with the end pointed at the ground, keeping pace with Ora.

"You've hidden yourself," she said, showing no fear. "In all that time, I thought you had finally given the Elders what they wanted without me having to hunt you down."

"You thought I was dead by my own hand?" Ora brought her hands together and rubbed her palms in circles.

"No, they knew you lived, but wherever you'd hidden was like a prison of your own making."

Her comment made Ora stop moving her hands and laugh. "Are you stupid? I wasn't stuck anywhere. I was waiting for the right time to defeat those simpletons you serve. Their mistake was sending only you to face me."

"I got you here, didn't I?" she asked, moving her sword so only the hilt pointed at Ora. "Or should I say, Henri got you here, because I'd be easy to beat since I'm weak and waste my time on mere mortals. Did he tell you that over and over again until it sounded like the truth?"

"You gain nothing from all the compassion you shower on these simpletons, so it is a waste," Henri said, making her turn around to see where he was. She looked at him standing nearby, leaning on their father's sword. "Only the darkness contains the truth."

She nodded, not taking her eyes off him, but she heard Ora moving quickly behind her. "You're right, brother," she said, waiting until the last second. When she turned around, Ora had jumped the last five feet between them, howling with her mouth open as if she planned to use her fangs once she landed on her.

Kendal turned toward Henri again, raising her blade and wanting to see his face when he lost what was most important to him. She felt Ora's breath on the top of her head before the screams stopped. Her aim was true and she held the sword steady as it split Ora's heart down the middle.

Unlike any of Kendal's other kills, Ora exploded, forming a cloud of red dust that caught fire and burned as it fell to the ground. Very little of Ora's essence remained, and it swirled in the wind, scattering away from Kendal like a small swarm of mosquitoes. Ora's remains seemed to be trying to cling to whatever life was left in her.

❖

"Let me go, or I'll kill her," Henri said, holding an unconscious Piper in front of him. To make his threat real he pressed his teeth to her throat. If Kendal rushed him, she'd never make it in time before he ripped into Piper's carotid artery.

"Not this time, Henri. This ends here and now."

"Have you learned nothing about me?" he asked, not lifting his mouth far from Piper's neck. "I don't grow attached to the weak, pathetic creatures like you do. Their only job is to worship me and give willingly all I need to exist."

"If you remember, you asked me to face you and fight. Let her go so you can prove how much better and stronger you are than I am."

"You won't kill me because your love for this girl is stronger than your hatred of me," he said, raising his head completely but not releasing Piper. "It may piss you off that I'm your brother, but I'm still Abez." He held up their father's sword so she could see the blade and the writing that must have been copied numerous times when he'd had it repaired. "Knowing that, can you bring yourself to kill me if I let her go? What would our honorable father say if he were here?"

"He was honorable, yet you killed him. That you're capable of such an act must have killed his spirit before his heart stopped beating. Nonetheless, considering the type of man he was, he would tell me that every man can hope for redemption, so you deserved your freedom and chance to make amends." Kendal tossed the dagger away from her. "Release her and I won't come after you." She dropped the katana next, leaving herself unarmed. "You're right, I can't kill you."

"Fool, I'll take her and bury you for being so fucking weak." He opened his mouth wide, ready to bite down on Piper's neck.

"I didn't say you deserved to live, brother," she said, stopping him. "Someone else deserves the kill more, and he's anxious to claim that prize." Henri squinted, but it was too late. He'd forgotten Charlie, the man he'd dismissed as insignificant, the man he'd laughed at. "I only wanted to see your expression before you have to face all the innocents you've killed. I hope they show you as much mercy as you gave them."

Henri tried to turn around, but Charlie stabbed him hard enough from behind to pierce his heart. Henri disappeared in a black cloud of smoke that dispersed quickly. He was finally dead, and wherever Angelina, Tomas, and Charlie's family were, enjoying the afterlife, they had peace.

"Thank you," Charlie said after dropping his sword and catching

Piper before she fell to the ground. "And forgive me if you had any feelings for him."

"My brother ceased to exist the moment Ora sank her fangs into him, so you've nothing to apologize for. You put the beast out of his misery."

Piper moaned as she started to become more alert, but she quieted down as if she recognized her touch when Charlie placed her in Kendal's arms. "Sleep now, my little one, you're safe." She triggered a pressure point at the base of Piper's neck that eased her back into stillness. "Remember everything I've told you," she said, and kissed Piper's forehead.

"I'll put her inside," Charlie offered.

"You need to take her home." She held Piper closer to her and inhaled the scent of her perfume. "Take care, and I want you to be happy," she said, kissing Piper's lips this time.

"Are you sure?"

"Charlie, you know that's the right thing. Piper deserves someone who can make her happy and fill her life with love and joy." She was too weak to stand with Piper in her arms, so she released her to Charlie. "Have one of the staff take her home, clean her up, and leave no trace of us behind."

"She deserves better than that from you." Charlie cradled Piper, his injured hand still bleeding.

"No, Charlie." She propped herself against the lattice that wrapped the bottom of the porch. "She deserves better than me."

Chapter Twenty-four

No!" Piper screamed as she sat straight up in her bed. The blinds were open, and it took her a minute to figure out she was in her own home, safe from any danger. Her shoes sat neatly by the bed, and she was in her pajamas. She felt well rested, so she'd obviously slept, making her question her overwhelming urge to cry.

"Hey, you're awake," Hill said from the doorway. She had a cup of coffee in one hand and a folded section of the paper in the other. "I was just coming to get you up. Want something for breakfast?"

"Why are you here?" She rubbed her face, trying to focus on why her heart was racing.

Hill sat in the chair by the window and stretched her legs. "I kept calling and you didn't answer, so I came over to see if you were all right. You know, Piper, I realize this is a gated community, but you really shouldn't leave your door unlocked if you sleep like the dead."

She had no memory of the previous night except coming home after she'd dressed and left Kendal's room. Why couldn't she remember? It wasn't like she'd gone out drinking or taken something that fogged her mind. "I must've been out for the night."

"You sure you're okay? You look a little dazed." Hill moved to the bed and sat on the edge, her fingers coming away wet when she touched Piper's cheek.

"I'm fine, just still tired, I guess." She reached for the cup Hill had placed on the nightstand, but it fell from her hand when she looked at the small glass sitting next to it. Someone had put the daffodil Kendal had given her in water and left it next to the bed for her to see. She could've forgotten putting it there, but the vase it sat in wasn't hers.

She suddenly remembered the strange woman standing behind Kendal and running her through with an old-looking sword.

"Are you Piper Marmande?" The question came through the intercom from a voice she didn't recognize.

"Can I help you?" Piper looked through the peephole to see who'd gotten past the security gate without being announced.

"I have news of your friend Kendal Richoux. May I come in?"

He kept his head bowed, his fingers long and pale as they rested on the button of the intercom. She was about to unlock the door when she remembered what Kendal had told her about letting anyone in. "Can you tell me from out there? I'm not dressed to answer the door."

"Miss Marmande, your friend's in trouble and needs you. But I'll understand if you don't want to help, and I'm sure she'll understand that you don't want to be involved." His hand dropped and the man turned to go.

"Wait!" Piper opened the door and stood just inside it. "Please don't go."

"You must invite me in, Miss Marmande."

Piper had found herself at Oakgrove to see Kendal's murder. Charlie had kept her safe, and she was now convinced Kendal had sacrificed her life to save her.

"Piper, come on. You're scaring me."

"We have to go." She fought with the blankets and Hill to get off the bed. "We have to go now."

"Okay, honey, we'll go. You just need to tell me where and I'll take you."

"Kendal...Kendal needs me." Being trapped on the bed frustrated her, and her tears were making it harder to escape. "Oh, God, Hill, I think she's dead. I saw so much blood, so much."

"Piper, you have to calm down and breathe. What about blood? Whose was it?"

"Kendal's. This man came here and this woman stabbed her."

"You aren't making a whole lot of sense, and I'm sure Kendal's fine. You just had a bad dream." Hill helped Piper out of the bed, and she ran to her closet to throw something on.

She was despondent on the drive out of the city, and Hill couldn't get her to snap out of her stupor. She made Hill press the buzzer, hoping to find Kendal in a good mood. The intercom was silent though the gate opened.

Her dread doubled when she saw Charlie standing on the porch.

He looked more relaxed, as if someone had lifted a weight from his shoulders. "Welcome back."

"Can you get Kendal for us? Piper really needs to see her," Hill said as she helped Piper from the car.

"He can't," Piper whispered. "I'm right, aren't I?"

Charlie nodded and tried to offer a warm smile. Kendal had left that morning, and it would be decades before she'd walk these grounds again, if ever. Oakgrove had been Kendal's refuge for only a short period before it became the harbor for her greatest pain. Coming back had only proved that she was still suffering.

Jacques had spent more time with Angelina, but Charlie suspected that Piper had reached deeper inside Kendal in the few weeks they'd known each other. Kendal had fallen in love, and once again Henri had stolen the beauty of her feelings from her. Charlie didn't agree, but he understood her decision to walk away.

"She's gone, Miss Marmande. I'm sorry."

"Where is she?" Hill demanded.

"If you have any questions pertaining to any business dealings, her assistant in the New York office will be available to help you. That's all I can tell you. I'm sorry."

Piper leaned against the car and cried. "She gave me her word. She promised me," she screamed at him.

He couldn't stand to see her suffer. He imagined that she felt the same pain that he had when he lost his family. "You were her main concern, Miss Marmande. She told me how special you were and how much she came to care about you. Perhaps you can use that as a stepping stone to find someone who can give you what Kendal could not."

Piper stared at him with eyes so dead, they didn't appear to belong to her. "There'll be no one else."

"You're young, so don't give up so easily," he said, a hand on her shoulder.

A slight smile tried to crack the corners of Piper's lips but wasn't quite successful. "I have a feeling you know all too well what I'm going through and that what I'm saying is true. As much as I fought it and didn't want to like her, I ended up falling in love with her. A life without her will be empty."

"You are wise for one so young. Be well, Miss Marmande, and feel free to visit here as often as you like. You'll always be welcome at Oakgrove." She nodded and turned to head back to the car door. "If only a magic wizard could lift your spirits," he said as he closed her door and bent down to the open window to smile and place his hand on her shoulder one last time.

"What an odd thing to say," Hill said, starting the car.

Late that night, the clue hit Piper like a blow to the chest. She moved silently past Hill, who was sleeping on her sofa, and headed to her car.

The bartender at Oz just continued to wipe her hands on the bar towel and stared at her after she asked to be taken upstairs. Not bothering with introductions, the bartender led her to the office door.

"Have a seat and Lenore will be with you shortly. Do you want anything to drink?"

"What are all these books?" She stood at the railing and looked at the shelves.

A beautiful brunette emerged from the stacks, holding out her hand and waiting for Piper to take it. "They're our true history, child, and the tales of our greatest heroes and warriors. I'm Lenore and this collection is mine."

"It's a rather odd spot to keep them, but you have an inordinate amount here." She barely noticed that Lenore had yet to let go of her hand because she was so focused on her eyes. What were the odds that Kendal, Charlie, the bartender, and Lenore would share the same unique pale blue color with the yellow flecks surrounding the irises?

"So I've heard, and from your presence I can tell Charlie has done his job well in guiding you here. What can I do for you?"

"I want to know what happened to Kendal."

"Are you sure? Kendal's story is a long one." Lenore guided her to a set of comfortable reading chairs and poured her a cup of tea.

"What can I tell you to make you believe how much I care about her? If she's hurt or needs me, I want to go to her, and if she's dead, I'll have something to look forward to when I die."

"Piper, may I call you Piper?" She nodded. "I've known Kendal for a very long time. She'd want you to choose happiness, even if it meant you'd find it with someone else, someone like your friend Hill, perhaps. She tries to hide her feelings, but she loves you a great deal."

"If our heads chose our loves for us, the world would make more sense, I suppose, but they don't. Our hearts make our choices, and we can only follow. Kendal's the last person my head would have picked, but my heart cannot live without her, not anymore."

"You sound like a poet, child. I asked Kendal once what she feared most," Lenore said, closing her eyes and smiling. "Her answer was not one thing but three. She told me she feared vampires, demons, and God. Can you guess why?"

Piper stared at Lenore, wondering if the book lover was also a whiskey lover because of the strange change of topics. "She has a strange but vivid imagination?"

"She's more of a straightforward tactician than a dreamer, but I found her answer interesting. Vampires because they're a major reason Kendal has lived for so long, and demons because they can alter the fate of humankind if left unchecked."

"Why God?"

"I would have thought because of what man does to his fellow man in the name of a supreme being, but she had a different reason. To believe in the concept of a guiding spirit who helps you in all things, especially in our darkest hour, is to believe in love. Love, though, not one of her answers, is what I think she fears most. I believe she thought it was the one gift she'd never allow herself to experience fully."

Piper sat back into the cushions and wanted to scream. "But I love her. Didn't she realize?"

"I believe she did." Lenore rose from her seat and offered Piper a hand up so she could walk her to a large library desk. "Piper, I need you to dig inside yourself and find the small child you once were, the one who believed in fairy tales." Piper looked at the closed book entitled *Asra*. "It'll take me a while, but I'd like to tell you a story." Lenore flipped it open to the first page and showed her a sketch of Kendal dressed as an Egyptian soldier. "Born decades before the Christ child, Asra came into the world destined to serve the first and only female pharaoh, and then the Genesis Clan," Lenore said.

Lenore flipped the pages of the great book as she told Kendal's story: who she was in every lifetime, and all the demons and monsters she had fought along the way. Piper filled in the pictures in her head by looking at a detailed illustration of every identity Kendal had taken. Page after page contained stories and pictures of the same beautiful eyes and flirtatious smile dressed in the garb of a warrior.

After a week Lenore stopped talking, making Piper open her eyes. As long as she had sat in Lenore's library, she hadn't tired of listening to her melodious voice weaving a tale of fantasy she was sure was meant to make her feel better. Lenore's staff had given her a place to sleep and taken care of all her needs as Asra's story unfolded. The way Lenore told it made her want to believe, but rationally she dismissed it all as fiction. The total silence surprised her.

"Well?" Lenore asked.

"I want to thank you for your hospitality and kindness, Lenore. Listening to you almost made me forget the pain of losing her."

"You don't believe me?" Lenore asked with a sigh.

"It's a wonderful story, but no. As much as I want it to be true, I know better."

"Why not allow yourself the pleasure of believing a little bit? What would be the harm?"

Piper smiled and shook her head. "Because I have to hang on to what little sanity I have left. The image of that sword slicing through her chest almost makes me crazy, and my grandparents don't deserve for me to wander off into a make-believe world of vampires and immortals to make it easier to accept the truth that she's gone."

"Then we have misjudged you," Piper heard a woman say from the shadows. The sun had just set, and she and Lenore were bathed in the soft light of reading lamps and candles, making it hard to see into the stacks. "Asra deserves a woman who believes in the totality of who she is and, more important, who she has been."

"Who are you? Show yourself," Piper said.

"She's no threat, Piper, be still." Lenore frowned in the direction of the woman's voice. "Would you like to come out, or have you developed a case of shyness after all these years?"

A beautiful blonde stepped forward, and Piper recognized her from the first pages of the book. "We've fought the Elders for naught, Lenore."

"Don't be so pessimistic, Morgaine. She's defeated two of her greatest enemies, and I have faith that love will be her reward." Lenore put her hand on Piper's forearm. "Piper, this is the Elder Morgaine. She's Asra's watcher and teacher."

"Look, ladies, this has been fun, but we've got to face reality— Kendal's gone." Piper stood up.

"If you walk out, she'll be dead to *you*," Morgaine said icily, "but being immortal means that you never die, Miss Marmande. Not ever. Leave, and we'll never acknowledge you again. Kendal's memory will be all you have left of her."

"Where is she, then?"

Morgaine handed her an airline ticket to Italy. "We leave in the morning. You can refuse my offer if you like, but with or without you I'm going to see her."

"She's alive?" Piper was almost afraid to ask.

"As much as the characters in Lenore's book."

❖

After a lot of apologies and explanations to her family, Piper met Morgaine at the airport. She still didn't believe she'd find Kendal, but she couldn't take the chance of not trying.

She peered at her traveling companion when they reached cruising altitude, jealous of Morgaine's looks and self-assurance. "Were you lovers?"

"Should I lie?" Morgaine asked, reclining her seat and closing her eyes.

"I'm not that fragile."

"Yes, we were, but I think I should've paid better attention that last time."

Piper swallowed hard, wishing she'd let Morgaine lie. "Why, you find someone better?"

Morgaine's laugh came close to sparking her anger. "No. No one's better. I just think the last time was simply that—the last. I don't understand why, but Asra will never have room in her heart for another, which means she'll never need another in her bed."

They didn't speak again until the plane started its descent. Had Lenore been there to ask what she feared, Piper would have answered, "disappointment." If Kendal wasn't on the other end of this journey, life would always be empty, lonely, and full of disappointment. But would that be a life worth living or one she wanted?

❖

"*Bona sera*, Kendal. What can I get you this afternoon?" asked the waiter holding his pen to his pad. She'd been sitting in the Piazza St. Marco for a week, always at the same table and always from when the café opened. The self-imposed exile reminded her that while people would always be around her, she would always be alone. Nature was punishing her, she guessed, for defying the true order of things for so long.

"A bottle of beer and a plate of figs, Tony," she answered in perfect Italian.

"That sounds so Egyptian."

Morgaine's velvety voice came from behind her, but she didn't turn around. She was probably there to deliver a pep talk, and Kendal wasn't in the mood. "I felt like returning to my roots."

Morgaine laughed and sat across from her. "Shouldn't you have gone back to Egypt?"

"It's not like I don't have more time than I know what to do with. That just might be next on my itinerary, but I'm sure my future vacation plans don't interest you. Why are you here?"

"I came to thank you on behalf of the Clan. I don't need to elaborate on how you saved the lives of countless future innocents." Morgaine put her hands over Kendal's and kissed her rather chastely. "And I've come to reward you."

"No, thanks. I did what I was trained to do so everyone can return to their lives. This is mine, leave me to it." She pulled her hands back, not ready to accept any type of comfort. She had avenged her father but lost Piper. The victory was hollow.

"What of love, Asra?"

"What of it?" she asked angrily before taking a sip of her beer, not wanting to lash out too harshly. If she didn't feel like crap, she would've laughed at the foolish question. "If you're serious, then I'll tell you it doesn't exist. It's a myth wrapped in flowers and pretty candy boxes. I've never given a damn how others define it, since I'll never be able to truly experience it."

"You've told special women throughout the years that life isn't worth living without another heart beating next to yours that cares more about you than anything or anyone."

"I've tried it, Morgaine, and I've come to equate love with someone running a sword through me. They hurt like a bitch, so I've sworn off both."

"What about Piper?"

"What about Piper?" She was really angry now. No matter how hard she had tried to forget Piper, she saw her in every lover's face in this romantic city. "I left her to find someone she could share a life with. If you want to reward me with something, watch over her and make sure she's okay, because I can't bring myself to do it. I want her to be happy, but I couldn't stand to see her with someone else."

"She deserves to know what happened, and to know you're not dead. Don't you owe her that much, since she loves you?"

"Piper's in love with the idea of me. She'll find someone soon who can give her the things I can't."

"But what if she wants you? Doesn't she have a say?" Morgaine reached for her chin and made her look into her eyes. "She's hurting, warrior mine, and only you can make that go away."

"How badly do you think she'll be hurting forty or fifty years from now when she grows weaker and older by the day and I never change? How badly do you think it hurts to know you'll never get to keep the love of someone who completes everything in you because you're a freak of nature?" She drained the bottle and wiped at the tears in her eyes. "I don't want to put myself through that again. Call me a coward, I don't care, but I won't do it. She's better off without me."

"What if you found someone you could walk the road of forever with? Would you take a chance then?"

Kendal smiled at her, the original forbidden fruit she could only taste but never sate her appetite. "I believe she's off-limits, or so you keep telling me."

Morgaine softly slapped Kendal's arm. "Would you be with me if you could?" She kissed her again with more familiarity and pressed her palm to her cheek. "Could you love me as much as you do Piper?"

"I love you and want more than anything not to hurt you." She dropped her eyes to the tabletop.

"That's answer enough, no need to elaborate. You love me, but you're *in* love with her."

Kendal thanked the waiter, who put down two fresh bottles of beer and a loaf of bread. "I guess age only makes us older sometimes, but no wiser in some arenas. Our only consolation is having the luxury of unlimited time to help heal our heartbreaks, especially when we drown them in such visual beauty." Morgaine raised her bottle to the sunset. "Be well, old friend."

❖

Morgaine watched Kendal walk toward the northern part of town. She hadn't been sure if Kendal was staying in the city or retreating to her old haunts with the setting sun, but now she knew Kendal was heading out of Venice into the surrounding hills. After she flicked her wrist, one of her men took off to follow Kendal. She was sure of the final destination but wanted confirmation.

Now she had to deal with her other lovesick bookend. Once this was over, the two would make a stunning pair, if only because they were able to bring out every conceivable emotion in each other. Their love burned so passionately because they instinctively knew what the other needed and what drove them. Frustration, anger within reason, jealousy, affection, and devotion were always the best ingredients for love, in her opinion, and Piper and Kendal had them all.

It surprised Morgaine that the flame had kindled so quickly, especially in Asra. It had flickered a bit at first, but the inferno had thoroughly consumed both hearts and would ravage them if kept apart too long. Though it would cost her with both Kendal and the Elders to put Asra and Piper back together, the world needed Kendal to keep fighting, not become despondent and give up.

"Maybe I can get her to pick up another sword once this little girl gets her hooks into her," she said softly as she opened the door of the suite she had taken at the Lido.

"Did you find her?"

"Not yet, Miss Marmande. Tell me, are you always this impatient?"

Piper tucked her feet under her in the chair by the window, apparently trying to contain her excitement. "Look, I want to believe all this mumbo jumbo you people have been feeding me, but I've been sitting here for hours looking at every freaking tourist who can afford one of those cute little hats ride by in a gondola. I'm about to go insane. I don't think it's too much to ask if you found her."

A knock at the door saved her from letting Piper see the size of her smile. "Oh, Asra, may the gods bless you and keep you strong, you're going to desperately need it," she thought before she opened the door. A young man whispered something in her ear, and she nodded and sent him on his way.

"Well?"

"Just some information about something else. Why don't you retire for the evening? Tomorrow we're heading out early for a hillside walk."

"I'm not here to sightsee, lady. I'm here to see Kendal." Piper stood up and ran her hands through her hair, pulling it when she got to the ends. "And when I find her, I'm seriously thinking of kicking her ass."

"Asra's the finest fighter in the Clan," Morgaine gently reminded her. "I don't think you have the skill to swat a fly off her, much less kick her ass, as you so poetically put it."

"She's also the idiot who left without saying good-bye. I already told her what thinking for me did for my disposition," Piper said, her arms crossed. "What?" she asked when Morgaine looked at her and smiled

"Listen to yourself, Miss Marmande. To talk like that, you must believe she's alive. That's the faith you'll need to guide you through life if you choose to stay with Asra. I'm sorry, if you choose to stay with Kendal," she said with a small bow of her head.

"I love her enough to believe in anything if it gets me back to her side."

"You will receive your reward for your faith, then."

Piper walked close enough to her to put her hands on her shoulders. "You love her as well, don't you?"

"Asra has found her mate in you, Miss Marmande. How I feel is of no consequence."

"You didn't answer my question."

She walked past Piper to the window. "She is my pupil. I may not stay with her like that." With as much of a neutral expression as she could muster, she faced Piper. "Even if the Elders allowed it, her heart would still seek you out. She loves you, Piper, and if you love her as much, I won't mind losing gracefully." She spread her hands out and shrugged. "Good enough?"

"Yes, and thank you for being honest. If I find her, I'll take good care of her."

"Then she'll never want for anything."

CHAPTER TWENTY-FIVE

"A re you ready?" Morgaine asked the next morning. She
looked at Piper and saw what Kendal found so attractive.
Piper wasn't only beautiful, she had an aura about her that reminded
Morgaine of life.

Piper nodded and smoothed down the simple dress she had chosen
to wear. "Sure."

After a boat and taxi ride, she walked with Piper down a deserted
country road. Ten minutes later, they'd seen only a few stray goats and
an occasional lone bird on the hunt for a meal. The incline they were
on was getting steeper, and she slowed to accommodate Piper's shoe
selection. Both of them stopped when they crested the hill, and the
sudden, unexpected flash of yellow made Piper's jaw click shut. They
were extremely out of season, but daffodils, thousands of them, filled
the hillside.

"She's good at disappearing when she wants to, even from me, but
when Charlie told me what kind of flower she had given you, I knew
instantly where to find her. If you want a chance, keep walking. I'll
leave you to it."

Piper shook her head and opened and closed her fists, trying to
relax. Without another word, Morgaine headed away from her.

Piper walked straight into the flowers, feeling guilty about the ones
she trampled. After about two hundred yards she stopped and pressed
her hands to her mouth to suppress a sob. If her mind had conjured up
a ghost, she didn't want to scare it away.

Kendal turned around. "Piper?" Kendal whispered into the wind,
but she heard it and almost fell over.

"Are you real?" Piper held her hand up in midair. "Please be real."
Kendal moved forward with the same powerful body Piper saw when

she closed her eyes, though it vanished when her nightmares started and she woke with vivid images of blood.

Kendal covered the distance quickly and wrapped her in a hug, making her world right itself. This was the warm, safe cocoon she thought she'd never find again after that horrible night at Oakgrove.

"Gods, how I've missed you," Kendal said, taking a deep breath.

"Don't say anything yet." Piper put her arms around Kendal's waist. "Just hold me." She pressed her ear to Kendal's chest and closed her eyes, smiling as she heard the beat of her heart. Every thump was like a balm. "Thank God I believed Lenore. She and your friends gave you back to me."

"I know what happened was hard, but it's over, and you're free to enjoy your life without fear. Forget everything you saw that night, and forget me. That's the most valuable gift I can give you." Kendal sounded sincere, and she seemed shocked when Piper pulled away and backhanded her in the stomach.

"You're such an asshole," she said, enunciating each word carefully. "Do you have any idea what I've been going through? I thought you were dead, and it was killing me, especially because I'd never get to tell you how I felt."

"Piper, I could—"

"No, you can't," she shouted. "You're going to shut the hell up and let me finish. You promised you'd come back, and I believed you. Finding you out here picking flowers makes me wonder why I love you." She wanted to say so much more but couldn't talk around her tears. "Why?"

"You may not believe me, but I left for you." Kendal reached over to comb her hair out of her face before wiping away some of her tears. "If Morgaine helped you, you know the truth about me. That truth means you also know why the Elders gave me life and how I serve them. I'm their slayer, and I won't subject you to that kind of darkness." She kissed Piper's forehead and held her tighter. "I wish I could make this my last lifetime because I'd jump at the chance to grow old with you, but I have to accept that I'm not the right choice for you."

"You're not willing to even give me a chance?" she asked, feeling better when Kendal tweaked her nose.

"I'm immortal, not perfect," Kendal said, smiling, "so even I'm prone to making mistakes. Leaving you for what I thought was a noble reason without telling you the truth is one of the biggest ones I've made in years. Can you forgive me?"

"Why should I?" She accepted Kendal's hand.

"Because it was wrong to leave you in pain," Kendal said, kissing her knuckles.

"But not wrong to leave me?"

"How did Morgaine convince you about all this?" She took a step back but didn't let go of Piper's hand.

"She had some help from Lenore and her book."

"Then think of the reality of who I am, my duties to the Elders aside. My body was frozen in time when I was twenty-four, but since then I've lived for over thirty-four hundred years. All those days, all the battles, and yet I've stayed the same. All the people who've been a part of my life are only memories, but the pain of losing them is still fresh in here," she said, tapping over her chest. "I pray for your happiness, but the small part of my heart that's selfish is trying to save itself the agony of letting you go. I'm not saying it'll be easy, but I can't imagine what it will do to my sanity to watch you slip away from me years from now when you'll be so engrained that you'll take a huge part of me with you."

"So you don't love me?" Piper let go of her hand and turned away from her.

"Life hasn't been easy or fair to you, but you can't believe that."

"Then say it."

"I fell in love with you that very first day in the Palace Café when you wanted to kill me and were so ready to fight me for what you loved, you woke me out of a stupor I didn't realize I was in. You made me remember that if I wanted to enjoy my life, it had to have meaning, and I did everything possible to spend time with you before I'd have to let you go. It would've been selfish to stay."

"You're wrong," Piper said, shaking her head and turning to face her again. "Leaving with my heart made you selfish, and making that decision without me makes you either an idiot or a slow learner. The selfish part of my heart refuses to walk away from you, and if you let go of your worries, I think the future, no matter how long it is, will bring you nothing but happiness. You'll never know unless you take a chance."

"You're a bit of a slayer yourself, Miss Marmande, since you've run through every argument I have. If you're willing to forgive me, I'll do what I've done for hundreds of years and not worry about tomorrow."

"I'm willing to forgive you."

"Thank—"

Piper pressed her hand over her mouth. "I wasn't finished. I'm willing to forgive you if you won't leave again, and you'll talk to me about any decisions you make on my behalf." She released Kendal and stepped back. "Think you can handle that, or is the modern version of the Southern debutante too much for you?"

"I promise." Kendal made an *X* over her heart with her finger, making Piper laugh. "As for doing your thinking for you, I'm not that much of a slow learner. Your fire is your most beautiful quality, and clearly you're the braver of us," Kendal said, bending at the waist and bringing their heads closer together. "I'll never waste another moment with you." Kendal paused after tilting her head, as if asking permission to kiss her.

Piper accepted, wanting to reconnect and show her what she felt was real. She put her arms around Kendal's neck and didn't stop the kiss when Kendal picked her up and cradled her.

"Are you ready?" Kendal asked, making her nod.

Piper recognized the small villa Kendal started walking to from the sketches in Lenore's book. It appeared ancient but still in good repair, with a great view of the water below.

"Don't mess up too many flowers," she ordered.

"You like them?" Kendal stopped almost at the center of the blooms.

She pulled the leather tie from Kendal's hair and watched it blow free in the breeze. How many of the village girls who lived hundreds of years ago had admired and become bewitched by the same beautiful locks whenever Antonio DeCristo walked these hills? It had been one of her favorite chapters of Kendal's story.

"They're my new favorites."

"I first encountered them when I lived here, and unlike the more sought-after flowers such as roses and orchids, these have a simplicity that makes me happy."

The explanation warmed Piper's heart more than the sun shining down on them. "They're beautiful, but strange."

"How so?" Kendal asked, smiling in a way she could only describe as mischievous.

"It's fall. They shouldn't be blooming in the wild like this until spring."

Kendal laughed and started walking again. "No, they shouldn't, but we have something in common."

"You didn't."

"I did. It was one of only two times I upset the Elders, but look at them. Don't they look like they should live forever?"

Piper noticed that all the flowers Kendal had stepped on bounced back and turned their petals toward the sun. It was hard to believe how long they'd bloomed.

"The idea's starting to grow on me."

Kendal put Piper down when they reached the villa, and even though she wanted to touch Kendal, she was glad they took a short tour. The place had been modernized, but not to the point of erasing the history Piper could almost sense the walls had witnessed.

She touched some of the things Kendal had brought there throughout her life, but she wasn't interested in long explanations as they walked to the bedroom. The view of Venice was beautiful as she briefly glimpsed it from the balcony in the master suite, but it couldn't compete with Kendal.

Piper finally found the courage to unbutton Kendal's shirt and drop it to the floor. She had to know that Kendal was all right, and as Kendal stood before her wearing only her pants and a smile, she saw no scars or bruises. Whatever power had kept her alive had wiped away any evidence of her injuries and put to rest any doubts about who and what Kendal was.

"I wanted you to touch me that day in New Orleans," she said, not moving when Kendal stepped behind her and unzipped her dress. "Your hands felt so good."

"I wanted to, believe me." Kendal kissed one shoulder before pushing the dress to the floor. "I was trying to be good. You did, after all, think I wanted you only for your body, and I try in all things to be noble of heart."

Piper turned around, wearing a set of pale blue underwear and enjoying the way Kendal was staring. With steady hands she unbuckled Kendal's belt and unfastened the buttons of her pants, letting them drop to the floor. "Let's hope you're not so noble-minded now."

With what seemed like the last of her resolve, Kendal took hold of her hands as she looped her fingers under the elastic of her underwear. "Are you sure?"

"You told me to wait until it meant something to me. I have."

She tugged the plain white briefs Kendal seemed to like to her ankles, getting her completely naked. "I waited for you." On instinct she sucked Kendal's nipple into her mouth, enjoying the moan that followed. "I love you, so it means everything to me to show you." She went willingly when Kendal lifted her off the floor. "You stir my passions, but more important, you own my heart, and you will for the rest of time."

Kendal laid her on the large bed, caressing the length of her with her eyes before coming to rest between her legs. The feel of Kendal's weight made the ache of every lonely moment she'd ever experienced disappear, and she wanted to rush when Kendal placed her hand on her chest.

"You're so beautiful, I hurt from wanting you," Kendal said in such a sincere way she felt desired.

She turned over a little so Kendal could unfasten her bra, feeling extremely sexy when Kendal stripped it from her body with a bit of impatience, as if she was tired of the barriers between them, no matter how small. The panties came next, and Piper took a deep breath to try to relax. For the first time in her life, she wanted to give herself without reservation.

"I love you, Piper, like I've loved no other before you." Kendal rested her weight on one elbow so she could run her fingers along Piper's eyebrows.

"More than Angelina?" she asked, closing her eyes at her lack of self-control. It wasn't the time, and her question caused Kendal to roll off her, but she didn't move far away.

"How much of the story did they tell you?" Kendal asked, lying on her side with her head resting on her palm.

"Actually, Lenore went through all things Kendal, and that particular chapter held so much pain it was hard to listen to. I understand now why you reacted the way you did when we met more than I did when I saw her portrait. I saw only someone who looked like me, but you've had to carry the weight of all that pain for so long. Meeting me must have brought it back to the surface." She didn't feel comfortable talking about being Angelina's replacement.

"Lenore updates her book from the journal I keep and from the reports Morgaine gives the Elders after events like you witnessed recently. She had to piece together the story about what happened at Oakgrove without a lot of help from me."

"We don't have to talk about it now if you don't want to," she said when Kendal sighed.

"You deserve to know the totality of who I am, and why I literally hid away after all that."

She placed her hand on Kendal's chest. "Nothing you say will change how I feel about you."

"I loved Angelina, but you have to understand how different things were then. In 1727, with very few exceptions, women's lives revolved around their families and social events. I don't mean to degrade them, but few females spoke up because they were afraid they'd lose a potential husband."

"I would've been single forever," Piper said with a smile.

"Not if we'd met." Kendal rested her head on the pillow and opened her arms to her. "Angelina was a beautiful young woman, and her uncle adored the written word second only to her. It took me a while to convince her that expressing an opinion and not hiding her intelligence wouldn't scare me away. Her broad knowledge attracted her to me from the beginning."

"Giving her the freedom to share her true self, and the way you courted her, must've made her fall head over heels."

"She was in love...but she was in love with Jacques St. Louis. Granted, he was who I was in that lifetime, but because of my brother, I'll never know if she could've loved..."

"Asra," Piper said, because Kendal obviously could not.

"I'd taken them to Oakgrove to let her go, because while Angelina was different, she still had fantasies of her prince walking her down the aisle, followed by children nine months later. I could've given her the big church wedding, but not the rest. That's why I had to break it off. The easiest way to do that was to tell her the truth."

"If you'd had the chance, and she'd accepted your offer, what then?" she asked, keeping her eyes closed.

"I probably would've stayed with her as long as I could keep up the pretense of Jacques. I live my life in short windows of time and don't get many opportunities to stem the loneliness." As she spoke, Kendal rubbed Piper's back soothingly, so she snuggled closer. "I should have protected Angelina and Tomas from Henri's viciousness, and it was hard for me to face my failure."

"What happens now that he's dead?" Piper asked, realizing this question frightened her more than her first one.

Kendal sat up, still holding her so they could look at each other. "If I'm completely honest, will you believe me?"

"Sure," she said, feeling anything but.

"You surprised me at first because it was like staring at my past come back to mock me, but after one short conversation, you showed me how very different you are in every way."

She smiled and tugged on Kendal's hands. "Is that a good thing?"

"I've finally become free about who I choose to be, so Kendal Richoux is only a name, but you didn't have the illusions of Jacques. I've been myself with you from the beginning, and you kept coming back. Lenore and Morgaine stripped away my only secret, yet here you are. You know me, and you want me for who I am. That's not only wonderful, it's humbling." Kendal lowered her head and kissed her. "You're the one I've waited so long for, and I love you."

"You're very patient," she said, biting down on Kendal's bottom lip softly. "Not one of my good qualities."

"Really? I would've never guessed that about you." Kendal eased her back down. "You're always so focused." Kendal circled her nipple lightly with her finger, making it pucker to a hard point. "So in control of your emotions when it comes to waiting for what you want." She repeated the action on her other nipple with the same result.

"I'd like to be coming now without a lot of wait time," Piper said, her breathing uneven after that brief touch. "I'm focused on that most at the moment."

"That's what you say, but I think you'd prefer a slow buildup." Kendal ran her finger up next, tracing her lips first before moving to her chin and stopping.

"Sounds like you're thinking for me again," she said, making Kendal laugh. "My life is much shorter in years than yours, Asra, but I've waited for you just as long. I want you to make me yours."

Her request brightened Kendal's expression. "Thank you," Kendal said before kissing her and dragging her hand down her body at a slow, sensual, and torturous pace. "Stop me if you need," she said, moving so she was between her legs. "I want you to always tell me what you want because I love you enough to give it to you if I can."

"You—" She stopped when Kendal sucked hard enough on her nipple to wake up every cell in her body. "I need you to touch me." She was about to protest when Kendal lifted her head, but opened her mouth willingly when Kendal moved up to kiss her. "I've got other fun parts," she said as Kendal rubbed her hard nipple under her palm.

"Don't worry," Kendal said, moving her hand away again, which made her crazy. "I'm a soldier, and my training dictates that I map the field." She placed her finger on Piper's lips, smiling when she sucked on it. "Familiarizing myself with the landscape is crucial." She offered the tip of her thumb next. Piper's nipple rolled easily between her wet fingers when she lowered her head. "Rushing means I might miss something important in my planning."

When Kendal placed both hands on the mattress, Piper looked like she was about to smack her. She knew she was driving Piper mad, but she wouldn't rush. Piper deserved her full attention, so by the time she claimed what Piper had offered, Piper would have no doubts as to how she felt.

Piper grabbed a fistful of Kendal's hair when she pushed herself up, relaxing her hold when Kendal pressed her thigh between her legs. She glanced down after feeling how wet Piper was. It'd be cruel to make her wait anymore, so she started to move down.

"No," Piper said, "don't leave. You promised."

"I'm not going anywhere," she said, kissing Piper again and rolling a little off her so she could slide her hand down the length of her. Piper's skin reminded her of the first time she'd touched silk, and she stopped at the soft blond hair of Piper's sex when she felt her quiver.

Piper opened her eyes, as if questioning why she'd stopped, and didn't seem to need an explanation when she spread her legs for her. "I want you to," Piper said, gazing up at her in a way that made her eyelids appear heavy with sleep, but her breathing was fast and erratic, as if she was having trouble keeping her desires in check.

She entered Piper with two fingers, but only the tips, before pulling out and moving them to the base of Piper's clit. "You're perfect," she said as Piper arched off the bed, trying to kiss her, sucking her tongue into her mouth when Kendal met her halfway down.

"Are you going to make me beg?" Piper asked, moaning when Kendal raised her fingers, skimming over her hard clit. "I will if you want, I need you so much." Piper clamped her legs shut when she increased the pressure, but opened them again when she let up. "Go inside," Piper said, bringing her feet up a little to allow her knees to fall open. "I want you inside me."

Kendal looked at Piper, thinking how different this was from their first meeting, and from the way Piper was smiling back, she'd guessed what was on her mind. "What can I say, you grew on me," Piper said, tugging Kendal's hair.

"Then let me fill the small piece of you that's still wanting." She entered Piper with a slow thrust, pausing to allow Piper to adjust to her.

The way Piper's sex pulsed around her fingers, she was glad for the stillness, wanting to memorize the moment.

"I've waited all my life for you, Asra," Piper said, keeping her hands around Kendal's neck and moaning loud and long when Kendal pressed her thumb to the diamond-hard clit.

Piper was so wet that her fingers moved easily as she set a pace to meet Piper's hips, which rose higher and faster off the bed. Their bodies fit perfectly together, and the enjoyment intensified because they didn't feel awkward or hesitant, even though this was new to Piper.

From the moment she'd met Piper, she'd seen the physical beauty, but in some cases beautiful women were only pretty casings for the worst kinds of demons. Piper, though, was full of fight and loyalty for those she loved and cared about, and that drive in her hadn't allowed Kendal to move on and leave Piper to her anger. Kendal knew Piper would be irresistible when she let go of the barriers around her heart and gave herself completely. If Kendal wasn't already in love, she would've fallen then.

"Look at me," Kendal said, thrusting her fingers in completely and holding them there, but still rubbing Piper's clit hard with her thumb. Piper opened her eyes and gifted her with such an open expression that she released the last bit of fear that kept her from giving Piper the commitment she deserved.

"What if you found someone you could walk the road of forever with?" Morgaine had asked her. She could easily answer what had seemed impossible to fathom only a few hours ago. Asked again, she'd say yes, even if forever consisted of sixty short years, if they were lucky. It was worth taking the chance because love gave her no other recourse.

"Can you see how beautiful you are in the way I love you?" Kendal asked, still moving only her thumb. Piper held her breath, as if trying to hold back the orgasm she so obviously wanted.

"I've never been so turned on in my life." Piper sounded as if she'd been running for miles.

Kendal pumped her hand three times, letting her thumb slam into Piper's hardness, and Piper hissed when she pulled almost all the way out, leaving only the night air caressing Piper.

"You own my heart. I hope you know that."

"Not the time for sappy, baby," Piper said, reaching between her legs to grab her wrist. "You turned me on, got me so wet I'm dripping, and I'm so hard it's making me crazy, so do something about it."

"I'm known for my deal-closing abilities," she said, moving her fingers in to the knuckles.

"Prove it." Piper arched her back, forcing her fingers all the way in when she squeezed her fingers around her wrist. "If you really love me, make me come."

"Whatever you want." She started slowly again, feeling Piper's wetness soak her entire hand, smiling when Piper pushed her onto her back.

The reversal of positions allowed Piper to move as freely as she wanted and let Kendal enjoy watching as Piper pumped her hips, varying her speed as if to hold back her orgasm a few times. When Kendal reached up and pinched her nipple, Piper leaned forward and rested her hands on Kendal's shoulders. With her eyes closed, Piper moved her hips, taking in the length of Kendal's fingers on every downward stroke until she moaned and stopped.

"Shit," Piper said as she squeezed Kendal's fingers, not seeming to stop the spasms and twitches as the remnants of her orgasm burned through her. "It's amazing that I've lived this long feeling so little." Piper rested her head on her shoulder, panting when she didn't seem to have the strength to hold herself upright. "I hope you're this passionate when I'm eighty, because I'm positive this won't get old."

"I may keep you here and naked until you're eighty. I love you, Piper," she said, pulling out and maneuvering them under the blankets, smiling at Piper's look of contentment.

"What about you, love?" Piper asked.

"What about me?"

"I want to touch you. It isn't fair not to return the favor," Piper said, appearing mortified when she yawned.

"Sleep now, little one. The Elders keep telling me to believe in eternal life, and now that I have you, I hope they're right. With you it'll take forever to show you how much I love you."

"For future reference, this is the perfect time for sappy." Piper closed her eyes.

"Don't worry, I'm taking notes." She kissed Piper's forehead. "We'll have plenty of time for all the things we'll do together."

"Promise me again," Piper asked, before sleep claimed her.

"I'll never leave you, love, and I'll always be here to watch over you."

EPILOGUE

They spent a month exploring parts of Venice and the surrounding countryside, talking and making love. It was incredible for Kendal to finally be with someone and not have to hide any part of herself, and to find acceptance in Piper's arms. Lenore had read Piper the Clan's account of her life, but Piper had also listened attentively as Kendal told stories of the people she'd met and the lessons they'd shared with her.

Her life before Piper had been full, and she'd tried to find people and things to bring joy into it, like her brief relationship with Angelina and Tomas. Now she was content to watch Piper sleep every night after they'd made love, holding her until morning. That so simple an act would bring her so much peace made her love for Piper grow.

While their time together quieted the warrior spirit in Kendal, it had brought Piper to life in a way that made her feel like nothing could penetrate the happiness she'd experienced. She'd never had a lover who took such time and seemed to get so much pleasure from trying to give her everything she'd dreamed of.

Kendal didn't have to tell her how much she loved and cherished her; Piper could see it in her eyes and feel it every time they touched. They hadn't been together that long, but Piper didn't doubt that what they'd found was permanent. That was why she'd asked Kendal the most daunting question the week before as they lay on one of the chairs on the balcony watching the sun burn the dew from the fields. She was that sure.

She kneeled next to Kendal and asked her to mix the elixir of the sun for the third time. Kendal didn't say anything as she explained her reasons. "I don't want to live forever if I can't share eternity with you, and I can't imagine leaving you in death to go on alone." This was the only way she could prove how much she loved Kendal, and was why they were back in the field of Kendal's daffodils.

The dawn wasn't far off, but Piper could see what Kendal was doing in the light from the full moon. Kendal had bathed her like Lenore had described Morgaine doing for Kendal in the pool of their oasis, and now she knelt before Piper mixing a multitude of ingredients and speaking a language she didn't understand.

Kendal dropped in the last item before looking at her. "Are you sure? Once it's done, no one can undo it. You will move forward in time, but you can't return to this moment."

It looked like water, but released a yellow vapor, so Piper assumed it was ready. She knew she could back out and Kendal would understand. "I don't remember very much of the French I learned in school, but a phrase came back to me this morning."

"You don't have to do this," Kendal said, obviously taking her ramblings as a sign of her uncertainty.

"Let me finish," Piper said, smiling. "Do you know what *toujours ici* means?"

"Always here."

"In Lenore's book, that will be the chapter title of our story. I'll always be here for you, my love." She placed her hand over Kendal's heart. "Am I sure? As sure as I am in my love for you."

Kendal handed her the chalice and said, "Then you'll walk at my side for as long as the world exists. For three thousand years I've lived and learned all I could, but it's taken me only a very short time to learn my most valuable lesson."

"What's that, my love?"

"That I cannot, and do not, want to live without you."

Piper held up the cup in a toast and smiled before she brought it to her lips, tasting it tentatively at first, then draining it when she felt like she was drinking in a cool flare from the sun. When the elixir had done its work, Piper opened her eyes on a new world, and her skin began to tingle as the sky lit with the first rays of sunrise.

Kendal focused on the small twitches in Piper's body, a sure sign that the elixir was bonding with every fiber, bone, and muscle. She laughed with Piper threw the cup away and held her hand out. When their eyes met, Kendal gasped.

For the first time since the elixir had existed, it failed to make the physical change that marked Piper as a child of the Clan. The other physical changes Kendal witnessed left no doubt that Piper was immortal, but her eyes were still green.

"What's wrong?" Piper gripped her hands with strength that only the elixir could provide.

"Your eyes," she said, as the legend Lenore had told her at the beginning of their training came to mind.

"We have a matching set, huh?" Piper asked.

"No, but it makes no difference to what's important." She didn't want Piper to worry.

Lenore had spoken of this as their training was coming to an end, outside Giza, in 535 BC.

"Before the first of the Elders perfected the potion you drank, Asra, one of the old ones from their tribe gifted with the sight of a seer told of a vision he'd had shortly before his death."

"What was it?" she asked, stopping her sword drill, as she usually did when Lenore spoke of demons and monsters.

"A woman will come to drink one day long from now, but she will keep the one thing that will set her apart from the rest of us. That will show her lover who she's awakened."

"Interesting," she said, laughing. "This doesn't sound like you, Lenore, but like one of those romantic tales you love to read when you think I'm not paying attention."

"This might be important to you one day, so listen closely," Lenore said. Kendal sheathed her sword and sat. "This woman will become an Elder and wield tremendous power."

"You, Morgaine, and the others have made it clear what my place will be, so thanks for the story, but I don't see what it has to do with me."

"The scroll states that the woman will join the ranks of the Elders with her green eyes and heart of a lion, though she'll be no warrior. Rather, she will join with the warrior and bring light to the darkness, beginning with her lover."

Kendal had laughed it off as a romantic tale back then, but the prophecy fulfilled itself right in front of her. She cried from the happiness of knowing she'd never be alone again. Piper was her salvation, and her love for her would outlast the stars. Mixing the elixir again might have broken her promise to the Elders, but it had proved that her choice was just. Piper was her fate.

"Are you okay?" Piper asked, looking at her as if she was worried.

"I love you." She kissed Piper and the sun started to rise.

Across the globe, after weeks of spells, another immortal gained a new surge of power. The young female vampire saw the cloud of red dust flying toward her and laughed. Her magic had finally worked. She opened her arms and accepted Ora's spirit and strength into her heart. The new Queen of the Vampires existed, and when the unholy union ended, she opened her eyes on her new world.

"Asra," she said.

The battle would begin again, but for now Asra and Piper had found their missing half in each other. Their love would make them strong, but not invincible.

About the Author

Ali Vali is the author of the Devil series, which includes *The Devil Inside*, *The Devil Unleashed*, *Deal With the Devil*, and *The Devil Be Damned*. Her stand-alone novels are *Carly's Sound*, *Second Season*, *Blue Skies*, and the Lambda Literary Award finalist *Calling the Dead*. Ali has also contributed to numerous anthologies, with her latest short story "Devil In Training" appearing in *Women of the Mean Streets*, published by Bold Strokes Books.

Ali is originally from Cuba and now lives outside New Orleans with her partner of twenty-six years. When she isn't writing, she works in the nonprofit sector. Ali is one of the 2011 Alice B. Readers Appreciation Award winners.

Books Available From Bold Strokes Books

Three Days by L.T. Marie. In a town like Vegas where anything can happen, Shawn and Dakota find that the stakes are love at all costs, and it's a gamble neither can afford to lose. (978-1-60282-569-7)

Swimming to Chicago by David-Matthew Barnes. As the lives of the adults around them unravel, high school students Alex and Robby form an unbreakable bond, vowing to do anything to stay together—even if it means leaving everything behind.(978-1-60282-572-7)

Hostage Moon by AJ Quinn. Hunter Roswell thought she had left her past behind, until a serial killer begins stalking her. Can FBI profiler Sara Wilder help her find her connection to the killer before he strikes on blood moon? (978-1-60282-568-0)

Erotica Exotica: Tales of Magic, Sex, and the Supernatural, edited by Richard Labonté. Today's top gay erotica authors offer sexual thrills and perverse arousal, spooky chills, and magical orgasms in these stories exploring arcane mystery, supernatural seduction, and sex that haunts in a manner both weird and wondrous. (978-1-60282-570-3)

Blue by Russ Gregory. Matt and Thatcher find themselves in the crosshairs of a psychotic killer stalking gay men in the streets of Austin, and only a 103-year-old nursing home resident holds the key to solving the murders—but can she give up her secrets in time to save them? (978-1-60282-571-0)

Balance of Forces: Toujours Ici by Ali Vali. Immortal Kendal Richoux's life began during the reign of Egypt's only female pharaoh, and history has taught her the dangers of getting too close to anyone who hasn't harnessed the power of time, but as she prepares for the most important battle of her long life, can she resist her attraction to Piper Marmande? (978-1-60282-567-3)

Contemporary Gay Romances by Felice Picano. This collection of short fiction from legendary novelist and memoirist Felice Picano are as different from any standard "romances" as you can get, but they will linger in the mind and memory. (978-1-60282-639-7)

Pirate's Fortune: Supreme Constellations Book Four by Gun Brooke. Set against the backdrop of war, captured mercenary Weiss Kyakh is persuaded to work undercover with bio-android Madisyn Pimm, which foils her plans to escape, but kindles unexpected love. (978-1-60282-563-5)

Sex and Skateboards by Ashley Bartlett. Sex and skateboards and surfing on the California coast. What more could anyone want? Alden McKenna thinks that's all she needs, until she meets Weston Duvall. (978-1-60282-562-8)

Waiting in the Wings by Melissa Brayden. Jenna has spent her whole life training for the stage, but the one thing she didn't prepare for was Adrienne. Is she ready to sacrifice what she's worked so hard for in exchange for a shot at something much deeper? (978-1-60282-561-1)

Wings: Subversive Gay Angel Erotica, edited by Todd Gregory. A collection of powerfully written tales of passion and desire centered on the aching beauty of angels. (978-1-60282-565-9)

Suite Nineteen by Mel Bossa. Psychic Ben Lebeau moves into Shilts Manor, where he meets seductive Lennox Van Kemp and his clan of Métis—guardians of a spiritual conspiracy dating back to Christ. But are Ben's psychic abilities strong enough to save him? (978-1-60282-564-2)

Speaking Out: LGBTQ Youth Stand Up, edited by Steve Berman. Inspiring stories written for and about LGBTQ teens of overcoming adversity (against intolerance and homophobia) and experiencing life after "coming out." (978-1-60282-566-6)

Forbidden Passions by MJ Williamz. Passion burns hotter when it's forbidden, and the fire between Katie Prentiss and Corrine Staples in antebellum Louisiana is raging out of control. (978-1-60282-641-0)

Harmony by Karis Walsh. When Brook Stanton meets a beautiful musician who threatens the security of her conventional, predetermined future, will she take a chance on finding the harmony only love creates? (978-1-60282-237-5)

Nightrise by Nell Stark and Trinity Tam. In the third book in the everafter series, when Valentine Darrow loses her soul, Alexa must cross continents to find a way to save her. (978-1-60282-238-2)

Men of the Mean Streets, edited by Greg Herren and J.M. Redmann. Dark tales of amorality and criminality by some of the top authors of gay mysteries. (978-1-60282-240-5)

Women of the Mean Streets, edited by J.M. Redmann and Greg Herren. Murder, mayhem, sex, and danger—these are the stories of the women who dare to tackle the mean streets. (978-1-60282-241-2)

Firestorm by Radclyffe. Firefighter paramedic Mallory "Ice" James isn't happy when the undisciplined Jac Russo joins her command, but lust isn't something either can control—and they soon discover ice burns as fiercely as flame. (978-1-60282-232-0)

The Best Defense by Carsen Taite. When socialite Aimee Howard hires former homicide detective Skye Keaton to find her missing niece, she vows not to mix business with pleasure, but she soon finds Skye hard to resist. (978-1-60282-233-7)

After the Fall by Robin Summers. When the plague destroys most of humanity, Taylor Stone thinks there's nothing left to live for, until she meets Kate, a woman who makes her realize love is still alive and makes her dream of a future she thought was no longer possible. (978-1-60282-234-4)

Accidents Never Happen by David-Matthew Barnes. From the moment Albert and Joey meet by chance beneath a train track on a street in Chicago, a domino effect is triggered, setting off a chain reaction of murder and tragedy. (978-1-60282-235-1)

In Plain View, edited by Shane Allison. Best-selling gay erotica authors create the stories of sex and desire modern readers crave. (978-1-60282-236-8)

A
Gram
of Mars

A Gram of Mars

Stories / Becky Hagenston

Winner of the 1997
Mary McCarthy Prize
in Short Fiction
Selected by A.M. Homes

Sarabande Books

LOUISVILLE, KENTUCKY

Copyright © 1998 by Becky Hagenston

FIRST EDITION

Managing Editor
Sarabande Books, Inc.
2234 Dundee Rd. Suite 200
Louisville, KY 40205

LIBRARY OF CONGRESS CATALOGING-IN-PUBLICATION DATA

Hagenston, Becky, 1967–
    A Gram of Mars : stories / by Becky Hagenston.
        p.   cm.
    Contents: A Gram of Mars — Close enough — Till death do us part — Holding the
fort — All the happiness in the world — Parking lot ham and other acts of God — Fugue
— Fishhook girl.
    ISBN 1-889330-21-3 (cloth : alk. paper). — ISBN 1-889330-22-1 (pbk. :
alk. paper)
    1. Maryland—Social life and customs—Fiction. 2. Arizona—Social
life and customs—Fiction. 3. Family—Maryland—Fiction.
I. Title.
PS3558.A32316G73   1998
813'.54—dc21
                                                98-14370
                                              CIP

Cover painting: "Eve" by Patrick Donley. Used by kind permission of the artist.

Cover and text design by Charles Casey Martin.

Manufactured in the United States of America.
This book is printed on acid-free paper.

Sarabande Books is a nonprofit literary organization.

for my parents

Acknowledgments

I am grateful to the following publications, in which some of these stories first appeared in slightly different form: *Antietam Review,* "A Gram of Mars"; *Witness,* "Close Enough"; *The Crescent Review* and *Prize Stories 1996: The O. Henry Awards,* "Till Death Do Us Part"; *TriQuarterly,* "Holding the Fort"; *Folio,* "All the Happiness in the World"; *Shenandoah,* "Fugue."

My thanks to Alison Moore, Sarah Gorham, A. M. Homes, and Linda Asher. Thanks also to Cathleen Keenan Church, Robert Hepworth, Lynda Majarian, Joyce McMahon, Julie Newman, Margo Rabb, and Lara Wright for your friendship, encouragement, and good advice.

Table
of Contents

Foreword

 T he box arrives in the mail—the finalists; ten sets of stories, ten imaginations, hundreds of voices, characters, lives exposed. How to pick a winner? What catches the eye, the ear, the heart? It is the fiction of illumination, fiction that refracts pivotal moments, fiction that throws life into relief and allows us to see ourselves all the more clearly.

Reading the ten finalists several times through, I found myself returning to Becky Hagenston's stories. In *A Gram of Mars,* Hagenston offers us tales of the heart at home, capturing the fractured experience of family and the often desperate need for connection. Set on the author's home turf of Maryland, where she grew up, and in Arizona, where she attended graduate school, Hagenston's stories bravely document the ways in which we fail each other and ourselves. In these fictions one comes to know the estranged father who collects rocks from outer space—meteorites—and the woman separated from her husband, who stalks the house she used to share with him, sneaking in one night and stealing little things, things "he will miss." In crisp, spare prose, Hagenston explores lost love, the conundrum of couples coming together and then coming undone, and the terrifying turn life takes when parents become children and children are forced into the parental role.

I'm always curious to know how a writer comes to a story and what propels the author to write—I phone Becky to congratulate her on winning the 1997 Mary McCarthy Prize in Short Fiction and to ask her a little bit about where her fiction comes from. At twenty-nine, Hagenston lives in Arizona and describes her stories as often starting from things that happen in the real life—"My mother was actually given a ham in a parking lot," she tells me, referring to the story "Parking Lot Ham and Other Acts of God." She goes on to say: "My characters don't always understand what's happening to them, what they've lost or even what they're looking for. These stories are guided by my own search for what's most important, the things I need for the happiness my characters don't always find."

In Becky Hagenston's *A Gram of Mars,* one is both comforted and challenged by the familiarity of the characters and the shared history that is life in the late twentieth century. Hers is a new and necessary voice in American fiction.

— A. M. Homes, July 1997

A
Gram
of Mars

A
Gram
of Mars

When my mother and father got married, his mother gave mine a rolling pin. She told my mother it was "Teflon-coated, so it won't stick to Ernie's head." My father keeps the rolling pin under his sink, which is twenty-five miles from my mother's sink. He holds it up now, saying, "Can you believe this thing lasted longer than our marriage? Can you believe that?"

I say it's some tough rolling pin.

"Teflon-coated," he says. "Too bad your mother and I weren't."

My father lives alone in a basement apartment one hundred feet from the Chesapeake Bay. From his kitchen window, I can see the pavement, snow-splattered hedges, cars slushing by. I feel half-buried.

This is the first time I've seen where he lives, the first time in two years that I've seen him at all. His apartment is bigger than I'd expected—he'd once described it as a little cave—but it's crammed with enough furniture to fill a house. My mother's basement is the land of dead grandmothers: all of their ratty old chairs, silver tea sets, and Norman Vincent Peale books ended up there. My father has rescued some of his mother's things and brought them here, to his own basement: the blue sofa, its legs chewed by generations of frustrated, declawed cats; the egg-white kitchen table; the glass bluebird that used to sit on my grandmother's piano. His parents' wedding picture hangs in the hallway, beside the thermostat. A picture of his favorite childhood pet, Ace the one-eyed retriever, is taped to the mirror in his bedroom, along with postcards I've sent from Arizona and a picture of myself standing in front of a saguaro that seems to be growing from my head like a prickly Dr. Seuss hat. There are things from my mother's house, too: two end tables, helixed with cup stains; the queen-size bed that used to be in the guest room; the plastic red-and-white-checked plates and saucers. Everything seems mismatched and displaced, as if the furniture itself is visiting from somewhere else and wishes it could go home.

"Do you want something to eat?" he says. He's rummaging under the sink, clattering pots and pans. "I think I'm going to heat up some soup."

"I'm not really hungry."

"Me neither," he says, clanking a pan onto the stove. "I eat when I'm stressed. That's what I do. Sometimes I go to the Horn and Horn for their all-you-can-eat buffet." He pats his stomach. "And I just gorge. Lately I've been a bottomless pit." By "lately" he means since he found

4

out my mother's getting remarried and selling the house, the house the two of them bought together and where she now lives by herself. I didn't tell him about these developments, and I don't ask how he found out. Neither of us has mentioned what brought me here, the phone call three nights ago when he told me this was it, he had the gun picked out, he loved me, he was sorry. And in this desperate threat I heard a specific request: Come back. *Now.*

I didn't tell my mother about the phone call. I said I wanted to visit and pack up some of my old things before she sells the house. "I'm so glad," she said. "I'll even clean up your room for you."

"Actually," I said, "I thought I would stay with Dad. If that's okay."

"Of course it's *okay,*" she said, like it wasn't okay at all. "I'd like you to save some time for me, though. And Tim."

Tim is her fiancé. She's sent me pictures of him—a large man wearing a camouflage jacket and glasses shaped like television screens. When I first got here, I called her, and Tim answered the phone. "Please hold," he said, as if he were her secretary. My mother asked if she and Tim could steal me away for dinner tonight, and I said *she* could steal me away, alone. "I'll meet Tim tomorrow," I said. I was using the phone in my father's bedroom, and I could hear him outside the door, pretending to look for something in the hall closet.

My father's sleeping on the sofa bed, and I'm staying in his room, which feels sepulchral, as if my grandmother's bone-colored curtains, hanging like sodden wings, have never been opened. The room smells damp and dusty at once, and the white bedspread has a worn, frayed look, which once seemed antique-y but here looks like poverty.

While my father heats up his soup, I go into the living room and look at all his office equipment, which he's already demonstrated for me, like a child showing off for a new baby sitter. "This is what happens when you

5

go away for two years," he said, over the whir of his photocopier. "You have to put up with your dear old Dad showing off all his new contraptions."

He calls the part of the living room that's nearest the kitchen "the office." He has a computer on a little gray desk, a printer, scanner, fax machine, copier, and file cabinet. Part of the office has spilled into the living room area; piles of manila folders teeter on the back of the sofa, next to stacks of stationery and business cards that say "Ernest Hopkins and Associates, Inc."

"I might have associates some day," he told me. "You never know. You could be an associate. Course," he grinned, "I couldn't pay you."

Under his name it says "President" in raised black script.

My father rewrites letters for credit card companies to send their late- and non-paying customers. His theory is that you have to make the customers believe you're on their side, that you're rooting for them. He roots for them. He's told me that lately he's been getting his own letters. "They're so clear, and so sensitive," he said, "it makes me sadder than ever that I can't pay."

When he and my mother were still married, he was the vice president of a company called Clearwrite, and he did essentially the same thing and got paid a lot more for it. After my mother moved out he said going to work was too painful—"acting normal all day, as if my life hasn't been shot all to hell"—and decided to start his own business so he wouldn't even have to get dressed in the morning if he didn't feel like it. Most of the time, he didn't. At least, this is what he tells me; I wasn't there four years ago when my mother actually left him crying on his knees in the dining room. I was at college in Pennsylvania, close enough to come home if I really wanted to. I didn't want to. My mother has told me that she drove back to the house later that night to see if he'd killed himself. She sat outside in the car with the lights off until she saw his

6

shadow moving around in the living room. Hunched over, she said. Carrying the dog.

He would call me at school in the middle of the night. "Please just talk to your mother, tell her I've changed," he begged. "Tell her if she doesn't come back, I'll die. Tell her I'll do whatever she wants." I would fall asleep with the phone against my shoulder and wake up in the dark to an insistent, metronomic beeping; for a few seconds, all I would know was that something terrible had just happened.

Now, listening to him putter around his kitchen, I wonder if he ever thinks about all the ways I've deserted him—first by staying away, then by leaving altogether. I want to believe that my temporary presence is all that's necessary to keep him alive, that just by showing up I have already done whatever is required of me. I hear the stove roar and catch, and the smell of gas floats out into the living room. My father appears in the doorway, holding a big metal spoon. He touches the spoon lightly to my left shoulder, then my right, as if knighting me. "I'm glad you're here," he says, and when I tell him I am, too, I almost believe it.

After he finishes his soup and the pan is soaking in the sink, my father wants to show me the bay. I don't own a heavy coat anymore, so he gives me his black jacket and a gray scarf, and we crunch over the thin snow to the water. It's March, the week before spring, and my father wants to see if the swans have come yet.

"They're late this year," he says. "Which is a good thing, because the bay's been frozen and they would've been out of luck. It's pretty amazing, isn't it? It's like they just knew."

"Pretty amazing," I say. My hands are already numb. I've brought out my automatic camera, and I snap a few pictures of my father in his tweed cap, staring out at the bay, his hands stuffed into his pockets, his binoculars around his neck. There are tufts of gray coming out of the bottom of his cap. He looks at me.

"My kid," he says.

I feel sad taking his picture, as if my snapping it is somehow going to create or accelerate his death. That is, after all, why I'm taking it—to have something to remember later. To preserve him.

I take a few more pictures of the bay, of the lighthouse far off, and of my father in his baby-blue windbreaker. He's wearing a short-sleeved shirt underneath. "Aren't you cold?" I say. My mother used to bug him about wearing short sleeves in the dead of winter.

"Oh, a little. Are you?"

"Oh"—I chatter my teeth together and hold out my blue hands—"a little."

"That's right," he says. "There are no mittens out there in Tucson." He looks through the binoculars again. "I've seen red foxes, too. And blue herons."

Last winter he called to tell me about the bald eagles flocking by the dozens to Conowingo Dam—not to mate, not for any reason, just because other eagles did it. This kind of behavior in the animal world enchants him; in the human world he hates it. My father thinks my mother's women's group talked her into leaving him. He says they were all gung ho about walking out on their husbands, so she did too. Not for any reason. Just because everyone else was doing it.

"I hope you get to see the swans before you leave," he tells me on our way back inside. I don't care much about seeing the swans, but I nod and say I hope so, too. We go down the stairs and past the building's laundry room. "A dollar to wash, a dollar to dry," he says. "I never thought I'd need quarters to do my laundry. But," he adds cheerily, unlocking his own apartment door, "it couldn't be any more convenient, could it? At least I don't have to lug my clothes down three flights."

I think of him hauling his tan trousers and short-sleeved shirts across the hall to the dark little room, stuffing quarters in the slots, and going back into his apartment with its view of the pavement and hedges.

"I almost want to eat again," he says when our coats are off and draped over the chairs. "I could almost go for some fried chicken. Could I interest you in some fried chicken?"

"Not right now," I tell him. "Why are you so stressed?" The words hover in the air between us.

"Oh," he says. "You know."

There are things I could say that could send him stomping out of the room, crying. "Because she's engaged?" I could say. "Because you ruined everything by not paying enough attention to her and now she's found somebody else to love?" There was a time when I would have said these things, when I had what felt like a rock inside me—a smooth black rock where my guts used to be. Cruel things just slipped right over it and out my mouth. But I don't feel mean any more, just tired and quietly sad, and so I settle down on the sofa. It still smells like my Grandmother Hopkins. Like baby powder and Chanel. I want to close my eyes and sleep for a long time. I feel my blood beating against the walls of my skin.

My father is bouncing, doing a little dance and snapping his fingers. "My kid's here," he says, as if he still can't believe it. "Hey there, kid!"

"Hey there," I say. I lift a hand at him.

"Right now," he says, "I'm so happy, I think I might pop. Your Pop will pop," he says. "What do you think of that?"

9

"Don't pop," I tell him.

"You know what?" he says. "I never showed you my meteorite collection, did I?"

"No, you never did."

"Well, I gotta show you that, hold on a sec." And he dashes down the hall. On his computer, toasters are flying across the screen. Earlier, he had shown me all of his screen savers. He told me that if you stare at a computer screen, knock your teeth together and hum deep in your throat, it'll set up a vibration in your head so that the screen will look like it's moving in waves. So we sat on the sofa together, humming and chattering our teeth and staring across the room at the computer.

"If anyone could see us," I said, between chatterings, feeling silly and happy.

"They'd think we were pretty weird all right," said my father. "Ooh, there it goes!"

I couldn't see it then, but now I try again, halfheartedly, with no luck. For a poor man, he has a lot of office equipment. He's explained that he's so far in debt, it hardly matters. "I just keep on getting new credit cards," he said. "I guess they haven't figured out I'm flat busted yet."

He comes back with three small square cardboard boxes and sets them down on the coffee table, shoving old newspapers onto the floor. "I keep meaning to recycle," he says. He sits beside me. The boxes are the size of ring boxes, with clear plastic lids. Inside each box is a piece of rock smaller than a pebble. My father is the president of the Harford County Astronomy Society. He's always loved astronomy, but it was a solitary thing for him until my mother left—just him and his telescope out in the back yard. He joined the Astronomy Society as a ploy to win my mother back, by proving that he did actually have friends, that he did go out and socialize once in a while. The ploy didn't work, but my father ended up with friends anyway. One of them owns a local radio station, and my father does a sixty-second Stargazing bit every Tuesday, to alert the citizens of Harford County to the celestial happenings of the coming week.

"Now this one," he says, pushing the box with the largest rock toward me, "is a piece of what landed in your Grandmother Hopkins's back yard in North Dakota when she was nine years old."

I've heard the story before but I ooh and ahh a little anyway. I pick up the box and turn it over. "Richardton, North Dakota. June 30, 1918," it says on the back, on a little white card.

"Her family huddled together in the back bedroom wondering what the dickens the Germans were doing bombing North Dakota!"

"How'd you get it?"

"Through a catalog," he says. "From a guy out there in Tucson. I could give you his number if you want. You could start up your own collection."

"Hmm," I say. I'm not interested in things from outer space. I remember, from some high school summer, my mother standing at the kitchen door in her nightgown and hollering down to the back yard: "I'm going to bed now, Ernie. You know, I never thought I'd feel jealous of a *planet.*" He was looking for Pluto. I don't know if he ever found it.

The next meteorite he hands me is what he calls "primitive, mysterious matter." It's just a little black speck under the plastic. "This is older than the solar system," he tells me.

"Wow," I say. I'm not even sure how old the solar system is. I peer at the box for what I hope is a respectful amount of time. My father is watching me intently.

"And this." He offers the last box to me on his palm. "This, believe it or not, is a piece of Mars."

"Oh, cool," I say, taking the box. "Looks like something you'd find in the driveway."

He's leaning toward me. His eyes are shiny seas of gray. "No spacecraft has ever brought back a sample of Mars," he says, and I realize I'm not giving him the reaction he's expecting. I realize this is something more significant even than primitive, mysterious matter.

"So how'd you get it?"

"Well." His face flushes down to his Adam's apple. This is the kind of thing that drove my mother crazy, this wild enthusiasm about things that didn't have anything to do with her. "What *happened* was that an asteroid hit Mars with such impact that it knocked pieces off, and they just floated around space for billions of years." He waves his hands in the air, sprinkling down invisible particles of Mars. "This one fell in France in 1815. And you know, it does look like something out of the driveway."

"How do you know it's actually a meteorite?" I ask him, and I feel a tightness in my chest, as if all my organs are squishing together. I think I might say something I shouldn't, something to bring him plummeting back to earth, where he belongs—something about my mother asking me to be her maid of honor.

"Someone saw it fall," he says. "If no one had seen that, it would never have been identified as a meteorite. Only twelve stones in the world have been identified as Mars rock, and this is the rarest one. It sells for three thousand dollars a gram. And I have a gram of it." He grins.

The part of me that is my mother comes skittering to the surface, hot-faced and furious. "This?" I shout. "You're living on Spam and Ramen Noodles and you paid three thousand dollars for a speck of rock? That you can't even do anything with? That you can't even touch for godsake?"

"Yep, I did." He's smiling, turning the box over in his hands. "I sure did." He looks at me. "Charged it."

"I can't believe this," I say. I'm thinking of the plane ticket that wiped out my bank account, and the hours at work I'm missing, and my tiny studio apartment with cinder-block walls. I'm thinking of telling him that I'm paralyzed by debt, too, unable to move away from Arizona even if I wanted to, which I can't tell if I do. And I'm thinking of the times I worried he might die of starvation or lose his apartment the way he lost his house. I have sent him care packages full of candy bars and coffee, things I stole from the restaurant where I work. I have tucked in boxes of macaroni and cheese, packages of pasta and dried fruit—as if the candy bars could disguise the fact that I am trying to keep him alive.

"It's pretty unbelievable, isn't it? I mean, what are the chances, first that it would happen at all, second that someone would see it land, and third that I would end up with it? It's about as near to impossible as you can get, and yet here it is."

"There it is," I say, and I look at the little rock a little closer. It could be from anywhere. It could be a pebble from somebody's shoe. "How do you know it's even real?"

He looks at me blankly. "Oh, it's real. That dealer's extremely reputable—he was written up in *Astronomy* magazine a few months ago. Do you want to see the article?" He starts to stand up but I say no, that's fine, I don't need to see it. "With all this hubbub about life on Mars, my little rock is worth even more than when I bought it. Not," he adds, "that I'd ever sell it."

"Oh, of course not," I say nastily. "Why would you do that?" I take a breath. "With what this is worth, you could get yourself out of debt."

"I'd probably need a Mars boulder to get out of debt," he says. "But I know, I know. It was incredibly stupid of me to buy this, but I bought it right after I moved in here, and it was the only thing..." He picks up the box, sniffs it absently. "I guess I'm too optimistic for my own good

13

sometimes." I don't know if he's referring to my mother, or to his financial situation, or to his $3000 piece of rock. "But I'm glad I have it anyway." He sets the box down and looks at it as if he expects it to walk across the table.

"Does Mom know you have this?"

"Nooo," says my father. "Actually, though, I have been getting some business lately. I'm not as bad off as I used to be. Some months are actually pretty good, and then some months I don't have any business at all. My theory about life," says my father, folding his hands together on his knees, "is that things pretty much even out. So when I'm happy, I appreciate it because I know it won't last. And when I'm blue, I know I won't be blue forever, either. And I also bear in mind the possibility of those nearly impossible things happening."

It almost makes sense when he puts it that way, and I find myself wondering: If something can begin millions of years ago on Mars and somehow, miraculously, find its way to my father—then why not something simpler, like happiness, which happens every day right here on earth?

❧

Two years ago, my father and I were living in the house together. I had just graduated from college and was waitressing at a Mexican restaurant, where I learned to talk to customers as if they were children at a birthday party. I was saving money so I could move away from home, and my father wasn't charging me any rent because, as he said, "Just having you here is payment enough. Just having somebody in the house to talk to." Even though he didn't want to talk about anything except my mother. She was living in a one-bedroom apartment across the street from Pappy's Pizza, where we used to go after church on Sundays when she didn't feel like cooking. Sometimes in the middle of the night I would hear him pacing downstairs. The front door would slam, and I'd hear his car back out of the driveway. In the morning he'd tell me he went to sit in the parking lot outside my mother's window.

"That's sick," I told him, but he said it was love. I told my mother and she said it was sick, too. She phoned him and told him not to do it anymore or she'd call the police.

"My father is stalking my mother," I told my friends.

He told me everything he'd worked for was going down the toilet. "My business is failing, and your mother's going to kick me out of my own house," he said.

"She *is* making the payments," I reminded him. "It is fair."

"Nothing about this whole situation is fair," my father said. "But at least you're here. If you weren't here, I don't know what I'd do."

To appease some of my guilt about not paying rent, I'd treat him to lunch at the Horn and Horn on Sunday afternoons. The abundance of fried chicken, shrimp, and corn bread seemed to cheer him temporarily. "Your mother used to tell me I ignored the family," he told me once, his mouth full of dinner roll. "But everything I did I did for the family, can't she see that? You can see that, can't you?" He had a milk mustache.

"Sure," I said, thinking: What does staring into a telescope for three hours every night have to do with the family? What do flight simulation computer programs have to do with the family?

My mother gave him two months' warning before she sent the sheriff to remove him from the house. *"Remove* me," he said. "Like I'm a wart. Like I'm a splinter, for chrissake." I brought home the paper every day, but he wouldn't look for apartments. "She'll have to drag me out to the sidewalk," he said. "Which would thrill her no end, I'm sure."

I asked my boss at the Mexican restaurant if he knew of any openings, at any other chains, anywhere else. When I told my father I was going to Tucson, his eyes got wide, and I thought he was going to beg me to stay. But all he said was, "You're lucky. I've always wanted to see Arizona. The pictures make it look like another planet."

"That's what I need," I told him.

Two days before the sheriff was supposed to come, I left him waving in the carport, holding Brandy the dog so close to his chest it seemed like he was trying to share her heartbeat.

I thought that the desert would change me, that the heat would burn away the old life and leave me with a new, unrecognizable one. I imagined myself dancing drunk on Mexican beaches; I saw myself flying along dusty highways with a handsome young man who loved me. I haven't been to Mexico, and while there was a handsome young man, I couldn't manage to love him back. I had hoped, by the time I saw my parents again, that I would be full of good news, that my life would have shifted into something I could explain and account for. But the old life hasn't burned away at all; if anything, the heat has simply melted down the same old sadness, so that when I see the sun pour over the Catalina Mountains, it is there, and when I drive through the saguaro shadows at twilight, it is still there.

My mother calls up and asks to speak to me.

"I want to know if you're getting hungry for dinner," she says. "If I should drive over there soon or wait a while."

"She wants to know when she should come get me," I tell my father, who's sitting at his computer, printing out a letter to Midwest Bankcard.

"You tell your mother I want to take the two of you out for dinner."

He leans back in his desk chair, and the laser printer starts whirring. "We could pick her up and take her to Pappy's, for old times' sake."

"Dad wants to take us to Pappy's." I leave out the old times' sake part.

"Cathy," says my mother, and I can almost see her wiping the back of her hand across her forehead, as if checking for fever. "You know he's going to get all sad and sentimental, and I won't be able to stand it."

"Please," I say, and I realize that I want this, the two of them together with me—before my mother gets remarried, before there are step-people ·and new addresses. "I haven't seen either of you in two years, and I can't even remember the last time we went out to eat together."

"I can," she says. "It was your college graduation, and your father kept offering me bites of his food."

"Well, that was years ago."

I wheedle until my mother relents. "Then you never have to see him again as long as you live," I say, and my father looks over at me.

"That's not what I want either," says my mother, and I want to tell her to make up her mind, but I don't.

"Great," I say cheerily, and give my father a thumbs-up, as if we have achieved some sort of victory together, defeated the other team.

It's dusk when we drive to my mother's house. The sky is the color of dishwater, and the landscape unfolds into unfamiliar shapes—schools where there used to be barns, shopping plazas where there used to be fields.

"I've missed trees," I say. "Regular, normal trees."

"Well, you've come to the right place," my father says. "We've got lots of those!"

When he isn't talking, he's humming. We're listening to his friend's radio station, Classic Country All the Time. He taps his fingers on the steering wheel. It occurs to me that his happiness is so desperate, it's not happiness at all. It's like gasping for air.

"Calm down," I say, and he stops humming but keeps tapping.

"I'm just glad you're here, and I'm glad we're going to dinner with Rita. It just makes my little heart go pitter-pat!" He thumps his hand against his chest. "And it makes me feel like I have a family again." He stops thumping. "It makes me feel like maybe I haven't fouled up my life as completely as I sometimes think."

On the radio, Pasty Cline is falling to pieces.

"Don't worry," says my father. "I'll be down again soon enough."

When my mother moved back into the house, she fixed everything that had fallen into disrepair over the years. She had the gravel driveway paved. She had the floor in the basement fixed so it wouldn't flood any-more. She cut down the giant pine tree and got rid of the rotted wicker furniture, de-slugged the picnic table. She had told me about these changes but now, standing in the living room with my father, I feel dis-oriented. The walls are all different colors—beige where they used to be blue, yellow where they were white.

While my mother hugs me and says, "It's so good to see you, Pump-kin. I missed you," my father holds the dog and looks around as if he doesn't know whether he's allowed to sit down.

"Hey, Brandy," he says, joggling her belly-up. "I've missed this doggie. I wish I had an apartment that allowed doggies."

I had forgotten how my father slips into baby talk when he's around the dog.

"I have some boxes of your things I found," my mother tells him. "You can get them when we come back."

"Oh, sure," says my father. "That's fine."

"Books mainly. Some tools from the utility room."

"You know what they say," says my father. "You can never have too many books or tools." He ruffs Brandy under the chin.

"I've just got to get my coat and Brandy has to hurry up," my mother says. "Hurry up" means go to the bathroom. Brandy leaps out of my father's arms and starts spinning around in circles. My father says he'll take her.

My mother is heavier than she used to be, pear-shaped, the way I remember her from childhood. After she left my father she lost twenty-five pounds and dyed her hair strawberry blonde. She started wearing fuchsia and periwinkle skirts that swished around her knees. The weight's back on, and her hair is brown-turning-gray. She's wearing baggy jeans and an apricot sweatshirt. I don't know what to think of her happiness, perhaps because I can't locate it on her body—I don't see any physical evidence that she is, as she tells me, happier than she's ever been in her life. "It's a grown-up happiness," she says. "I like myself so much I don't even care if I'm a little tubby." On the coffee table, I notice, is one of her ubiquitous learn-to-love-yourself books.

"He's making me nervous already," she whispers. She goes down the hall and comes back wearing a gray coat she got at Goodwill for four dollars. She's always getting bargains at Goodwill and telling me about them. The coat's got a fake fur collar, and she lowers her chin in it and frowns.

"You don't have to whisper," I say loudly. "He can't hear us."

"I know," she whispers.

"He's been all right. How did he find out anyway? About you getting married."

"I sent him a letter." She shoves her hands into her pockets as if she's already cold. "Which maybe wasn't a great idea, but I thought he should know. Has he said anything?"

"Not really." My mother gives me a look that says she doesn't believe me, but I raise my eyebrows at her and she looks away. I am wondering if I can bear to come back here in a year for her wedding. It occurs to me that I want to punish her for being happy.

The back door slams, and there is the sound of my father stomping through the kitchen and the jingle of Brandy's leash as he unhooks it from her collar. When he comes into the living room, he's holding her and she's leaning against his chest and panting.

"This little dog is just a bundle of love," says my father. "Aren't you, Bran?" He strokes the wiry fur under her chin. He never used to say things like "bundle of love" or kiss the dog on the nose, like he just now did. "That's right," he says when she licks his face. "Gimme some of those dog germs." He sets her down and she turns in a circle, then plops down at his feet. "She's so smart, too. Rita, after you moved out, she'd sit in the chair by the window waiting for you to come home from work. Around six o'clock she'd start whimpering. She did that for weeks and weeks."

"She's pretty sensitive," says my mother, in a singsong voice that seems to come from too far up in her throat.

"A bundle of love," says my father again, and my mother is already moving toward the front door.

🐾

"Crank up the heat," I say when we're in the car. My mother passes me one of her gloves so we can share.

"There's no mittens where Cathy comes from," says my father. He looks into the rearview mirror. My mother is a fuzzy gray shape beside him.

"Humpf," she says. She turns halfway around. "You thawing out a little, Snookie?" she says, and pats my knee.

"Doggone it," my father says suddenly. "Whatever happened to muffs? Remember muffs?"

"They were before my time, Ernie."

"Ha!"

"People need to do things with their hands now," my mother says, looking out the window.

"Watch your language!" says my father.

"Girls wore them," my mother continues, humorlessly, "because they were supposed to be dainty and helpless."

"That so," I say. I feel a familiar irritation growing up through me like a weed, spreading from my stomach into my legs, up to my arms and into my brain. I had forgotten how my parents, when they're around each other, simply become more extreme versions of themselves. I feel myself slipping back into adolescent nastiness. I cross my arms and throw my legs up on the seat. When we'd gotten into the car, my mother had offered to sit in the back, but I told her no. I liked the idea of the two of them up there together, the backs of their heads side by side. My father likes it too, because he says, "What a night! The sky's all pretty and mysterious, and Cathy's in the back seat, just like years and years ago."

My mother looks at him and then looks straight ahead. "It's not the same," she says. "It's not just like years and years ago at all."

I know she's trying to squelch his nostalgia before it suffocates her, before it makes her mean.

"Well, it's close," says my father good-naturedly. "It's as close as I have, and I'm grateful for it."

21

✦

Pappy's Pizza has become a chili restaurant, the Hard Times Café. My father says, "It's my place!"

Inside, we're told we have to wait ten to twenty minutes. High school kids with their arms and legs twined around each other are taking up all the benches, so we stand near the restrooms. When the doors open, I can smell bubblegum air freshener.

"Ernie, will you please stop bouncing?" says my mother. "It's giving me a headache."

"I'm buoyant so I'm bouncing," my father says. He looks at me. "Did you hear about the two kids, one littler than the other, who go into a restaurant, and the bigger kid says, 'I'm the party of six and he's the party of four.'" He grins. "I'm the party of fifty-one and you're the party of twenty-five."

"I was going to do something really grand on my fiftieth birthday," says my mother, "but I didn't. I guess there's always fifty-one."

"You don't have to wait till your birthday," I tell her. She's looking sad; her glasses are down on her nose and she's staring at her feet.

"No, you're right."

"You're doing grand things," I say quietly, while my father is examining a menu at the hostess stand.

"Yes," she says, and smiles.

At the table, my father says to order whatever we want. "Even lobster. If you want lobster, then order lobster!"

"They don't have lobster," says my mother. "They have chili."

"Well, whatever you want. Maybe they have lobster chili!" He nudges me. "That sounds like a taste treat, doesn't it?"

They don't have lobster chili, so I order the Three Alarm and a beer.

I can't recall ever drinking beer with my parents before. I decide to get drunk.

"I looked up your street on the computer," my father's saying to me. "Imagine, one little disk with every street in the United States on it."

"They have a computer program for that?" says my mother.

"Oh, sure. When I found your street," he says to me, "I said out loud—'There she is!' It was so exciting. I'll show it to you."

"Okay, thanks," I say, even though I don't think much of computer programs. My mother doesn't, either. She used to say things like, "If you spent as much time with me as you do with that computer." She used to threaten to unplug it, to smash it, to set fire to the disks and watch them melt.

"Back home, it's already like eighty degrees," I say. I tell them how I ride my bike to work every day, and about finding a lizard in my closet, and how sometimes you can see snow on the mountains when it's ninety-five degrees in town. The more I talk about this other life, the farther away it seems, like a movie I watched once a long time ago. It becomes easier to make things up, and so I lie about still having a boyfriend and applying to grad school.

"You're so brave," says my mother. "When I was your age, I never would have been able to drive across the country, just pick up and move to someplace I'd never been before. I went right from my mother's house to my husband's."

"That teensy little house in Apopka," says my father. "With the dryer in the kitchen. Sounded like a jet was taking off every time we ran it."

"You guys should come out and visit me someday," I say.

"I'd love to do that," says my father. "I'd like to see the observatory out there."

"I wouldn't mind staying at a resort," says my mother. "If I ever have

23

the money. And if I can ever get the time off work, which doesn't seem too likely."

"How is work?" says my father, and my mother goes on about whatever it is that she does, something about quality control and staff enthusiasm.

"Enthusiasm is important," says my father. "I wouldn't mind some more of that myself."

My mother narrows her eyes at him. "You seem pretty enthused to me."

"Well," says my father, and then starts hacking into his napkin. "Hoo," he says. He looks up, teary-eyed.

"You choke?" I ask, thumping him on the back. "You need to be Heimliched?"

"If he can talk he doesn't need to be Heimliched," says my mother.

"I *know* that."

"I think I'm just coming down with something," my father says. "Some blasted cold or something."

"Well, it's no wonder," says my mother. "Traipsing around in short sleeves."

I order another beer and slug it down. My parents don't drink, not for any religious or moral reasons, but just because they never bothered with it. I see my mother looking at me, and I excuse myself and make my way across the blue carpet to the bathroom. Inside, I look in the mirror, searching for the clues that tell me I belong to these people. I look until my face is a blur, like some abstract painting, until it means nothing. I walk back through the restaurant, stepping over the carpet as if it were the ocean, and the table where my parents sit seems suddenly to be floating, small and lost, like a life raft.

After dinner, we go back to my mother's house. While she's down in the basement searching for my father's box of tools, he and I sit on the sofa together, looking around at the walls where my 4-H paintings of mallard ducks and eagles used to be. I didn't manage to get drunk, just soggy-headed and sleepy.

"I'm going to miss this house," my father's saying. "Even though it's not mine anymore, I'm going to miss knowing your mother's here, and thinking about her here." He looks at me. "I know we all went through a lot of crap in this house, but there was good stuff, too."

"There was a lot of crap," I agree. "I seem to remember mostly crap."

"That's a shame," says my father, and he looks at the wall again.

Downstairs, there's the sound of something metal falling on concrete.

"You need any help?" my father calls.

"No," says my mother, already at the top of the stairs. "There's books in the study, but I haven't packed them up yet. You can get a box and do that if you want." She sets the box of tools on the floor in front of my father.

"I was just telling Cathy I'm going to miss this house."

"I'll probably miss it, too," says my mother, looking down and touching the box lightly with her foot.

"I'm kicking myself for not being able to pay my part of the equity. At least then I'd get some money out of the sale. At least it wouldn't seem like I've just *lost* it—like a lot of things." He's tapping his foot on the carpet, wringing his hands. His head is bowed and I can see swipes of gray-white hair across his bald spot. This is how I remember him from the years just after my mother left: wilted and anxious, his voice small and squeezed up out of his throat in a whimper. I want to say: What about things evening out? What about this afternoon, when you were so happy you couldn't stand still?

"Ernie," says my mother, like a warning. "I am not about to get into this with you now."

"Oh, hell." My father wheezes into his hand. "I'm just uptight because I'm going to need a new clutch soon and those things are so blasted expensive."

"You're upset because of your clutch?" says my mother.

My father sits there on the sofa, his elbows resting on his knees, his head so far down it's as if he's preparing for an emergency landing. "Oh, hell," he says again, and I feel all the old meanness come back, scampering through me like an animal with claws.

"If you need money for a clutch so bad," I say loudly, louder than I mean to, "why don't you just *sell* something?"

"I'll be all right," my father says. He lifts his head. "Don't worry about me."

"I'm not," I tell him, and I feel what I was going to say—*Just how much does that dumb rock mean to you?*—drop down a little, from my throat into the space between my heart and my stomach. I feel it there, glimmering and useless and mine.

My father is struggling up from the sofa, coughing, his face bright red. "Let's get to those books," he says hoarsely.

"It's a wonder you haven't gotten a cold sooner," says my mother. "You never did know how to dress warm."

"Oh, well, it's just a cough."

"You know," she says, "when you get a cold, your cough will linger for about three weeks."

"Really?" My father sounds surprised. He sits back on the sofa. "Really?" he says again.

26

"Tim's coming over in a half hour." My mother looks at her watch, and my father stands up again.

"Gotcha."

We go into the guest room, all three of us, and pull my father's books off the shelves where they have been for thirteen years, books he hasn't missed at all, which he is now packing up as if he needs them to survive.

"It's my high school astronomy book!" he says. "And my mother's *Oxford English Dictionary.* I forgot all this was here."

"This is yours," says my mother, handing him another one.

"The Life of Charles Lindbergh!" cries my father. "Oh, boy!"

I know that what she's doing is trying to clear away this old life, to get rid of all reminders and evidence of my father. I also know that to him it is something else entirely—she is giving him gifts.

"Thank you," he says to her.

I'm flipping through *The Life of Charles Lindbergh,* but I'm thinking of all the things my mother will never give back. I'm thinking how strange it must be to know there's someone out there who knows what you sound like when you sleep, where you misplace your keys, how long your colds last. Things you don't know about yourself, things you'll never have the chance to find out, while somewhere in the world, or in the same room, someone is walking around with knowledge they have no use for anymore.

Alone in the car with the heater blasting, my father and I do not say a word. Two boxes of books and tools are rattling in the back seat. My father flips on the radio, but Classic Country All the Time is just static now, and he turns it off again. "It was nice seeing Rita," he says finally. "Nice being out with my favorite gals."

"It was nice," I say. I crane forward, looking for a light traveling through the sky—something to make a conversation out of—but the sky is marbled with ghostly clouds. I cast about for something else to say, but I can't ask him if he's glad I've kept his secrets. And I can't ask him if he will be okay now, when I have done nothing at all but show up, two years late. I can't tell him that I am not happy in the desert—which looks like another planet, yes, but feels like earth when he is singing his sad life to me across all the miles I traveled to get there. I can't tell him that my worst fear is a future as empty and terrible as this, and that sometimes I think I can feel myself being pulled toward it, caught in the orbit of his sorrow.

And he can't tell me that he still loves my mother and will keep on hoping for something nearly impossible to happen to make her love him back again. He can't tell me if he doesn't have enough money to pay rent, or if he needs me to send him another care package of chocolate and macaroni, or what will happen when the credit card companies finally wise up and stop sending him cards.

He can't tell me he wishes I would stay.

Beside me, my father is breathing slow and regular as a child, and I wonder suddenly if he's fallen asleep. But his eyes are open, fixed on the road. For a moment, I believe I know what he's thinking—he has seen the woman he loves, and his daughter is beside him, and for now everything is just as simple as that. He lifts one finger in a half-tap and holds it above the steering wheel for a moment before letting it fall back again. When he sighs, I lean back in my seat and try to think of nothing. The sky vaults over us and silence settles down, like a pact we've made together, like a precious, immeasurable weight.

Close Enough

The girls always call between two-thirty and three in the morning, but Janice is never prepared for them. A feeling of doom wakes her, beginning at the top of her head and exiting the soles of her feet, like a bolt of lightning. In the dark, briefly, she can't figure out what disaster has occurred, or to whom. Then the phone rings again.

Maud is the third girl in six months to wake her up this way.

"Janice?" says a small, shaky voice. "Is Davey there?"

"Oh, honey," Janice says, sitting up in bed. Is she hung over? Her

29

heart is still thudding; she takes a breath. "Just a minute, let me check."

She swings her legs over the side of the bed and stands up faster than she means to. In the dresser mirror she sees herself as a wavering blob of white. She slept in her slip. Crossing the room she steps on something cold—her belt buckle—and then something slippery—her hose. She flicks the switch and floods the room with light. Her clothes lie strewn across the room, inside-out, hollow-looking, like moltings off an animal.

"Davey?" she says. She knows already that he isn't home. Davey is thirty-one years old. When he isn't living with a girlfriend, he lives in his old room. "Davey?" She pushes the door open. The bed is piled high with her laundry, stacks of towels like miniature buildings.

"He's not here," she says to Maud. "But I'm sure he's fine."

"Oh, I'm sure he's fine, too," says Maud bitterly. "He's just never not come home before and I'm pissed."

Usually they cry and beg Janice to tell them what they've done wrong. Are they too clingy? Too independent? Do they smother him? Ignore him? What? What have they *done?* And Janice will calm the girl down, tell her she's done nothing, nothing wrong, that Davey is just that way. She'll apologize for her son's heartlessness. She'll wonder what *she's* done wrong.

"You've got to stop introducing me to these sweet little girls and then treating them like dirt," she'd told him. "It breaks my heart. Did I raise you to treat girls this way? Did I?"

"I *like* them all," Davey said. "I don't ever mean to be mean to anybody. It just sort of happens. They're never who I think they are."

"You mean they're not perfect," said Janice. "Get it through your thick skull—nobody is."

"Even me. *Especially* me," he said, and grinned at her. "I can't help it."

When he was little, girls breathless from giggling would call up and say, "Is this where the boy who looks like Donny Osmond lives?" And when Janice said yes, did they want to talk to him? they would scream and hang up.

"He's probably at his friend Jim's house," Janice tells Maud now.

"He probably got drunk and met some slut," says Maud. "I mean, no offense—your son is so sweet, but then he can be such a complete asshole. I waited for him at Friday's, waited three fucking hours and got drunk by myself, and some bald guy kept asking me out, and I was like, 'No, no, I'm meeting my boyfriend. Any second now.' And he was like, 'Oh yeah, right.' I mean, it was humiliating. And then he didn't come home, didn't call, nothing."

Janice prefers comforting the girls who cry. "Davey's not perfect," she says. Her throat feels sticky and dry. She forgot to brush her teeth last night and wants to do it now, and drink some water. The clock radio is glowing 2:37.

"Damn straight he's not," shouts Maud, as if she has a right to be mad at *Janice.*

"Perhaps," Janice says coolly, "you should discuss this with Davey next time you see him."

"I'm sorry," Maud says, and Janice is pleased to hear her sniffle a little. "I'm really drunk and really really sad and . . . and I don't know. You know?"

"I know," Janice says soothingly. "I do know, dear. I've been through it myself."

"Yeah?" Maud says, and Janice wishes she hadn't said anything. She has, on several occasions, poured out her love life to one of Davey's girls, explaining how Davey's father was a drunk who was never around; how they'd left him in Oklahoma when Davey was thirteen and driven to Tucson to stay with her mother, and had just stayed on after she died. She'd told them about her succession of boyfriends—the rich one who'd offered to marry her because he liked the way she cleaned his house; her boss at the bank who'd made a pass at her, then had her fired; the married man; the younger man; the man who worked as a clown. She made some of them sound worse than they were; she omitted all the ones she'd dumped. She told them about her current husband, Arnold, who drives a truck and is gone for six weeks at a time. But she doesn't want to talk about this now. Last night, she and Arnold had one of their long-distance fights, which was why she'd gone out. So she wouldn't have to be home if the phone rang, or if it didn't. She'd been so drunk when she got in that she hadn't even checked to see if there was a message, but she sees now that the red light on the machine isn't blinking.

"Just get some rest," Janice says.

"Fat chance," says Maud. "Listen, I'm sorry I woke you. Call me tomorrow? When I'm back to normal?"

"Of course," Janice says.

"And if you see that son of yours, you tell him he's being a big dumb jerk, will you?"

"You bet," Janice says, and she will, too, and Davey knows it—which is why he'll stay away. In a couple of weeks, Janice will come home from work and he'll be lying on the sofa watching some game or other, drinking the Heineken she bought for Arnold. She'll let him move back into the spare bedroom, and she'll charge him rent, and in a month or two he'll bring a girl over for dinner, and it will start all over again.

❦

After they hang up, Janice goes into the bathroom and drinks water from the sink, catching it up with her hands. She isn't hung over; she's still drunk. Not karaoke-drunk, like she was earlier, but muddy-headed and sad, almost how she'd felt before she started drinking. She brushes her teeth and takes two Anacin and goes into the living room.

The last time Arnold was here, over a month ago, Janice slept on the sofa for half the nights he was home.

"You've started sleeping on a diagonal," she told him the first morning. "I was hanging off the bed!"

"You should have kicked me," he said. He was standing naked in the hallway. Janice hated it when he walked around naked. He looked like a giant child—a six-foot, fuzz-haired toddler with a yellow mustache.

"Yeah, well," Janice said. "I wanted to, believe me. Go get dressed. I can't talk to you like that." There were times when she felt more like his mother than his wife, and not just because he was eleven years younger than she was. He expected her to wait on him, to make him breakfast every morning even though she had to go to work and he got to sit around the whole week. And there was always some ailment that made it necessary for him to lie on the sofa and whine; his back hurt or he had a cold or a stiff knee. The first year of their marriage, Janice hadn't minded. She was, as she told her friends, crazy, out of her head in love. She and Arnold stayed up all night drinking, and she would come to work rumpled and exhausted. Arnold was so *fun,* she would say, and so kind. Not like Gary, her first husband, who wouldn't know a good time if it bit him, who flew into rages if there was crud in the sink or if he couldn't find his socks.

The second year, she began to suspect that what Arnold really wanted was to be taken care of and cleaned up after. Now, after three years, even the fun seems like another thing to be tended to, along with his knee or his back.

"He's just a big old baby," Sheila had said last night at the Mockingbird. Sheila is one of Davey's girls from years ago; sometimes she and Janice go out to the bars on the east side of town. "Even Davey doesn't like him."

"Davey likes him just fine," Janice lied. When Davey first met Arnold, he pronounced him a loser. "He doesn't say anything," Davey said, and Janice said what did he know? "I know a loser when I see one," said Davey. When Arnold and Davey were around each other, which wasn't often, Davey puffed up like a threatened cat while Arnold seemed to shrink. His mouth would pucker and vanish; his neck retreated into its collar.

"If he was my husband," said Sheila, "I'd tell him to take a hike."

When Janice was with Sheila, she smoked and drank too much and said things she didn't mean, like how she was going to be gone when Arnold got home tomorrow for their anniversary.

"I'll go on vacation," she said. "And I'll leave a note on the kitchen table: Lasagna is in fridge."

"Make him cook his own lasagna," said Sheila.

"Oh, he wouldn't. He'd starve to death. I'd come back from Cancún or wherever and he'd be this skeleton on the sofa, watching football."

She only talks this nasty about Arnold when she's with Sheila. This is partly because of the amount of tequila they consume together, and partly because Sheila is always saying, "You deserve a husband who comes home every night and takes you places. That Arnold is always sitting on his butt complaining. What do you want with that?" "Yeah," Janice would say. "What do I want with that?"

"We'll go someplace together," Sheila said last night. "We'll take a vacation and let old Arnie fend for himself."

"Okay!" Janice said, but of course they wouldn't. She and Arnold would go out to dinner, and maybe this weekend they'd drive up to

Flagstaff, where they'd gotten married. Most likely, though, they would just sit around Janice's apartment getting drunk. Sometimes it shocked Janice how much they drank together; the day after Arnold arrived, the kitchen floor and counters would be teetering with green bottles, like some tiny emerald city. He filled her apartment with empty food boxes and empty snack bags; when he left, she always felt as if she'd been robbed.

Davey dumped Sheila four years ago. As a way of making up for her son's insensitivity, Janice had taken her to happy hour and told all about her first marriage to Gary. She said the usual: she'd been too young, they were high school sweethearts, back then you just went from your parents' house to your husband's, you did what everybody else did. She leaned forward with her elbows on the bar. She shook her head, swishing her hair in her face. She felt oddly, appealingly tragic. She rolled off her reasons as if they were excuses, summing it all up with: "I was just dumb."

"And you've got the pictures to prove it," Sheila said. "Davey showed me some. You had a beehive up to here." She held her hand a foot above her head.

"Don't remind me," Janice said.

"It was just last *week*," Sheila said dismally. "Just last week he showed me all his childhood photos and I thought, I've got him now! You don't show just anybody pictures of yourself being potty-trained."

"You'll be fine," Janice said. "There's other fish in the sea."

"Yeah," said Sheila. "But we live in the desert." She rocked back on her barstool, nearly flinging herself into a glossy-faced couple. "Oh, sorry," she said. Sheila was not the sort of person Janice would have chosen to be friends with: she was the big-haired, blue eye-shadowed type, a woman who wore high heels and ankle socks with denim miniskirts. When she wasn't talking about Davey, she talked about her tan, and her nails, and whether or not she should get her bazooms enlarged.

"You could just work out," Janice told her. "Lift weights."

"So that I can have pectorals where I don't even have breasts? No, thanks."

Secretly, Janice was glad Davey had dumped Sheila—she thought he could do better—but she was also surprised to realize she liked the girl: she was Janice's confirming, conspiring little voice made flesh; she was the fun-loving, drink-till-you-drop girl Janice had missed her chance to be.

Sheila took Janice out to clubs that featured bands of tuxedoed Mexicans playing synthesized versions of "YMCA" and "Celebration." Sheila, who styled hair for a living, would meet her friends from work there— young, moussed girls who wore dusty-rose lip gloss and high heels with their jeans. They would talk about the butts that walked by. "Getta loada him," they would say. "Gimme somma that." Janice, to her complete shame, loved it. She did tequila shots with the girls—Cammy and Tammy, could that be right?—and doled out Camel Lights, and once, in a moment of exquisite intoxication, she even danced to the theme to "Fame" with a short, Tahitian man.

"Go, girl," called Sheila, Cammy, and Tammy.

Sheila was the one who'd first taken her to the Mockingbird four years ago. It was tiny and lit with red light bulbs, like Janice imagined an opium den might be. They played only fifties and sixties music, and while there were never any of what Sheila called hubba-hunks, she thought Janice might like it. Janice did like it. She always ended up dating men who couldn't dance—or *wouldn't* dance, claiming they looked stupid or didn't know any "moves." Her ex-husband Gary had never danced with her either, and she kept shouting this over the music while she and Sheila were twisting.

"What?" Sheila screamed.

"Gary! He would never *dance* to this stuff!"

Sheila thrashed her hair across her face and spun around on one of her little pink heels. It was while they were drifting off the dance floor, mopping sweat from their foreheads, that a tall man with a yellow mustache and a red polka-dotted necktie touched Janice on the elbow and asked, "Do you want to dance?" Later, Janice told Arnold it was the necktie that got her. "I was willing to overlook your personality."

"It was false advertising," Sheila said last night at the karaoke bar. "You meet him dancing, he's wearing this totally cool tie, he looks like a fun sort of guy, right?"

"Then you marry 'em," Janice said. She was feeling sloshy. "And whammo. Dancing? Why would he want to go dancing when he can plant his big fat butt in front of the television? He's worse than Gary, cause Gary never pretended to like something he didn't. But Arnold made me think he was fun!"

"Old fat weirdo," Sheila said.

"He's younger than me."

"Bullshit." Sheila spat this so forcefully that a drop of spittle landed on Janice's cheek. "You are so goddamn young. And you should be out there, having a blast."

"You know why we were fighting tonight?" Janice said. She pointed her margarita umbrella at Sheila. "I'll tell you why. Because he just sort of assumed that I could get tomorrow off. And I said, 'No. You never told me you wanted me to take the day off *tomorrow*, you said try to get Monday off and I did, and I'm taking comp time to do that anyway.' And he just clammed up the way he does when he's pissed. He started mumbling in his little clam-voice. And when he does that, that's it. If he wants to talk about it he should talk. Don't give me this silent, pouting shit. So I hung up on him."

"All right!" Sheila slapped the table.

"Well, first I said, 'There's no point running up this phone bill if you're not going to say anything. So if you have something to say, say it.'"

"Shit or get off the pot," Sheila said.

"Right. But he didn't, so *click*."

"Buh-bye," Sheila said.

That was when they started talking about how Janice should run off and leave him on their anniversary. Sheila dragged Janice up to do karaoke to "I Feel the Earth Move," and then they went over to the Mockingbird and twisted, but Janice couldn't manage to enjoy herself as much as she felt she should. Also, Sheila was beginning to annoy her. She was doing her closed-eyes, sultry look-at-me dance, where she ignored the music and just slunked around, lifting her hair up off her neck. When Sheila hadn't had a date in a while she got this way: desperate, Janice thought, with a strange, gleeful meanness. She pictured Sheila twenty-five years from now, divorced and dancing in these same places.

"Don't just stand there!" Sheila was screaming above the music; the disco ball rolled green and red and blue lights over her skin, making her look like an alien. "Dance!"

"I'm sorry," Janice shouted in Sheila's ear. "I'm going home."

"Come *awn*." Sheila stopped mid-slink. "You're just going to go?"

"Yes!" Janice yelled.

"Fuddy-duddy!" Sheila called after her.

Once in the car, Janice realized she shouldn't be driving; the oncoming headlights were starbursts against her window. She drove as slowly as she could, squinting. Janice had never driven drunk until she met Sheila, and she thought angrily that somehow Sheila would be to blame if anything horrible happened to her. She imagined Arnold coming home tomorrow afternoon and finding the apartment empty, the trash cans full, no snacks in the cabinets, no beers in the fridge. He would call her office, pissed off. "I'm sorry, you didn't know?" Meg, her assistant, would say. She imagined herself in the hospital, unconscious, connected to machines. She thought of Davey standing by her bedside, holding her hand. But this was somehow harder to see, and she found herself thinking of Davey lying in the hospital, his room so crowded with sobbing women that Janice couldn't even make her way to the side of his bed.

She passed the car dealerships, the Walgreen's, the all-night coffee stores. The palm trees seemed pressed flat against the black sky, like cardboard cutouts. When Janice had arrived in Tucson, the palm trees were what thrilled her first—it was like being on vacation!—then the mountains, with their rivers of shadows running green and gold and blue. While Davey was at school, she would drive into the pincushion saguaro fields and tramp through the desert as far as she dared, out into the prickly world. Now, turning left without thinking, it occurred to her that she didn't see things anymore so much as feel them move past her, like the ghosts of people she once loved.

❧

Janice considers having a shot of whiskey and going back to sleep, then decides to make coffee instead. There's a thin gleam of gray light under the orange curtains. In two hours she'll have to get dressed and go to work, so she can spend all day saying, "Garrett Labs, this is Janice," in her best secretary voice—friendly and chirpy, emphasis on the *this*. She knows she sounds much younger than fifty-one; men are always flirting with her on the phone, asking her personal questions until she says kindly, almost apologetically, "You know, I *am* married." She won't tell them this until they've asked her out.

39

The coffeemaker sputters and hurls mud-colored drops into the pot. Janice can feel a vague dread drifting like smoke through her body.

One time, after she'd been up all night consoling someone named Helen, Janice asked Sheila, "How many times did you call me in the middle of the night?"

"Once," Sheila said. "Once was enough."

"Hmm," said Janice. She seemed to remember several calls from Sheila. "I always think someone's dead. I think it's the police, telling me that Arnold's been killed, or Davey's been mugged, or, or—"

"Terrible things," Sheila said.

"I just think—Oh! It's happened! And I don't even know what it is."

She thinks of phoning Maud—who is certainly wide awake, half-wishing Davey was mangled somewhere on his way to meet her, that there has been some larger, more obvious tragedy than the fact of his not loving her. She thinks of Arnold, somewhere between Santa Fe and Tucson. She used to follow him on road maps, tracing her finger along the blue and red lines. When they talked on the phone, she would stare at the dot of the town where he was. Now, her maps are stuffed somewhere in the closet, and she has only the vaguest idea of where he is at any moment, somewhere between one dot and another.

Her orange curtains are glowing like jack-o'-lanterns, like something beginning to ignite. "Look," she says to no one, and considers the possibility that the thing she's been dreading might be nothing more tragic than loneliness.

Later, when Arnold is gone again and Davey is on her couch with a half-empty bottle of Heineken, Janice will tell Sheila that their trip to Flagstaff was very pleasant and relaxing, and then she'll say she needs to hang up, she can hear dinner bubbling over in the kitchen. She will not mention sleeping on the sofa, or the argument she and Arnold had because he won't look for a different job. She will not complain about his silences, or his whining about his knee, and she will not say that when he left she told him she was glad to see him gone. She will not repeat what they said to each other when they were both so drunk they could hardly see. She will not offer any warnings or ask for any advice.

Then she will go back to the living room and sink onto the sofa beside her son, and ask who's winning. When she realizes he's asleep, she will inch closer, until she can see the pores of his skin and the way his eyebrows ruff up at the edges, like black feathers. In that pocket of time between one girl and another, when Davey has forgiven her for calling him a louse and she has forgiven him for being one, she will feel blameless and new. She will look at her son, his ankles crossed on the coffee table, his eyes closed in a dream that doesn't include her or anyone she knows, and think this might be close enough to happiness.

Till Death
Do Us Part

1

When Joyce was seven, the Reverend Sewickley performed the second of her mother's four wedding ceremonies, to the first of three stepfathers. Joyce was disappointed to realize that her mother's new husband would be Fat Henry; she'd thought that the Reverend would marry her mother, that he would live with them in their apartment in Baltimore and take her to the zoo. "He's already married, dummy," said Kathy, who was ten and didn't want a stepfather. "Besides, he's about fifty years old." Joyce didn't care. If the Reverend married their mother, he would let her ring the church bell every Sunday.

Their mother made her own dress from a Butterick pattern, and miniature versions for Joyce and Kathy. The fabric was called seashell pink, and with the leftover scraps, their mother made herself a wide pink headband. Joyce and Kathy got bows for their ponytails. While Aunt Gretchen played guitar and sang a song she'd written herself, Joyce walked down the aisle, feeling like a princess even though her shoes pinched her. She fluttered pink petals from her basket and waved at her Sunday School teacher, Mrs. Cook.

Joyce thought that getting married was a fine thing to do, as long as you could hold still. She was under strictest instructions not to scratch herself or yawn. It wasn't easy. The Reverend looked over at her once and smiled, and she could almost hear his voice in her head, saying her name in his gentle drawl: "Joy-ous," he called her, and she was.

The reception was in the Ebenezer Church hall, where last month they'd had the big Oyster Fry, like they did every March. White, fold-out paper bells were thumbtacked to the ceiling, and pink streamers wound their way around the bookshelves and paintings of Jesus. Doris Sewickley had made cream cheese and olive sandwiches on pink bread, cut into little triangles. The silver punch bowl was filled with Hawaiian Punch.

After the cake, Joyce and Kathy went outside and hunted for toads in the mulchy ditches by the basement windows, which is what they did every Sunday after church while their mother was talking with the Reverend and Doris. They each caught one, and Kathy's left a damp brown smudge in the palm of her white glove when she let it go. Joyce deposited hers in her pocketbook. Later, she would give it cake.

They walked up the weedy hill and through the iron gate to the cemetery. Joyce stomped over to a gray marble gravestone three rows down, bunched up her skirt, and threw herself down on her knees in the prickly grass. "Hello, Agnes," she shouted to the ground. Even though Joyce and Kathy didn't know who she was, they felt sorry for Agnes, for having to go through an entire life with that name.

Mrs. Cook said that when you died you went to heaven, where flowers bloomed all the time. Joyce preferred to think of it as a zoo. In her heaven, camels stepped carefully among the roses and pandas nibbled the daffodils. She wasn't clear if they were under the ground or in the clouds, but she liked to believe that heaven was beneath her feet, so that if she stomped hard enough, all the dead people would pause on their elephants and wonder what it was. Her father—who was farther north, under dirt much colder and harder than this—would call out her name, and sad Agnes would start to laugh.

Kathy was sitting on her knees in a way their mother said destroyed ligaments. "I won't call Fat Henry Dad, no matter what," she said. "And I won't move to that stupid house in the middle of nowhere."

Joyce had her ear to the ground. "Shh," she said. "I'm trying to hear the dead people."

2

Joyce and Kathy's mother married George on a Saturday in November. They had moved back to the city, out of Henry's house in the middle of nowhere. Joyce was back at her old school, and they didn't have to drive an hour to get to church anymore. Not that they'd been going much—Christmas and Easter, mainly. Fat Henry said religion was boring.

"I don't *go* for the religion," said Joyce's mother. "I go for the rest of it." She'd made George promise to go, too. George had a little boy named Andrew, who was just big enough to toddle up the aisle with the ring.

"I bet he swallows it," Kathy said.

Joyce giggled. "And they have to get it out of his poop."

Kathy frowned. Kathy was fourteen, and suddenly things offended her. Joyce had to be careful now, especially where boys were concerned. The mention of certain boys would send Kathy flying to her room, an unrecognizable whirl of hair and shrieking. Then she would lock the door and get on the phone until their mother threatened to call the fire station to break the door down. Joyce didn't know what to make of it.

In the vestibule before the ceremony, the Reverend Sewickley called Joyce a lovely young lady, and Joyce blushed because she knew it was true. Her mother had splurged on turquoise taffeta gowns and pearl chokers. The dress—scoop-necked—looked better on Kathy, who was beginning to poke out in front, but Joyce felt radiant. Her hair was swept up on her head, and little ringlets bounced beside her pearl earrings.

She was the only flower girl this time. Kathy was a bridesmaid, positioned between Aunt Gretchen and George's sister. George's brother was the best man, and the ushers were Uncle Ted and Cousin Charlie. As she walked down the aisle, behind little Andrew, she imagined that the entire wedding party was giving off a pale light that the people in the congregation could see. The Reverend's smooth head gleamed like something holy. Joyce thought she might die from happiness.

George was a bank teller, and he had already taken them to Ocean

City and King's Dominion. And Joyce had always wanted a brother; admittedly, not one like Andrew, who cried when you looked at him, but he would grow up eventually, and perhaps they would be friends.

As she was thinking this, tossing out her white and turquoise flowers, little Andrew stopped short, as if realizing that he should have been afraid a long time ago. Joyce collided with his tiny tuxedoed back.

"Keep *moving*," she hissed, and gave him a push.

Andrew swung around, opened his mouth, and bleated. His lips were shiny with drool. The ring box fell off its velvet pillow and landed at the puffy feet of Mrs. Cook, who picked it up and tried to push it back into Andrew's fist.

"No!" he screamed, batting her hands away. He plopped down in the aisle, legs straight out in front of him, and howled. George rushed over and swept the boy up by his armpits.

"He's wet himself," he announced, and Andrew screamed louder. Joyce's mother ran from her place at the end of the procession and hefted Andrew into her arms, heedless of his damp bottom.

"I *told* you he was too young," said Kathy loudly.

Their mother swung around and mouthed, *"Shut up."*

The Reverend Sewickley stood with his hands on his thick hips, shaking with laughter. Joyce glared. He was in charge here; he was supposed to settle things down, put everything back in order. He could ask Mrs. Cook to cart Andrew off to the nursery, where he could cry all he wanted. But Andrew stayed. George joggled him in his arms while they said their vows. When they kissed, squishing Andrew between them, the congregation murmured *"Awww"* and clapped. Joyce squeezed the handle of her empty basket and stared at her shoes. As far as she was concerned, the wedding was ruined.

Kathy was no longer interested in looking for toads or visiting Agnes. She was preoccupied with applying lip gloss and flirting with Robbie Russell, whom she had known since she was six and had, until recently, only addressed as Turd Face. Joyce found it sickening. She went outside and peered into the ditches by the basement windows. It was cold, and she couldn't squat comfortably without ruining her dress. "Here, toad," she said halfheartedly, but no toad came.

The clouds were thick like milk behind the steeple, and the weather vane—a brass rooster—twisted creakily this way, then that, as if it didn't really care if the wind blew or not. There was the faraway smell of burning leaves. A jack-o'-lantern, damp and rotten, grinned a mush-toothed grin on the porch steps of the house across the street. Joyce wondered why anyone would want to get married in dreary November— or, for that matter, at all.

3

"This is it, I *swear*," said the girls' mother. It was the night after Christmas, and the church glowed with white candles and smelled of pine air freshener and wax. The day before, the Sunday School had had a pageant, and there was still hay on the floor by the altar. The girls' mother was standing in the vestibule, under the rope that led to the bell tower. She was wearing a white suit and a white velvet hat, which Joyce was bobby-pinning to her hair. The short veil reached just past her chin.

"Ow, you jabbed me," said her mother, turning around. She pulled the veil back from her face. She and Joyce were almost the same height.

48

"Anyway," she continued, "if this doesn't work out, I'll just stay single. Not that I think it won't work out," she added hurriedly. "I'm sure it will." She cast her eyes down at Reverend Sewickley, who was picking tinsel off the carpet. "You must think I'm pathetic."

"Not at all," said the Reverend. He stood up, looked about vainly for a trash can, and put the tinsel in the pocket of his robe. "I think your persistence is admirable. You're grasping happiness when you find it"—he clutched at the air—"and if we don't go after happiness, what're we here for?"

"Is that what I'm doing?" said the girls' mother.

"I should hope so," said the Reverend.

"There, you're done," said Joyce, sliding in one last bobby pin. She took a step back. "You look beautiful."

Joyce was sixteen. She was, to her complete shame, in love with her cousin Charlie, seventeen. She hoped to dance with him at the reception—which was going to be at the Holiday Inn—but not if she had to do the asking.

Her mother touched her veil. "Well, I am happy, some of the time," she said. "I just know that I deserve better than a husband who ignores me or yells at me."

Life with George and Andrew had proven more trying than life with Henry. While Henry would lapse into trances over Cheerios, staring dumbly at a *Popular Mechanics* flopped under his bowl like a place mat and not speaking for hours at a time, at least he was docile. George had a temper that Little Andrew—as he would forever be called—was fast beginning to inherit. Sometimes they would both throw figurines.

George got a job in Nevada and wanted the girls' mother to go with him, but in the end he and Andrew went alone, and the girls' mother moved with her daughters to an apartment in the suburbs. She met Jerry at a yard sale, pricing end tables.

Joyce's mother had erased all traces of George and Andrew, the same way she had disposed of any paraphernalia that might evoke memories of Fat Henry. She didn't even buy Cheerios anymore. "A person needs to start fresh," she'd said grimly, tossing her wedding album into the trash. Then she bought other people's discarded objects to fill the spaces left by her own.

Moving around so much had made it difficult for Joyce and Kathy to keep friends—particularly boyfriends—and Kathy had once accused their mother of deliberately destroying their own chances for love, out of petty bitterness. "It isn't fair," she said. "Just because you're a failure at relationships, why do you have to make us suffer?"

"Because I can," said their mother.

Joyce had stayed out of her mother and Kathy's battles. She preferred to shut herself away in her room with her unique tragedy, which no one could possibly understand or appreciate, and which Joyce herself could not even define. She sat on her bed and smoked, blowing clouds out her open window and watching them vanish into the maple tree above the roof. While Kathy and her mother screamed in the kitchen, Joyce lay on her floor and wished her real father was still alive so that she could go live with him. She used to believe that, had her father lived, he and her mother would still be married. She was no longer so sure.

Her father had died when Joyce was one and Kathy was four. Kathy said she could remember him, or parts of him—a gold watch, brown leather shoes, his voice floating down the hallway, singing "I Feel Pretty." Joyce's mother hadn't thrown away all remnants of her father; there simply weren't any. Except the wedding picture, which showed a tall, geeky boy with snaggle teeth grinning beside a poofy-haired girl in a dress that looked like it was made of icing. Sometimes Joyce doubted that these were actually her parents. She wondered if her mother had found the picture at one of her yard sales.

Now that Kathy was away at college, Joyce and her mother had reached a kind of understanding: Joyce would not smoke in her room and her mother would not make her change high schools for her senior year. She and Jerry were going to get a larger apartment in the same complex, and in a year and a half Joyce would go away to college, to live the kind of life she was meant to be living. To meet some boy besides her cousin she could fall in love with.

❧

When the service was over, the lights came on, and smoke from the white candles hung in the air like a low fog. "I don't suppose anybody has a fan?" the photographer wanted to know. Nobody did. The photographer was a friend of Jerry's. He dabbed his eyes with his hanky. "I'm not crying," he said to Joyce. "Although it was a gorgeous ceremony, and I did feel a little weepy partway through. Did you?"

"Kind of," said Joyce. "But it's not like it's the first time I've seen my mother get married. Are you all right?"

"It's my contact lenses, I'll be fine when the smoke clears. Would you mind pointing me in the general direction of the tree?"

Joyce took the photographer by his bony elbow and escorted him to the tall artificial mountain pine, from which dangled the handiwork of Mrs. Cook's Sunday School class: clothespin shepherds, pipe cleaner wise men, Popsicle stick mangers. This was the first year the Reverend had invested in an artificial tree—to the outrage of several elderly members of the congregation, who declared it a "sacrilege." Old Mrs. Ely called it "spitting in the eye of God," but somebody pointed out that she'd said the same thing about television and now she had three. Still, the Reverend was sensitive about it.

51

"It really looks just as nice as a real one, if not nicer," he was saying now to Cousin Charlie, who was admiring a tinfoil star. "And there's no pine needles to pick up."

"It's less of a fire hazard," Joyce added, depositing the photographer at a nearby pew so he could squeeze out his hanky and change his film. At home, her mother and Jerry had put up a horrifying aluminum tree that Jerry's family had used in the fifties. It had its own spotlight, which rolled rainbow colors across the silver branches. It made Joyce think of something from a cruise ship disco.

"Okay, I think I've got everything under control," the photographer announced. "If you all don't mind, I'd like to get a couple shots in front of the tree. You two." He pointed at Joyce and Charlie. "Why don't you just stay right where you are, and if we could only find the bride and groom—"

"Here they are!" cried the Reverend, herding them over.

Joyce's mother and Jerry allowed themselves to be arranged in front of the tree, between Joyce and Charlie. The photographer pulled out a piece of mistletoe from his pocket and handed it to Jerry. "Now, Jerry, what I'd like you to do is hold this over your lovely bride's head and steal a kiss. And these two are going to lean in—that's right—lean in and make kissy faces toward the bride and groom!"

"You're kidding," said Charlie.

"How hokey," said Joyce. She felt suddenly sick.

"Oh, come on," said the photographer.

The flash went off, freezing Joyce, Charlie, her mother and Jerry in a photograph that would make Joyce wince every time she saw it, for the rest of her life.

"That was really stupid," Joyce said to Charlie, but he had already wandered off to talk to Kathy's boyfriend, Philip, whom she'd brought home for Christmas break. Philip was tall and gaunt in a way that made Joyce think of Abraham Lincoln. She wasn't envious of Philip himself, but of the way he looked at her sister, and the way when they were watching TV in the den he would rub her knees distractedly, as if he couldn't help it.

Joyce pushed her way past the people milling in the aisles and went outside. There was a limousine parked by the curb. The driver was reading a magazine. Pieces of slate rolled off the church's roof and landed with soft thuds in the old snow. People began pouring out of the church, hugging Joyce, their voices launching puffs of steam into the darkness. Jerry and her mother emerged, laughing and waving, then scrambled into the limousine and were whisked away. Joyce crunched across the church parking lot with her sister and Philip, under the frosty stars.

4

"You're the same age I was when I had you," Joyce's mother said to Kathy after Kathy's bridal shower. They were cleaning up the wrapping paper in Kathy's living room. Joyce had started off folding it neatly like her mother insisted, but finally gave up and stuffed it all in a Hefty bag.

"I know. You've said that before."

"I'm just glad you didn't run off without finishing college, like I did."

"You've said *that* before, too."

Joyce had been noticing a certain irritating sentimentality about their mother lately. It was as if, by pointing out the way her daughters' lives differed from her own, she was holding up her failures for their inspection and forgiveness. Assuring herself that she had been a good mother, successfully steering her girls clear of the mine field of her own mistakes.

"I hope you like the book. Joyce, you might want to read it, too."

Joyce nodded and carried a tray of empty cups into the kitchen. Her mother had given Kathy a book called *Making Love Last.* Now that she was happily married, she had become preoccupied with searching out the root of her previous unhappiness and bad luck. She read self-help books and went to retreats where everyone cried, hugged, pounded pillows, and ate candy for four days. Joyce couldn't talk to her at all anymore; every complaint had some corresponding chapter in a book about people just like herself.

When she came out of the kitchen, her mother was moving aside a Victoria's Secret box so she could sit on the sofa. "You know," she said, sinking into a pile of tissue paper, "it's not so much *marrying* the right person as *being* the right person."

"Oh, for chrissake!" said Kathy. "No offense, but I'm sick of all this really helpful advice. I know what I'm doing."

"I think you should have married Philip," said Joyce. "You've only known Brian six months."

After two and a half years of Philip, Kathy had accused him of being predictable and average. "If Philip were a color," Kathy had said, "he would be beige. You can only live with beige for so long."

"There are worse things," was all Joyce could think to say.

"If you like Philip so much, *you* marry him," said Kathy now. "I'm crazy, wacko in love. Isn't anybody happy for me?" She stood swaying in the middle of the living room floor, under the hanging light. It occurred to Joyce that there were certain words that could knock her sister over, and she wanted to use them. She wanted to hurt her mother, too, sitting amongst the tissue paper like some ceramic figure held together by glue. She felt the words rising like a tornado from her stomach: You're turning out just like her, casting people off like clothes that are suddenly the wrong color.

Knowing she possessed this power to wound her mother and sister made her feel dizzy, and she was opening her mouth to see what might come out of it when her mother spoke up loudly.

"Of course," she said, rustling on the sofa. "We couldn't be happier."

Jerry gave Kathy away when she married Brian. They got married in a small Methodist church in Pennsylvania, in a town between the Amish farms and Hershey Park. It was May, and the air smelled of pasture when the wind blew from one direction, chocolate when it blew from another. "A land of contrasts," the Reverend had sighed appreciatively. "Glorious." The Reverend was not going to perform the ceremony, but he and his wife Doris sat holding hands in the third pew, beside Aunt Gretchen and Uncle Ted. The Reverend had retired, and he and his wife had moved to the country. The Reverend had told Joyce and Kathy to call him Dan.

As a child, Joyce hadn't considered this other life of the Reverend, the life that existed apart from Sundays and her mother's weddings. And she had always viewed Doris Sewickley with undisguised animosity— she was, after all, the woman who kept the Reverend from falling in love with and marrying her mother. "Say hello to Mrs. Sewickley," Joyce's mother would say. Then, helplessly: "She's shy," as Joyce untwisted herself from her mother's arm and ran off.

"It's all right," Doris would tell her mother. "I was shy, too."

Joyce had tried to make amends, without ever mentioning the reason for her hostility. Doris had been in and out of the hospital for chemotherapy, and Joyce made it a point to bring her magazines and catch her up on the kind of things the Reverend wouldn't think to tell her—like how old Mrs. Ely had boycotted the new red hymnals because red was the color of the devil, and how one of the men fixing the roof had fallen in love with Ellen Wilcox, the organist, when he'd heard her practicing one Saturday afternoon. She did this partly out of guilt, partly out of genuine affection. Doris accepted Joyce's sudden kindnesses as calmly as she'd withstood her rude stares. Two rows in front of Doris and the Reverend—she could never bring herself to think of him as Dan—Joyce's mother sat proudly, her gloved hands reminding Joyce of a day long ago, when she and Kathy had hunted for toads in the mulch.

Kathy's reception was held in an old barn that had been converted into a restaurant. Waiters and waitresses dressed in black and white drifted between the tables, refilling champagne glasses and baskets of warm bread. The deejay, a friend of Brian's, was telling everyone to get up and dance. Joyce's mother kicked off her shoes and hauled Jerry over to the floor, where they twisted until she got a splinter and they had to sit down.

Joyce was sitting between Brian and Charlie, for whom she still harbored a mild residual crush. She had never danced with him at the Holiday Inn and so, having revealed nothing, could now chat easily about classes and her plans for the summer. She'd won a scholarship to the University of Connecticut, where she was studying English literature. She had no real plans for the summer, but she told Charlie that she was thinking about going to Spain, to see the running of the bulls. Joyce lied when she drank. She took another gulp of champagne.

"Not that I would run with them, of course," she told him. "I'm not an idiot."

"That's so cool, though," said Charlie. "I'd love to do that."

"You know," Joyce confided to Charlie's ear. "Kathy says that if Brian was a color, he'd be magenta. That's why she married him!" It had never seemed so ridiculous before. "Personally, I think it's lust," she added, and felt her face flush. She had never said the word "lust" to a young man before.

"Looks like your sister's getting sloshed," Charlie said.

Kathy was laughing too loud. "I got gravy all over my sleeve!" she shrieked. She held up her arm for Brian to inspect the damage.

"Don't worry," he said.

"Who's worried?" Kathy said. "Next time, I'm wearing blue."

"Next time?" said Brian.

Charlie was leaning in close to Joyce, watching.

"Blue." Kathy nodded and took another swig of champagne. She held up her glass. "Yoo hoo, Mr. Waiter Person!"

Kathy's mother came over and stooped down beside her daughter. "Honey, why don't we cut the cake now? You don't need any more champagne."

"Let them eat cake," Kathy agreed. Her mother helped her to her feet, and Brian strode ahead of them to the cake table.

The deejay cut off the music and tapped his microphone. "Hey, everybody! It's cake time!"

"What's she doing?" Charlie asked.

Kathy, instead of following Brian to the cake table, had run laughing past the stunned deejay, out the front doors and into the cornfield behind the restaurant. The guests rose to their feet and shuffled as a mass to the window. Joyce stood next to the Reverend, who was shaking his head in bewilderment. She could see her mother's face, blank and pale as an egg. Jerry was behind her, holding both of her shoulders as if she might split in half if he let go. Joyce wondered if there was some bulleted list in one of her mother's books with instructions on what to do when your oldest daughter runs away from her wedding. What to do when—as Joyce watched with a strange thrill—your oldest daughter trips through a corn-field in the late afternoon sun, leaving her shoes and veil in the stalks.

Brian sagged against his father's shoulder. The best man ran out-side and, as everyone watched, Kathy threw her arms around his neck and kissed him on the mouth, hard.

All those tuxes look the same, she said later. How was she to tell?

5

Joyce watched Adam and his father playing horseshoes with Jerry and the Reverend, under the gold-washed trees. Adam's parents had insisted on having the rehearsal dinner at their house, and there were cubed cheeses, baby quiches, and shrimp cocktail laid out on picnic tables on their wooden patio.

Adam hadn't swept Joyce off her feet or made her forget herself. She would not describe herself as "crazy, wacko in love." She loved him—not madly, not crazily, but sanely and contentedly. It didn't matter that certain young men made her feel woozy, like Cousin Charlie had, or that she sometimes fell in love in elevators. That, she decided, was a sickness similar to the flu. It passed soon enough, and then you recovered and went on with things. It was what got people like Kathy and her mother into trouble.

Joyce's mother was pleased because Adam came from a "healthy fam-ily environment." His parents had been married for thirty-four years, and he'd grown up in this farmhouse on a Connecticut country road that was still unpaved, five miles from Nathan Hale's house. Joyce couldn't remember what Nathan Hale had done, but she liked that his house was still there, after so many years. There was something reassuring and permanent about it.

Adam had grown up climbing these same trees, playing with the horseshoes that were now thudding and clanging across the lawn. In this place, Joyce had the same feeling she sometimes got when she went back to Ebenezer Church—that it could be ten years ago, or sixty, or a hundred. That every moment was present and intact, swirling seamlessly into right now.

Sometimes it seemed to her that she had left pieces of herself under furniture that had never belonged to her, and in schoolyards with children who had never learned her name. It made her sad, as if there were small ghosts that looked like her, wandering lost in places they didn't recognize. She had tried to explain this to Adam once, when he was showing her the remains of a rocket he and his brother had built in the barn when he was nine.

"I don't have any relics of my childhood to show you," she'd said. "I couldn't take you to any tree houses or point out any tire swings I used to play on. It was like, with every new father, everything just began again. My mother would give away a lot of stuff, so she wouldn't be reminded of whoever it was she had just divorced. And she threw away a lot of photo albums, so I'm not even sure what certain people looked like anymore."

"Well, you've turned out great," Adam had told her. "And maybe if your life hadn't gone that way, you wouldn't be the person you are now."

"Maybe," said Joyce, doubtfully.

"Besides, we've got about sixty years ahead of us to collect relics."

Joyce was always relieved when he said things like that, even if she herself was not entirely convinced. Now, pulling a cube of cheddar cheese from its red-frilled toothpick, she squinted toward the lawn and imagined her sons and daughters playing on this same grass. It was much easier to picture these people who didn't exist than to imagine the older version of herself who would be right here, watching them.

Joyce could see the absence of Doris in the Reverend's face, in his sudden jowliness and pale cheeks. His smooth head still reflected the stained-glass greens and blues of saints and saviors, but his eyes sagged at the corners. It had been easy to convince the Reverend to come to New London for the wedding. He and Doris had lived just across Long Island Sound in Providence, he told her, fifty-two years ago. The service was held in a nineteenth-century church with dark beams and windows that flared in the August afternoon light. Adam's uncle was performing the ceremony, but the Reverend was giving what he called a Marriage Meditation, between the scripture reading and the exchange of vows.

"We are here," said the Reverend, "not only to celebrate the marriage of Joyce and Adam, but also to celebrate our own vows, our own commitments." His voice caught. He cleared his throat. "To ourselves, to each other, and to God."

Joyce thought of Kathy in the cornfield. She thought of Henry, of George and Little Andrew, and of all the vows made and broken in the search for happiness. She knew that if she turned around she would see her mother and Jerry holding hands in the first pew. If she turned to her left, she would see Kathy, tall and lovely in lavender. Kathy had decided that—at least for now—her particular brand of happiness did not include a husband. Next week, she was going to England to study business at the University of London. Joyce and Adam would spend two weeks on Cape Cod and then fly over to visit her.

She thought of the Reverend, on his knees in front of Doris's grave in the Ebenezer churchyard, four rows away from sorry Agnes.

And there was a moment, as Joyce waited for the preacher to say "Do you, Joyce, take Adam," when she believed herself entirely capable of saying no, she didn't; no, she wouldn't, and running down the aisle and out the wooden doors, into that less predictable life. She thought of the pastor's three vixen daughters, blonde and sulky in the third pew, turning around to watch her go. And their mother, a beat behind, rising to her feet; her own mother clapping a hand to her mouth; Adam's parents rattling their pew with astonishment; the ushers tripping over each other and the bridesmaids dropping their white and lavender bouquets. Adam wilting in his white tuxedo. By the time she'd finished rolling out this scenario in her head, the time had come to say the expected things, and she said them. Adam pulled back her veil and kissed her, and she knew she had never really had a choice at all.

After the reception, Joyce and Adam put on shorts and sweaters and made their way down to the beach, where the other members of the wedding party were drinking beer and throwing themselves into the Sound. The best man, Adam's brother Todd, was running down the sand toward Kathy, who stood knee-high in the surf, giggling in her underwear. She shrieked as Todd lunged at her. They fell into the water and Joyce could see, flashing between the gray foam, a heel, Todd's denim rear end, and a white knee. Then two dark heads rose out of the water, attached to two sets of shoulders. Kathy and Todd started paddling toward the floating dock, where three of the ushers and two more bridesmaids were huddled together, half-naked, whooping and shivering.

"Come on." Adam tugged at Joyce's sweater. "Let's jump in."

"It looks kind of cold," said Joyce.

The Reverend was waddling down to the beach in his pale blue swim trunks, black shoes, and black socks. "You two should be out there," he said. He had a yellow towel draped over his shoulder; it swooped out across his white belly like a kiddie slide.

"That's what I've been telling her," Adam said, squeezing Joyce's hand.

The Reverend shook his head. "You don't know what you're missing." He shuffled on down the sand. Moving faster, he kicked off his shoes, threw down his towel and, gaining momentum, flicked off his socks in a few quick hops. He threw himself face-first into the water and splashed out to the dock, where the young people were now jumping up and down and clapping. Todd caught hold of the Reverend's wrist and hauled him aboard.

"Amazing," said Adam.

"He's seventy-three," said Joyce proudly, feeling almost as if she had created these happy human beings gamboling in the waves, the way she'd made herself see her future children on the lawn. The way, years ago, she'd populated her zoo heaven with daffodils and elephants. There was something miragelike about the scene. If she tried to step into it, it might shatter like glass, or melt. Or perhaps the people would be not quite as happy as they seemed from here; perhaps Kathy and Todd were really arguing on the dock, and the Reverend was horrified at all these young people gallivanting half-naked.

"You're worrying," said Adam. "Your forehead's doing that twitchy thing. We just got married! What could you possibly be worrying about?"

"Nothing!" Joyce laughed. "Maybe my forehead just does that on its own now." She took a breath and tried not to think anything. When she'd asked her mother what she'd thought on each of her wedding days, she'd said she'd been too happy to think. But then, look what had happened to her. Wasn't it better to be rational, and clearheaded, and recognize the risks involved? Wasn't that better than plunging blindly into forever, only to have forever last three years? Or, in her sister's case, a year and a half?

The sky was turning the blue-gray of dusk, and the lighthouse cast a rippling light over the water and across the curve of beach. The wind blew cold and damp, and Joyce sneezed. She and Adam were huddled at the picnic table, under a blanket Todd had left behind. The members of the wedding party began to make their way back to the shore. They pulled on their clothes and scurried back to the inn at the top of the hill.

"He's still out there," said Adam softly.

The Reverend was a pale shape, fading to gray. Big Band music floated down the hill from the inn and out across the water—or at least Joyce imagined that it did, that it reached the Reverend and reminded him, as he stood facing Rhode Island, of a night like this fifty-two years ago.

The Reverend raised his arms in the air and twirled in a half-circle, then back again.

"Is he dancing or praying?" Adam asked, and Joyce shook her head. From here, it was impossible to tell.

Holding
the Fort

Alone in her parents' house for the first time since her separation, Alice feels a weird, exhilarating freedom she doesn't recognize from any part of her childhood—a sense that there is nothing at all preventing her from doing whatever she wants, if she could just figure out what that is. She stands at the kitchen window, watching the back yard roll out into the woods. She's slightly drunk. Earlier, she sat at the kitchen table in her bathrobe and drank two vodka tonics, which she'd never liked before and still doesn't. She feels as if she's rooting around for some trapdoor into the life she's supposed to be living now: single, footloose and fancy-free, that sort of thing.

Alice's parents take a European tour every August. Usually Mrs. Parrott from next door watches the house while they're away, but this year Alice volunteered. She told Glen he could clear his things out of their house while she was gone. "On vacation," she said, trying to sound mysterious. Glen told her he'd be moved out by the following Wednesday. "It's no hurry," she told him. "I'll be gone for two weeks." Her parents' house is a half hour away. She was going to tell Glen she was off to someplace sunny, but he didn't ask.

When she told her parents that she and Glen were splitting up, her father had said sometimes people are better off living apart, and her mother had gone very quiet and vanished into the bedroom, as if this were something Alice was doing to her deliberately. Alice didn't mention the part about Glen deciding he was in love with someone else. That was too humiliating.

"Marriage is hard work," Alice's mother is fond of saying. "It's like a recipe you have to throw everything into, but in the right amounts. And you have to watch it so it doesn't boil over or freeze or turn goopy." She has another saying, about sex being like scrambled eggs one night, filet mignon another. "And both are fine," her mother says. "There's nothing wrong with scrambled eggs." Alice's mother never said what happens when your husband, after four years of perfectly good eggs and filet mignon, suddenly decides he wants nothing but pork chops, night after night after night.

❦

Alice drives her parents' car to the grocery store, still feeling fuzzy from the vodka. While standing in the checkout line she realizes there's a possibility of seeing Glen here: The store is on his way home from work, and it's already past five. Alice herself would be coming home from her editing job at the university press—where she would like to believe she's indispensable, but suspects it isn't true. "I can take some manuscripts away with me," she'd offered, but her boss Marjorie told her not to worry, to just go have a wonderful time with her hunky husband. Alice hasn't gotten around to telling anyone at work about her and Glen yet. "I will," Alice told Marjorie, with what she hoped was convincing enthusiasm.

Her plan was to simply lounge around her parents' house for two weeks—read, rent movies, think about things and come to terms with them—but after two days of this she's just restless and slightly miserable. She thinks there's something else she should be doing.

Her cart is full of things she doesn't even know if she likes—cayenne-flavored linguine, strange-looking canned sauces, water chestnuts, kiwi, toffee-flavored coffee. The man ahead of her is tall and handsome in a red-haired, ruddy way. He plunks a gallon of whole milk on the moving belt, then a box of sprinkle-covered cookies. That's all he's buying. Dessert for him and the wife? Or maybe a late-night snack while he watches a movie all by himself. At what degree of loneliness does one strike up conversations with strangers in the checkout line? Handsome male strangers. The cashier, she realizes with some alarm, is also handsome and male, and she feels suddenly conspicuous—a woman who has been dumped—and wonders if there is anything at all about her to signify that she is different from the person who has been coming here for years and years, the happily married person who didn't even consider the possibility of a Patsy.

She had seen Patsy before, at Glen's office Christmas parties. "Patsy in purchasing," he called her, as if there were lots of other Patsies who worked there. Alice hadn't suspected, not once, not ever. When Glen was trying to tell her about the two of them she'd said, "People get crushes even when they're married, it doesn't mean anything, it goes away." Alice had had crushes, too. And they did, they went away.

"It's not a *crush,*" he said, and only then did she understand that her husband was having sex with this woman, was kissing her and frolicking naked with her and falling in love.

"Ah, Alice." He sighed, and looked at her as if she were dying and there was nothing anyone could do. "I know you're mad, I know you must hate me." He said other things, about never wanting to hurt her, about wanting to be friends—or *stay* friends, he wanted them to stay friends.

"I don't think," Alice said slowly, "that's such a hot idea." Was she mad? She must be, but all she could feel was something that was almost fear, a slow freezing. She took an inventory of herself, to determine if some piece of her was suddenly missing. She couldn't tell.

She wanted to ask Glen, How do you find the time in a day for things like this? When you're supposed to be working, or at the grocery store, or home eating dinner with the person you married? But she couldn't bear to know the ways these things worked, as if knowing would somehow make her an accomplice to her own deception. She decided there must be a sort of balloon of time floating around, just for affairs. It contains them and keeps them safe, and the wife never knows a thing.

Alice considers having a crush on the cashier, coming back here every week and standing in his line and finally making conversation, going out, sleeping with him. This could happen. Glen used to flirt with her when she was working at Barnes & Noble, standing around her register and asking questions and being charming, and look what happened to them.

The cashier looks young, maybe twenty-five. Not too young. Patsy is older than Glen, but not much—late thirties, Alice guesses, though she could be as old as forty-five. She's one of those women who used to be eternally tan and has the thick, leathery skin to show for it. She's not what anyone would call beautiful—short, slightly stocky, shoulder-length hair that's trying to be red.

Alice imagines that sex with the cashier would be pleasant and that he would be kind, but by the time he asks her if she found everything okay she has already decided it would never work. She smiles, a little regretful. Nothing at all is at risk. "Yes," she says, "I found everything just fine."

At midnight, she calls their house. If Glen answers she'll hang up immediately, but the machine picks up—"Hi, nobody's home. Leave a message." Alice frowns, annoyed. He's changed the message. It used to be her voice—"Hi, *we're* not home." She imagines he's with Patsy somewhere, wherever it is that she lives.

It takes twenty-five minutes to get to the house, and she parks across the street and turns off her lights. The house is dark, the driveway empty. She sinks down in the seat as if there's somebody who might see her. A dog barks somewhere down the street. She rolls down her window a little and closes her eyes, and when she opens them her neck is sore and the sky is beginning to bloom a dusty yellow. The driveway is still empty. From here, the house looks friendly, beautiful in its red-brick ordinariness. The roof, which Glen repaired last year, slants at an alarming angle (all those times he was up there, cleaning out the drain-pipes!) toward the driveway.

Glen had volunteered to move out. "You keep the house," he said, and she had thought of saying, No. I don't want it. But she did want it. She had found it, and she wanted it. She wanted the red-brick ordinariness and

69

the windows with their curtains that match the carpets and the careless shrubbery in the front yard. She wanted the blue mailbox with the red flag—which is sticking straight up, she notices now, like a salute.

She feels suddenly sad at the thought of him tending to such small things, with her gone. Remembering to put up the flag.

The light is beginning to touch the windows. She can see the blue curtains in the living room. She wants to stay right there and watch the house—her house—until she has seen it at every hour of the day, until she has memorized it from the outside the way she knows it on the inside.

But there are other things she should be doing. She drives back to her parents' house, and when she sees Glen's black Jeep go by she feels an odd thrill as he passes without noticing her, as if she is suddenly invisible, or disguised.

There's a message on her parents' answering machine.

"Sweden calling!" says her father. "I was worried we might wake you, but I guess you're already out and about."

Then her mother's voice: "Hi, honey! Hope everything's well. It's raining here. Had a choppy time on the ferry last night, but we're fine."

Alice can't imagine what her parents do for two weeks alone together every year. She seems to remember, from when she lived at home, the three of them just sitting around in separate rooms, watching television or reading or talking on the phone. While her friends' parents were getting divorced, Alice's maintained a sort of detached camaraderie, like people in a boardinghouse who are civil when they pass on the stairs, but don't really go out of their way to get to know one another.

The trips were her mother's idea. Alice was fifteen the first time they went away, leaving her with their neighbor, Mrs. Parrott. They came back bubbling with stories of lochs and castles, laden with shortbread, tam-o'-shanters, woolly sweaters. Since then, the trips had been a ritual; the planning for the next one began almost as soon as they got off the plane. Stacks of brochures arrived in the mail, and they poured over them, her father tapping at his calculator, her mother wondering aloud if such-and-such a place would be too expensive that time of year, or too crowded.

There was never a question of taking Alice along.

"You'll have your chance," her mother said. "You'll have your romantic European getaways."

Glen wanted to go to Hawaii for their honeymoon, which Alice thought was cliché but she agreed. She'd been imagining someplace gray and castle-y, someplace with canals and moats, where women wore scarves on their heads and you bought things from markets. Instead, they took walks on the beach under a metallic-blue sky and drank fruity coconut drinks. It was very romantic in a predictable, unsatisfying way. In the years since, there hadn't been the time or money to go anywhere.

If she had been able to pack Glen off to Scandinavia or the Mediterranean every summer, would everything have been different? They could be having a choppy time on a ferry right now, and Patsy in purchasing would be out of luck.

✦

It's hard to know what to do during the day. She sleeps late, wanders through shopping malls, goes to movies. She calls her and Glen's house for messages and is relieved and disappointed when there aren't any. Part of her wants to hear a gooey, dirty message from Patsy.

At night, she drives to the house and parks across the street. She

71

tells herself there's nothing strange about this—it is, after all, her house, and she has a right to know what goes on there. Or what doesn't go on— Glen hasn't been home at night. She wonders if he's already packed up and moved. In which case, he should at least leave the porch light on. He should at least make it *look* like somebody's home.

There had been a burglar once. He came in through the basement while they were sleeping, and in the morning the TV and the VCR were gone, and the dresser drawers were open and rifled through. Alice still feels sick thinking of the burglar right there, in the bedroom while they were asleep.

"He could have killed us," she said to Glen.

"But he didn't."

"He was watching us!"

"He wasn't watching us. He was too busy stealing. Relax," he told her. "All he got was replaceable things. And it's not like we watch TV that much anyway—we'll hardly miss it."

But that same day he went out and bought a new one, with a VCR built right in.

"For convenient, one-trip stealing," said Alice bitterly. "I think we should get a dog."

"We don't need a dog," Glen said. "I'll protect you!"

But she was the one who suddenly couldn't sleep at night. She was the one so tired and distracted, worrying about a stranger taking their television, that she didn't even notice her husband was falling in love with somebody else.

The fourth night, his Jeep is there, parked at a sloppy angle in the driveway. From across the street, she can see him sitting indoors, in front of the flickering blue light of the television, and she feels literally heart-broken—as though something has cracked open and is rattling around inside her chest, loose. She wills him to stand up and come outside, to stand on the front porch and look across the street, but of course he doesn't. He just sits there on the sofa, with the curtains wide open.

"I don't want one of those fishbowl houses," Alice had told him the night after the burglary. She pulled the draperies shut. "I don't like the idea of people staring at us when we can't see them."

"But that," said Glen kindly, "would make it even *less* likely for some-one to break in, wouldn't it? If they could tell somebody's home?"

"I don't think I'm being unreasonable," she said.

"I didn't say you were."

It had always seemed to her that their personalities complemented each other, that her sensible down-to-earthness served as a ballast for his occasional recklessness. She loved that he did things she never would—like skydive, or quit his job before he had another one. She thought it indicated optimism. Now, for the first time, she considers the possibility that it was nothing more than stupidity.

Glen is holding up the remote, pointing it toward the set. She's glad he left the draperies open, glad she can watch him—oblivious and alone and unprotected.

The next night there's a red car parked behind the Jeep and she knows it's Patsy's. It's the sort of car a woman like that would drive—flashy, shiny, expensive but nothing special. The curtains are open but the living room's dark. She thinks of Patsy moving through her house, using the coffeemaker and watching the television, opening the medicine

73

cabinet and seeing her Anacin and tampons and pink Mary Kay containers.

She feels, for the first time, that there's something she could do, but she can't think of what it is. At two, the car is still there, and Alice drives home.

*

"Are you holding the fort?" says Alice's father.

"The fort's still here." Alice is in the living room; there's a pile of laundry on the floor where she dropped it to answer the phone. From the window she can see Mrs. Parrott, tiny and pink-haired, waving a green hose over her lawn.

"We were thinking," says her father, "that maybe next year, maybe you might want to join us. We were thinking it might be nice."

"Oh," says Alice, slightly stunned. She wonders if this means her parents have given up on the possibility of her ever having a romantic European getaway of her own. "Did Mom come up with that idea?"

"She did, actually. But I agree completely. It would be a good . . . family experience, we think."

Then her mother: "We'll pay for it, of course, don't you worry about that. We'd just love to have you along. We were thinking maybe Scotland."

"But you've already been to Scotland."

"But *you* haven't."

"No," says Alice. "I've just been to Hawaii. Maybe Scotland would be fun, we'll see."

Her father gets back on the phone, tells her the temperature is a refreshing fifty-four degrees and that tomorrow they're off to Copen-hagen. "Copen*hah*gen," he says. Before they hang up he recites their itinerary and reminds her to pick them up at the airport on Saturday.

Alice regards her laundry on the floor and decides to leave it there. Across the street, Mrs. Parrott has become slightly tangled in the hose; it's wrapped around her ankles, and she turns in a bewildered circle before managing to untangle it. Mr. Parrott was dead before Alice was born; Mrs. Parrott used to tell her highly romantic stories about how they met, one of those love-at-first-sight on a crowded train things. Alice feels suddenly sad, and she's not sure if it's for Mrs. Parrott or herself. She wanders through the house, checking the locks, closing the curtains.

Patsy stays for the weekend. Alice wonders if they'll go out for bagels on Sunday morning like she and Glen used to, if Patsy knows yet that the only kind he'll eat is onion.

Of course he'll move in with her. He'd asked Alice to move in with him three months after they met.

"Too soon," warned her mother. "You should live by yourself first."

Alice was living with her parents after college to save money. She'd had every intention of getting a place by herself, but why should she, when she was in love and it was all inevitable anyway? She moved into Glen's apartment. And then one day on her way home from work she'd seen their house—her house, where she will soon live by herself, just like her mother wanted.

On Wednesday, Glen is still there. She can see him inside, moving around, watching television. Patsy hasn't been over the past two nights, and Alice wonders if there's trouble in paradise, if someone has given someone the old heave-ho. What if Alice comes back on Saturday and Glen is still there, as if nothing ever happened? What if he says he's sorry, he's so sorry, he loves only her, can he stay?

She's still wondering this when the lights go off in the living room. But the curtains are wide open so anybody can look right in, can step around the shrubbery and put their face to the window and see the corn chip bag on the coffee table, and the socks on the floor, and the two empty beer bottles—drinking alone!—and tell that whoever lives there isn't very careful or aware, that he's one of those people who just assumes he's always safe.

She enters through the basement, using her key.

When she pulls the metal chain above her head the room fills with dusty, orange light, and everything looks like it always did—olive-green washer and dryer, clothesline, Glen's metal shelf of tools. She takes off her shoes and can feel the cement floor, cold and hard, through her socks. Upstairs, the house is silent.

She isn't sure what she wants to do, but certain vicious, TV-movie scenarios occur to her: suffocating him in his sleep, tying him up, leaving him helpless. Or seducing him, seeing how long it takes for him to realize who she is. She goes up the creak-less stairs, holding her shoes by the heels, and flicks off the light at the top. Their burglar had left the basement light on. Alice had found this strangely insulting, as if he wasn't even making an effort to be sneaky, as if he somehow knew how oblivious they were.

The basement door opens into the kitchen. Alice locates the flashlight in the junk drawer next to the stove, and when she switches it on the room fills with drippy-looking shadows. There are two crusty bowls in the sink. The dishwasher (she opens it) is full of clean dishes. The shadow of the microwave fills an entire wall. She had never thought to wonder yet who would get what—the microwave, the matching ceramic dish set, the curtains over the kitchen window—but now she does. Moving through the living room, she waves her flashlight over the accumulations of their four years together, and she sees objects to be divvied up. He will take the sofa his mother gave them, she will take the bookcase. He will take the credenza, which she never liked anyway. He will take the television. She will take the rocking chair and the big mirror in the hall, a wedding gift from her parents.

It occurs to her, suddenly, that she will never live here again. She will take what's hers and go someplace else, where she doesn't have to find a way to fill the empty spaces Glen leaves behind. It's a joyful knowledge, and she wants to wake Glen up and tell him, the way she'd told him she had found the perfect house for them, the perfect place to live.

There's some evidence of Glen's packing—a cardboard box with his overcoat and a pair of his boots in it, sitting in the hallway next to the closet. She stands just outside the half-closed bedroom door and can make out the sound of his breathing. The window over the bed must be open—she can smell the oleander bush outside, hear the twittering of crickets. She turns off the flashlight and pushes the door open.

In the moony light it looks like there might be two people in the bed, but when she moves closer she sees that it's only Glen, with the covers thrown off next to him. He's scrunched up on his side of the bed, not sprawled across it as she would have thought, and she feels a sudden twinge of fear for his helplessness—and for her own—as if they have failed to protect one another from innumerable, nameless dangers. She wants to crawl into bed with him, and in the morning everything will be normal again, like in those movies where at the end you find out it was all a dream. She moves closer to the bed. Glen's face is pale as marble in the watery moonlight, something foreign and breakable. She thinks of all those nights she stayed awake, vigilant, while he slept peacefully beside her—tired, she knows now, from sneaking around and falling in love, too tired to care about someone breaking in.

The duffel bag he takes to the gym is on the floor and she picks it up. She takes out his shorts and T-shirt and running shoes, then changes her mind and puts one of the shoes back. The closet door is open, and their clothes are hanging like limp ghosts. Certain things are missing—his blue suit is gone, and his gray one. She takes one of his black work shoes and puts that in the bag, too. She takes the alarm clock and his watch from the nightstand. She takes his glasses and leaves the case.

While he sleeps, she moves silently through the house, shining her flashlight, taking objects and putting them in the bag—coffee filters, the batteries from his Walkman, the light bulb from the bathroom. She takes the toilet paper, the can opener, the remote control. Small things. Replaceable things that he will notice missing, that he will miss.

All the Happiness in the World

I n the photograph, Gina and the man she's fixing to marry, Richard the Accountant, are wearing matching red sweaters and seem to be holding each other up by their waists. Behind them is a Christmas tree, loaded down with bulbs and plastic elves, glittering away, and through the open curtains I can see part of their New Jersey front yard, which looks pretty much as I expected: dead trees and snow. Both Gina and Richard are wearing big glasses and remind me of bugs. Her hair is short and close to her face, like a small helmet, shiny as the back of a beetle. She's about

79

armpit height on Richard, who's grinning like he's the happiest, luckiest guy in the whole world. Gina's previous fiancé is my own sweetheart, Eddie, so I show him the picture and he says they deserve each other.

Sometimes I think that maybe Eddie is not completely and entirely over Gina, on account of he's always asking what she's up to and have I heard from her. Still, I know he was never able to stand certain of her habits, like how she'll throw spaghetti strands at the wall and how if you're eating across the table from her, she'll reach her little pinky over and pick food out of your teeth. She's done this to me, too, but I never minded.

"What the hell *happened* to her?" he says, and I know he means, Where's her big hair? Where's her tight little tank tops? Where's my hot-blooded, fiery-tempered Italian vixen? I'm wondering the same thing.

We're in the kitchen, at the white table, and there's flounder defrosting in the sink. Eddie's got a cigarette in one hand and a glass of chocolate milk in the other, and that'll tell you something about Eddie.

I read him the letter, skipping over the first part, where she tells me how Richard hates this picture because he says it makes him look goofy. I read, "You tell what's-his-face our baby broke another tooth." I leave out the part where she says, "You tell him she got all her stupidness from *his* side of the family." The baby she's referring to is the bunny, Tangerine, which Eddie gave her three years ago. Tangie's always chewing on her cage and yanking her teeth out. Gina has enclosed a photograph of the rabbit. "I love you, Aunt Nancy," is written on the back, with a little paw print.

"Aww," I say, holding up the picture.

"Ain't that thing dead yet?" says Eddie. Eddie has never given me a pet, and we've been together over a year. Eddie has also not proposed to me, but this is fine because we're young and in no hurry.

I read, "We've just picked out the wedding invitations, and they're a real pretty silver color." The ones she and Eddie had were beige, and I still have mine in my scrapbook; I don't know why. I read, "I understand there are people who'll be kind of skeptical, considering what all went on before. My mother says I'm insane."

"She is insane," says Eddie. "They're both insane."

Eddie hasn't met my mother yet. He says it's too far to go, all the way up to Roanoke, but it's less than a day's trip and I make the drive myself twice a year with no trouble. He'll meet her one of these days, he says. The one time she and my father flew down here, Eddie went camping in the Everglades with his buddies, Mike and Jeff, who are nice enough but they always get Eddie drunk and he comes back Sunday night smelling like a swamp.

"Well," I say. "Says here her mother wants to send them off to Paris for their honeymoon." I don't read the part about Gina refusing to go to Paris, where everybody speaks French, or that they're going to Dollywood. She writes, "I'm going to send a letter to Dolly and ask her to show us around."

Eddie rocks back in his chair until he's leaning against the sink. "Paris," he says. "That's very hoi-tee toi-tee." He and Gina had been talking about going to Walt Disney World, a place I've never been and wouldn't mind going. But I suppose when Eddie and I do get around to our own honeymoon—not that I'm in any hurry, still having plenty of childbearing years ahead of me—we probably shouldn't go someplace the two of them almost went. I think a cruise would be nice.

"Why don't you read the whole thing?" Eddie says.

"Some of it's personal," I tell him, and he makes a snorty sound and squashes out his cigarette and lights another one.

The part of the letter I'm skipping over is the part that says, "Rich and I failed our marriage test. One of the questions was, Does your future husband/wife have habits which annoy you? and Rich said yes. He can't stand it that I chew on my split ends at dinner. And there was another question about if your future wife/husband has enough hobbies and Rich said no. There were other questions like that, but those are just two that stick out in my mind real big. So I went out and got me a needlepoint set, and I'm also making Rich's dad a wreath out of shotgun shells and a camouflage bow cause he's a hunter. I've gotten real crafty."

I read the part about Rich's father being a hunter.

"Does she say anything about me?" Eddie wants to know.

"No," I say. "Why would she?" I skip over the part about her asking if Eddie's gotten off his lazy butt and found a job yet. Which he has, or at least he's trying real hard, and a person can't do much more than that, can they?

❧

I didn't used to like Eddie. When Gina was dating him I used to call him Rat Boy, because his nose is somewhat pointy and his hair's sort of grayish brown and his eyes are what some people might consider beady, if you didn't know him. Back then we worked together at Morrison's Cafeteria down the road, all three of us, Gina and me on the line with our hairnets and plastic gloves, plopping Salisbury steaks on the plates of the geezers who go to that kind of place. Eddie was in the back, a dishroom technician he was called.

When I wasn't working there, I was busy flunking out of the community college, not being able to decide how I wanted to make my mark in the world. I tried business, which sounded like it could come in useful but required entirely too much math, and psychology, which sounded useless but interesting and required entirely too much going to the library, and finally I gave up altogether. I still haven't decided how to make my mark in the world, but now I have a good job as a customer service representative at a hospital supply company. I take orders over the phone for heart trays and catheters and bedpans and what-have-you, and so I feel like I am, indirectly, saving lives each and every day.

Gina and I got to be best friends after I'd given up school and started working full-time. We'd take our breaks together, and that was how I learned about her hair-chewing habit. After a while we decided we might as well get a place together, and that was how I learned about how she'll throw spaghetti against the wall to see if it's done. "It's an Italian thing," she said. We liked to sit on our little porch at night, three stories up, and drink wine coolers and smoke cigarettes and eat spaghetti with our fingers. I would point out where the various stars and planets were, and she would crane her head around until she could see them, too. I showed her how to find the two stars at the bowl end of the Big Dipper and continue the line they make until you run into the North Star.

The only class I hadn't flunked out of and actually enjoyed was Astronomy 101, and I still listen to Star Facts on the radio every Sunday night at eight P.M. Sometimes I would lie to Gina and say I saw things I didn't—the Swan Nebula or a globular cluster in Sagittarius, things I liked the sound of—that the Star Facts announcer had said to be alert for.

Gina would tell me stories about her ex-boyfriend, Craig, who pissed her off one day when they were driving down the road, so she just opened the car door and got out. Said she got scraped up pretty bad but she didn't care, she just had to get out of that car. Course, he came right back for her and apologized, which was what she'd been counting on. That's the kind of thing I wish I could do. Not that I'd have any reason to, Eddie being just as sweet as pie. I didn't have any of those kinds of stories to tell her, never having had what you could call a real boyfriend and certainly not one who'd drive me to such extremes.

Gina told me I'd meet somebody some day. She told me I was a diamond in the rough.

Physically, Gina and I are about as opposite as two people can get, her being five feet tall and curvy as some of the rivers out here, and me approaching six feet in a way you'd have to call rectangular. Eddie is two inches shorter than me, and while in the beginning he used to say things like there being more of me to love, now he seems to prefer me sitting.

I remember when Gina told me she had the hots for Eddie. We were sitting on our porch, and it had just rained so the air was all steamy and junglelike, and the smoke from our cigarettes was hanging in the air. I remember leaning back on my elbows and being dripped on from the awning, and that's when I said, "You mean Rat Boy?" It just came to me, like that. Rat Boy. We both keeled over laughing, and wine came out her nose and she said, "He's not a Rat Boy, don't you call him that." And she said she'd had a premonition, she was going to marry Eddie. She said she'd always liked that name.

When Eddie started coming over, he and Gina would disappear into her room and I'd put the radio on in mine or go out onto the porch. I'd dangle my legs over the side and look up and pick out the constellations for myself. Sometimes a man in the apartments across the parking lot came out and set up a little telescope on his balcony. Sitting out on the cold cement, I wished I had a telescope myself, so I could get a closer look at all that mysterious twinkling. Nights I drank wine coolers, I enjoyed the spectacle even more, and started waxing sentimental about me being nothing but a speck, etc.

I wondered what in particular the telescope man was trying to see. Sometimes I'd try to puff out something resembling the Ring Nebula and send it over toward the telescope man like a smoke signal, but it always dissolved as it passed over the railing. It was all just a way of not thinking about Gina and Eddie locked up together in her room, doing things Gina would tell me all about later.

"He likes me to kiss him right here," she told me, twiddling the top of her ear. "Isn't that something?"

I said it was something, all right. And it was all very interesting at first, until it sank in fully that these activities were getting in the way of her being my friend. I wanted her to tell me again how I was a diamond in the rough and some day I'd be happy, but she was too busy with Rat Boy.

Now, let me explain first of all that in my mind, Rat Boy and my Eddie are entirely different people, though they may look similar. Rat Boy was annoying and vulgar and wouldn't give me the time of day, and neither would I give it to him. But my Eddie possesses many fine qualities.

1. He has a genuine way with children, though you wouldn't know it to look at him. But I've seen him out in the parking lot with the kids from across the way, playing kickball with them and being careful not to bean the littler ones.

2. He's got a lot of talents, artistic-wise. He can draw pictures of people you'd swear would just up and talk to you, pictures of movie stars mainly, particularly Marilyn Monroe. He writes his own songs on the guitar, with lyrics pertaining to moons and slow rivers and his lady love—meaning me. He doesn't sing these songs to me directly, but he used to, and on occasion I will still hear him humming something that sounds like it didn't come off the radio.

3. He's never lied to me, or led me to believe things were other than they are. I don't ask exactly how things are because when the time comes, I believe he'll tell me.

I could go on.

Gina will tell you he's a good-for-nothing who's too lazy for regular work. She won't tell you the reason he lost his cafeteria job in the first place is directly related to his being with her. Eddie got fired for being late too many times, and the reason he was late was because he was always getting drunk and sleeping over. Gina worked the seven A.M. shift, and she always managed to haul her sorry self out of bed, though I could hear her whining and slamming things around. Eddie and I both started at eleven. At about twenty till, I would put on my uniform and just go out the door, real quiet. Gina got mad and said why didn't I wake up Eddie, and I would say he's a grown-up he should be able to wake up all by himself. I really did not like Eddie at that point, but that was just because I didn't know him and also because he was taking away all the fun I used to have with Gina, all our nights of patio-sitting and spaghetti-throwing and staring at the sky. So it's understandable, and I have no reason to feel bad about it now.

Gina let Eddie move in with us. As a sort of thank-you, he bought her Tangerine, the bunny, who on her first day in our apartment managed to pull her front teeth out by chewing on the bars of her cage. Gina went into a fit of hysteria, screaming and crying and dialing 911. She was not fit to drive, and Eddie was also not fit to drive, being all juiced up, so I took Gina and the bunny to a veterinarian's office. We sat there for two hours, Gina sobbing and calling herself a bad mother the whole while. When we got home, Eddie was on the sofa, lying in a pile of snack wrappers. "I ain't paying for that thing to get shots or nothing," was all he said.

I remember thinking Eddie had some nerve.

So Eddie ate our food and drank our wine coolers and smoked our cigarettes. I was highly peeved, but bear in mind that I had never even actually held a conversation with him, and so had no real way to judge his character.

Eddie and Gina ended up getting engaged. They were out at Neptune Beach, necking and so forth, and Eddie said something to the effect of him loving her so much that if she ever left him he'd throw himself into traffic at rush hour, and she said something to the same effect, and next thing she knew he'd asked her to marry him and she'd said yes.

The two of them went off to visit their respective parents together and spread the glad tidings, and when they came back they were both sunburned and Gina was crying her brown eyes out. Turns out, while they were on their trip he and Gina had started arguing about whether to stop at the Howard Johnson's or the I-Hop, and Gina pulled the same stunt she'd pulled with Craig: she stepped out of a moving car. Eddie let her, and what's more, he drove a mile or so on down the road, with the door swinging open before finally turning around and coming back. That's Gina's version. Eddie told me the car went out of control for a while, it was nothing deliberate.

I prefer to think of it as a big misunderstanding.

But I didn't hear about this business until later, and at the time all Gina told me was, "My mother says if I marry Eddie I'm throwing my life away." She was heaving and bawling and Eddie was bringing in their duffel bags and coolers. "She says she won't even show up. And my father says whatever my mother says." She dropped onto the floor, just crumpled onto the linoleum in what looked like a very painful way, and it's just another thing I always admired about Gina: her ability not to let pain get in the way of a passionate gesture. After she'd been down there a while, I pulled her up into a chair.

"What do they know," I said. "What about Eddie's parents? What did they think?"

"Oh," she said, drawing the back of her hand across her eyes and leaving a smudge of mascara all the way to her wrist. "They were just real sweet. Said of all Eddie's girlfriends, I'm the only one they could stomach knowing he was married to." She said they all went to New Smyrna Beach and had a great time, playing Frisbee.

By the way, I have not met Eddie's parents yet either. He says they're just normal parents, and that one of these days I can go home with him for Christmas. They still have to get used to the idea of him not marrying Gina, since they'd liked her so much, he says. Which I can understand, of course. Maybe this'll be the Christmas one of us gets to meet the parents of the other one; I'll ask in a few days. It's only December fourteenth, no sense putting any pressure on him.

Since Gina's parents were so dead set against her getting married, Gina was that much surer it was the right thing to do, and ASAP.

"Nothing fancy," she said. "We'll just get some invitations printed up at the copy store, and I'll find me a dress at Fashion Bug." Eddie's parents, enthusiastic as they were, made a point of telling them they'd have to swing the whole thing themselves, financially, since they were still in debt, paying off their mortgage. "I thought maybe an outdoor wedding, since neither of us is particularly religious," she said.

Eddie pretty much went along with what she said. He still hadn't found a job and wasn't looking too hard. Much as I hated the bunny smell and, yes, Eddie's trash laying all over, I was sort of sorry that I'd have to get my own place. I guess living with the two of them made me feel like I had a life alongside my actual one. Also, Gina was my only friend.

I helped Gina send out the invitations, licking and stamping like a good sport, since Eddie said he'd have no part of it. He said he was all for getting married but he had no patience for details. Gina and Eddie had never had what you could call a peaceful relationship, and I was used to their bickerings and hollerings, but after the invitations—all twenty-two of them—were sent out, that's when they started threatening to rip each other's heads off. Gina said you're nothing but a lazy asshole and Eddie said oh yeah? Well, you're a psycho bitch. Then Gina said you're just a ugly rat boy, everybody says so and Eddie said that so?

I crept out onto the cement patio, but I could still hear them, loud and clear. I remember looking across the way at the telescope man and wishing he would swing his telescope my way and see my eyes big as swimming pools, and wonder who I was and what I was doing outside all by myself this time of night. I waved to him now, a big hello, but he was busy with Jupiter and the rings of Saturn and such. After a while, I heard the front door open and slam and then a great deal of banging and doorbell ringing, then dead quiet.

"You can come in now, I threw the dumb ass out," Gina yelled. "Out on his dumb lazy ass."

I looked over the railing and could see the shadowy shape of Eddie, making his way across the parking lot under the yellow lights. He was walking real slow, jingling his car keys and carrying a pillow under his arm. And that, I believe, was the first time I actually felt a pang for Eddie, a deep-down aching pang. I remember bringing my hand up to my chest, and not knowing why.

The next morning, Gina went off to work and around eight, there was a lot of pounding on the door and I, knowing full well who it would be, answered it. Eddie was all puffy-eyed, and his pillow was dirty. I let him in and we had a couple of beers at the kitchen table and just started talking. Not even about Gina, but about his older brother who was shot in the head when Eddie was fifteen, and about how he never felt like his parents loved him, etc. I took his hand and got another one of those pangs.

Eddie said he'd never told all this stuff to Gina, but he could talk to me like he couldn't talk to her. He said he'd never realized how pretty I was.

As I was saying previously, nothing remotely approximating this had ever happened to me. Not that I'm making excuses for what happened with Eddie and me, because there's no way of predicting when love'll hit you like a ton of bricks and change everything. No way at all.

89

I skipped work that day. Eddie and I drove out to the river, past Methodist Hospital, where I was born and which I now supply with heart trays, catheters, and bedpans. We lay out on the hot grass and I told him how I love the water but never learned to do much more than doggy paddle. Eddie told me he'd teach me to really swim someday. He hasn't exactly got around to it yet, but I'm starting to realize that someday covers a lot of territory.

I told him how I'd been born and grew up here, and how when my parents moved to Roanoke I opted to stay put, feeling the closest thing to independence I ever had. But, I told him, the people I knew had left town, going north mostly, and I was feeling blue and friendless when I met Gina. This was a way of letting Eddie know I didn't want her to be mad at me. Eddie said we'd be real delicate.

As it was, we went back to the apartment and got a little carried away. When Gina came home from the cafeteria, smelling of deep fry and holding a sack from the 7-Eleven, there we were—me and Eddie, flat out on the sofa, kissing. We were fully clothed, and the television was going, so it was nothing serious. I sat up fast and started straightening my shirt, and Eddie was grinning in a way I used to find highly annoying but didn't anymore.

"You," said Gina, "deserve each other." Had it not been spoken in such ill will, I would have thanked her. Eddie kissed me again, hard. Gina put the bag on the kitchen table and went into her room and slammed the door. Considering what Gina is capable of, this was like seeing a hurricane level all the houses on your block except for yours.

Eddie was watching the closed door of Gina's room. "She don't understand," he said loudly, and I had to allow that she didn't. I tried to kiss the top of his ear, but he hauled himself off the sofa and shouted to Gina's shut door, "She don't know how to be happy for two people in love."

Later, when I looked in the grocery bag, I saw a six-pack of Seagrams Wild Berries and my brand of cigarettes, and it registered that Gina had been hoping for some Girl Talk, and what kind of a friend was I? And I guess there was a part of me that wished she could be happy for me, having found what she'd always said I would. I suppose she hadn't counted on it being in the person of Eddie. Her Eddie, now mine.

The next day, Gina was gone, sticking me and Eddie with the full month's rent—which was all the worse since Eddie was at the moment between jobs. It's not true, what Gina says about how Eddie doesn't work. He's cleaned offices at night and done some courier-ing, and to help me pay the rent that one month, he delivered pizzas for a couple of weeks. So Gina doesn't always know what she's talking about.

When she left, she took Tangerine but left a pile of droppings in Eddie's and my bed, which used to be just my bed. At work, she glared at me like she wished I was dead and I started wishing it, too.

I got a job cashiering at Kroger's. Eddie and I found ourselves a one-bedroom place that doesn't have a cement patio, so I have to go outside and sit on the curb by the parking lot, which is what I imagine I'll do tonight, while Eddie's watching TV. We live on the first floor. Sometimes we can hear the couple upstairs throwing each other against the wall.

I'm not inclined to fight with Eddie. I think that what Eddie and I have is different from what he and Gina had, not only because I am not so fiery-tempered, but also because I understand Eddie in a way that she did not. I don't expect him to change into anything else.

Every once in a while, I would see Gina at Kroger's, buying cigarettes and wine coolers and bags of spaghetti, some of which I knew would end up on her wall. Wherever her wall was. She would always come to my register and then act like she didn't know me. I'd say, "How're you doing today?" and she'd say, "Fine," and I'd say, "Paper or plastic?" and she'd say, "Plastic." That was it, for about six months. Until the time last year when she comes to my register and unloads her red basket and tells me she's in love, she's moving to New Jersey with an accountant named Richard. Bygones could be bygones, she said.

We met at the El Torito and drank about ten margaritas apiece and were best friends again, just like that. Her true love was already in New Jersey, having got a job up there starting that very week.

She asked about what's-his-face and I said he was fine. She said did I know how humiliating it was to have to mail out a retraction to those wedding announcements? I said no and she said she hoped I never would. "I made them pretty lighthearted," she said. "They said 'Ooops, I goofed!' or something." She told me some of the reasons she dumped him were because (a) he never got around to getting her a ring, (b) he never got around to getting a job, and (c) he once said to her, "I just want to have sex with you and then I want you to leave me alone," which is the sort of thing I can imagine Eddie saying, though he hasn't said it to me. According to Eddie, he was the one who dumped her, on account of all those habits he found intolerable. I didn't mention this to Gina.

Gina asked if me and Rat Boy were going to get married and I said first of all, he's not a Rat Boy, and second of all, we're young and there's no point rushing into things.

"You were the one that called him Rat Boy first," said Gina. This was after about four margaritas, lime and then strawberry.

"Well, that's just because I didn't know him," I said.

I could see Gina's face twitching like she wanted to say something else but wasn't going to let herself. We drank some more margaritas, and by the time we left we were both crying and hugging each other and promising to write every day. Which we haven't, we've written each other maybe twice in the last year, and this letter is the first I've got from her since my birthday in July. But I know she's busy, making her plans. We talked on the phone once, and I told her about my new job, and she said she's working in a bookstore and likes to wink at the men that buy sex books. She says a lot of them do.

There's not much more in the letter, just some stuff about not wanting any sequins on her dress and how she's teaching Richard to do the hillbilly stomp. She tells me I'd better be at the wedding, it's May fourteenth, and I can bring old what's-his-face. I wonder if I should go. I wonder if I should ask old what's-his-face if he wants to go.

Eddie's watching me. "She says stuff about me," he says. "What's she say."

"No. All she says is she's really happy and she's got a great big ring." I just made up that part about the ring. Eddie tries to grab the letter out of my hands and the picture floats down to the floor. He picks it up.

"Even though she looks like a big old geek," he says, "she's still awful pretty." I know he's thinking that if the two of them were still together, she wouldn't have changed into this other person, she'd be the same big-haired little spitfire, and she'd be his. I see him picturing her in my chair, instead of me.

And where would I be?

This is the thought that keeps me awake nights, listening to the air moving in and out of Eddie. I don't touch Eddie when he sleeps. He gets startled, bolts up in bed, tells me don't you touch me when I'm asleep. So I stay safe on my side, the side by the window, and I can hear the cicadas, the cars going by, the dogs next door. The world going on.

According to the Star Facts man, tonight is the best night to see the

Geminid shower—between midnight and dawn—if it's not too cloudy, which I'm hoping it won't be, and if I can stay awake, which I have a feeling I will. One thing I like about the meteors is that I know I'm seeing something that's really there, something that's happening right now, maybe only sixty miles up. When I told Gina that a lot of the stuff we were looking at might not even be there anymore, she said that's crazy, it's like a big lie. A big lie in the sky, she said. I said I'd never thought of it that way.

Eddie's smoking another cigarette and through the smoke he's looking at me, seeing all the ways I'm not Gina. Don't ask me how I know this. I wish she hadn't sent the picture. I would like us both to still be able to think of her in the same old way, and perhaps miss her in the same old way, but now she's become something else. Something like a dead girl, and you can't compete with a dead girl. It will be a while before I write her back, telling her we're sorry we won't be there on her big day, but we wish her the best, we wish her all the happiness in the world.

Parking Lot Ham and Other Acts of God

Carrie Baxter was hefting the first sack of groceries into the trunk of her car when she heard a voice close behind her: "Wait." She turned around, and there was a man wearing a long gray coat and red mittens, holding out a ham. He pushed it toward her in its plastic net bag, saying, "I just wanted you to have this ham."

"'I just wanted you to have this ham,'" Carrie says later that day, to the ladies in her living room. "Can you believe that?"

"And you took it?" says Josephine Thurman, creaking on the blue and beige sofa. Sometimes Carrie worries about Josephine's bulk damaging the springs—not that the sofa is *hers;* it belongs to the parsonage, like the rest of the furniture, but she feels responsible for it. Josephine is balancing a plate of sandwiches on her lap. There's a smudge of jelly on her pinky, which is twiddling the air like a caterpillar. "I'd be careful taking pork products from people you don't know."

"It was a smoked ham," says Carrie. "I thought it was nice."

"What were you wearing?" asks Margaret Glover, leaning forward and squeezing her hands together. Margaret is Carrie's own age, thirty-one. She works part-time in the bank on the corner of Main and High Streets, where Carrie's daughter Wendy catches the bus. Margaret's son Gerald catches the bus there, too. He's twelve years old and in Wendy's first grade class. Two winters ago he'd fallen through the ice of the pond behind his house, and when Margaret's husband pulled him out he'd been almost dead, frozen as a Popsicle. It wasn't Margaret who told Carrie this; Carrie learned it from Wendy, who had gleaned more information on her first day at school than Carrie has in five months.

"What was I wearing?" says Carrie. "That coat I always wear. The plaid one. It's a nice coat," she adds. And it is—she'd bought it back in Connecticut two winters ago, before Neil had even decided to be a minister. Before she'd known she would be a minister's wife. It's true that now they're poor, but she hadn't wanted to believe it showed yet.

"It is a lovely coat," says Helen Nester. She's ninety-two and lives on Nester Drive, in a house all the children in town like to think is haunted. Wendy had told Carrie that Helen Nester is a witch; you can tell by the way her eyes go in different directions.

"After I took it," says Carrie, "the man said, 'I've never done anything like this before in my life.'"

"Sounds like something you'd hear from a blind date," says Beth

Ann. She drops her sandwich in her lap and giggles. Beth Ann works at the Jack in the Box and always smells faintly of salt and grease. Her boyfriend Stan lives in Libertytown, five miles away. She'd brought him to Christmas Eve service three weeks ago. Afterward, they'd sped off together on his motorcycle, Beth Ann's trench coat fluttering out behind her like dragon wings. Carrie had felt strangely jealous.

"He said, 'The Lord told me to give you this.'"

Actually, he never said anything about the Lord, but Carrie is getting annoyed that the ladies won't see things in their proper light, and she figures bringing the Lord into matters can only help her side. In fact, the man had been sweetly bumbling, had blushed when he shoved the ham at her, there in the parking lot of Pantry Pride. She tries to imagine how he must have seen her: a slightly pudgy woman in a red and yellow coat and ankle boots, brown hair in a bun, like a librarian. Like a minister's wife. It bothers her suddenly that she must have seemed so unattractive, that there was no possibility at all that he might have been flirting with her, or that his kindness was not entirely selfless. The man had actually been quite handsome. She keeps this part to herself.

"Hallelujah," says Emily Graves, and Carrie gives her a grateful smile.

"Exactly," she says.

Emily had been the first to come over to the parsonage and introduce herself last August. The trees were still dripping from a thunderstorm the night before, and Emily's head was covered in a blue plastic rain bonnet. She stood on the front steps, clutching a crockpot with yellow pot holders. "It's a beef stew," she said. Then, as if apologizing: "I'll need the crockpot back." When she dragged off her bonnet, her hair sprung out of it like dandelion fuzz. She reminded Carrie of a baby chicken.

Carrie led her through the clutter of cardboard boxes, down the hall to the kitchen, and cleared off two chairs and a space on the table.

"You'll have the place looking like home in no time," said Emily, glancing around. "Reverend Yost and his wife did quite a bit of renovating."

"Did they?" said Carrie, wondering what they could have possibly fixed up. The entire house seemed dim and musty. There was paint chipping off the walls. There were cold, black doorknobs and hallways that went nowhere, and all but one of the eight fireplaces were boarded up. She had to light the stove with a match, which made her nervous, and she'd seen a bat hanging on the side of the house, next to the flaking green shutters.

"Bats won't hurt you," Neil had said, and Wendy decided to start a zoo: bats and cats. She had the cat already, a gray kitten with briar-matted fur which she'd found clinging to the screen door.

"Neil isn't here," Carrie said, because Emily seemed to be craning her neck toward the hallway. "He and our daughter went over to the church to put some things away."

The night before, they'd all gone together, and Neil had walked up to the pulpit and tilted his head back; he seemed to be scanning the ceiling for angels. The windows were so high up that all the saints seemed slightly too squat, the way people in movies looked when you watched from the front row. Wendy ran circles around the sanctuary, and Carrie sat in a pew three aisles back, her hands clasped around one knee. The air smelled of old wood and dust and ancient carpeting, and she took deep breaths of it, as if her body could absorb holiness through her lungs and her skin. Outside, the rain sounded like bacon frying, and tree branches scraped against the stained-glass windows.

Churches made Carrie feel equal parts peaceful and nervous: peaceful because there was something soothing about candles and stained glass and the murmur of voices, nervous because there were forces at work which she couldn't explain and which had nothing to do with her. When she bowed her head and closed her eyes, what was supposed to happen? It seemed to her that everyone else was in on some secret, and she had to pretend to be in on it, too. Especially now, as the minister's wife. Now, when she lifted her head and opened her eyes, she would have to look serene and blessed, not anxious and confused.

Everything in her old life was tinted with a kind of hazy, warm light; she missed her house with the dishwasher, and her friends at work. Here, everything was either too dusty—like the church and their house—or too sweet, like the perfume rising off of Emily Graves. There was no downtown to speak of—just an intersection and a blinking red light. A bank, a school, a corner store that must have been there since the fifties. A Methodist church. Washington, D.C., where Neil drove every morning to seminary, was two hours away.

Carrie had been unpacking all morning; she realized suddenly that she must be terribly sweaty. Emily was staring at her, tapping herself on the chin with one finger as if keeping time. Carrie scooted back a little in her chair and smiled in what she hoped was a friendly, open way.

"I was thinking," said Emily, directing her finger away from her chin and toward Carrie. "It might be nice to have some of the ladies come over and help you unpack." She nodded eagerly and Carrie did the same.

"That'd be great!" she said, trying to sound enthusiastic.

That next day, when the ladies came over for the first time, Carrie had taken the boxes she didn't want them to see—of chipped, mismatched dishes, and her smutty romance novels—and had hidden them in the basement. She let them unpack the silver tea set and the dish towels, the Dr. Seuss books, and some of Wendy's toys, and when they were finished she served them Earl Grey tea and vanilla wafers.

Josephine and Emily settled themselves on the sofa, Helen propped herself in the red rocker, and Margaret made herself comfortable in the recliner. Beth Ann vanished and returned with a dining room chair, holding it out as if she were a lion tamer. There was one chair left, the gold one that spun around, and Carrie sat down. "Well!" she said.

It all reminded her of the kind of parties she'd had as a child, arranged by her mother. She would gather up all the neighborhood children Carrie was too timid to befriend and serve them ice cream and bring out board games like Payday and Life and Sorry. The children would all end up playing with each other, and Carrie would go to her room and shut the door.

"So," said Margaret finally, looking around the room as if what she were about to say was written on the walls. "What did Reverend Baxter used to do...*before?*"

"Well," said Carrie. It was strange to hear him called that. "He was in advertising. We both were. He did a lot of ads for color film. I mainly wrote copy, that sort of thing."

"How exciting," said Helen Nester, rocking forward, her black shoes leaving the floor for a moment as she rocked back again. "Color film."

"You know," said Josephine, heaving one leg over the other, "Reverend Yost's wife had prayer meetings every Tuesday afternoon."

"They weren't really *prayer* meetings," said Beth Ann. "We'd just get together and shoot the breeze. Eat snacks."

"We did pray sometimes," said Emily. "We prayed for Astrid Stuber's gallstone."

"We did," said Helen. "God rest her soul."

Carrie wanted them to be her friends, but she hadn't understood them. Now, after five months, she still doesn't. They have their Tuesday after-

100

noon meetings while Neil and Wendy are at school, and Carrie provides trays of crackers and Muenster cheese; she does her best to appear interested in Josephine's theory about purple choir robes being more inspiring than white ones, in Emily's bunion, in Gerald Glover's crayon drawings, in Beth Ann's plans to marry Stan and have five sons. It seems to Carrie that the more she's around these ladies, the less they know her, as if her true self is creeping away into the shadows, down the hallway.

There is a part of her that wants to be the best minister's wife Wickerville, Maryland has ever had. She wants to be known for her charm and her compassion and her sympathetic ear—none of which, as yet, she's had a chance to employ.

Then there is that other part of her that wants to be run out of town. There are certain things she's never done before, and now she suddenly wants to. Smoke cigarettes, for instance. Walk around in a bikini. Drink martinis in the tub. Flirt with strangers in parking lots. She wants to tell the ladies all about a wicked, tawdry past that isn't hers, complete with topless bars and Parisian opium dens, if there are such things. Topless Parisian opium dens. She wants to be Wickerville Methodist Church's dirty little secret: the minister's wife who just gets in her red Toyota one day and keeps on driving, forever and ever, amen.

❦

In the letters she writes to her friends back in Connecticut, Carrie tells about the owls that live in their eight chimneys, and the coughed-up balls of mouse fur and bone they leave on the sidewalk in the morning. She says Wendy likes her school and has befriended the hillbilly twins who live next door. She wrote about the welcome party the congregation had thrown them in the church hall, complete with Hawaiian Punch and sugar cookies. To her friends at her old job she said she was a woman of leisure, giving tea parties to old biddies. "And having an affair with the milkman, of course," she wrote to her best friend Dana. "There actually *is* a milkman, and he's about a hundred and four. I live in the town that time forgot. It's like a fifties movie or something."

When Dana came to visit for a weekend in October, she'd dragged Carrie up and down Main Street so she could look at the antique shops and the dime stores. "This town," she said, "is so cute I can hardly stand it. And everybody knows you! Good *morning*, Mrs. Baxter." She giggled. The air was cool and damp, and soggy brown leaves stuck to the bottoms of their shoes as they walked.

"People are finally starting to call me Carrie, but now I'm not sure what to call *them*." Carrie sighed. "If we turn left here," she said, "we could go to the cemetery and see Mr. Tommy Bowhand, who's ninety-seven years old and still sits in front of his mother's grave for hours every day."

"God, that's awful," said Dana, turning left. Mr. Tommy Bowhand wasn't there, so Dana sat on his metal folding chair, after wiping the dew off with her coat. She leaned forward and looked at the grave in front of her with its fresh flowers. Carrie shoved her hands in her pockets and stared up at the milky sky and the black V of geese tilting across it.

"Do I seem different to you?"

"No," said Dana, standing up. "You still seem like you."

"I don't even have a job," said Carrie, as they squished across the grass, back toward town. "I used to be a high-powered advertising executive, and now I can't even find a stupid secretarial position. I've been volunteering at the day-care center, handing out fucking Fig Newtons."

"Watch your mouth," said Dana, and Carrie blushed. "First of all, you were not a high-powered advertising executive; you were a copywriter."

"Ah, same thing," said Carrie. "I felt important."

"Well, now you're important in a different way."

"Because *he's* important."

"Do you want me to hit you?" said Dana, smacking Carrie on the shoulder. "You live in this great little town, everybody knows you, you have the coolest house, a great kid, a great husband, blah blah blah." She smacked Carrie on the shoulder again. "So shut up."

During Neil's sermon that Sunday, Dana whispered to Carrie behind her bulletin, *"That's* the guy who was cheating at Uno last night? *That's* the guy who used to run through the office shouting, 'How do you fix the copier?'"

Carrie looked up at the pulpit. Neil did look splendid in his black robe, standing under the big wooden cross. He didn't read his sermons, he memorized them. Sometimes in the middle of the night she could hear him downstairs, pacing and saying things she couldn't quite make out. When he preached, his voice lifted and rolled through the air over the green hats, the brown hats, the pink scalps, and stiff-sprayed hairdos.

After church, they all stood outside in the sun, and Neil shook hands while Carrie introduced Dana to the ladies and to Mr. Tommy Bowhand. Wendy went scrambling through the graveyard with the hillbilly twins, Melissa and Melinda.

"This," said Dana, "is the life."

"I suppose it's *somebody's* life," Carrie agreed quietly. "I just can't tell if it's mine or not."

Not one of the ladies has ever asked why Neil decided to become a minister in the first place. Carrie's glad, because she would have to lie. The truth, she knows, is too close to what they would want to hear. It would prompt similar stories from the ladies themselves. Carrie would have to hear again, for instance, about Helen Nester seeing a wee little fairy when she was nine, about Beth Ann's miraculous knack for picking winning lottery numbers, about Emily's guardian angel, and about how Margaret can speak in tongues (though she refuses to do it, pleading shyness).

The truth is that Neil had seen a vision. At least, that's what he'd told her, one night last year when she was in the bathtub and he was sitting on the furry blue toilet seat, watching her.

"What do you mean, a vision?" said Carrie. "You mean like a dream?"

"What it was," said Neil, "was that I was sitting in my office, eating my egg salad sandwich, and the wall just kind of dissolved." He made waves in the air with his hands. "Into this glowing goo. And there in the brightness was this form. And...and I knew." He shrugged.

"You knew *what?*" said Carrie. She felt all the heat in her body draining out into the bathwater. She turned on the hot water and Neil waited until she turned it off again.

"I think I'm supposed to be a minister," he said.

Sitting there in the tub, Carrie had had a vision herself—of the three of them stewing in a cannibal's pot, of three shrunken heads on three poles.

"Are you crazy?" she said, squeaking forward in the tub.

"I hope not," Neil said good-naturedly. "I've done some checking into it. If I get accepted at the Wesley Theological Seminary in Washington, D.C., I could be a lay preacher while I'm still in school. We'd get a free house."

"A free house," said Carrie.

"Yep." He nodded his head, tapped his foot on the tile.

"And then what? We go to Africa and you convert savages?"

He laughed too hard. "I'm going to be a *minister*, not a missionary.

104

We just have to move to Maryland. There haven't been savages sighted in Maryland for at least twenty years."

"Oh, ha ha," she said, thinking, My house will have to be clean *all the time*. It was almost as frightening as cannibals. The only ministers' wives she had ever known seemed always to be baking something or organizing hayrides or leading youth groups. Carrie had never even read the Bible the whole way through. She believed in a vague and powerful goodness, but she didn't know the rules of this power; she didn't know how to approach or address it. She and Neil went to church occasionally, but that was mainly so Wendy could have Easter and Christmas pageants. So she could make macaroni crosses and learn little songs about getting along with everybody.

"It's up to you," Neil told her. "If you don't want me to apply, I won't."

What could she say? She had friends, she knew her way around town, she enjoyed her job writing copy for soap advertisements. She knew where to buy fresh bread and where to get her oil changed. How could these solid facts compare to a vision? And she wanted to believe Neil's vision was intended for her, too. Sometimes she felt as if the life she wanted was happening someplace else, in some other state or country. Maybe now she would find out where.

This morning, in the parking lot of Pantry Pride, Carrie had felt the closest she ever had to a kind of knowledge she couldn't name. A warm reassurance that everything would be all right, one way or the other. That the things she wishes for—whatever they are—are not as complicated or impossible as she'd believed. What she hadn't told the ladies was that she *had* been wishing for something; as she'd tossed the mackerel, cat food, soy burger, and mushy on-sale bananas into her cart she'd been thinking: Steak! Chicken! Asparagus! and nearly crying, because the world was unkind and unfair. And suddenly a man in a gray coat with a ham balanced it out again. Not on any grand scale, not with any trumpeting or glowing goo, but something had happened. It all seems ridiculous now, especially with Margaret asking her what she'd been wearing.

"Once I found twenty dollars," Beth Ann is saying. "Somebody'd left it in the ATM machine."

"That doesn't count as finding," says Margaret. "That was at somebody else's expense."

"Expense," says Helen Nester. "I get it. That's very funny."

Carrie doesn't understand what finding twenty dollars has to do with her ham. Are they saying it all has to do with luck? She wants the ladies to leave. Usually, after about an hour, the conversation is reduced to Josephine muttering about Minnie Yost's heavenly crumpets and Helen Nester wondering aloud if she's left her stove on, but now everyone is chattering louder and faster. Helen's talking about the fairy again, and Josephine is telling her there are no fairies mentioned in scripture.

"An angel, then," says Helen, which starts Emily going.

Wendy will be home soon; Carrie starts listening for her, but instead of her stomping on the porch and the clanging of her empty lunch box, she hears the jingling of keys.

"Hello, ladies." Neil is pushing the door open with his foot so he can hold on to his books and his briefcase. He shuts the door and stands there under the hall light, grinning. Neil likes the ladies; he knows they adore him. Carrie imagines that the older women think of him as the son they always wanted and the younger ones, possibly, desire him in unholy ways. He is, after all, thirty-three years younger than their previous minister, and the ladies are always commenting on his blue eyes.

"Like ice mints," Josephine said. "Like Paul Newman," said Beth Ann, smiling in a way Carrie found inappropriate. Her husband doesn't look like Paul Newman, but he doesn't look like a minister, either. He looks, she thinks, like an intrepid young journalist. Which, in college, he actually had been. Carrie is still trying to reconcile the two Neils—the Neil who stands at the pulpit and says things like, "Turn to page 234 in your hymnals," and the Neil she'd married, who watched football and drank Budweiser and told bawdy jokes once in a great while.

"Hello, Reverend Baxter," the ladies say all at once, like a choir, and Carrie can see Neil's face flush. She knows he likes it when they call him that.

"My last class was canceled. Some of the guys were going out for lunch, but I decided to come home."

"How sweet," says Beth Ann.

"Carrie was just telling us about her miracle ham," says Margaret.

"What ham?" says Neil, pulling off his jacket. "Just a minute." He disappears down the hall and comes back again, wiping his palms on his trousers. "What ham? I missed the ham."

"Maybe you could use it in your sermon," says Helen Nester.

"It does seem very biblical," says Josephine.

Neil is staring at Carrie with his eyebrows raised.

"It's in the refrigerator," she tells him. "Somebody gave it to me."

"He said the Lord told him to," Beth Ann pipes in.

"This is interesting," says Neil, though Carrie can't tell if he really thinks it is. "How about that."

"Do you think," says Beth Ann, in a timid whisper, "we could *see* it?"

"Oh, for God's sake." Carrie rises suddenly, sending a spray of crumbs off her lap. "There's nothing to see."

"We'll charge a quarter!" Neil says. "Put a sign on the front door—See the Miracle Ham, twenty-five cents!"

The ladies are chortling now, even Josephine, who's holding herself around her waist with one hand.

"He gave it to *me*," says Carrie, shriller than she meant to. From here, standing, the ladies remind her of children. They are all clutching their plates on their laps, staring at them as if they might spin away. Their mouths are slightly open. "The ham is mine."

It occurs to Carrie that this is her chance to go crazy, to act in a manner unbefitting a minister's wife, to show them all that the person doling out trays of crackers every Tuesday is not really her at all. She can feel her true self creeping back out of the shadows, ready to be run out of town.

"We were just kidding," Neil says merrily.

He is smiling at her; the ladies are smiling at him. Carrie knows what they see: the Reverend Baxter, calm and charismatic, holy and sexy. And when they follow his eyes and look up at her she knows what they see now, too: a scattered, ranting woman, raking her hands through her hair, pulling out her bun. She wishes her hair were long enough to froth around her shoulders, but it isn't; it bunches at her neck like a warm animal. She feels almost drunk, and when Neil says, "Carrie," half amused, half like a warning, she tells him, "You don't have to believe my ham any more than I believe your vision. Or your wee little fairy," she says to Helen Nester, then feels horrible when Helen ducks her head. But the thing is, she believes all of it. "I'm sorry, I didn't mean that," she says, and walks fast through the swinging doors to the kitchen. The silence follows her like a web spun out of her heel, cocooning the entire house. She goes out the back door and walks down the concrete path, past the maple tree and the green and yellow swingset, glittering with icicles.

After that day in the bathroom, neither she nor Neil ever mentioned his vision again. She had gotten out of the tub, dried herself, made dinner. As if everything were the same; as if the world was just as solid as it had always been, and walls didn't dissolve and angels didn't appear, and the things you understood to be true were still true.

But he did start the seminary; he did change their lives. There are times when she wonders if he has seen it again, that vision of his; if he's been given any proof that this—being here—was what it meant. She can feel it between them like a ghost only he can see—a jealous, possessive ghost who whispers in his ear when she and Wendy are in the room, distracting him, sending him off muttering to his study. In the five months they've been here, they've made love only twice; he tells her he's tired, he has to get up early, he has to stay up late. But he doesn't sound tired late at night, when he's talking out loud downstairs. He doesn't look tired on Sunday mornings, up at the pulpit, glowing with energy and good will. He didn't seem tired just now, either, standing there watching the ladies adore him, adoring them back.

She tucks her hands into the sleeves of her sweater and walks carefully over the icy grass, past the defunct water pump and toward the gravel road, which leads up the hill to the fire station. The sky is turning the murky gray of dirty paint water. If she walks to the top of the hill, she will be able to see the white steeple of the church, or perhaps in the fog she will only be able to see the black slate roof, or nothing at all.

A door slams behind her. The ladies are leaving. Carrie imagines them shaking their heads, their hats bobbing like winter flowers. She understands that she has become something else, something worth whispering about. She hears one, two, three car engines start, rev, fade down the street. She hears Wendy clattering up the porch, turns toward the house, and sees the kitchen light flick on. The daisy curtains part and Neil's face appears, then the small face of their daughter. They both move away from the window; the kitchen light goes out. After a moment Neil appears again, a shadow between the curtains. Does he think she can't see him?

Wendy will be flopped out in front of the television already, watching cartoons, her boots and socks strewn over the living room floor. Carrie should be in there. She should be making ham sandwiches for her husband and her child, telling the nice story of the nice man who gave the ham to her, to them.

And she will. But first she will walk a little farther into the foggy air, toward the top of the hill. And if Neil is still at the window, and if he watches her long enough, he will see her disappear completely.

Fugue

Some fathers on Saturday afternoons fix the car or spray weedkiller on the lawn. Mine would take the air apart and put it back together with a fugue. The dismantling and reassembly of an entire household's molecules was something we all performed periodically, though not as gracefully as he did.

On summer evenings his organ music got stuck in the screen door and floated on top of the cat's water dish. If the music was loud enough it drifted into the garden, where it got caught in the cornstalks. We'd eat it for dinner and pick it out of our teeth. The owls that lived in our six chimneys coughed it up on the warm sidewalk. When the air turned cool, we raked it up together and stuffed it into garbage bags. We packed snowballs of it and sent it sailing. It always came back, though, in some form or other.

Our musical house began with an advertisement in the back of a magazine. In just two years, it promised, you can assemble your own electronic recital Schober organ, at a fraction of the cost of buying one. There was a grainy photograph and an order form. Six weeks later, the first cardboard box arrived.

My father brought it inside, and we followed him into his study. He set the box down beside the green vinyl sofa and looked at it. Then he scooted it against the wall with his foot.

"I think I'll put it here," he said.

Inside the box, swaddled in bubble sheets, were several instruction books, a soldering iron, some clamps, small wooden boards with mysterious metal knobs poking out of them, and a coil of blue wire.

"How long did you say this would take?" asked my mother, gently pulling a rubber-handled clamp away from my sister Molly's drooly mouth.

"Two years." He plopped down on the floor and flipped through a booklet.

"We could have bought a piano," said my mother.

"What I'd *really* like someday is a pipe organ. We could put the pipes in the living room. Maybe when I get the speakers I'll put one in here and one in the living room." He looked at the boards as if he wanted to eat them.

We left him in there. He came out to collect the boxes every two weeks. He scurried out from his study like a bug from under a bed and then scuttled back inside again.

There were three plates at dinner now. When we went to church, people asked, "Where's Howard?"

"He's sick," said my mother. Or: "He had to go out of town. On business." When his boss called, my mother explained, "His mother died. He had to go to Bismarck for the funeral." Then: "His brother had a nervous breakdown, so he has to stay and make sure he doesn't try to kill himself."

Very late at night, I would hear a door open downstairs and a gentle padding to the kitchen. The refrigerator would open, and there would be quiet munching noises. Sometimes a toilet would flush.

My mother got a job. She was a secretary at a big factory that produced lipstick, eye shadow, and a white cleansing cream that smelled of eucalyptus. She would come home crying, with free samples of mauve and gray eye shadow.

Many of the church people felt bad for us. My mother had finally admitted that my father had witnessed a brutal crime during his business trip to Rome to deliver a seminar on the Fast-paced World of American Advertising, and that he was hiding in a small village, somewhere in Portugal, until things blew over.

The Aimses sent their teenaged daughter Debbie over to baby-sit us after school. During the day, Miss Edith Reynolds and Miss Grace Reynolds, spinster sisters in their mid-seventies, took turns watching us.

Miss Edith read us the Bible and Dr. Seuss and told us that if we looked very hard at the ceiling, we could see angels floating around the hanging light. I looked, and I thought I saw them. Fat baby angels, naked and smiling.

Miss Grace directed her grandmotherly wisdom toward my sister's thumb. "Does your thumb taste nummy?" she liked to ask. Then she would tell Molly that she was going to suck her thumb right down to the bone, and the skin would never grow back. Erosion, she called it. "Just look at the Grand Canyon," she warned. I deduced that the Grand Canyon must be a flat, thumblike wasteland. I pulled my sister's thumb from her mouth periodically, to check for that mysterious process, erosion.

113

I was in the second grade, and by the time I got home from school there was only an hour left of coddling, cajoling, and religious instruction to endure before Miss Grace or Miss Edith packed up her satchel (full of flash cards, Dr. Seuss, handpuppets, Little Golden Books, and other paraphernalia intended to transform my sister into a precocious smart aleck) and turned matters over to Debbie.

My mother had explained to Debbie and the Misses Reynolds that the study—which was in the back of the house and overlooked the weedy patio—was a storeroom, with boxes balanced precariously throughout, and implored them to stay out lest something topple. This explanation was good enough for the Misses Reynolds—who had seen enough storerooms to know that they're always full of cobwebs, musty books, and boxes of doll parts—but not for Debbie. With the moxie of a demented teenaged sleuth, she set about getting to the bottom of things.

Debbie was going through her Nancy Drew stage; she said she didn't believe our father was in Portugal. "I think he's dead," she told us. "I think your mother killed him and fed him to you for dinner."

For a while, I thought she might be right. I went through periods when I forgot what had actually happened to my father. So I went straight for Debbie's stomach with my fists, wanting to both punish her for lying and beat the whole truth out of her. She used the eucalyptus cream my mother gave her, and when I flew at her in my tantrums, the scent rose out of her like dust from an old carpet.

After a few months, Debbie came up with a new theory about my father, one that bore some small resemblance to reality.

"Witnessed a crime, my foot. Committed one, more likely! And I don't think he's in Portugal *or* dead—I think he's right *here.*" She leaned forward, her nostrils fanning excitedly like a tiny bellows. Debbie had a real talent for working herself into a fit. Many years later I saw her on a soap opera, heaving and fanning her nostrils in this same way while she denied having an affair with someone named Derek.

Her first suspicion was the basement. She was convinced that we had some sort of Mafia set-up going on down there, something to do with counterfeit money hanging from the clothesline, dripping onto the bones of unlucky meter men.

One afternoon, she dragged me down there with her and was disappointed to find only a cat box, rusty sleds, a pogo stick, and the washer/dryer. Underwear hung from the clothesline.

"We make counterfeit underwear," I giggled, but Debbie was not amused.

"Don't get smart with me, missy," she warned. "There is definitely something weird going on here." She frowned and squinted, as if trying to read something that was written on the surface of her brain.

"The storeroom!" she cried, slapping the side of her head with her hand. She ran up the steps and I ran after her.

By now, I imagined, the study had been turned into a laboratory, with beakers of gurgling purple froth, brains in jars, marsh gas hissing from cauldrons. And hunched over a squirming nest of wires and panels, a man in a labcoat with wild eyes and disheveled hair cackled with delight and soldered another wire into place.

"We can't go in there," I gasped at the top of the stairs.

"Come on. What gives?" She leaned down so that her eyes were inches from mine. "Have you ever been in there?"

"Sure I have," I said, trying to sound casual. "It's just boxes."

"Boxes of *what?*" she asked, moving closer and slitting her eyes. Her breath smelled like butterscotch. I glared at her.

"Bodies!" I yelled. "Bodies of babysitters and salesmen and . . . and *puppies!*" Debbie loved puppies.

115

Her eyes got wider and she took a step backward. "Liar."

"Chopped up."

"Rachel, you're a weird kid."

"We have to chop them up so they'll fit in the boxes."

"You're *sick*. I'm telling your mother."

"Tell her." She stared at me. "Tell her tell her tell her!" I screamed, running to my room. I slammed the door. I was turning into a crazy person, just like the madman in the study. And there was a part of me that wished Debbie *would* go in there, would open the study door and see that—if?—my father was just fine. I wondered if he'd heard anything, if maybe he'd lifted his dazed head and let a wire hang there for a moment, unconnected.

I tried to remember what he'd been like all those months ago, before the first box arrived. I knew he used to go to work grumbling, gripping his burgundy briefcase, and come home the same way. He would leave the briefcase on the dining room table until my mother made him move it. When I asked what was inside, he scowled and said boring papers, nothing anybody needed to know about. This question always seemed to depress him.

He must have eaten dinner with us, because I could remember my mother telling him he should help with the dishes once in a while. After dinner he would disappear to the study with his boring papers, but this was all right because he always came out again.

"You're lucky," my best friend Ellen used to tell me. Her father drove a truck and went away for weeks and weeks. But he always came back and took her to the movies and McDonald's, and sometimes they would invite me along and I would think *she* was lucky. Now I really thought she was lucky. I even thought Brian Kruger was lucky. Brian Kruger's father was dead, but at least he was in heaven and it was easy to picture heaven. I couldn't picture exactly where my father was, so I placed him in several settings.

The laboratory was one, with the monster of wires rising up from a stretcher. And Miss Edith had given me another idea. She told me about a place she and Miss Grace used to pass on their way to school in upstate New York, a dark, stone place where people called nuns prayed by candlelight. Maybe he was chanting in the dark, kneeling before this thing as if it could save him, or at least bring him a little happiness.

Miss Grace, when she wasn't fussing over my sister's thumb, told us unsettling stories of castles and witches and young girls who had spells cast on them and had to be rescued. My father didn't fit the criteria for fairy-tale enchantment, not being a nubile maiden in a tower and not, as far as I knew, in possession of a spinning wheel. Still, there did seem to be some kind of spell cast on him, and I didn't know how to undo it. Neither did my mother.

That evening I told her Debbie was getting curious, and couldn't we just please bring him back? (As if this were a magic trick that had gone on too long, and he was trapped in some netherworld cabinet.) My mother frowned, like she always did when I mentioned him, and her lips got very small and white. In a voice that didn't sound like hers she said, "He's very busy."

"What if Debbie goes in there?" I asked, feeling almost breathless.

"It's locked," she said flatly, and it occurred to me for the first time that she wanted to get inside, too.

During summer vacation, I was usually home for the hallowed, secretive event we had come to call Box Day, every other Tuesday. On those days, the Miss Reynolds du jour came in later, at lunchtime; my mother told them she liked to spend one morning every other week with us. Actually, she went to work as usual and made me and Molly promise not to burn the house down or fall out a window. Around ten, the doorbell rang and my father ran to the door and flung it open, panting and bug-eyed. He took the box into his arms as if he were holding a newborn and carried it into his study.

At first my mother was afraid the mailman would talk. Then she remembered that he kept a beehive and was rumored to have a python in his tub. She reasoned that the eccentric are less attuned to odd behavior than normal people.

Things ran fairly smoothly for over a year on this system. Then, about a year and half after the first box arrived, there was a shattering, resonating eruption of sound from the study.

Miss Edith let *The Cat in the Hat* tumble off her lap. "The smoke alarm!" she sputtered, leaping up as best she could. Then she dropped to the floor, entreating us to do likewise. "Smoke rises," she panted, as if already overcome. After checking behind her to make sure that we had obeyed and were ready to evacuate in an orderly fashion, she commenced creeping toward the front door, twenty feet away.

I followed her powder-blue bottom, which smelled like an old sofa and seemed to be made of the same material. Behind me, my sister was inching along with some difficulty. Her thumb was still in her mouth, and she had managed to capture Buffy the cat under the other arm. She propelled herself with one elbow.

Upon reaching the front door, Miss Edith reached up and grasped the doorknob, gave it a frantic twist, and tugged the door open. She wriggled onto the porch and scrambled to her feet. With surprising agility, she hauled my sister and me from our crouched positions and flung us face-first into the lawn. We landed heavily. Buffy and Miss Edith's glasses flew into the rhododendrons.

"Poor things," she murmured to the ground, stroking our heads with her bony fingers. "First your father gone, now your house up in flames."

Mr. Bick next door was raking leaves and rushed over to see what the hoopla was. Miss Edith had let us up and was rooting around for her spectacles.

The fire engines came, three of them, with sirens screaming gloriously. Somewhere in the midst of the ruckus my mother arrived, frantic and babbling. "My husband's in there!"

"She's ranting," explained Miss Edith to a fireman standing by with a hose. "You're ranting, dear." She patted my mother on the arm.

"Get off me! Howard!" she yelled, making for the front door.

My father emerged, a fireman leading him gently by the arm. His hair was long. He'd grown a beard. He blinked in the sunlight. "Wha?" he said.

My sister's thumb fell away from her mouth and she started to cry.

"Howard!" My mother ran to him, then stopped short. "Oh, God."

"The speakers work," he said happily. "Geez, it's bright out here."

"There's no fire," the fireman who'd rescued my father said helpfully. "That wasn't the smoke alarm."

"It was my speakers. Hey—you kids have gotten big."

"I'm in the third grade," I told him.

Neighbors had gathered to gawk. My mother was shaking.

"Does it take this?" she shouted. "Does it take a disaster to bring you out of that room?"

"It wasn't a disaster—" said my father meekly, but he was cut off.

"The babysitter's been looking for bones in the basement, and Molly's trying to suck all the skin off her thumb because she wants to see her skeleton, and Rachel thinks you're some mad hatter!"

"Scientist, Mom," I corrected.

"Every day I go to a job I *hate* and leave our children home with an idiot teenager and senile old women."

"I'll be going now, see you Sunday," mumbled Miss Edith, slinking away. My mother took no notice.

"Do you know how much of our lives you've missed? And what a spectacle you've made of us?" She gestured wildly to the crowd. "No, he *hasn't* been in Portugal, okay? He's been in his damned *study* building a damned *organ.* Are you happy? Go home!" she screamed.

The yelling went on for weeks. When the boxes arrived, my father just put them in the study and left them there, unopened. I went in there once, to see what he'd created. Against the wall was a wooden frame, gaping with yellow, orange, blue, and green wires. It looked like the inside of a magnificent animal, killed and splayed open in the process of digesting jungle plants, arcane tropical fish, seaweed, and the veins of hummingbirds. The keyboards gleamed below a panel of white and black plastic levers that said things like "trumpet," "oboe," and "chimney flute." Some of the names sounded like Italian desserts: *flautino, dulciana, vibrato.*

"The speakers still need a lot of work," said my father. I turned around. He was standing at the door, looking sad. There were eight unopened boxes on the floor. It reminded me of Christmas.

❦

When the music began, it stomped into the house like an uncouth houseguest. It put its feet on the furniture. It belched and blew its nose in the tablecloth. It ate with its hands.

Then, like an urchin sent to charm school, it learned grace. It tapped on the door before barging in. It told jokes. It amused and enchanted guests. It presented us with lovely bouquets of Bach and Beethoven. It stood on its head, showing off.

One afternoon it shivered through the air and knocked the crayon out of my hand, so I ran down the stairs and asked the man hunched over the keyboards, "What's that called?"

"Jig Fugue. Fugue in C Major," he said, bouncing wild musical mumbles against the wall, startling the cat into the corner.

"Are you playing that on Sunday?"

"No, not this piece."

The eighty-seven-year-old church organist had passed away, and my father was going to replace her. His first Sunday was two days away. When he wasn't perusing the classifieds, lamenting his disinclination toward telemarketing and manual labor, he was practicing. Now he stopped mid-fugue and gave a little sigh.

"Enough of this stuff. Back to work." He pulled out a dogeared book called *Best-Loved Hymns*.

"I liked the other thing better," I said loudly, over the music.

My mother had come in the front door and was standing in the hallway. "Why don't you play something you can dance to?" she wanted to know. "A waltz or a tango or something. Did we ever waltz or tango?"

"Hmm, nope," said my father, squinting into "We Are Climbing Jacob's Ladder." "Gotta practice, Marybeth. Gotta live up to the tradition of old Catherine Nelson."

"She wasn't all that good." My mother disappeared down the hall, carrying her shoes and a small plastic bag. She had been promoted at the makeup factory and could now deposit her samples of Seafoam eye shadow and Twilight Blue mascara in the medicine cabinet without whimpering. "You're much better." The medicine cabinet shut with a metallic clink. The music stopped.

"You think so?"

"Of course, she was *arthritic.*"

My father grinned and started from the beginning.

When he played, the light came into the church at wild, impossible angles. The reflections of sheep and saints ricocheted off the preacher's bald head. The ivory robes of the choir sang in shades of pink and gold. Above us, the chandeliers chimed an echo of violet, green, pale orange.

I looked over at my mother to see if she had noticed anything, but she just sang. Her voice was high and sweet, a voice we sometimes forgot she had. She was standing next to the open window, and a bee hovered level with her nose. She didn't notice. The bee rose toward the roof, the music flying on its feet.

My father's hands were skipping over the keys. His back was slightly hunched; his fingers were splayed like a frog's or a ballet dancer's and his mouth was almost closed.

The organ he was playing was one of those old ones with the knobs you pull out and the wooden pedals that sometimes stick when it rains. It had only one keyboard. I told him it wasn't as nice as his, but he said it was fifty years old and was full of so much music it could practically play itself; he was just reminding it of the notes, he said.

He reminded it of five songs, and after the service the preacher and the members of the congregation came over to congratulate him while we stood outside in the sun.

My father blushed. "I kind of messed up there in the second verse of 'Holy, Holy, Holy,'" he said modestly.

"Pishposh," said Miss Edith.

"Yeah," said my mother. "Pishposh."

We left the Misses Reynolds and the other congratulators to go home to our warm house that smelled like roast beef. My parents went into the kitchen to fix the gravy and mash the potatoes. Molly curled up on the sofa with Buffy.

I walked down the hall to the study. The door was always open now, and the windows behind the green vinyl sofa were open as far as they went, which was halfway. The late spring air lifted the pale green curtains, then let them fall. They looked like they were breathing. Mr. Bick was mowing his lawn in his yellow shorts and black socks.

The organ against the wall looked as if it were napping but wouldn't mind being woken up. I climbed up on the smooth wooden bench and looked around. From here, high off the ground, I could reach all the switches and keys and levers, but the pedals were too far away. I felt big, puffed up with the air that was coming through the windows. I flipped the little metal switch to "on." The organ hummed. It was awake.

What should I play? I pushed all the levers with the strangest names: *bourdon, gamba, nazard, zink*. And there were black levers, too, that said things like Swell to Pedal, Great to Pedal, Great to Swell. I pushed Swell to Great, because that's how I wanted the music to sound. I decided to try for "Happy Birthday"; it seemed simple enough to play right off. I knew exactly how it went. I spread my hands across the keys the way my father did and, humming, brought my fingers down. It made a noise hauntingly similar to the one that had scared Miss Edith into evacuating us. I tried again, one key at a time. It still wasn't "Happy Birthday."

"Do you want to learn how to play?" My dad was in the doorway. There was a smudge of flour on his forehead.

"I don't know. I think so."

He came over to the bench and sat down beside me.

"Is it hard?" I asked.

"It is at first."

"Will it take a long time?"

"If you want to be any good it will."

I thought a minute. "I won't get stuck in here like you were, will I?"

He frowned. "Was I stuck in here? Is that what you thought?"

I swung my legs against the bench and looked at the pedals. They were made of pale yellow wood, with smaller black ones in between. "You didn't come out for a long time."

He didn't say anything. Mr. Bick's lawn mower sounded like a swarm of bees. "Tell you what," he said finally. "I will personally guarantee you that neither one of us will get stuck in here. And if you don't like it, you can stop any time you want. Okay?"

"Can you teach me that fugue? That's what it's called, right?"

"That's what it's called." He picked up my hands and placed them on the cool plastic keys. "But I think you'd do better starting with a waltz."

Fishhook Girl

For years after Annie Stokes disappeared, I kept seeing her. She loped down sidewalks, hanging off the arms of longhaired boys; she waited wearily at bus stops. I saw versions of a future Annie I would never know: pregnant in the grocery store, homeless in the park. I saw her old and pale and staring at me from a wheelchair, with plastic-looking eyes, as if she had aged forty years in ten. Now, listening to her voice on my answering machine, I realize I never actually expected to see her again.

My boyfriend Thomas is hauling things in from the car. He shuffles into my living room and stands in front of me, holding the blue cooler with both hands. He's red on his cheeks and the top of his head, places he missed with the sunscreen.

"Hey it's me," Annie's saying on my machine. "Surprise surprise."

"Who is it?" he says.

Thomas never met Annie, but I've told him about her. "She sounds like a flake," was his reaction, which pleased me at the time.

"One of the other science instructors," I tell him now, with a vague toss of my hand.

"I'm in Greenridge Hospital, so come by if you feel like it, okay?" Annie's voice is warbling and small.

"She sounds awful," says Thomas.

"I hope you feel like it," Annie says. Then she laughs. The machine beeps and whirs, and then my mother is telling me to give her a call when we get in.

"She's fine," I say, with no idea whether she's fine or not. She should have said what she's doing there, why after vanishing for fifteen years she's in a hospital twenty miles from where I saw her last.

"Let's get some air going in here," Thomas says, disappearing into the kitchen. "Open some windows, and I'll finish unloading. Then you can go see your friend, and I'll go home and take a nap. Sound like a plan?" He reappears, wiping his hands on his shorts.

"Sounds like one," I say. Thomas likes plans. The trip to the Appalachian Mountains was part of his plan to convince me to marry him. Within this master plan were many sub-plans: the wilderness trek, the campfire, the two bottles of Chianti.

Thomas goes back to the car for another load and I move through the apartment, pulling the windows open. We have been gone five days, long enough for my apartment to feel suffocating and dusty. The hiking shoes Thomas forgot to take with us are on my floor; one of his white T-shirts, stained yellow in the armpits, lies on my bed. It's always surprising to find evidence of his presence here, as if he is someone I just made up, as if he did not even exist. But he *does* exist, and when the other guy I'm sleeping with comes over, I make it a point to hide anything of Thomas's.

I open the bedroom window and lean out, looking over the rows of black roofs and the oval pool glinting in the late afternoon sun. I should go see Annie now, get away from Thomas and from this apartment which seems, in my absence, to have grown smaller as well as hotter and dustier. The phone rings and Thomas answers it, the way he does automatically now. "Hi, Carrie!" he says exuberantly—my mother's name—and I shout, "Tell her I'll call her back later, after the hospital."

"Friend from work," Thomas says in a low voice. I find my car keys under the rubble on the dresser and am out the front door, waving to Thomas. He lifts a hand at me, points to the phone.

"Let me tell her," I say, denying him permission to spread our happy news.

I met Annie the summer I was afraid of everything. I was eight years old but looked younger—my first day in Mrs. White's third grade class, she suggested I might be in the wrong room. "No," said my mother cheerily. "This is where they said down at the office." It was mid-September, two weeks after school had started. My father, a minister, had been transferred from a church in Wickerville, Maryland to one six and a half hours away. We'd driven through the Alleghenies, through tunnels gouged out of mountains, and arrived in flat, grassy Greenridge. The elementary school was arranged in something called quads, and my mother led me through them with her hand on my shoulder, saying things like, "What a pretty school, Wendy. Isn't this fun?"

Later, Annie said she remembered me that day, standing like a doofus in the middle of the classroom with my mother beside me, holding my book bag. "I thought you looked like a little farm girl," she said.

"I've never even been on a farm."

She shrugged. "Well, that's what you looked like."

And I must have seen her, too, though I can't remember; can't remember seeing her on the school bus, either. I was too busy being afraid of everything: afraid of our brand-new house, which had siding the color of chicken fat; afraid that I would wake up in my pink room and my parents would be gone, vanished in the night. And what if burglars broke through our shiny new doors and took me away? I had nightmares about scorpions in my bed (the result of too much *Wild Kingdom)* and would wake up kicking at my covers. Every night, sometimes twice, I went down the hall to my parents' bedroom to wake them up; they took turns searching my bed, telling me over and over that nothing was there, couldn't I see?

The outside frightened me, too; I worried that Japanese beetles would fly into my ear, that ticks would suck out all my blood, that I would be stung by bees and wasps. And at the third grade picnic my mother warned me to watch out for fishhooks, so that was one more thing to be afraid of.

My first memory of Annie begins here; it fades and shifts, changing slightly every time although I can never be sure exactly how. In the latest version—recounted to myself along the drive north to Greenridge, past the plazas and strip malls—my mother and I are walking through the woods at Gunpowder State Park in late September. The leaves are just beginning to golden. "You should put your sandals on," my mother says, near the lake, swinging her hand in mine. "So you don't step on a fish-hook." And then, as the first twinge of panic comes over me, we are in a clearing where a little girl, with brown hair past her waist, is sobbing on a small boulder. And she looks like a mermaid, though I don't know if I thought that then. But that's the image now: a child mermaid, marooned on a rock. Her family clusters around her. The father kneels with a first-aid box. And somehow I understand what has happened, and I hear the voices separate from the rush of water.

"You should've watched where you were stepping," the father says, swabbing the girl's heel with a Handiwipe.

"Is she all right?" asks my mother, in a memory now washed-out, like the pages of a picture book that's been left lying open in the sun for years and years. She steps forward with a twiggy crunch, but no one seems to hear her, or see us.

"I suppose you'll have to get a tetanus shot," says Annie's mother.

"And you'd better get one soon," says her sister. "Else they'll have to take your foot off—to *here.*" She karate-chops her knee.

"Way to go, Bucktooth Annie," chants her brother, flapping around the rock.

"Goddamn it, Ted, will you shut up?" Annie's father swats the air as if his son is a mosquito he wants to squash.

My mother herds me on gently, saying, "She'll be fine, don't worry." I stoop to put on my sandals, and when I look up Annie is staring right at me. She stops weeping long enough to grin and stick out her tongue, a gesture nobody else sees. Then she's crying again, and I'm not sure I saw it either.

The next Monday, Annie bumped up the bus aisle with her Scooby-Doo lunch box, plopped down next to me, and said: "I saw you on

Saturday," as if it were an accusation. Then she just stared at me, and I felt for the first time what I would feel for the rest of our friendship: that she expected something of me, something interesting, and quick.

"Can you sit on your hair?" I asked, and she said she could but didn't feel like it. I nodded. "You stepped on a fishhook," I said reverently. This seemed to please her. She wiggled down in the seat and put her knees up; her feet—white-socked, tennis-shoed—dangled against the back of the seat in front of us.

"It hurts a little to walk," she said, smiling but managing to sound bored. "I had to get a shot."

"My name's Wendy," I told her.

Annie looked at me. "Like in Peter Pan."

"Right!" I said, not mentioning that my given name was Gwendolyn.

My parents were relieved that I'd finally made a friend. My mother made it a point to call up Mrs. Stokes and introduce herself as "the mom of Annie's little friend Wendy." I cringed when she did this, and wondered if Annie had even told her mother I existed. "Oh, we're looking forward to meeting Annie, too," my mother said, and winked at me.

My parents were relieved also when I stopped waking them in the middle of the night, a development they attributed—correctly—to Annie's influence. When I asked Annie what she would do if a bug flew in her ear, she said, "It wouldn't. I'd smash it first." And if the house burned down? "Jump out the window." And if there was a scorpion in her bed? "That's stupid," she said.

And so I relaxed; or rather, I directed my anxious energies toward more important matters, like making a good impression on Annie. I brought her Reese's Peanut Butter Cups and M&M's, as if she were a stray dog I was trying to bribe and tame with treats. She accepted without a word, popping the candy into her mouth and chewing with her eyes clamped shut.

We sat next to each other near the middle of the bus. We wanted the back—who didn't?—but that was the territory of screaming boys like Annie's brother Ted. And the front was too tame. Annie's sister Kelly sat by herself in the seat behind the driver. The Stokes children gave no indication that they recognized each other.

When I was introduced into the Stokes household, Annie's siblings treated me like one of their own: they ignored me completely. Ted was in fourth grade and Kelly in sixth. Ted played with his friends outside, throwing a beachball against the side of the house, while Kelly drifted about in baggy overalls, long before they were fashionable, with teen magazines clutched to her chest. As an only child, I envied the idea of a brother and sister, if not the reality of Annie's. I envied her parents, who were swarthy and angular, while mine were pale and gnomelike.

The difference between the Stokes family and mine, it seemed to me, was best illustrated by our basements. In mine there was the family room with its green rug, black-and-white TV, and white stucco ceiling. There was the guest room down the hall, where we kept boxes of Christmas decorations and, stuffed in the closet, a life-size Santa doll that would heave forward at you when you opened the door. At the end of the hall was my father's den, where he wrote his sermons on yellow paper and once, during the *Jaws* era, attempted a blockbuster novel about a glacier that destroys New York City.

Annie's basement was dim and musty, like a basement should be. It reminded me vaguely of the Wickerville basement, except that was moldy from flooding so many times, and my mother wouldn't let me go down there by myself because there weren't any lights. In Annie's basement there was a bare light bulb and a rusty chain, which we would not be able to reach without a chair until we were fourteen. Boxes of dusty, leather-bound books, all with frontispieces and inscriptions like "To Cyn-

131

thia from your Loving Roger, Christmas Day, 1908," filled one corner of the room. Against one wall was a big green bookcase that had been converted to a dollhouse. We played with that dollhouse until we were thirteen years old, by which time the game was called Boarding House, and the object was to make every doll go to bed with every other one. There were albums of sepia-tinted photographs of dark-haired men and women standing in front of big black cars or leaning against the rails of ocean liners. We found yearbooks and corsages, moth-eaten gowns, faded satin shoes, and paintings that we thought must be priceless masterpieces. There was a wine rack with a dusty black bottle of champagne that Annie's parents had bought when she was born, which they were saving for her wedding.

We appointed ourselves caretakers of this abandoned, underground world while upstairs Irene Stokes spoke on the phone in hushed, urgent tones, sipping rum from a teacup. Sometimes, when we would burst up the basement steps, she would be propped against the door frame between the kitchen and the living room, as if waiting for something to happen or trying to recollect what she should be doing next. She didn't have a job, unlike my own mother, who taught at a preschool. Sometimes Irene volunteered at the library, and she seemed exotic even then—stamping and stacking in a low-cut red dress, her dark hair tucked behind her ears. Annie said that her mother had once been a debutante, which meant she'd worn frilly, off-the-shoulder dresses and had a lot of boyfriends. In the basement there were pictures of her, corsaged and swathed in tulle, standing next to some crew-cut boy with a great big neck who was not—Annie informed me significantly—Mr. Stokes.

Peter Stokes owned a major meatpacking business and was descended from Belgian royalty—illegitimately, Annie confided. Neither of us knew what the word meant, but it sounded dangerous and wicked.

Mr. Stokes reminded me of a pirate. He smoked cigars and lounged half-reclined in his burgundy leather chair, facing the television and reading the *Wall Street Journal*. When I came over he would tip his paper down and say, "Whaddya say, Wendy?" and I would take this question seriously, believing it required a careful response. Before each visit to Annie's house, I would flip through the newspaper or an almanac, searching for some piece of information worthy of Mr. Stokes. "Did you know that it hasn't rained in _____ since _____ ?" I might say. And Mr. Stokes would consider this. Or I believed he was considering it; Annie finally told me that her father had called me a know-it-all. After that, I just said, "Hello, Mr. Stokes."

Annie's brother Ted looked like their mother—small and dark and spindly, which on Irene could pass for elegance but gave him the look of a nervous spider. Later, in high school, I tried to have a crush on him, influenced by reading teen romances in which things like this were inevitable: a young man, oblivious for so many years, falls wildly in love with his little sister's blossoming best friend. But even as an adolescent I knew I could never love a boy who flew into rages and (according to Annie) knocked up at least two girls he hardly knew.

Kelly, the eldest Stokes child, spent most of her time shut away in her room. She would emerge with her face and hands blackened, and stare at us as if she wished we were dead. Annie suspected her sister of practicing black magic. One Saturday when Kelly was out, we snuck into her room and found a drawing pad and some sticks of charcoal under her bed. The drawing pad was full of pictures of fruit and candles, and a few mountain scenes. No voodoo dolls.

And then there were the absent relatives, living out their individual traumas and tragedies in places like Toledo and Las Vegas. There was Aunt Dottie—who, as Annie said, certainly was. She was in a hospital for people who had "imbalances" and talked to imaginary people. Sometimes she would call up and make Mrs. Stokes cry. It seemed that the phone was always ringing, that some sibling or cousin, aunt or uncle, was alerting Annie's family to yet another misfortune, breakdown, or medical dilemma. Annie would act out her family's little dramas in basement performances, assuming the roles of her mother and father, as well as whichever whining relative might be on the other end.

"Really, Ruth, I don't think it's anything to worry about." (Pretending to vacuum with one hand, drink rum with the other.)

"But Irene, my *stools* are *hard.*"

To someone who had no cousins and whose grandparents were all dead by the time I was three, this was the kind of eccentricity I craved. I pressed my parents for juicy tidbits about my own heritage.

"Well," said my father, after a moment of careful thought. "I had a great-great-uncle in Sweden who got gangrene in his fingers. There were no hospitals nearby, and if he waited too long, the infection would spread and kill him. He asked his wife to chop his fingers off, but she was only able to do one before she fainted dead away. When she came to, he'd done the rest himself."

"No gangsters? No madmen? Aren't we related to any royalty somewhere?"

"Your Grandmother Leary met the Queen of England," said my mother. "She went over to London to help promote the Girl Scouts— they call them the Girl Guides over there—and she was presented to the Queen."

But this wasn't quite what I was looking for, either. I told Annie about the Swedish man, naming him Karl and improvising so that he had to chop off his entire arm. I added a bitter Nordic storm and howling wolves. And the wife was not his wife, but a beautiful Danish princess, named

134

Helga, who'd escaped from her castle in Copenhagen, and whom Karl had rescued and taken back to his cabin, en route tripping and infecting himself in the jaws of a rusty bear trap.

Annie listened patiently. We were, of course, in her basement, and for once I was the one performing while she sat on the ratty, taupe couch.

"That's pretty incredible," she said. "And they fell in love and got married?"

"Yes," I said eagerly. "Only they couldn't get married legally, since she was betrothed to the evil Thor, back in Denmark."

"And she had a baby?"

"Yes!" I cried. "A beautiful little boy, named Erik. But Helga died giving birth, and Erik—when he was twelve—wandered into a storm and froze, and bears found his body and sat outside the cabin eating bits of him while poor Karl watched helplessly from the window." I thought this last part was inspired. Annie tilted her head.

"They had windows?"

"Yes," I insisted.

"That's so sad," Annie said. "How did Karl find another wife?"

"He didn't! What with Erik no longer around to chop wood for him, he died alone during a winter storm, like the one he'd rescued Helga in."

I felt flushed and giddy. Finally, Annie Stokes: consider yourself outdone! I hadn't performed as skillfully as she did, or acted out the various parts or mimicked the voices, but Karl was better than Dottie any day.

Annie had been quiet—with envy, most likely.

"So," she said finally. "How exactly are you related to these people?"

In my enthusiasm I had killed everyone off, without leaving them any progeny.

"Oh," I muttered. "Karl had a brother."

Annie nodded. "That," she said, "is quite a story."

I roll down the car window and the breeze is warm and smells like pasture—midsummer air, the air Annie disappeared into. What do you say to someone after fifteen years? *I thought you were dead* seems inappropriate. So does *What makes you think I'd want to see you?* I wonder suddenly: *Do* I want to see her? Will seeing her make any difference, to either of us? Perhaps she's tried to kill herself. Or maybe she's dying and wants to tie up loose ends, say her last goodbyes. Of these two options, I prefer the suicide scenario. Then I could be angry, try to shake some sense into her. Also, it would make me feel stronger than I do right now, more in control. It shocks me to realize I have fallen back into my old habit: holding my life up next to Annie's to see which is the superior one.

There's also—and this occurs to me with an almost physical pain, right by my heart—the possibility that the person on the phone was not Annie at all. What if I've turned into one of those people whose fantasies become ghosts in their real lives—mysterious voices, glimpses out of the corner of their eye? Messages on their answering machines. Can you wish a person back into existence?

I had a car accident once because of a girl crossing the street with long brown hair swinging in her face; I stared after her and swerved into a blue Subaru. "I thought I saw my sister," I blurted to the other driver. I gave him the insurance information and drove my mother's dented car home, shaking behind the wheel. I've seen Annie in shopping malls, in airports. Each time, my heart falls into my spine before I realize this one is too old, that one too young.

The hospital is ten minutes from Annie's old house and forty-five minutes from Towson, the Baltimore suburb where I live. My plan when I was younger was to move to California, as far from Maryland as possible, but a scholarship to University of Maryland nixed that, and then I got a teaching job at a community college. Then came Thomas, and here I still am. What had Annie thought when she looked me up in the phone book, as she must have, and found me? Was she surprised at all?

I think of things that would surprise her.

My big fat engagement ring, for instance? Or the fact that I'm cheating on Thomas with a former student, a boy ten years younger, and that I haven't figured out what to do about him after I get married?

Annie would not find Thomas surprising. "A dentist?" she might say. "You must look adorable when you're having drool vacuumed out of your mouth. Was it love at first rinse?"

I imagine myself saying yes it *was* love at first rinse; that I never had any doubts, then or now. By telling her this I might begin to believe it myself.

She would be happy for me.

Two nights ago, in the Appalachian wilderness, Thomas and I lay on a blanket looking at the full moon. "It looks smaller," he said, "don't you think? Than it looked earlier? But it's not."

"What do you mean? Sure it is."

"No, it's a proven fact. Because people think it should look smaller when it's right overhead, our minds warp it into what we expect. But if we'd measured it before and then measured it now, it would be exactly the same size. I know," he said, "because I've done it."

"You've measured the moon? You're the only person I know who's measured the moon."

"Well, thank you," he said, though I hadn't necessarily meant it as a compliment. Thomas is big on proven facts.

"As far as I'm concerned, it's smaller now. I don't care if my mind's gone and warped it." But it made me wonder what else my mind had gone and warped. It made me wonder if I knew any proven facts at all. I'm wondering the same thing now—what facts can I tell Annie? I am engaged, I am good at my job, my soon-to-be-husband loves me. What else can I bear to hear myself say?

Thomas and I had talked about getting married once before, and then we discovered that he wants three children and I want none, and he started saying things like, "Don't you ever wonder what they would look like? Our offspring?" and I started saying things like, "Maybe we should reconsider this."

"Reconsider what?"

"You and me. Happily ever after. Maybe it shouldn't happen."

"Maybe," he said. "But I think it should." And then we didn't talk about it again.

Lying there in the dark on the piney ground I heard Thomas say, "What do you think of one?"

"One what?"

"Instead of three and instead of none. One kid."

And because I knew Thomas loved me, and because I was drunk from all the wine, and because part of me believes Thomas makes me happier than anyone else ever could, I said one kid sounded all right to me.

That's when he disappeared into the tent and came back with the big fat engagement ring.

And it was a relief—everything would be simple now. I'd break up with the Boy. I'd marry Thomas and be happy. A wave of love tingled the surface of my skin; I understood how people can decide to spend the rest of their lives with each other, how the future can seem like a big red carpet rolling out in front of you.

In the tent that night, after making love and telling each other all the stupid, sweet things we could think of, we talked about our one kid.

We talked it right into adulthood; we gave it a job and a house and happiness, and when we lay back in the darkness, I felt this child as a shadow wedged between Thomas and me, taking up all the air that belonged to us. I looked over at Thomas, and in the darkness his profile looked like the Boy's—whom I have never spent an entire night with, whom I do not love and who probably doesn't love me, who is passionate and kind but not so bright, whom I have no business being with but who makes me oddly, inexplicably happy. And why shouldn't I be happy, all the ways I can? Thomas's breath got lower and slower, and when he slept I unzipped the tent and crawled out of it. The stars splashed out in a vast arc over my head, a blur of meaningless twinkling, and the moon—bigger now, no matter what Thomas would say—was falling below the trees.

❧

I turn the radio on and off and on again, flipping through the stations, singing loudly as a way of not thinking. I have just made the turn where, if I'd gone the opposite direction, I could be at my lover's house in ten minutes. But I don't think of him as my lover, which sounds like something out of a soap opera, but just as the Boy. I don't think about his name.

When things started with him, I'd only been on two dates with Thomas. I was in the Safeway, buying French bread and Brie and garlic for our third date—dinner at my apartment—and the Boy was there, standing in the beer aisle holding a red basket with Doritos and olives in it. When he saw me his face flushed, as if I'd caught him doing something he wasn't supposed to do. "Hey Gwen," he said shyly. The whole semester, he'd avoided calling me anything at all.

He looked into my basket and said something to the effect of, "Yum. You sure know how to shop. Better than I do," and glanced shamefully

139

at his Doritos. Then he looked me in the eye, and all bashfulness vanished. "Maybe later you could come over. I'm having a party. Not a big party, just a couple of friends."

"I can't." The Boy stared at me, half-smiling. "But maybe next time you're having a party, you could give me a call." I scrounged a pen from my purse and wrote my number on the back of a V-8 coupon. Giving it to him was like issuing a dare to both of us.

That night, I slept with Thomas for the first time—my first time with anyone in over a year. I didn't usually sleep with men on the third date, but I didn't usually get propositioned in grocery stores by handsome ex-students, either—or give them my number and tell them to call me. It was as if I'd discovered a trapdoor, secret to everyone but me. I was the one who started unbuttoning Thomas's shirt, leaning close, smelling his warm, garlicky breath, putting my lips on the space between his ear and his chin. He tasted like soap. "Do you want to lie down?" he said after a moment, hoarsely, and I led him down the hall to my bedroom, feeling desirable and young in a world full of possibilities. Thomas slept the entire night with his arms wrapped around me and his chin buried in the back of my neck. But when I awoke, it seemed as though I'd already betrayed him, as if already there was something to betray.

Two days later the Boy called. I went over to his apartment and we sat on his shabby, college-boy sofa. His roommates were out. I imagined what he must have said to them: *My biology teacher's coming over—beat it so I can score.* He offered me a beer and I took it, feeling more nervous than I had with Thomas. The Boy is handsome—tall and dark-haired, lanky but not thin, the kind of man who always seemed like my type. Sometimes I find myself thinking that in ten years, he'll be beautiful. In ten years, however, I will be approaching middle age, married with one kid.

He offered to show me his college film projects, but I said no, why can't we just talk? Which translated into, why can't we just kiss? His boldness surprised me; he scooted over and started to stroke my arm, telling me how soft my skin was, how beautiful I was, how he used to get hard-ons right there in the front row of my Biology 101 class. He kissed me and I kissed back. He smelled faintly of a spicy cologne. He reached his hand up under my shirt, earnestly groping, and I nearly laughed.

"What?" he murmured, nibbling my neck. "What are you smiling at?"

"Because I like it," I said, which was not a lie. And because I was acting like a fool, and because in three hours I would be going out to dinner with Thomas, and when he asked me what I did today I would say, "Oh, just graded some papers. Not much." And because he would never know anything about this.

We didn't have sex that time; I had visions of him high-fiving his roommates when they came home and then never calling me again. It seemed important that he call again. And when he did, a few days later, I told him to come over to my place.

I let him try to impress me. He told me about applying to law school, and about his plan to go to Paris and learn French, and how he can build an entire car from junkyard scraps. He looked at me after revealing each new thing, as if checking to see if this made him worthy of my approval or respect. Or maybe he was just seeking permission to grope me further. His uncertainty made me feel powerful, but it was more than that. It made me someone else, someone created for this young man to adore, someone wise and wonderful. He didn't ask me about myself, and I didn't offer any information; it was as if we both understood that it was his job to try to win me over, and mine to remain mysterious.

Thomas wanted to know everything about me. On our dates he asked the questions, plumbing the details of my life: "What sort of shampoo do you use?" he asked. "Do you polish your toenails? What's your earliest memory? Your favorite candy bar?"

It was a process of revelation that was both comforting and frightening. I loved that he wanted to know these things, but at the same time, it was like I was being tested, as if he sought some miraculous combination of details by which he would recognize his True Love.

So I told him stories. I imagined the woman Thomas would want most, and I thought about what shampoo she would use (something herbal) and what candy bar she would eat (Almond Joy—nutty yet sophisticated); and her earliest memory would be of trees and her mother's face, not peeing in the yard at her fourth birthday party. She would be calm yet reckless, and fully formed. She would be exactly the way I feel when I'm with the Boy, only she would be with Thomas instead.

I slept with the Boy that night because there was nothing left to say, and because I understood, suddenly, that on my part this would be effortless. It was like stepping into a river that isn't strong enough to carry you away.

After he left me lying naked on top of my sheets, I reached for the phone and held it until the dial tone clicked off; there was no one to call, no one, no one. That's when I started missing Annie again. Really missing her, like I hadn't in all the years she'd been gone. I could feel a loss that reached all the way into the tips of my fingers, hollowing me out.

There had been other times I'd missed her, of course: when I lost my virginity, and at my high school and college graduations—those milestones of adulthood. I'd missed her when my mother and father split up—suddenly, though my mother said it had been a long time coming. But there had been other friends, other people to take Annie's place, drifting in and out. Sometimes I told them about Annie—her crazy family, her mysterious basement.

I've told Thomas about her, too.

"You make her sound like somebody out of a fairy tale," he said. "The Fishhook Girl and her evil, ugly stepfamily. Except they were her real family, which is even worse."

"They weren't evil. Just a little screwy."

"But they pretty much drove her out of her own house, didn't they?"

"Well. That's sort of what she led everyone to believe."

"And you never heard from her again after that day? That's so weird. Did you check the basement?"

"Very funny," I said testily.

The idea disturbed me: Annie hiding in her basement, or asleep—enchanted, waiting for someone to find her and wake her up, and lead her back to the world.

I cross into Harford County, driving toward those towns with the wholesome, happy names: Hickory, Churchville, Fountain Green, Greenridge. It seems the landscape has sprouted new shopping malls just in the past few months—and 7-Elevens, and Red Lobsters, and mega-plex movie theaters. I imagine Annie in the car with me, but it's her sixteen-year-old self beside me, wearing feathered hair and Jordache jeans. I remind myself to tell her they tore down our elementary school to make a TGI Friday's. I think of asking her if, when she's out of the hospital, she wants to go to the mall and look for people we used to know. It would be nice to have her with me, proof that everything can turn out fine, for everyone.

I used to make this drive often, when my parents were still married and living in Greenridge. My father quit the ministry while I was in college, and they moved out of the parsonage and into a solar-powered house on the other side of town.

My mother hated that house. She said it was a nightmare. The solar power didn't work, and the wood stove heated only the add-on room. Later, when I asked her if the house had anything to do with her and my father breaking up, she said it just made her more aware of what their marriage had become: something that meant well, but just didn't work.

Now, my mother lives by herself near the Eastern Shore, in a house that smells of candles and woodsy incense. After the divorce, she decided she'd had enough of preschoolers and got her real estate license. She's lost weight and dyed her mud-blonde hair auburn, and she wears crystals under the fancy suits she buys at Red Dot sales. I once passed her in the Harford Mall and didn't recognize her until she grabbed me by the elbow.

My father lives in Phoenix, Arizona, and gives seminars to business people on how to "Speak to Succeed," "Say What You Mean—Get What You Want," "Be a Leader!" That sort of thing. He loves it. He lives in a pink stucco apartment complex with palm trees and hanging vines all around. There's a swimming pool. When I went to visit him, I stared out the plane window at the brown flatness and thought it looked like a place to vanish. I considered moving there but couldn't stand the stultifying heat, which coated my body like Saran Wrap. "Ah, it's good for you," said my father. He was wearing a safari hat and sunglasses and was tan for the first time in his life.

We went out to dinner with his girlfriend Susan. The restaurant was dim and had what looked like debris dangling from the ceiling—sleds and carousel horses and hubcaps. There was a cow skull hanging above my father's head.

Susan kept smiling at me but not saying anything, and the candles on the table cast shadows that made her look sad around the eyes. I smiled back and didn't say anything, either.

"How's your mother?" my father asked me after a silence, and I told him she was fine, she says hello. Which was true: "Say hello to your father," she'd said when she dropped me off at the airport. They speak of each other now as if their identities can only be defined by their relationship to me—my mother, my father.

"She's taking yoga," I told him, then wished I hadn't when he smirked. I didn't tell him she was meditating and doing New Age-y candle burning. I thought, My parents have become people I don't even know.

When I first told Thomas about my parents, I described them the way I was used to thinking of them: preschool teacher and minister, happy and uncomplicated.

"Your parents sound great," Thomas said. "We should have them over for dinner."

"Except my father lives in Phoenix."

Thomas stared at me.

"They're actually divorced. My father has a girlfriend and my mother's into crystals and stuff."

"You didn't mention that part," he said.

"Well," I said. "I keep forgetting."

❦

The parsonage is close enough that I could drive past it if I wanted to. Past its chicken-fat yellow siding and its one-car garage. I took Thomas by the parsonage recently, just to show him what it looks like, and there was a pink Big Wheel in the driveway. "You should knock on the door, tell them you used to live there," he said. But I said I'd rather not. We went

145

by the Stokes's old house, too, and if I was going to knock on anybody's door it would have been theirs. I even got out of the car. I was used to thinking of Annie's house as sprawling, big as a mansion, but it was just a regular two-story colonial. There were orange curtains hanging in the room that used to be Annie's. "Go on," Thomas said.

"No," I told him, getting back in the car. "I just wanted to see it."

I'd do it now if there was time: go down into that basement, just for a minute. So I can tell Annie what it looks like now. I could reassure myself that there is nothing important still there, that nothing has been left behind. But this would take me ten minutes out of my way, and what if those are the ten minutes that matter? The ten minutes when Annie decides that I'll never come, that I don't care if she's sick or injured or dying, that I have finally given up on her?

❧

During the summer between eighth grade and high school, Annie became convinced that her mother was having an affair. She insisted we act out various scenarios and confrontations in her basement, with her taking all the dramatic, hysterical roles. At first we acted out the scenes with Boarding House characters—the Sunshine Family father as Peter Stokes, the Bionic Woman as Irene—but then Annie decided we were too old for dolls. And though I didn't agree, and tried to keep things interesting by throwing everyone into Barbie's Dream Spa together, Annie had lost interest. "Let's put Peter in a dress and send him up to seduce Donny Osmond," I said once, and Annie stared at me as if I were a failed joke.

"Peter, keep your goddamn voice down." Annie was lying on the sofa, one leg thrown over the top of the cushions. Her basement was as cool and dim as a cave. She held a pencil between two fingers and brought it to her mouth, inhaled, blew out imaginary smoke. "I told you, I was out with Ellen."

"Bullshit." I lunged toward her, fists out like a boxer.

"No, you idiot." Annie sat up and threw the pencil on the floor. "Can you imagine my father bouncing around like that? He would be sort of calm, but with rage in his eyes. Rage and disbelief. Can you do that?"

"Rage and disbelief." I turned in a little circle. "Why can't I be your mother this time?"

"Because you didn't overhear them. I did."

"Well, you could tell me what to say." I pressed the back of my hand against my forehead. "It's not that I don't love you, Peter."

"She did not say that."

"But I love another even more! I love—" I cast about for a suitable love object. "Mr. Handy! Our daughter's social studies teacher!"

"Ha, right," Annie said.

"I call him Randy Handy."

"I'll bet you do," Annie said.

"It could be him."

"My mother ipping Mr. Handy. And he probably still would've given me a C." Annie lay back on the sofa. "Ipping" was one of the code words we'd created for the things that were happening to us, as well as the things we were afraid might never happen. We had words like *nod* (boy), *tacky* (good-looking), *bag* (like), *card* (love), *eek* (to make eye contact with), *ick* (to simply see in passing), *ock* (to speak to), *gob* (to kiss), *pag* (pregnant) and *ip* (which was what you did to get pag). "You sound like a caveman," my mother remarked one time, passing through the kitchen when I was on the phone. "Oonga oonga."

"Maybe," I said, "she's not having an affair with anybody."

147

Annie swung both her legs up on the sofa, so that she was upside down with her hair hanging on the floor.

"Oh, she most definitely is."

"Move over," I said, and sat beside her.

"She exhibits all the signs in that Cosmo article, 'Is He Cheating?'" She hardly comes out of her bedroom for anything, and she always looks totally distracted, more so than usual. Plus all those times the phone rings and nobody's there? How do you explain that?"

"I don't," I told her. "I never tried to explain it."

"Exactly," Annie said, and hauled herself to a sitting position.

According to Annie, all hell was breaking loose in the upstairs world: Kelly, she'd informed me in a reverent hush, had tried to slit her wrists; Ted had knocked up a girl in the eleventh grade; and now Peter was accusing his wife of sleeping around. I never told anyone else these things, and Annie knew it. I carried the Stokes's secrets around like something stolen, something that could be taken away from me and returned to their rightful owners.

♦

I'm thinking of how to present my life to Annie in its best, most flattering light, and I am suddenly afraid I will not be able to remember the truths I've created for myself, that one of the real truths might slip out. Out loud in the car I say: *I teach Biology 101 at a community college.* Like a game show contestant. *I enjoy tennis, travel, and gourmet cooking.* The tennis part is true, sort of. *And my name is Gwen, please, not Wendy.* I smile widely at oncoming traffic. *My fiancé has his own dental practice.* This is a lie; he works at one of those insurance-managed offices. *He has no*

148

idea that sometimes, while he's at work, I'm having sex with a former student on the bedspread he gave me for Christmas.

It's a relief, sometimes, to think that there is no one who knows everything. So I can never turn into just one thing—just what someone knows about me. I can be three or four or ten stories, none of them completely true, none of them exactly right. And so trying to decide what to tell Annie is just making up a new one—scraps of fact held together by lies, a moon whatever size I want to make it.

In the tenth grade, Ted introduced Annie to the joys of alcohol, marijuana, and hallucinogens, and they hung out in parking lots with his friends, getting stoned and watching inanimate objects breathe. She said sometimes when she got home she would go down to the basement, and it would seem as if the dolls in the Boarding House were talking to her, warning her of something. "Warning you not to fry your brain?" I said, and she narrowed her eyes at me. It didn't escape me that, as far as Annie was concerned, I was a big disappointment. She had tried to re-create me into a Wild and Naughty Preacher's Daughter; she wanted me to hang out the window of a speeding convertible, hooting and hollering and waking the dead. She wanted me to smash bottles in the street and come home at all hours. I liked this idea, too—at least, I liked the sentiment behind it, that I could be more than I appeared to be. One afternoon after school, I let Annie dress me according to her vision, and I tottered around her basement in her black heels and ripped jeans, feeling more like a freak than a floozy, since none of her clothes fit me right. Annie had grown busty and long-legged, while I still had the stubby proportions of my mother. We drank the champagne that was meant for Annie's wedding, and I threw up all over her red halter top, which I had stuffed with her father's monogrammed hankies. The young men we were supposed to meet that night for raunchy fun ended up going to some headbanger party with each other.

Annie blamed my failure to attain rough lawlessness on my parents, and of course she was right. I had grown up in a world of psalms, meat loaf, and doddering old biddies, a world my parents still inhabited. Certain things simply did not occur to them; they saw what they were accustomed to seeing. When I came home the morning after Annie's failed makeover, it was no effort at all to convince them that my hangover was a bad case of the flu, and my mother tucked me into bed with a hot water bottle. There were days when I wished I didn't have such innocent beings for parents; that wasn't one of them.

A couple of months before Annie's sixteenth birthday, Ted went after Irene with a steak knife. Or so Annie told me, one Saturday afternoon when we were down in the basement, listening to Van Halen. The basement smelled faintly of pot. When Annie wasn't getting stoned with Ted, she was busy dating boys with names like Jake and Tony and making enthusiastic plans to never attend college. The more Annie told me of her dating life—her ipping life—the more mysterious it seemed, as if our codes were now codes only to me—symbols of all that was unknown and unapproachable. I, meanwhile, had baffled and alienated her by enjoying chemistry, biology, and the dissection of cow eyes and fetal pigs. "It's cool to see how things work," was all I could think to say. I was starting to wonder about the possibility of launching myself into an Annie-less world.

When she told me about Ted, I felt a familiar, shameful thrill, and I wanted to squelch it. I stared at her skeptically. "Ted did what?"

"He went tearing through the house, calling her a dirty whore," said Annie. "He stabbed her mattress twice. Now he's in an *institution.*" She twirled her finger beside her head. "And my parents are waging the third world war every night, keeping me up till all hours. I have to get out of this hellhole."

I was stuck on the image of Ted chasing Irene. I wanted to believe it. "He really actually did that?"

Annie nodded. "You think I'm lying?" she said.

"I don't know," I admitted, and before I could say another word she was gone, flying up the steps, shouting, "Mom! Hey, Mom!"

"Wait!" I shrieked, flying after her before there was time to wonder why it mattered to me at all.

"You're out of luck," said Annie, breathless, when I caught up with her in the kitchen. "Nobody's home." She leaned against the counter, pulled open the cutlery drawer and took out a knife. And I thought, in a brief flash of fear, that she would do something terrible to me for not believing her, but she just touched the blade gently and looked at me. "This was the knife," she said, "that he stabbed her mattress with." She put it back in the drawer. "If I don't get out of here, I'm going to turn into my fucking Aunt Dot. Completely bonkers." Annie looked at me and shook her head. "You can't imagine what I have to deal with every day. You really can't. Stuck in this hellhole," she muttered, so quietly I almost couldn't hear her.

"So leave," I said.

"Leave where?"

"Run away." My heart pulsed in my forehead.

"I know," Annie said smoothly. "I was planning on it." Her eyes flickered. "On my birthday. Sort of as a little present to myself."

Annie's birthday was in June, just before the end of the school year.

151

"That's perfect," I said. "Everyone'll be cutting anyway. What are you going to do?"

"Just go. Just take off."

"What, hitchhike or something?"

The year before, a senior girl named Jackie had run away and was gone for three months before detectives found her and hauled her back home. There were rumors that she'd slept with truck drivers and gotten beat up a few times. She dropped out of school and got a job at the Texaco station. We'd see her there, sitting inside her little glass booth, staring out at the cars with raccoon eyes.

"I'd prefer not to hitchhike," Annie said.

"You need a plan," I told her, feeling a sudden strange, sparkling power. "Let me help you."

I told myself it had nothing to do with her, with her friendship or her approval. This was my opportunity to have a Secret Double Life. This would be as much my adventure as hers. I devised a plan. On the morning of her birthday, I told her, I would pick her up as usual, in my mother's Toyota. I would have a knapsack of her clothes with me. I would take her to the bus station, then continue on to school and act innocent.

"Like you do so well," said Annie. "Just don't get nervous, because you turn red and everybody knows you're lying."

"Don't worry," I said coolly.

I threw myself into the project with gusto, plotting back routes to the bus station in the next town, researching fares. I snuck around my house, pilfering maps from bookshelves, retrieving old Triple A books from my parents' closet. I hid these under my bed the way other teenagers stashed drugs. I borrowed the car to go to the mall and went instead to the bus station, where I snuck around in sunglasses, stuffing brochures into my purse. I took my loot to Annie's house and spread it out on her basement floor.

"Holy shit," Annie said.

"Yes," I said, feeling mature and proud of myself. "This is what I found out. If you want to go, say, to Los Angeles, that's going to cost you a hundred and twenty-five dollars. But if you're only going to New York, that'll be a measly twenty-five bucks. One way, of course."

"Of course," Annie said. "I like the *idea* of Los Angeles." I nodded. I felt like a travel agent. "But that's too cliché, everybody runs away to Los Angeles—don't you think?"

"It is sort of cliché," I agreed.

"Same with New York," she said. "Plus it's too close."

I shuffled through the maps. Most of them were from our vacation to the Smokey Mountains five years ago. "Nashville?" I suggested. "Grand Old Opry?"

"Not hardly," Annie said.

"Denver," I said, pulling open a big, yellowed map of the southwestern states. "One hundred and twelve dollars away." This was the oldest map in my collection; it was from my father's trip across the country back in the 1950s. "Denver, Colorado. You've got your mountains, you've got your skiing."

"Ooh," said Annie, leaning forward on her knees. The map looked like it would disintegrate if you touched it. It looked like a treasure map. "I'm liking the sound of that. Can I take this?" She put her finger down on the map, somewhere in California.

"Okay," I said, though what I was thinking was *absolutely not.*

"You're the coolest," Annie said. "All I need now is cash. Or credit! I could steal Irene's Visa."

"No way." I'd read enough mystery novels to know this was foolish. "That's too easy to trace. Has to be cash. Cold hard cash." My voice sounded different to me—older, braver. Annie was looking at me expectantly, and I felt a flash of childish joy: I had made myself indispensable. "Don't worry," I said. I'd been asking neighbors if they needed their dogs walked or their children baby-sat, but I wasn't about to tell Annie that. "I'll think of something."

"I need a hundred and twelve bucks in six weeks," Annie said. "So think fast."

"You could help me fold these," I said, indicating the papery sea of highways on the floor.

The second Sunday in May we had Homecoming Week at church. It was weirdly hot that year, and my father enlisted me to stand in the church foyer and dole out paper fans—made of flowery printed cardboard—to people as they came in the door. They took them gratefully, pausing to tell me how tall I'd grown (not an inch since age thirteen) and what a nice young lady I was turning into. I smiled sweetly, cooed over the toddlers, and complimented the old ladies on their stupid-looking hats.

Sitting there, looking around at the same faces I had seen for years and years, faces of people who had stayed and people who had gone away and then returned, I felt despair settle over me like a dusty old blanket. I stood and sat with the rest of the congregation, but I was thinking of my father's map of the southwestern states, of the brown parts that meant mountains, and the blue twist of the Colorado River. I was thinking of the black dots of Las Vegas, Denver, Los Angeles. I was thinking that I would visit Annie, wherever she ended up. Or maybe I would go live there, too.

I had made sixteen dollars baby-sitting.

I bowed my head when everyone else bowed theirs, and prayed, *Please let me find a way to make enough money.* I didn't know if I believed in God, but I stood and took communion, let my father place the piece of bread in my mouth. *Please,* I thought, as I tossed back the grape juice. But the despair didn't lift; it just turned in circles and settled down in the pit of my stomach.

Following the Homecoming service there was a potluck in the church hall, so everyone could eat and mingle and catch up on recent happenings and old times. I made myself useful setting up the tables and mixing iced tea, jostling elbows with Birdie Butterfield, who was trying to plug in her crockpot of meatballs. Birdie was twenty-two but looked older, wrapped in a frumpy pink dress with puffed-up sleeves that made her look like she had breasts growing out of her shoulders. "It's my grandma's Swedish recipe," she said to somebody, maybe me.

"Wendy," said my father, bustling over. He'd taken off his robe and was wearing a blue suit. His hair was wilting into his eyes. "Would you run get more paper plates from the office?" He tossed me the keys, on a red crab key chain. "And napkins, too, might as well."

The paper towels, plates, and napkins were all stored in a gray metal cabinet in the church office; the Homecoming before, we'd run out of napkins and discovered the extra supply chewed into confetti in the kitchen cabinet. "Mice," said my father, shaking his head.

I clipped down the hallway, past the clumps of people exclaiming over how so-and-so hadn't changed a bit, not one bit, pumping each others' hands, flapping their fans, yammering that it wasn't the heat so much as the *humidity.* I was sweaty and tired and wanted to go home and wait for whatever miracle I'd tried to invoke.

The office was across the hall from the nursery, which was open and empty. On the walls were big, old-fashioned paintings of Jesus holding children on his blue-robed knees. Stacks of wooden blocks formed a miniature fort on the table. There was a faint scent of baby powder and urine.

My father didn't actually use the church office to work in—he wrote and memorized his sermons at home—but he hung his robe in the closet there, and sometimes he'd take home some of the dusty, brittle books from the shelves, books with glossy color illustrations of bearded men parting seas and wielding staffs. I'd rarely been in the office, and when I looked around, I felt something similar to what I'd felt the first time I saw Annie's basement, something like awe. The communion glasses, which my mother would take home and run through the dishwasher, were on the desk, too—juice-stained, looking like something out of chemistry lab. Draped across a green-cushioned chair was a banner made of burlap that spelled REJOICE in gold felt. On the massive wooden desk were boxes of envelopes so yellowed they probably wouldn't seal; stamps with outdated postage; a big black typewriter with round keys. Mr. Dugan, the persnickety treasurer, had left the four emptied collection plates stacked neatly at the corner of the desk, where they glinted like crowns. And next to those—a green fabric bag, squashing a pile of bulletins. Mr. Dugan usually counted and logged the collection money right after the service—but there hadn't been time yet to count it, and I had seen Mr. Dugan outside, chatting with the recently widowed Beatrice Anders.

The green bag was huge, bulging. How many more dollars than usual were in there? I pulled it open, stuck my hand in. Envelopes. But I could feel cash, too. All the money not in envelopes went to the cemetery fund. Weren't there plenty of Greenridge Methodist loved ones in that cemetery, and plenty of people today who would have donated generously? I pulled out a one dollar bill, and a five. It was like rooting for the prize in the bottom of the cereal box. A twenty. I put back the one and five and concentrated on the larger bills: another twenty, a ten. As I pillaged the treasurer's bag, I felt a strange, exultant thrill: the preacher's daughter—

stealing! As if I were no longer Wendy, but a delinquent version of myself. When I remember this now, it's as if I'm watching myself from slightly above, or from off to the side. I see myself pull out another ten, and another, and a twenty. And even when I have enough for the bus ticket, I pull out a few more tens and some fives—for food and lodging. For souvenirs, I actually think, and movies. I sift through the bag to make sure there's still plenty of cash left. I close up the bag, fold the money, take off my white flats and put the bills in the toes of my shoes. I see myself open the file cabinet and take the paper plates and napkins, and then I shut the office door behind me and stride back to the church hall, my small-heeled, money-stuffed shoes clipping along the fake-marble floor. I'm smiling, unsullied by guilt.

The church hall smelled like meatballs. Jell-O molds quivered on the dessert table, next to chocolate cupcakes, lemon squares, brownies. I took the plates and napkins into the kitchen and stood in the doorway, watching as my father said grace and the congregation lined up to make their way around the tables. Everyone looked beautiful, charming, and kind. The babies were adorable, the old women were plucky, the old men were dashing. My mother and father caught sight of me at the same time, and from two corners of the church hall I was beamed with rays of love. I squiggled my toes in my shoes and wondered if this was what was meant by grace.

When I got home, I hid the money in the ballerina jewelry box I kept in my closet, along with the other junky, childhood things I hadn't had the heart to throw away. And that night, as I was falling asleep, I thought of that money and imagined it glowing in the darkness of the jewelry box like a prophesy of the future. Annie's future, and mine.

At first, I didn't tell Annie what I'd done; I wanted the knowledge all for myself, at least for a while. And I wanted to surprise her, mystify

157

her, make her realize that she didn't know me at all, that she had no idea what sort of things I was capable of.

By Wednesday morning I couldn't stand it anymore. I picked her up for school as I usually did, in my mother's car. When we were on the road, driving toward the cinder-block fortress of Greenridge High School, I said in my lowest, most mysterious voice, "Start packing."

"Why?" Annie said suspiciously.

"'Cause you're going to Denver, baby, that's why! I have the loot."

"Quit talking like a gangster," Annie said.

"I am a gangster," I told her. "Well, sort of. There were no weapons involved." And it all came out in a rush, everything—the potluck, the plates, the green bag, the money in my shoes. "Can you believe it?" I cried.

"Watch the road," Annie said. We got to a stoplight and I sank against the seat with a sigh. On the radio, someone was singing that he'd been waiting for a girl like me.

"Well, shit, Wendy," Annie said finally. She sounded slightly annoyed, as if she were scolding me. "I can't believe you would do that."

"It was right *there,* calling me."

"I mean, don't you worry about burning in hell or something? Isn't that one of the Ten Major Sins?"

I took a deep, slow breath. "There are no Ten Major Sins," I said. "And anyway, God told me to do it."

Annie eyed me suspiciously. "I thought you didn't believe in God."

"What the fuck?" I yelled, trying to shock her into silence with a rare exhibit of profanity. I slammed my palm on the steering wheel. "What about *'Thank* you, Wendy'?"

"Thank you, Wendy," she said sullenly. "So where is it, anyway?"

"Don't you worry your pretty little head," I told her.

Annie couldn't leave on her birthday after all. My mother would need the car that week because the woman she carpooled with was on vacation; then Kelly came home from college to visit, and Annie decided that somehow, miraculously, they might actually *like* each other now. She called me on her birthday to tell me they were going shopping together, and that was the last I heard from her for a week. For her advance birthday present I'd given her a copy of *Let's Go USA*. "Aren't you psyched?" I'd said.

"Yeah," she said, riffling through the book with a bored look on her face.

From downstairs, we could hear the bass thrumming of Ted's guitar. He'd been released from the loony bin after a couple of days, but Annie said her father had swept through the basement and found all the pot and the Rolling Rocks he'd stashed. He also found the empty bottle of Annie's wedding champagne and as punishment sentenced her to a summer of volunteer work at the library.

I, meanwhile, had wads of stolen church money crammed into my jewelry box. It had occurred to me that if Annie suddenly decided not to run away, I would not be able to spend it. I would have to give it all back. I had stolen it for a high and noble purpose—to launch my best friend into her new, independent, and adventurous life. That I had managed it at all was an unexpected triumph, which Annie could spoil on a whim.

With school out, Annie started working at the library every day, and my parents thought I should make myself useful as a candy striper. So I didn't see Annie very much—she was getting home just as I was going off to the hospital to feed old people pears and pudding—but sometimes I'd stop by the library before my shift, wearing my uniform ("Well, look, it's Peppermint Patty," Annie would say), and ask her what was new. I'd preface sentences with "When you're in Denver," and I'd wonder how cold it got there, and if she'd find some cute ski instructor to marry.

"We'll see," Annie said.

Sometimes, before I went to sleep, I would take out the maps from under my bed, spread them on the floor, and trace my finger along the red and blue lines—and the highways looked like arteries, the rivers looked like veins, as if the whole country was some magical, living animal and I was stuck living in a sweat gland. I'd been to Hershey Park in Pennsylvania, I'd been to Delaware and New Jersey and the Smokey Mountains—which were more like fuzzy green hills—but I'd never been anywhere like the Continental Divide, or the Rio Grande, or Pike's Peak. I had never been anywhere that could be depicted in wavy brown lines. I was jealous of Annie, wickedly jealous. Why did my adventure depend upon hers? But it did—that she couldn't see this indicated a selfishness on her part that infuriated me.

On the first of July I came to the library and startled her out of a Judith Krantz novel. "Listen," I said, smacking my hand on the check-out counter. "Are you going or not? Don't get wishy-washy on me now."

"Think what we could do with all that money," Annie said. "Just think of it."

I didn't say anything.

"I'm going," Annie said. "I am going. I was thinking of asking Kelly what she thought."

"Are you nuts?" I cried.

"Or at least going to visit her up in Philly or something."

"That's not running away," I said. "That's visiting. I wouldn't have robbed a *church* if you were just going to visit your sister." I was trying to keep the panic out of my voice. "I'll come over tonight and help you pack. You can get the bus tomorrow, okay?"

"Okay," Annie said.

She lay on her bed reading magazines while I stuffed her clothes into her khaki duffel bag. Kelly had gone back to Pennsylvania the day before; Ted was probably out driving around with his headbanger buddies. We could hear the television through the floor: Irene watching a movie while Peter read the paper. Even Annie had lost interest in their scandals and secrets. In the subterranean world of the basement, the goings-on upstairs had gleamed with wickedness and mystery; now that we spent all our time upstairs, her family had acquired the same dull sheen as my own.

The next morning Annie slammed into the car, humming. "Hey," she said, and lugged her backpack onto her knees.

"I have your clothes in my trunk," I said.

"Well, no shit," Annie said pleasantly.

"Do you have that *Let's Go* book?"

"No, I forgot it." She unzipped her backpack and rooted through it. "I have that map, though. Somewhere in this mess. Never mind."

"Don't lose that," I said.

Annie nodded. I rolled down my window. It had rained the night before, and the wind blowing through the car smelled like damp earth breathing. The sun was a watery yolk in the sky above the alfalfa fields.

"You're going to have fun," I said, just to say something.

"I'm not going on a fucking vacation," Annie said. "I'm running away from home. We could both get in huge trouble, you know that?"

I nodded. I hadn't been thinking in terms of huge trouble.

"Roll up the window, please. It smells like horse shit in here."

I rolled up the window. There was a long silence. The bus station was in Aberdeen, ten miles north of Greenridge. I'd made this drive before, on my fact-finding mission, and there was a part of me that believed it was all part of an elaborate game.

Annie made a low noise in her throat, like she was going to be sick. I wished she could be as enthusiastic about her leaving as I was.

"Are you all right?"

"Peachy."

"Look, *I'll* go if you don't want to," I said, and something whirled up in my stomach that was not quite terror and not quite love—something I would not feel again until fifteen years later when I was letting Thomas shove that ring on my finger and all I knew was that I was doing something drastic and irreversible, and that the rest of my life would come from this.

"I want to," Annie said sharply. "You have the money, right?"

"I have it."

Sometimes I think about my other, phantom life, reeling itself out in the shadowlands of possibility. I know how it begins: I get out of the car instead of Annie; I take the duffel bag from the trunk, and the manila envelope of money; we hug each other; I give her the car keys and say, "I'll call you from someplace." I disappear.

❦

I have not been to Greenridge Hospital since my candy-striping days, and as its orange bricks come into view I feel a familiar teenaged dread—of feeding those old people pudding, of worrying that I will never have adventure and love in my life. I feel a familiar jealousy, too—of Annie—and mixed with it a guilt that is fifteen years old, a teenager itself. I feel those fifteen years suddenly gone, and I have to remind myself that I'm a grown woman, a person with her own life.

I think Annie will recognize me, though there was a time when she wouldn't have. I became Gwen in college, bid goodbye to Wendy forever in a whorl of tequila and cigarette smoke. I watched her rise to the ceiling and disappear, like a banished ghost. Gwen dyed her hair black, wore short black skirts, smoked unfiltered Camels. Gwen lost twenty pounds and passed out in the shower. She fell in love with fiercely smart, bitter young men who told her she was like the air, the sea, a shadow, the light of their lives, then dumped her when she was too drunk to care. In the pictures from those years, I look wildly out of focus, as if I'm in constant motion. I wear a hard little smirk.

I think that Annie will see both that Gwen and this one, and under the layers she will see Wendy, too—like pages in the books I teach, where you peel off one transparent layer after another, past muscle and organs and veins right to clean, white bone. I want to think that if Annie is really here, she will be glad to see all of us.

Over the years, I have finished Annie off in a number of ways. Sometimes I place her by the side of the road, under a clump of purple flowers where no one can ever find her. Or she falls asleep in the snow, on some Colorado mountain pass, and is transported into the unknown with frost on her hair and eyelashes.

I try not to think about how she got to these places.

The task of bringing her back to life is more complicated; it involves weaving a past for her, filling in the fifteen years of blankness. Is she married? Does she have a child? Where did she disappear to? And so I am forced to think of what I don't want to think about, to wonder if she was hurt or kidnapped or raped, if she ever spent nights alone and cold, cursing my name.

163

And if she was, and if she did, what can I say to her now?

When I tell it, there is only one version of this story, no matter who I tell it to: Annie told me she wanted to run away and I tried to stop her. I threatened to tell her parents. We argued. She relented, finally: she'd stay. I didn't tell her parents. She left.

"I wish I'd told them," I said to Thomas. "Just so they'd have watched her more carefully, you know?"

"It's not your fault," Thomas said, everyone says, and I let them all do their best to convince me, and I do my best to be convinced.

❦

Two days after Annie left it was the Fourth of July, and I woke up to see my father standing over me saying, "Honey, there's somebody here about Annie. Get dressed." I came downstairs and there was a police officer in the living room, sitting on our blue sofa. My father was in the rocker across from him, pitched forward at an alarming angle.

"Wendy," he said, rocking back, and held out his hand. I went toward it. "Wendy," he said again, and I understood suddenly that Annie was dead, that I had bundled her away to doom.

"You know," said the police officer, speaking slowly, as if I were retarded or might not understand English, "your friend's been missing for a couple days now."

I nodded. Maybe she wasn't dead! Or maybe she was, and they didn't know it yet.

"And we think," the officer went on, "that you might be able to help us find her. Do you think you can do that?"

"Yes," I tried to say, but it came out *"Ahhh."* I sank onto the ottoman. My mother appeared then, shouldering her way in the front door with two paper bags of groceries, her purse swinging from her elbow. "Did they find her?" she said, rushing forward in a clatter of baked-bean cans and keys.

Annie would have appreciated all this drama on her account.

I took a breath. "She's in Denver," I said. My father was creaking nervously in the rocker, and my mother gripped me firmly by the shoulders. "She took a bus. She said she was going to take a bus." My mother's fingers dug deeper.

"We know," said the policeman, in a normal voice now, "that she did not get on a bus. She was seen getting into a white"—he consulted a pad of paper—"Ford Escort."

"But she had bus fare!" I cried. "She had over a hundred dollars!"

"Where," said my father, "did she get a hundred dollars?"

"I don't know," I mumbled, staring hard at the floor. I could feel my parents looking at me, and suddenly I wanted to tell, I wanted them to know what I'd done: I had become someone else, without them even noticing. It would be like jumping out of a box, or pulling away a curtain.

"You don't think she *stole* it, do you?" said my mother, horrified, and that's when I said, louder than I meant to, "No, she didn't steal it. *I* did." My parents went pale; the policeman sighed heavily. And suddenly, without knowing exactly why, I broke down sobbing, and confessed it all. Or almost all. I didn't say it was my idea, or that I'd driven her to the bus station, driven her out. I told them that she'd needed and wanted my help.

"Holy shit, Wendy," said my father. It was the only time I've ever heard him cuss. "You *stole* from the collection plate?" I was crying so hard the room was spinning. I slumped off the ottoman and curled on the floor.

"I'm horrible," I gasped.

The consensus among my parents and the police officer was that I should make reparations, take responsibility for my actions. The next

Sunday I had to stand up in front of the congregation and apologize. I do not remember what I said, just that it ended with, "And of course I'll pay it all back and I'm sorry." And then I ran crying up the maroon rug, past the drop-jawed acolytes and the choir director and Mr. Dugan and my mother and right out the front door. I stalked up the hill to the graveyard, hating Annie and my parents and myself most of all, and when I threw myself down on the grass between the headstones I believed I would die right then—as a glorious revenge on everyone. Was Annie dead? I wished she was. I wished she was hovering around, regretful but impressed by everything I'd done for her. I squashed my face into my arm and tried to suffocate myself. From down the hill the organ began; then came the voices, which sounded like one faraway voice, rolling out the windows like a fog toward someplace I was too small and wretched to reach.

The congregation's reaction to my confession was sympathetic. I had, after all, just lost my best friend. And I'd been sucked into a web of thievery as well, through misguided but purely noble intentions. I got a job at McDonald's and worked there the rest of the summer to pay off my debt to society. My parents couldn't ground me because I didn't go anywhere. From time to time I would catch them staring at me as if they were trying to make out where they'd seen me before. "Are you all right?" they would say. "Are you sure?"

Although it seemed as if my secrets were out, I realized I still had some. What they were, I couldn't say, but I held onto them the way I held onto Annie's secrets back when I believed in them. At work I fried fries and wrapped burgers and bid people have a nice day; then I went home and climbed the stairs to my pink room and lay on my bed in the dusk, feeling the darkness expanding and making room for me. I thought I could actually feel the old Wendy being shoved away, as if by some strange weed.

Annie's picture ran in the paper. The photograph was from freshman year, when her dark hair was short and freshly permed. The Stokeses hired private detectives, who would come to my house and ask me questions. I caught snippets of news: she may have been seen in Cedar Rapids, and in Topeka. Then nothing.

I visited the Stokeses with my parents once, soon after Annie left. We sat in their living room chairs, listening to the rain outside. The light coming into the living room was thick and white; from the window, I could see the front yard vanish into mist. The air smelled faintly of Peter's cigar smoke, like residue from a dream. The basement would be musty and damp, and I wanted suddenly to be down there, trampling out the ghosts of Annie and me.

This was the first time we'd all been in the same room together—was that possible? I had contrived to keep our parents apart, feeling that somehow the presence of my parents would tarnish the mysterious, shimmery glow of Annie's. Now, all four of them just seemed tired and old. I felt tired and old, too. Irene, who I always thought of as feline and fashionable, was wrapped up in an ugly magenta dress that displayed her bulging middle to full effect. Peter was just a stout, whiskery man. Did Irene ever have an affair? Was Peter descended from Belgian royalty? Did Aunt Dottie bite people? Did Ted attack Irene? Sitting there on the Stokes's living room sofa I felt sick with a sadness that came floating down from my head to my stomach, like a big gray parachute with a hole in it. Were they really so strange? Annie would have stayed; I knew this and wanted to say it.

"You know," said Irene, lifting her head from her husband's shoulder and looking me straight in the eye, "you're still welcome here any time, Wendy. We miss having you around."

Peter nodded and so did I, and I understood that I would not see any of the Stokeses again.

Years later, the summer after college, I drove by their house slowly, staring at the curtainless windows and the Mayflower truck in the driveway. The Boarding House was lying on its side at the curb, next to piles of Hefty bags.

I walk toward the glass doors of the hospital, a reflection of myself that splits open with a whir. I am shaking, suddenly cold. I can't remember the version of my life I've rehearsed; what if I simply cry? The secrets are pushing themselves out of me; if I tell Annie then I'll tell Thomas, there will be no stopping me. I'll grab strangers on the street and sob out everything—that I don't want to marry Thomas but am afraid no one else will ever love me, and if I don't marry him I'll be doomed to a series of useless flings with unformed boys. That the Boy I'm sleeping with makes me feel in control—in a stupid, shallow way, like having a dog on a leash. That I'm sorry, sorry, sorry for making Annie leave when she didn't want to go. It's like that magician's trick with scarves, where he pulls one after another from his sleeve, and just when you think that's the last one, out comes another.

There's a white, kidney-shaped reception desk and I move toward it, over the beige carpet. It occurs to me now that I don't know if Annie has the same last name. When I ask for her, the small man behind the large kidney-desk says, "What ward, please?"

"I don't know."

"Do you know who her doctor is?"

"No," I say. "I don't know."

The man taps something into a computer and shakes his head. "Doesn't look like she's been admitted here." He looks at me. "Are you sure it was this hospital?"

"I'm sure," I tell him. "That's what she said. Did you type her name right? S-t-o-k-e-s?"

"No Stokes," he says, and I nod and step back to let an elderly man inquire the way to the gift shop. The thought comes to me again that the person on the phone—the "me"—was not Annie at all, but someone else who thought she needed me, or simply a wrong number. Or maybe she was here and then she left. And if she was, she might come back. She must know I would come; I'd be waiting here. She must have things to tell me.

In the lobby, I settle into one of the cheery-pink, health-inspiring chairs. The elevators ding open and closed, and people move over the carpet—bandaged, damaged, bearing flowers. I stare at them all, as if looking hard enough might bring Annie's face to the surface.

Outside, the sky has faded to Prussian blue, the color of sleep. I consider calling my machine for messages, in case anyone phoned since I've been gone. I could call and listen to the message that brought me here, play it back again. Or maybe another call has already erased it. I swivel in my seat a little to look out the window and watch the reflections moving around—and from here they are all Annie. All the Annies I knew and the ones I never did, walking through the sky. And I understand that this may be the last time I will be able to conjure her, and that all the things I need to say will have to be said to the people who need to hear them. I suppose I have lured myself here because there was one last story about Annie Stokes I needed to believe—that she is alive, and she forgives me. That when I tell Thomas I can't marry him and tell the Boy

I can't see him anymore, she will cheer me on. And when I tell her that I'm ready to leave, to go someplace new and see what happens, she will tell me what I need to hear: Be careful. Send postcards. I'll miss you. Keep in touch.

About
the Author

Daniel Snyder

Becky Hagenston grew up in Maryland and received her M.F.A. from the University of Arizona. Her stories have appeared in numerous journals, including *TriQuarterly, Shenandoah, The Crescent Review, Antietam Review, Folio, Press, Witness,* and *Carolina Quarterly.* She has received an O. Henry Award and a Bread Loaf scholarship, and currently resides in Las Cruces, New Mexico.